1492 A111

D0437351

Alpine Branch Library
PO Box 3168
Alpine, WY 83128
307-654-7323

EVERLASTING LANE

EVERLASTING LANE

ANDREW LOVETT

MELVILLE HOUSE
BROOKLYN · LONDON

EVERLASTING LANE

Copyright © 2013 by Andrew Lovett
First published in 2013 by Galley Beggar Press Limited, London

First Melville House printing: January 2015

Melville House Publishing   8 Blackstock Mews
  145 Plymouth Street   and   Islington
  Brooklyn, NY 11201   London N4 2BT

mhpbooks.com   facebook.com/mhpbooks   @melvillehouse

Library of Congress Cataloging-in-Publication Data

Lovett, Andrew.
    Everlasting Lane / Andrew Lovett.
      pages   cm.
    ISBN 978-1-61219-380-9 (hardback)
    ISBN 978-1-61219-381-6 (ebook)
    1. Boys—Fiction.   2. Outcasts—Fiction.   3.Villages—Fiction.
    4. England—Social life and customs—20th century—Fiction.
    5. Domestic fiction.   I. Title.

PR6112.O815E94 2015
823′.92—dc23
                                                2014012463

Design by Christopher King

Printed in the United States of America
1 3 5 7 9 10 8 6 4 2

For Carole and Wynne

nunquam refero

PART I

A Game of the Imagination

1

I was nine years old the night my father died. Or ten.
I don't remember.

'Peter?' My mother's voice. 'Peter?'

'What?' I was half-awake, half-asleep. 'What is it?' Like the moon: half sunlight, half midnight. All moon.

'Peter.'

'What *is* it?'

I was in my bed, eyes closed, my mother's breath on my face. And I could see her tears like stars, for although my eyes were closed I believed them open.

She took me in her arms; pulled me to my feet.

'What?' My heart thumping in the darkness. 'What is it? Where's Daddy?'

I was led by the hand into the brightly lit corridor. 'Peter, you know Daddy's been poorly a long time—'

'No!' Struggling in her arms. 'No!' Louder: 'No!' Screaming: 'No, no, no!' Twisting, turning, pounding with my fists. 'No, no, no!'

'Peter. Come and see him, Peter.' I wrestled free. 'Please don't do this.'

I ran to my room, the door slamming behind me, and I hid, cold and breathless, beneath sheets and blankets.

From the landing, silence. And then a terrible howl rising from the silence, filling the night. And then long, trembling sobs fading away. A door closed. My mother cried alone.

So, how do I begin?

It was 1975 when he died. Or 1976. I don't know. It was definitely a year in which I was ten.

As they lowered his coffin into the warm ground, my mother's face crumpled up like old tissues, her tears drying in the spring sun, her make-up all blotchy.

A tall man with sharp, little teeth and shiny, black eyes took my mother's hand. 'This is a terrible, *terri*ble tragedy,' he said. 'If there's anything I can do.'

'Peter,' said my mother, 'this is Doctor Todd. Say hello.'

'Peter,' he beamed. 'Your mother's told me so much about you. I didn't get the chance to really know your father, of course, but I believe he was a wonderful man.' A fat cigar burned bright between his knuckles. 'A *wonderful* man. And so devoted to you. And to your mother, of course …'

Stooping, he pinched a clump of soil between forefinger and thumb, tugged it from the upturned pile and tossed it into my father's grave. He plucked a red handkerchief from his breast pocket to wipe his fingers clean.

'I'm so alone,' said my mother. 'So completely alone.'

I missed my father very much but sometimes it was nice having my mother to myself. I couldn't remember the last time she'd hugged and kissed me and told me she loved me. And she told me stories about my father. He'd been in the war fighting the Germans before she'd even been born. 'He always told me,' she said, 'that he waited to marry someone who hadn't been alive then: someone, I don't know, clean.'

She was only young and very beautiful but she had this sore leg that hurt when she was tired or sad and I would fetch a stool so she could rest it. I would look at her smooth, copper hair curling at the shoulder, her autumn eyes shining, and think of bonfires and fireworks, of blackberry picking and everlasting misty mornings.

But sometimes she would look at me like a mad man and shout: 'Peter, tidy your bloody room!' She would grab fistfuls of paper. 'Throw away all this rubbish!'

'But I—'

'Just keep what's important and throw away the rest!'

'But I don't know—'

'And I don't know how I'm supposed to cope with you running around under my feet all day long!'

Or I'd stare at her and she'd shout, 'For God's sake, Peter, you wouldn't say "boo" to a goose!' or, 'Don't just stand there crying like a baby!' And her face would move so close to mine that I could smell her breath and see my own startled reflection in her eyes.

A few weeks after the funeral, I returned home from school to a kitchen full of pots and pans, and a table laid with the best mats and the nice plates with the gold edge. And beside each mat not just one knife and fork but several. And there were three places laid. There were three of everything.

There were three knocks on the front door.

'Hello, Peter,' said Doctor Todd.

'Peter!' My mother, stepping into the hallway, wiped her hands on her apron and struggled to unpick the strings tied across her tummy. Beneath the apron she wore the green dress my father'd bought her, a golden necklace and the butterfly earrings that sparkled if she laughed. 'Doctor Todd,' she said, 'Clive, you're,' glancing at the hall clock, 'right on time.'

'It pays to be punctual,' said Doctor Todd. 'I abhor lateness. Ha!' And as he laughed, the house filled with the smell of cigar smoke stinking it up like a dead cat.

My mother laughed too: 'Ha-ha-ha,' her hand waving politely in front of her face.

'These are for you,' he said, pink roses appearing from behind his back. 'A token of my—ahem—esteem.'

'Oh,' she murmured, 'they're lovely!'

'Yes,' said Doctor Todd. 'Red, I thought, perhaps too demonstrative; white, too cold; and yellow, too ambiguous.' He touched her shoulder and kissed her cheek. She blushed when she caught me looking. 'Goodness,' said Doctor Todd, touching her earrings. 'These are very pretty.'

'I've got a bit of a thing about butterflies,' she said, smiling nervously. Doctor Todd chuckled. 'Well, anyway,' she scooped a strand of red hair behind her ear, 'the flowers are lovely, Clive. Thank you but you really shouldn't … I'll put them in some water.'

'And, Peter, how have you been? Behaving yourself, I hope.' He showed his teeth. 'Ah, of course, the enigmatic Peter I've heard so much about. A gift,' he announced, presenting me with a small box, 'to help you,' and he tapped me on the head with each word, 'or-ga-nise yourself.' It was a watch with a thick strap and little hands ticking.

'What do you say, Peter?' called my mother from the kitchen.

'Thank you.'

'You'll think of me every *time* you look at it,' he said, 'eh, Peter?' and he nudged my shoulder. 'Ha!'

'That's so kind, Clive.' My mother stood in the doorway watching us. The evening sun played like music in her hair.

Doctor Todd cleared his throat, his face suddenly pink. 'I couldn't help but notice a *Lipton's* on the corner. If it's not too …Why don't I go and buy us a nice bottle of wine?'

'If you're sure,' said my mother. And then she smiled. 'Yes. That would be lovely.'

'Perhaps Peter wouldn't mind keeping me company, eh, Peter?'

'What a good idea,' said my mother. 'Peter, why don't you get your coat?'

'I know, Peter,' said Doctor Todd as we walked along, the setting sun stretching our shadows, 'you like games, don't you? Why don't we play a game? Let's see. I know, why don't you tell me the very first thing you remember. I mean your very earliest memory.'

Well, I couldn't have answered that even if I'd wanted to. I didn't really have any memories of when I was very little. It was just like a big, black hole. Sometimes I would try to re-member things. I'd poke my head into the hole but all I could hear were echoes and I would feel all giddy standing there on the very edge. The only really earliest thing I could remember was this one day after we moved when it started snowing and my father took me into the garden. I ran round and round trying to catch it. The snow, I mean. It was nearly over the top of my boots. And I could remember Daddy grabbing me and lifting me into the air. It seemed so high and I was laughing and screaming, and he was laughing. And then he hugged me really tight. And then I could even remember looking across to where my mother was staring at us through the kitchen window, tears on her face.

There was this photo on the TV of my father from when he was in the army. I could barely remember him being well, sat all day in front of the television, the curve of his ribs through the top of his pyjamas, thin hair turning to snow. He'd lift his unshaven face and smile his skeleton smile: 'How was school today?'

'Okay.'

And I'd go out and ride my bike up and down the rain-soaked street until teatime.

And I could remember how I would lie in bed and hear my mother pleading with him to stay. And later I would listen to her pacing back and forth, muttering to herself; and to my father's breath hissing like steam.

But I didn't say any of that to Doctor Todd.

He bought a bottle of wine and gave me ten new pence for Blackjacks and Fruit Salads. 'Could I have a receipt?' he asked the lady.

On the way back, Doctor Todd said, 'And how are things at home?'

I chewed hard, my teeth all sticky and my tongue turning to liquorice-grey.

'Ah,' said Doctor Todd. 'I see.'

It was a proper dinner with three courses, four if you counted the cheese. I had to turn off the television.

Doctor Todd sat with a straight back and forked cubes of meat into his puckery mouth. Between chews he asked me about school ('So, do you have many friends or one particular close friend?') and my hobbies ('Your mother tells me you keep a scrapbook. I'd love to take a look') and some things I didn't even understand ('Tell me, Peter, do you ever find you're awake when you thought you were dreaming?'). And as he talked, his eyes gleamed and he caressed his sideburns like a pantomime villain.

I turned my arctic roll to mush with my spoon.

'Peter!' said my mother, tapping my arm. 'When Doctor Todd asks you a question, you must answer. And make sure you're telling the truth.'

'Not to worry. Peter will talk when Peter's good and ready to talk, isn't that right, eh, Peter?' The smell of smoke was making me sick. 'Do you know, my mother would never—*never*—have allowed me to even sit with my elders, let alone *speak* at the table.'

'I am so sorry, Clive,' said my mother. 'It's just sometimes he has a very vivid—'

'Yes, yes,' said Doctor Todd. 'With regards to that, Peter, do you think you ever find it hard to distinguish between—'

And I tipped my pudding to the floor with a crash. Ice cream bloomed on the kitchen tiles from beneath the shattered bowl.

And so I was sent to bed.

And so, how do I begin?

2

I awoke from shuddery dreams of frozen desserts: icebergs of vanilla, mountains of soft sponge. I crept down to my secret step, my tummy grumbling like that waste ground behind *Lipton's*.

'It's perfectly understandable.' Doctor Todd's voice spread like oil. '*Perfectly.* You mustn't blame yourself.'

'I know, I know, but I feel so alone. There's nobody I can talk to.'

The television was black, and candles, like those ones we'd used in the power cuts, flickered through Doctor Todd's smoke. I could see my mother's leg resting on that stool I told you about. I could hear her sniffing into her hankie.

'Well, that's what *I'm* here for,' said Doctor Todd. 'You can talk to me about anything. *Anything.*'

'I know, Clive. I don't know how I would have got this far without you. But Peter—'

'No "buts",' said Doctor Todd. 'You're not being fair. You've said it yourself, you need some time. It's for your benefit. And Peter's too, of course.'

'I know. I know.'

'I mean, isn't there *any* other family? Of course, I know about his grandmother but I'm sure—'

'His grandmother?'

'Yes, I'm sorry. But surely there's someone who'd take him off your hands ... for a while.'

'Off my hands?'

'Yes. I mean who wouldn't *love* to spend some time with Peter?' said Doctor Todd. 'He's such a ... such a character. It would do him the world of good. Besides, you've said it yourself: you need a change, a new beginning, and this is your opportunity.'

'But she—'

'That's enough,' scolded Doctor Todd. 'You mustn't be selfish. You really need to think about what's best for Peter.'

'Maybe you're right,' she murmured. 'This could be my last chance.'

'Exactly. Ex*actly*.'

'I could take him to Amberley. Wouldn't that—?'

'Well, no, I'm not sure that would be such a good ... What I *meant* to say was that I could take him if you like, if there's someone there ... I'll get him there,' he said, 'safe and sound.'

'No, no. You mustn't. I've imposed too much—'

'Nonsense,' said Doctor Todd. 'It's been,' his shadow leant towards hers, 'an absolute,' was that the sound of, 'pleasure'?

The tennis ball went bobbling across the back lawn. I was always challenging myself: the further I punted the ball with my father's golf club, the higher my score. But I couldn't concentrate. I didn't even know why until, tick by tick, I remembered the watch clinging to my wrist. Doctor Todd's watch. The seconds were speeding. I could see them and feel them, frantic-tick-ticking deep within. I shook my wrist. And again. Harder.

I released the watch, placed it on the path and returned to my game. But I couldn't shake it out of my head. I could still see the hands spinning, you see, the numbers changing, the time passing.

I could hear Doctor Todd speaking to me in my head: 'So, do you have many friends or one particular close friend?'

There was sweat on my face and tears began to prickle my eyes. It was like I could feel myself crumbling, blood thick and throbbing, noises exploding in my head, lights flashing like blades.

'Your mother tells me you keep a scrapbook.'

I raised and tested the golf club. I lifted it higher and swung it through the air.

'I'd love to take a look.'

The head of the club hit the watch with a crack, splitting its ugly face.

Again.

Again and again. Crack. Crack. Crack.

I smashed the watch into its smallest.

Tinest.

Pieces.

And then my mother, thunder and lightning, staggering towards me. 'Why?' she cried. 'Why must you always … ?' And then pain as her stick went splintering across my shoulder. Once. Twice. And I really did cry, spinning as I fell. She turned her back, stumbling away before I'd even hit the ground.

When I found her at the top of the stairs, head hanging down, hands covering her face like the soil across my father's grave, she said, 'I've decided,' her voice all muffled. 'We'll go to Amberley. Clive's right: it'll be good for both of us. A new start.'

'There's no grandmother.'

'What?'

'You were lying.' I knew she was. 'I haven't got a grand-mother!' My dad always told me how she died when he was still in the war.

'Peter.' My mother sighed and raised her head. She looked like an alien, her eyes all dark and swollen. Her hair was wild. 'Heaven and Earth are full of things you've never even dreamt of. I deserve a second chance, Peter, don't you think? Doesn't everybody deserve a second chance? Well? Don't just stand there blubbing: say something!'

'I don't want to.'

'Don't want to what?'

'I don't want to be with you,' I said. 'Someone else … Someone else would love to spend time with me. I'm such a character.'

She kind of laughed when I said that with her shoulders all shaking. 'Unfortunately, Peter,' she said in a kind of wet whisper, 'there isn't anyone else. I'm the only mother you've got.' And then she sniffed and said: 'I just thought we needed a break. A little holiday. And then everything will be like it used to be. You'd like that. Wouldn't you?'

★

Doctor Todd, in a safari suit and a silk cravat, came to see us off. 'If you're absolutely sure,' he said, smoothing his sideburns before touching my mother and kissing her cheek. 'You'd best leave right away. *Right* away. It's a hot day and the *roads* are atrocious. A*tro*cious.'

'Yes,' said my mother. 'The sooner the better. Peter,' she snapped, 'stop chattering and use the toilet.'

Doctor Todd glanced at my wrist. 'Where's your watch?'

'Come on, Peter. You know what you're like.'

When the car door closed, Doctor Todd's face appeared

leering against the glass, his terrible teeth gleaming. 'Off you go, then,' he said, and the engine roared.

The day *was* hot and the car stank of fresh leather. My stomach gurgled and churned as we passed the hospital with the pretty nurses, and weary mothers shunting prams along the pavement. Everything was different: the colours had all changed, the sun was bright. I saw daffodils, and sunlight falling through the branches of trees. I saw people on their way to work: people for who this was just another day, people whose daddies were fixing cars or mowing lawns or rolling pens back and forth across office desks. The car slid across the lanes and the motorway swept us away from town.

I kept a scrapbook, of sorts, like Doctor Todd said, bits and pieces pasted on paper. I always wanted to control things, you see, the things that happened and put them in order just like the kings and queens on the classroom wall. But it was so hard. I could never tell what mattered. I couldn't control the world any better than I could an armful of snakes. The hills and fields unfolded like pages and the contents of my scrapbook shuffled all higgledy-piggledy across the back seat of the car. I scrambled to collect everything and hurry it back between the covers.

But why was it so frightening? I mean, you know, when everything got all muddly? Grown-ups always pretended that everything *could* be answered or explained or justified. But if you ever looked at the face of a lady who'd lost her child or a child that'd lost its mummy or daddy you might think that, well, maybe, life is all confusing and messy and wouldn't fit between the pages of a book no matter how hard you tried. Maybe it'd be better if you just closed your eyes and went to sleep and dreamed. And then when you woke up, if you had to wake up, you might as well just forget about trying to make everything make sense and lie in your bed, eyes wide open, waiting for another day to start.

I saw handfuls of sheep scattered across the hillsides, and villages small enough to put in my pocket: so small that I imagined ruling over them, bringing destruction whenever the mood took me. The people would scream in terror at the wild world I'd made.

'Peter,' my mother's eyes flared in the rear-view mirror, 'what is it? What are you saying?'

'Nothing!' and I slapped the back of her seat. Sometimes I wondered what it would be like if I really could kill someone.

She twisted around, her finger jabbing at me. 'Are you *try-ing* to cause an accident?' She spun back to the road and I sat plastered with fear to my seat, her spit on my face. 'Not long now,' she muttered. 'Amberley: two miles. Thank God. As soon as we get to Everlasting Lane—'

Everlasting Lane? I hadn't heard that name before. It took me by surprise. How long would we have to drive down an everlasting lane?

'It's just a *name*, Peter!'

And then we passed the sign—Amberley—and everything changed.

I made up stories, you see, and filled my scrapbook with the people I knew: a widowed mother; a lost child; the woman, smiling, her shadow sliding back towards the large house; the young man taking a match to a bundle of secrets. And now the swinging chain, turning, creaking, the air still. I made a world where summers were warmer, where the winters were whiter, and even love seemed better.

I can't promise that this is the way it was, not exactly, only that this was perhaps how it sometimes seemed to be. Because it's a strange kind of courage, isn't it? The courage to let someone die; to let them die alone without a word. And you should tell her that I'm sorry because, in the end, I didn't do the right thing at all. But, you see, although I believed them open, my eyes were closed.

I stood in the doorway of the little white cottage as my mother ruffled through her handbag and produced a bundle of keys. I heard church bells: chimes rising into the spring sky, and a tumble of silver notes. I heard the turn of the squeaky lock. The branches of a weeping willow rose and fell; birdsong twinkled in the taller trees.

And, so, this is how I begin.

My father died when I was nine years old. I must have been nine because I was ten when I went to live in Everlasting Lane.

It was all so long ago, how could I ever forget?

3

The cottage in Amberley made me think of an old library: dusty and undisturbed.

I sat at the kitchen table, lurching from thought to thought, watching my mother's every move. She brought out biscuits and lemonade and perched on the yellow worktop to watch me eat and drink. I wasn't hungry but ate anyway, forcing mouthfuls of digestive down my throat. The table-top was plastic and patterned to look like wood. It was funny because there was something familiar about it just as there was about the floor tiles and the cupboards and the yellow curtains tied up with blue knots at the window.

The kitchen smelt empty. Opening a brown cupboard, my mother cleared a space among old packets and tins for beans and bread; in the fridge she placed butter, milk and cheese. The fridge shuddered as she switched on the power and at the same moment a memory flickered across my brain. I found myself building towns of coloured paper, my feet swinging clear of the kitchen floor, large blocks of pale afternoon pasted on the walls. There was a smell of fresh paint and brushes soaking upended in old jam jars. I could hear my father singing and I could see myself, my tiny self, giggling with glee at his funny voice and thoughts of hippopotamuses and glooorious

mud as he slipped ginger cake into the oven and warmed co-
coa in the pan.

I could hear my mother's footsteps upstairs stomping on
the old floorboards and the Hoover rattling against the skirting and whooshing under the beds. I listened out for the sudden silence that would follow the end of her housework. You
see, something was about to happen. Something only I knew.

My father stood behind me admiring my work.

I wondered how much I knew about this man. Not much.
He had a moustache and his tummy hung a little over the
rim of his belt but he was tall and proud like the soldier he'd
once been. He never talked about it but at least I knew what
a soldier was. I'd seen pictures and read comics and, sometimes, my mother told me stories. But he wasn't a soldier any
more. He was a businessman and I didn't really know what he
did or understand that world of suits and ties and secretaries.
There were no comics about businessmen. He was so much
older than me I couldn't imagine the world through his eyes.
He was a mystery; a mystery in my own house, but I never
thought to ask. In my dreams he never changed. He was never
ill and he was never dead. He was always Daddy and that was
all that mattered.

'Peter,' he said, smiling, 'have you seen this trick?' He moved
to the opposite side of the table and—

'Peter?' I flinched. My mother's eyes were scorching me, a
whisper of smoke rising from my hair. 'What is it?'

A sip of lemonade washed down the last stubborn bite of
biscuit. I shook my head. 'I've been here before.'

'Peter,' she frowned at my confusion, 'why don't you remember?'

'Who lives here now?' I demanded.

'We do.'

'Yes, but whose house is it?'

'Well, your grandma lived here awhile,' she said. 'But now it's ours.'

'And we live here?'

She nodded.

My mother clunked my suitcase up the narrow stairs. If the downstairs was small, the upstairs was smaller still and the wooden chair onto which she sank filled most of the landing. I nearly toppled backwards but she seized my wrist. The shadow of the gloomy, green drape hanging behind her slid across her face.

'You nearly had a nasty fall,' she said.

She produced a brass ring from which rattled an assortment of keys. She removed four. 'Bathroom,' she said, handing me the first. I fitted the key, unlocked the door and returned the key to my mother. 'Mine,' she said, and I repeated the task a second time. 'Yours.'

I twisted the third key into its lock. As the door opened the room coughed out a puff of stale, stuffy air. My mother jerked back the curtain and pushed open the tiny window. 'Oh, Lord,' she said as a triangle of light fell across the room and its contents. 'This,' she said, shuffling an armful of clothes from the pink eiderdown, 'is, apparently, where your grandmother decided to store all her junk. She was a devotee of *Woman's Weekly*,' my mother went on, a stack of magazines threatening to slip from her grasp, 'and clearly reluctant to throw away a single edition.' Sniffing the bedding she said, 'And a change of sheets is in order, methinks.'

She winced as she lowered herself to her knees. She reached beneath the bed and began tugging free toys and books. 'Your old Action Man,' she cried, 'your Robin Hood set, your Rupert annuals. Oh, and look who we've got here!' It was a piggy bank, pink and smiling, forgotten pennies rattling around inside. And then a tattered glove-puppet. 'Goodness me, Peter, you were always "Pinky-this, Perky-that". You drove us to despair.' She slipped the toy onto her hand and wiggled it as if it were talking. 'Pinky-Perky-Peter we used to call you,' she said in a squeaky voice. 'Don't you remember?'

I shrugged and scowled at the pig. I wondered whether I wanted to remember.

'Look,' she sighed, removing the puppet from her fingers and reaching back under the bed, 'I know it's not much, but sort out your pictures and things, it'll be just like …'

She now held a skipping rope. It looked nearly new. She caressed its silky strands and wrapped it around her fingers like beads.

'That's a girl's toy,' I said.

Alone in the living room, afternoon sun speckling the air, I counted porcelain animals roaming the shelves in packs or lurking alone between the spines of tattered books. A clock squatted on the mantelpiece, its hands still. Kneeling before the TV I scrawled my name across its dusty screen.

I studied a row of photographs that sat along the sideboard. They made me feel happier. Photographs always did. It was like I could pretend that they were real and the room around me was the picture. Like when you look in a mirror and see the world where everything is backwards, so that your right hand is your left hand and all the writing looks funny and mysterious. It's like another world where the things that happen are opposites and if you're sad in the real world, then you'd be happy in the mirror, and if you were lost in one world, then you'd be found in the other. And the people who were dead might be alive and everything would be different and better.

Some of the photos were black and white, others pale and coloured. Some I'd seen before at home, stacked in a box in the garage, damp-dry at the corners. Others I hadn't seen before, like this one with my father and mother sitting side by side and smiling for the camera but the picture was torn like a third person had been removed.

I couldn't guess who.

'What are you up to?'

I jumped. 'Nothing.'

My mother held a lemonade in each hand, bubbles rising. 'Don't worry,' she said, passing a glass to me and tugging a duster from her back pocket. 'It just needs a good clean.' The yellow cloth swept across the television's blank eye, erasing dust and signature in a single swipe. She went to the window and glowered at the tangle of weeds that had once been a garden.

I stared at her. She'd changed her clothes. She was all made up like a younger person, with pink cheeks and a storybook smile. She wore a T-shirt, red, white and blue like an American flag; and proper jeans, flared ones, almost like a teenager. But her eyes, when she turned to smile at me, were the same smoky shade as always.

'Where is she now?' I asked.

'Who?'

'My grandmother.'

My mother shuddered as if tasting something sour. She fiddled with an earring. 'Maybe, when you know me better,' she said.

'I *do* know you.'

'Oh, Peter,' she said, joining me on the sofa, 'you don't know me at all.' She took my hands in hers. 'I was thinking about what you said. You know, about not wanting to live with me.'

'But I—'

'No, it's all right. I was wondering what it would be like if you could live with someone else. Someone who wasn't cross all the time.'

And then she explained. We were going to play a game, she said, a game of the imagination. She told me how she was going to be my Aunt Kat (with a 'K') and how my mummy had gotten very tired and had decided to take some time to sort herself out because I knew what it was like when *I* was tired and how grumpy *I* got, didn't I?

I nodded. I didn't want to make her cross.

'Do you know why people play games, Peter?'

'Because it's fun?'

'Well, yes, sometimes, but sometimes it helps them discover something too.'

'Like Hide and Seek.'

The game had rules, of course—just like with that man in *It's a Knockout* who tells everyone the rules before he blows the whistle—but in this game you could change, you could be anything or anyone you wanted because the past and the things we'd done, which I'd always thought were carved in stone, might as well be carved in water. And it was a strange game, yes, but a good one because, as she explained, if you were losing, you just returned to 'Go' and started all over again.

But then she said how she wanted us to keep ourselves to ourselves and that people in a village had big noses and would want to poke them into our business given half a chance and I wasn't to tell anyone anything and even when I went to school—'Yes, Peter, school. Did you really think you wouldn't have to go?'—I needed to be careful because the game, she said, and the rules were secret. 'And if people ask questions,' she said, 'never answer.'

'Why?'

22

She groaned and then laughed. 'Do you know something, Peter Lambert?'

'No. What?'

'*You* ask too many questions.'

'But *what* do I call you?'

'I told you: you can call me Kat—'

'Why?'

'—with a "K".'

'But why? It's not even a proper name.'

'Of course it is. You are your name,' she explained, 'and your name is who you are. It's just sometimes you need another name to make yourself something more, something better. Your dad understood that,' she said, 'but I let him down. And now I'm making up for it. Well, what do you think?'

Well, sometimes, I didn't know what to think.

'Let me look at you,' she knelt down. 'Oh, Peter, your daddy would be so proud,' as if seeing me for the first time. Her fingers teased my hair. And then, 'Oh, Peter,' she said, 'I'm sorry.' And then, 'It's all right,' as she reached for me. 'Don't cry. Big boys don't cry.' And I didn't.

Hardly at all.

'Listen, Peter,' she said, her smoky eyes filling the room, 'can you keep a secret?'

'Yes.'

She put a finger to my lips. 'Then keep it.'

A butterfly fluttered among the thick, green leaves of the overgrown garden. Gardens at home were mirrors, reflecting other gardens, other houses and other small boys, but this garden backed onto trees. Not like the skinny trees at home either. These trees were thick and old with dark stories stuffed into the lines of their rugged faces.

Having turned it onto something big, thumping and full of summer, Kat, as I was supposed to call her, slipped a radio onto the seat of the rusty garden chair. 'There used to be a scythe,' she said, squinting at the chaos before her, 'but I'd hate to take you home with less legs than when you arrived.' And then, turning her back on the jungle to survey the rear of the house, she cried out: 'Oh, no. Look! The local yobbery have put a brick through a window.' A jagged black hole gaped from the first floor. 'Oh, Peter, is nothing sacred?' she sighed. 'I won't rest until I've done something about that. Can you entertain yourself, Peter? Yes?'

'What about Doctor Todd?' I said.

Kat sighed again, 'Ooooh,' as if I'd stuck her with a pin. 'Listen, Peter, my suggestion to you is that you don't worry about Doctor Todd. In fact, that's not even a suggestion,' she said. 'It's pretty much an order.'

That seemed too easy.

'Okay?'

I nodded.

'I'll not be long,' she said. 'Now be good.'

Left alone I couldn't resist plunging into the overgrown garden, like Doctor Livingston, I presume, or Doug McClure, fully expecting to discover the ruins of some dark forbidden temple or one of those Japanese soldiers that never know the war is over. I had to keep my wits about me, of course. You never knew what dangers might be lurking deep within the undergrowth: lions, probably, ready to rip your throat out; snipers, a pot-shot from the shadows; maybe aliens.

I tightened my grip on my gun and, with my walkie-talkie pressed to my ear, I could communicate with HQ and keep them alerted to my progress: 'I am approaching the nest,' in a whisper, twisting the dial. 'Over. I must be absolutely silent,' I went on. 'Over. Who knows what I might find,' I concluded. 'Over and out.'

There was a burst of activity. I crouched and gazed in wonder at the mighty beast rising in to the air, leathery wings beating over the land that time forgot. Awed by its ancient beauty, I—

'What the hell are you doing?'

The pterodactyl vanished. My gun, I discovered, was only a stick, and the voices of my comrades were static crackling from Kat's wireless. It took a moment to remember where I was and a moment more to find the source of the question.

A pale, freckle-faced girl was leaning over next-door's fence. She had long, golden blonde hair and big ears. I had the uneasy feeling she'd been watching me for some time.

4

The girl frowned at me with serious eyebrows.

'What the hell,' she repeated, as if I was retarded, 'are you doing?'

'Playing.'

'Playing? Is that what you call it? Is that why you're muttering to yourself like a demented baboon?'

'I ...' I stared at my feet, blushing.

'I asked you a question, dimwit.'

I prayed she wouldn't climb over the fence. But she did. One long, spider-thin leg appeared and unfolded itself. And then a second. She slid down into the overgrown flowerbed. 'Thanks for your help,' she said, straightening her dress and glaring at me with pale blue eyes. 'Frankly, it's nice to know that chivalry is so far from being dead.' Her knees were grazed and dirty.

My heart thumped and bumped like a body falling down stairs. I studied the buckle of my sandal and the earth beneath my feet with a sweaty concentration that would have delighted my teachers. I finally looked up past her grubby knees and faded yellow dress. She was a year or so older than me and a head taller. Of all the challenges I'd faced that day, she was the toughest.

'I'm Anna-Marie,' said the girl. 'Anna-Marie Liddell. And,' she said, as if discovering something hairy in her salad, 'who the hell are you?'

'Peter.'

'Peter?' she said with disgust. 'What are you doing here?'

'I ... I live here,' I said. 'With my ... with my ... my aunt.'

'Since when?'

'Since ... today.'

'Oh.' She considered this information whilst using her little finger to free something green from between her teeth. 'You're not Oliver Twist, are you? I mean, you're not some awful, Victorian orphan?'

'No.'

'Why don't you live with your mum or dad, then?'

'I ... My dad's dead.'

Anna-Marie looked away. 'My dad is in sales,' she said. 'He's away a lot, but it's very lucrative. So what's she like, then, this aunt? She'd better not be a horror like Mrs Winslow. Mrs Winslow hates me.'

'Why?'

'It's a long story,' said Anna-Marie. 'Anyway, now she says I'm "bad news". That's what Tommie says. Do you know Tommie?'

'No.'

'He's at his dad's for the holidays and who can blame him,' said Anna-Marie, pausing to chew a nail. '*I* say that Mrs Winslow is an ugly old trout. And she is.'

'Oh!'

'Mrs Winslow is Tommie's mother,' she explained. 'Tommie's a bit of a spud but his dad doesn't live with him so I look out for him. To be kind.' She looked at me again. 'You're a bit of a non-entity, frankly.'

'What?'

'Are you simple?'

'No.'

'You must be if you don't even know what a non-entity is. Perhaps you were dropped on your head as a baby. That would explain why you run around talking to yourself and don't even know what the simplest words in the English language mean.'

My lips were tight, my face hot with shame. So I kicked her. Hard. On the shin.

'Fuck-a-doodle-duck!' she cried. 'What was that for, you lunatic?'

She sat down, flattening the tall grass, and unrolled her grey sock. 'I think you must be deranged,' she said. She tapped the faint mark with her finger. 'Good kick, though.'

The sun tickled my head and the bare skin of my arms. A cat appeared, smooth and black, following the flies and raising a curious paw. Bees bobbled up and down between the weeds, stalks swaying beneath their weight.

'Are you standing there all day?' asked Anna-Marie, her voice gentler than before. I sat down. She flicked the hair from her face and smiled. Her teeth were white and straight, and two deep dimples burrowed their way into her cheeks. I felt a flicker of electricity.

'Are you clever?' she asked. 'At school, I mean.'

'I don't know.'

'I have an excellent vocabulary,' said Anna-Marie. 'They did a test. But I have a blind spot for numbers. I don't let it bother me. Maths is boring. There's no … variety. Everything's either right or wrong. There's no grey areas.

'I like English: reading and writing, but don't get me started on children's books.' I shook my head. 'All those animals running around in hats and jackets with their bottoms hanging out,' she said. 'I mean, why do they even wear clothes? They should at least wear them properly, I mean trousers, don't you think?' I nodded. 'And what about their names: Mr Toad, Badger, Rabbit? I mean, what are all the *other* rabbits called?

'Anyway, I don't read kids' books. I read grown-up books like Agatha Christie and Frances Hodgson Burnett. I like mysteries. I love books where anything can happen,' said Anna-Marie, 'don't you? Like somebody says they laughed their heads off or it's raining cats and dogs. I used to write stories myself and ... Well, in a story that can happen. It could really rain real cats and dogs. Literally. That's much more interesting than normal rain.'

I smiled.

'The impossibilities,' she said, 'are endless.'

'What's your school like?'

Anna-Marie wrinkled her nose. 'It's all right, I suppose. The teachers don't like me much and the headmistress is awful, but I'm going to secondary soon anyway. And I'll be glad to go. I've had enough of baby school.'

'Well,' I said, 'what do you want to be when you grow up?'

Anna-Marie gave me a withering stare. 'Oh, please,' she sneered. 'What's this: 'Conversation for the Under-Fives'? You are such a child.' She plucked a tuft of grass from the lawn and brushed it against her cheek. 'In fact,' she said, 'I'm going to be a teacher.'

'A teacher?'

'Yes, and I know what you're thinking but I don't mean like a normal teacher. I mean a good teacher. Do you know that game *Consequences*?' I didn't. 'We play it in school sometimes. Well, it's like that. Children don't know anything about consequences. They think they can just do any old stuff and that's all there is to it. What they need is someone to teach them about the consequences of what they do. Do you know what I mean?'

I didn't.

'I want to be an astronaut,' I said.

Anna-Marie snorted. 'Your chances of ever becoming an astronaut are about the same as mine of growing an extra head.' She glanced up at the cottage. 'Sorry about the window, by the way. I didn't know anyone was living here, obviously.'

'We keep ourselves to ourselves,' I murmured.

Anna-Marie gave me a funny look. 'Oh, you do, do you?'

'Who used to live here?' I asked.

'Well, when we first moved here there was this little old woman—Mrs Whatnot or something. She was nice enough. She used to say I was an angel and give me sweets and stuff,' Anna-Marie smiled, 'until they carted her off. I don't know much about it, to be honest. You know what adults are like. As if I cared.' She touched her bruise again. 'Cockaleekie soup,' she murmured, and then, 'You've probably never heard anyone swear like that before, have you? Properly I mean. I'm the best swearer in school. My mum hits me whenever I do it but it's funny 'cause I learnt them from her in the first place.'

She closed her eyes with a sigh, her face smooth and peaceful like a china god. We sat in silence, listening to the breeze rippling in the trees and somewhere the rusty joints of a child's swing. White sheets rippled on the Liddells' washing-line like a sailing ship. The cat crept closer and wrapped its slinky back about my neighbour's arm. 'This is Kitty,' she said. I fiddled with the buckle of my sandal and watched Anna-Marie, waiting for her to speak again.

'Pillock,' she said.

'What's a non-entity?'

'It doesn't matter,' she shrugged. 'Besides, you may not be one. Time will tell.' She caressed her shin one last time. 'I know,' she said. 'Come on,' and she leapt to her feet, grabbing my hand and pulling me up. 'You're coming with me.' My heart thrilled to her dry, determined grip.

'Peter!' It was my mother. 'I've put some cardboard in the window,' I mean Kat, of course, 'cleaned up the glass,' calling from inside, 'and I'm going to phone a man in the village about,' stepping from the back door onto the patio, 'the gar— Oh,' she said, seeing Anna-Marie for the first time. 'Hello. Who's this?'

'It's Anna-Marie.'

'Anna-Marie Liddell,' said my new friend, smoothing the creases out of her dress.

'Oh, well, I hope Peter's not bothering you.'

'He seems harmless enough,' laughed Anna-Marie.

'Don't you believe it,' said my ... said Kat.

'Can I go out?' I said. 'We were going to—'

'Well, I'm hardly keeping you a prisoner, am I? I want you to look around,' she said. 'See what you can find. It's baked beans with cheese on top—just how you like it—for tea, so make sure you're not back too late.'

'Don't worry,' said Anna-Marie. 'I'll look after him, Mrs—'

'Kat,' said Kat. 'With a "K",' and then she smiled at me just like an aunt would and said, ' 'Bye, Peter.'

And I said, ' 'Bye, Kat.' It was new and strange but it was kind of nice.

As Anna-Marie and I walked along I nearly began to believe what Kat had said about my having lived there before because nothing I saw seemed entirely new. Hadn't I once hidden beneath that willow tree waiting to spring out on my mother as she hung the laundry? Wasn't that pothole the one I had tripped on whilst chasing a pigeon and skinned my knee so badly that Daddy had had to bathe it in *Dettol*? Why did the low branches of that tree remind me of hiding myself among its green leaves and giggling as my parents bellowed out my name below? But if it was true why was I not sure? The memories were more like dreams than things that had really happened.

'So,' said Anna-Marie, 'that's the notorious aunt, is it?'

'Where are we going?'

'Kirrins'.'

I remembered when my dad, sat up in bed waiting for the nurse to come, was telling me about that funny feeling French people get when they've been somewhere before when they haven't really. Now that I could remember quite clearly: the sickening warmth of the room, the smell of medicine and Daddy's dry voice saying, 'Sometimes the mind likes to play tricks on people, Peter. Just like you do.'

'What's *Kirrins*'?'

'It's a shop.'

'Why? What are we going to do?'

Anna-Marie smiled. 'Something reprehensible.'

By the time we reached the sign that welcomed us to Amberley, wedged tightly into a wall of yellow bricks, I had decided that it was Kat who was playing the trick. After all, if we had once lived here, why had we left?

Along Hayes Road, the road that wound through the village itself, were rows of tiny cottages with black roofs and white walls wrapped in vines and creepers, their small front gardens brimming with flowers and shrubs. Anna-Marie hopscotched along the pavement, the loose rubber of her plimsoll flip-flapping. Occasionally she paused, frowning with concentration, to slip her hair back behind her ears before tossing her stone and skipping off again in pursuit, me trotting to keep up.

We passed the village green, the yellowing grass revealing the brown earth underneath, and the pond, scum collecting in the bottom, the dry bed rising to meet the water level. We passed *The White Hart*, where a row of old men, skins dark and cracked, sat muttering and drinking, squinting at the sun; and beer, Coca-Cola and cheese and onion wafted across the road.

Anna-Marie said: 'Where did she get that limp?'

'What?'

'Your aunt. She's got a limp, hasn't she? I mean I'm not saying she's Long John Silver or anything but you can see it.'

We left the pavement and crossed the road towards a pokey shop: trays of shrivelly fruit and buckets of droopy flowers lay outside and in its window a plastic sheet protected the insides from the glare of the sun. Above the door a sign, its black and white paint all scratched and peeling, read: KIRRINS' GENERAL STORE.

'She should use a walking stick or something,' said Anna-Marie as she took the handle and leant her bottom against the door.

'What's "reprehensible"?'

Anna-Marie sighed. '"Reprehensible": naughty, wrong, blameworthy, disobedient, wayward, mischievous, impish. Anto-nym,' she added with a wink as she pushed against the glass panel, 'good.'

Oh. Well, that was all right, then.

5

A bell rang and a man's voice called out: 'Greg! Shop!'

Anna-Marie nudged me. 'That's *him*!'

'Who?'

'Sssh!' she said. 'Come on.'

Down the central aisle, tins and packets of food to one side and powders and soaps to the other, she led me to a shelf of old-fashioned toys and games: bat and ball sets; compendiums of snakes and ladders, Ludo and chess; colouring books featuring teddy bears in dresses and cardigans; whistles and yo-yos, and beside each item a little Christmas fairy holding a small piece of card on which was written the price. The fairies looked uncomfortable and sweaty in their glittery, ruffled dresses and lacy butterfly wings.

'Aren't they sweet?' declared Anna-Marie with a sigh. 'Each one's painted differently,' she went on. 'This one's got curly red hair and this one's got short blonde hair and green eyes and this one's got jet-black hair and the one with the wand here, look, that's my favourite, she's got long blonde hair and blue eyes and freckles: just like me!'

It did look a little like Anna-Marie. But not much.

Next to Anna-Marie's fairy was a box of jewellery with different necklaces in it and bracelets with little love hearts hanging off them, and I noticed this one thing: a ring. It had a big jewel on it, like a diamond or a ruby, but it was orange. With a ring like that, I thought, people would think Kat was the Queen of England. I wondered how much it would cost.

'My dad tried to buy it for me once,' said Anna-Marie, 'but they're not for sale,' she meant the fairies, 'just the crappy toys next to them.'

And then, like a Venus fly-trap, her hand shot out, grabbed her favourite fairy—snap!—and stuffed it into *my* pocket, where it lay, the point of its wand stuck into my leg. Anna-Marie winked again. 'Well, Peter,' she said loudly as she escorted me to the shop counter, 'unfortunately those dolls are not for sale, so we'd better just buy some sweets.'

A tall man with a large stomach and dark patches beneath his armpits had appeared.

'Good afternoon, Mr Kirrin,' said Anna-Marie. 'How are you today?' Her smile sparkled. Mr Kirrin only grunted and wiped a handkerchief across his pink forehead. His snowy white eyebrows remained fixed.

With a finger to her lip, Anna-Marie studied the sweet jars that lined the high shelf like something out of 'Ali Baba and the Forty Thieves', comparing pear drops with liquorice allsorts; wine gums with pineapple chunks. And what about sherbet lemons? Mr Kirrin's face grew redder and his head shinier. Eventually Anna-Marie was decided and delivered another smile. 'I'd like a quarter jelly babies, please.'

Mr Kirrin struggled to reach a decision of his own, glancing at me from time to time as if for help until he turned and bellowed towards the back of the shop: 'Norman!' There was no response. 'Norman!' The voice we'd heard as we'd entered the shop remained silent.

The shopkeeper fetched a small stepladder. He was tall but still needed an extra inch or two to reach the required jar. He walked, I noticed, a bit like my mother—I mean Kat—and just snapping the stepladder into shape caused him to wheeze like a hamster's squeaky wheel. As he climbed the two or three steps necessary, each breath made me wince.

Anna-Marie smiled.

He grabbed the jar and held it to his chest with one hand whilst using the other to come down. The ladder creaked as it took Mr Kirrin's weight. He placed the jar on the counter before us. He frowned at Anna-Marie. She smiled at him.

They were like David and Goliath about to have some ancient battle, with rules written deep in the desert sand that whipped about them. Mr Kirrin looked like some old boxer who'd been knocked out so many times he must have wondered whether he shouldn't just lay down and save his opponent the trouble.

He was a desperate man. Of course he was. It was hardly a fair fight.

Whatever strength he had left Mr Kirrin drained it as he twisted the top from the jar. Sweetness burst into the air. I breathed in feeling my toes tingle. Hefting the jar at an angle, Mr Kirrin emptied a fistful of jelly babies into a bowl—they rattled like gravel—and then a couple more—plink, plink—as he guesstimated a quarter.

He balanced weights and nudged the scales with his pudgy forefinger, before turning to Anna-Marie and addressing her directly for the first time that afternoon: 'Just over.' His voice rasped with defeat.

'That's fine,' said Anna-Marie.

The bowl on the scales had a kind of lip, like with a jug, and Mr Kirrin tipped the jelly babies into a small paper bag. He twisted the corners into tight knots and placed the bag in front of Anna-Marie. His great knuckles leant upon the counter and a single drip of sweat fell from his upper lip. The hot patches beneath his arms had begun to sag. Anna-Marie waited just a moment before her hand jumped into my pocket and, to my alarm, produced the fairy.

'And this, please.'

Mr Kirrin's face was a sky full of storm. He snatched the tiny doll, clutching it deep in his fist. 'I have told you before,' he said, his temper bubbling, 'they are *not* for sale.'

Anna-Marie's lip was stiff, every bit as cross as Mr Kirrin. 'Well,' she said, 'I'd better just have the jelly babies,' but then: 'Oh, shoot,' she said, 'I haven't got my purse. Peter, could you lend me … Sorry, how much is it? Maths isn't my strong suit.'

'Yes,' I said, 'I've—'

'Oh, well, never mind. I'm awfully sorry, Mr Kirrin. It looks like I won't be buying anything. To*day.*'

'Did you hear that voice?' asked Anna-Marie as we left the shop and poor Mr Kirrin. 'When we first went in? You know who that was, don't you?'

I shook my head. I wasn't sure how I was expected to know.

'That was Norman.'

'Norman who?'

Anna-Marie met my blank expression with disgust. 'Norman Kirrin,' she said. 'How many Normans do you know?'

Well, in fact, I didn't know any.

'I'd give anything to get that fairy,' said Anna-Marie. 'I don't know why the old ogre won't sell it to me. He's very fond of me.' I must've looked doubtful. 'Why wouldn't he be?' she said, tossing her pebble. 'I'm very two-faced.'

But I was thinking about that ring. I hadn't seen a price but I was already wondering how many pennies were floating around inside that piggy-bank. It hadn't sounded like much but it was a start. I thought how good it would be to be able to buy it for Kat. No, not good. It would be better than good. It would be reprehensible.

★

As we made our way back towards Everlasting Lane the sun burned like a roaring lion, the fiercest it'd been since raising its head above the horizon that morning. Sunlight bled at the edges of the long shadows creeping across our path. I felt as if I'd woken in one world and crossed into another and never even noticed the two meeting at the border.

'We'll go back along the river,' instructed Anna-Marie, and we descended a steep bank hidden behind trees to the side of the bridge.

And I felt tired. I couldn't quite remember when I'd last slept. It seemed unreal how the day had stretched, gathering everything like a mystic band.

Anna-Marie asked, 'Do you like living here?'

'I suppose,' I said.

'But you'd rather be with your mother.'

I picked up a stick and tapped it on the ground as we walked. 'I suppose.'

'You really have quite a vocabulary,' said Anna-Marie.

'Do *you* like living here?'

'Do you know,' said Anna-Marie, 'for such a spud, you are reasonably adept at avoiding questions you don't want to an-swer, but I wouldn't want you to think I hadn't noticed. In answer to *your* question, however, I can certainly think of a lot worse places to be. I like the lane,' she said. 'Everlasting Lane. I like the sound of it.' She repeated it: 'Everlasting-Lane,' letting her tongue curl about its syllables. 'What if … ?' Anna-Marie stopped and looked at me, weighing me up. 'What if it really did last forever?' she asked me. 'The lane.'

'What do you mean?'

'Me?' She threw her head back as she walked along. 'I don't mean anything.'

I thought about the lane wondering whether it really could last forever, whether you'd see Australians and kangaroos, Eskimos and igloos, Red Indians and buffaloes. I walked and wondered and, in my mind, tapped out our route around the world with my stick.

As we reached the point along the path that backed onto the trees separating us from Kat's garden, I saw a strange thing. On the opposite bank was a field, and in that field I could see a man—close enough to see but too far off to see clearly. He was standing right in the middle of the field turning and looking first to the north, then to the east, then to the south and so on, each direction in turn, round and round, as if waiting for something to leap out at him from beyond the horizon.

'Who's that?'

'Who? Oh, him. That's the Scarecrow Man.'

'What's he doing?'

Anna-Marie shrugged. 'I don't know,' she said. 'Scaring crows?'

We slipped between the trees and through a rusted old gate into Kat's back garden. We heard a voice barking: 'Anna-Marie! Where are you? Come here! Right now, Anna-Marie!' It threatened to jump angrily over the dividing fence.

Anna-Marie scowled. 'Now that,' she hissed, 'is my mother. I'd better go.' Half way down the garden path she stopped, turned to face me, and said, 'I'm sorry about your dad.' And then, 'Who's your favourite Roller?'

'What?'

'Roller, numbskull—your favourite Roller? There's Les, Derek, Eric, Woody or Ian! Who's your favourite?'

'Woody,' I said. I liked the sound of the name.

'Hmm,' said Anna-Marie. And then, 'See you tomorrow, numbskull!' With that she ran off, her plimsoll slap, slap, slapping on the dry garden path.

I glanced up at the cottage. There was a light on in one of the upstairs rooms and I could see where Kat had stuck that strip of cardboard in place of the broken pane. There was something odd about it but for now I was too tired to think what it was.

I entered the kitchen through the back door only to be swallowed up by smoke and a burning smell rising from the baked beans bubbling on the stove. Leaving the door open and seizing a wooden spoon, I investigated the thick orange lump at the bottom of the pan. I wrapped a tea-towel around my hand and lifted the saucepan from the hot coil.

'Mum!' I called, and then, 'Kat!' I popped my head into the lounge. No. I went to the stairs and called up: 'Kat! Kat!'

Perhaps she was asleep. I ran up the stairs, thumped once on her bedroom door and plunged in. No: the room was empty. My bedroom? No. Locked in the lavatory? No.

I returned to the kitchen and attempted to wave the lingering smoke into the garden.

'Peter?' At last. 'What's that terrible smell?' Kat was descending the stairs, a teacup in her hand. 'Oh, my goodness,' she said examining the contents of the pan. 'I must've fallen asleep. Lucky you came home or I might've set the whole place on fire.'

She scooped what was left of the beans onto two plates and grated cheese over the top of mine.

'What's up with you?' she said as she put the plates on the table. 'Cat got your tongue?'

6

'Is it much further?'

'No,' said Anna-Marie. 'It's over there.'

I followed Anna-Marie's finger, through nettles and trees, across the river. I could just make out a … a fence. 'It's a fence.'

'Well, yes.'

'Oh.'

When I'd seen Anna-Marie, wearing a denim skirt and a white T-shirt with tartan trimmings, lurking outside the front door that morning and promising me 'a secret' I hadn't thought of, well, a fence.

'Come on,' she snapped, tugging my sleeve.

So, on we went. The fence disappeared but I could see a roof, grey slate, two or three stories up. 'It's a roof.'

'Yes, yes,' said Anna-Marie. 'Come on. Come on.'

And now the building itself came into view: red bricks and white-framed windows; the ground floor, also white, jutted out. The fence reappeared, a bit more of the roof and a smooth lawn sloping down towards the river. A little further and a chimney emerged. And then another. And then another.

We reached a point opposite the building where our view of the lawn was blocked by the thickest wall of nettles yet rising as high as our chins. We couldn't see the chimneys or the fence any more but it was the best sight of the building. Anna-Marie stretched to improve her view, stamping her feet in frustration, as close to the nettles as she dared, willing them apart. But they were so dense and tangled that eventually she sighed. 'We can sit down a little further up,' she said grudgingly, 'but we can't see as much.'

There was a path, of sorts, where the nettles weren't so thick and someone, I guessed Anna-Marie, had made their way on previous expeditions.

'Follow me,' and, arms above her head, Anna-Marie shimmied sideways through the nettles. When I raised my arms, my T-shirt exposed the bare belly above my shorts and I was soon aware of the gentle touch of the poisoned leaves. I followed, smarting and yelping in pain, whilst my companion laughed and laughed at my complaints. By the time we emerged and settled beneath a great Frankenstein's monster of a tree, I had decided to keep my suffering to myself.

'Phew,' said Anna-Marie throwing herself down on the grassy bank beside the living river. 'I'm crackered.'

I rested on a tree stump, listening to the birds, and watching midges and butterflies playing in the sun. Anna-Marie slipped off her plimsolls and socks and slid her feet into the cold water. It twinkled between her toes.

'Won't we get caught?'

'Not if you shut up we won't,' said Anna-Marie. 'Well?' she said. 'What do you think? Isn't it beautiful?'

And it was kind of beautiful. The red brick glowed like fire in a grate whilst the lawn and the tall trees that stood to either side produced a splendid light of their own. It was like a deep and peaceful dream far from the distant fury of the waking world.

'C–c–come on in,' she said, 'the water's f–f–freezing.' The

only water I'd ever put between my toes had been warm and soapy. But she patted the ground beside her. 'I insist,' she said. And, once I'd joined her, 'Well done. Now, take off your sandals and I ... will show you some magic.'

Her lips were amused but I couldn't read the look in her eyes at all.

'Now, close them—your eyes—tight. And put your feet in the water. Oh, come on, it won't kill you. Good. Now, keep your feet very still. Now, wait and you will feel the water ... turn ... to stone. Don't move or you'll break the spell.'

'It's cold,' I said. 'It ... It tickles.'

Anna-Marie giggled. 'I know,' she said. 'Now, don't move,' she warned. 'It pinches if you move.'

'What is it?' I asked meaning the strange building.

'That,' said Anna-Marie, 'is the Lodge.'

I peered at it. 'But what is it?'

'Well,' Anna-Marie paused, 'it's a hospital.'

'A what?'

'A hos-pea-tal.'

'A hospital?'

'Of sorts. Listen, you are *English*, aren't you? Should I make sure I use,' she raised her voice, 'ea-zee-words.'

I frowned. It didn't look like any hospital I'd ever seen.

'I'm so sorry,' said Anna-Marie. 'I didn't realise you were an expert. When you kept asking what it was, I naturally assumed you were a moron.'

'Well, what sort of hospital? What are the people patients of?'

'Oh, very grammatical,' congratulated Anna-Marie. 'They are patients,' she said, 'of life. It's a very serious condition. The worst thing is that most of them don't even know they're ill. They're the ones who suffer the most I think. Anyway,' she explained, 'they come to take the waters.' She suddenly smacked

43

me, hard, on the back of my head. 'Look,' she snapped, 'do you think I'm making this up?'

'No,' I grumbled rubbing the point of impact.

'Okay,' she laughed. 'Let me show you around. Over there, look, to the left, are the stables. I don't mean for horses. It's been ... what's the word? ... converted. It's rooms and whatnot now and you see that clock, well ... well, you can't really see the clock from here, but if you go a little further along, you can just see it. It's two hundred years old and keeps perfect time. Over there,' she went on, 'is a tennis court, but they don't use it much anymore, at least I've never seen anyone play, that's why there's no net and all the chairs are scattered about.'

'What chairs?'

'Well, you can't *see* them. You have to use your imagination ... if you have one. There are three floors and the patients either have their own rooms or they share, but they aren't like hospital wards or anything like that.

'Those big doors open out onto the garden. Surely even you can see that. And there's a piano in there and comfy chairs for the patients and a television and everything. The piano may not work. I've hardly ever heard anyone play it.'

'Where are the patients?'

'They're in bed, of course. It's a hospital, not Colditz.'

'What do they look like?'

'You'll see. Oh, don't look so worried. They're not deformed, if that's what you mean. At least not on the outside. It's life, Peter. No one's immune.'

'How do you know so much about it?'

'Well, I've got eyes, haven't I?' She put her hands to her face in a panic. 'I'm sure I remember putting them in this morning. Oh, oh, what a relief!' she exclaimed. 'They are there after all.'

The day was warm and getting warmer. Anna-Marie seemed quite content to sit, wait and wiggle her toes in the smooth flowing water, the shadows of leaves drifting back and forth across her face like camouflage. I tried to match her peaceful expression.

'Look. Someone's coming.'

The big doors opened from within. A short, fat woman in a pink smock with a horse's behind came out onto the patio. She scraped two heavy plant pots across the flagstones so that first one and then both of the double doors were wedged open.

'Who's that?'

'Oh, what does that matter?' barked Anna-Marie and my lips zipped themselves shut.

The woman fetched a garden chair from a pile stacked against the wall of the building and opened it with a snap that echoed in the still air. She positioned it on the edge of the patio facing the river. She then fetched a second and a third and so on until she had placed maybe half a dozen chairs in a row, each a couple of feet from its neighbours.

She disappeared back inside only to return a few moments later, her arm looped through that of an old woman with thin white hair, blinking as she shuffled out into the bright sunlight. She was wearing a nightgown and a knitted top with bright buttons. The fat woman led the old lady down to one of the garden chairs, folded her thin bones into place and then left. Within a minute she was back, this time escorting a younger man with a big round face. Several times the lady in the pink smock departed and returned until she had assembled her patients like battalions on the living room carpet, heads nodding like dandelions in the wind.

Anna-Marie pulled an apple from her back pocket and bit a chunk. 'So, what do you think?' she asked mid-chew, gazing across the water and wobbling her toes in the cool river. 'Do you know I can't think of anything you could do—anything—that wouldn't be better if you could do it there. I mean, if *I* was ill then this is just the sort of hospital I'd want to come to. Wouldn't you?' A butterfly appeared, its wings pink and I watched hypnotised as it settled like a ribbon upon Anna-Marie's silky-smooth hair. 'I said, wouldn't you?' She flapped her hand, her long, delicate fingers, once, and it, the butterfly, scuttered off across the river. 'Peter, I'm trying to …

'What are you gawping at, dimwit?'

'I … I …'

'You know,' she said with a yawn, revealing the contents of her mouth, 'I think this weather's getting to you. I'm not surprised you're the first. Your grip on reality seems so … tenuous.'

'No, I—'

'How *is* the weather on Planet Peter? Is it barmy?'

Anna-Marie had gone home for tea. It was school in the morning and her mother insisted on an early night. And that's how I found myself alone in Kat's garden among the brambles and tall grass, staring at the upstairs window: the upstairs window on the left with the pink curtains and the broken pane. I could see where Kat had stuck that strip of cardboard. Yes, there was definitely something odd. I counted the windows and then counted them again. It didn't take long. There were only three of them: the bathroom window, my window and the window with the pink curtains.

Was I the stupidest boy who'd ever lived, I wondered, or just one of the stupidest?

My mind entered the cottage through the back door, crept through the kitchen where Kat was scrambling eggs and up the creaky stairs. On the landing to the right was her bedroom door and the window that overlooked the drive; to the left, the bathroom and my door. My curtains were blue and the bathroom had a blind and that rippled glass so you can't look in and spy on people when they're naked. Kat's curtains were all flowery and they faced the front anyway. None were pink.

And then I remembered when the beans had been burning and I'd been looking for Kat all that time and Kat hadn't been upstairs but *had* been upstairs. And then I remembered the four keys on Kat's key-ring.

But there were only three doors.

And then I remembered the big, green drape. And then I wondered what it was hiding.

PART II

Every Story Needs a Secret Room

7

Mi name is Peter Lambert. I am 10 years old. I live in Everlasting Lane. Today is mi first day at ~~new~~ mi new school. Mi teacher is Mr Gale who is very nise. The hedmistres is Mrs Crapenter who is very nise. I sit next to Tommie who is very—

My piece of paper was whipped from beneath my pencil. I'd already written 'ni ...' on the table-top before I realised. Mr Gale adjusted his glasses and stroked his blue tie as he read my work.

'Well, I can see what you're getting at ... But you've got yourself into a bit of a rut, haven't you, Lambchop? And this handwriting: typical left-hander but *how* old are you?' Mr Gale's meaty fist crushed my work into a ball and tossed it in the direction of—but not into—the bin. 'Tell me something about your*self*, not all this ... this ... this *crap* about how nice everybody is. Besides,' he added, wandering off among the desks, a red tick here, a red cross there, 'I'm not that nice.'

Maybe he was right. Ten minutes into my first lesson he'd christened me Lambchop and I wasn't pleased. I didn't feel like a Lambchop and I didn't want to be one. It's like Kat said, a name is important but—

'Lambchop!' boomed Mr Gale.

Never answer. If I don't answer, I thought, he'll have to call me 'Peter'.

'Lambchop!'

I held my breath.

'Lamb*chop*!' But I couldn't ignore a teacher—not three times.

'Yes, sir?' And Kat had said I was my name and my name was who I was. Maybe I was a Lambchop after all.

'Excellent, Lambchop. I thought we'd lost you there; away with the fairies. But, what I'm wondering is why you're here at all. A new child on the first day of summer term? It could completely bugger up the finely tuned balance of my class. Anyway,' he said, 'best get on. Have a fresh piece of paper.'

My name is Peter Lambert. I am aged 10 years old. I live in Everlasting Lane in a vilag called Amberley. I have moved here from …

I'd squeezed Kat's hand as we'd stepped into the entrance of Dovecot Junior School. A jolly woman with ginger hair had appeared. 'Good morning, dear,' she said. 'Can I help?'

'Hello. This is Peter,' said Kat. 'Peter Lambert. He's just moved into the village. And, erm … He'd like to come to school … Please.'

'Oh, yes,' said the woman with a wide smile. 'There was a letter from county, wasn't there?' When Kat said nothing the woman enquired: 'And you're his mother?'

'Of course,' murmured Kat through gritted teeth. 'Yes, of course.' I might easily have reacted if she hadn't squeezed my hand. For a minute I'd completely forgotten she *was* my mother.

'Wonderful,' said the woman. 'Well, hello, Peter, I'm Mrs Ingalls, the school secretary.' And then to Kat: 'You'll need to fill out a form.'

As Kat completed our details, twice scrunching up the form and asking for a replacement, Mrs Ingalls said, 'You know, you really are quite familiar, dear. Do I know you?'

Kat smiled but said, 'Oh, Peter hasn't got any uniform or anything.'

'Oh, don't worry,' said Mrs Ingalls. 'We can dig something out of lost property, can't we, Peter? Of course, we can.' She presented me with a school tie, red and white stripes, an infant tie with elastic to loop around your neck. 'Now, now, Peter,' said Mrs Ingalls. 'Don't be like that. Keep it under your collar and no-one will ever know.'

'Now that,' said Kat, 'is always good advice.'

Mr Gale had brown hair, a thick neck and a large head. He seized my tiny hand in his fist.

'Who's this?' he said.

Mrs Ingalls introduced me. 'This is Peter Lambert,' she explained. 'He's just moved into Everlasting Lane,' before departing with a smile and a gentle, 'Good luck.'

'Welcome to Dovecot, Peter,' said Mr Gale. He turned me to face the class, gripping my shoulders until his fingers pinched. 'Mr Gale's class,' he boomed, 'this is Peter. Peter *Lam*bert. Peter, this is the class. Say, "Good morning", the class.'

I wilted beneath the glare of twenty-three strangers. 'Good morning, Mr Gale,' they chanted. If the eyes of one suspicious ten-year-old can slice and dice you, 'Good morning, Peter,' the eyes of twenty-three can turn you into mincemeat.

'Say, "Good morning", Peter *Lam*bert. Lamby-Lambert.'

'Good morning,' I said, face boiling.

'Peter,' said Mr Gale, 'Mr Lamby-Lambert, I, for one, am glad to meet you. But, my, your shoulders are tense.' He examined my neck. 'Aha, I think I've discovered the culprit.' He pulled on my elasticated tie revealing it to everyone. The class squealed with delight. 'No, no, class,' said Mr Gale wagging his finger, 'there is nothing to be ashamed of in not being able to tie a tie.' I tried to interrupt but, 'Even at the age of nine,' he continued. 'I only learnt to tie my shoelaces a week ago last Thursday.'

He put me next to a boy with curly black hair and thick-framed glasses. 'Do you know Winnie?' said Mr Gale. 'He's not the sharpest knife in the drawer but is, nonetheless, still too clever for his own good. You two must be neighbours.'

There was no spare chair, so I was given a stool, and sat head and shoulders above the rest of the children. Mr Gale might just as well have given me a flag to wave—I couldn't have felt any more stupid. Then he snapped his fingers.

'Lambchop!' he exclaimed. 'Of course! That's what we'll call you!' Well, I'd been wrong. *Now* I couldn't feel any more stupid.

*My name is Peter Lambert. I am aged 10 years old. I live in Everlasting Lane in a villag called Amberly. I used to live in L_____.
Now I live with ~~my arnt~~ my ~~mother Kat mumm Kat arnt~~ ...*

I dropped my head into my hands. It wasn't my fault. I'd lain awake all night dreaming of gloomy green curtains and—

'Hmm,' said Mr Gale, 'a lot of crossing out. And what are all these ... these ... these doodles?'

'Doors, sir.'

'Doors? What sort of doors?'

'Secret doors.'

He gave me an odd look. 'Well, perhaps we should just …' And, before I could object, my piece of paper was scrunched and sailing through the air, landing two feet shy of the bin. 'Piss-sticks!' said Mr Gale.

In morning assembly, the headmistress, Mrs Carpenter, read a Bible story. She had all these wrinkles and curly white hair. Her dress was purple and green, and a tiny silver cross hung on a thin chain about her neck. Time thickened like porridge as she spoke and the hands of the hall clock struggled until she closed the book and looked up with a satisfied smile.

'Put your hands together,' she said, 'and close your eyes.'

After the story, the prayer and a hymn, Mrs Carpenter read 'notices'. Following an instruction from, 'Mr Waterberry, that nobody should play on the swings until the broken seat has been replaced,' and a reminder that, 'although you are allowed on the field at lunchtime, footballers must pick up and replace all divots without exception,' I was welcomed. 'You may have noticed a new face in the third year today.' Everyone turned to look. Little children in the first row swivelled, stared and gasped in amazement. 'I am sure you will all welcome Peter Lambert to Dovecot, and, if you see him looking a little lost, perhaps you will stop and offer him assistance. After all, as Jesus said …'

I looked around to see Anna-Marie at the far end of the row behind mine, a grey, thready cardigan draped over the shoulders of her blue checked dress. Her lips were thin and her eyes, dark and angry, glared at the headmistress.

•

'Well, Lambchop,' said Mr Gale, 'this is a special day, did you know that?'

'No, Mr Gale.'

'*No*, Mr Gale,' he repeated. 'Well, today is the first day of a new term and, therefore, it is the day in which we ... we ... we *fin*ish the work we didn't quite finish last term.' The class groaned. 'Hey, hey,' he responded, 'you're not here to enjoy yourselves. We've got to finish the old before we start the new. History folders out.'

A hand, attached to the arm of a pretty girl with shiny raven hair, shot up. 'Lambchop,' continued Mr Gale, 'you know, I always say history is like geography: if you don't know where you started, how do you know you're travelling in the right direction? Right? I ... What *is* it, Smelanie?' said Mr Gale. 'You sound like a hamster.'

'I've finished *all* my topic work, sir.'

It was Mr Gale's turn to groan. 'Right. Then you, Smel-a-nie, should write a story entitled *The ... The ... The Secret Garden*. No ... *Goldfish. Garden* or *Goldfish.*'

'But which?'

'Garden, goldfish, rubber, pencil, window, door. I really don't care. You decide.'

'But how many sides?'

'Smelanie, you mustn't allow your creativity to be stifled by such petty considerations. But if you could have it finished by lunchtime on the dot that would be great. Okay?'

'Yes, Sir.'

'Lambchop?'

'Yes, Sir?'

'What are you staring at?'

'What? Nothing, Sir. Sorry, Sir.'

'Splendid.'

•

The curly-haired boy nudged me. 'Are we really neighbours?' he whispered. His jumper was baggy and shapeless, his tie ske-wiff and a top button pulled tight across his throat. One side of his grubby white collar poked up into his cheek.

I told him I lived in Everlasting Lane.

Mr Gale coughed and the boy put pen to paper, blue ink staining his fingers. He wrote two words.

'That's where I live,' he said, attempting to slow the flow of ink with a scrap of well-used blotting paper. 'Where are you from?'

When I told him he said, 'I used to live in London. That's where my dad lives.' His eyes twinkled behind heavy lenses. 'He says it's much better than living in Amberley.'

'Oh,' I said. 'Are you Tommie?'

'How do you know?'

'Anna-Marie told me.'

His face blazed bright red. His lip stiffened. And he punched me.

'What is it, Lambchop?' asked Mr Gale looking up from the blackboard.

'Nothing, Sir,' I said, rubbing my arm.

'Right. Good,' said Mr Gale, 'but maybe writing: *I must keep my Neanderthal outbursts to myself*, thirty times during playtime will encourage you to contain your enthusiasm.' He returned to his chalk. 'Oh, and as Winnie's causing you a bit too much excitement, why don't you move that big ol' stool next to Smelanie? You won't find self-control so much of a struggle under her influence.' Smelanie—I mean Melanie—Finch blushed as she slid her pencil case, rubber, ruler, gonk and dictionary to one side.

Tommie turned around as I moved my stool and settled into my new place, his lenses flashed with anger as he mouthed: 'I hate you!'

I must keep my nandatarl outbursts to myself,
I must keep my narandatall outbursts to myself,
I must keep my nanatall outbursts to myself,
I must keep my nranndatawl outbursts to myself . . .

It just wasn't a word I knew, although I turned Smelanie's dictionary inside out trying to find it.

8

Melanie Finch wrote feverishly all morning long and even glancing at the clock didn't slow her down. Her pen flashed across the page leaving dazzling loops and curls. It made my own writing look rubbish but when I asked to borrow a rubber, Melanie puffed.

'You're not allowed to use a rubber.'

'What?'

'You're supposed to use a pen,' she hissed. She wrestled my pencil from my hand, '*Pens* are for writing,' and shoved a pen in its place, '*pencils* are for maths, and crayons,' she returned to her story, 'are for babies.'

'Why?'

'*Why?*' She looked at me as if I was demented. 'It's the *rules*,' and with an exasperated huff she turned her sharp little shoulder blade towards me.

As the lunch bell rang, Melanie's hand was a skyrocket. 'Finished, Sir!'

"Finished, Sir!" squealed Mr Gale, marking books. He didn't look up as he said, 'Well done, Finchy. Leave it on the ol' desk.' A thick finger indicated a tall, untidy pile. 'I'll look at it later.'

'Couldn't you read it now, sir? *Please?*'

'Tell me, Finchy, does the last sentence read *and then I woke up and it was all a dream* or words to that effect?' He still hadn't looked up.

Melanie's voice, when she did answer, was soft as snow and twice as cold. 'I didn't have enough time.'

'Oh, Finchy, you know how I feel about all that Alice-in-Wonderland-crap,' said Mr Gale. 'Now, put it on my desk and I'll look at it later.'

Melanie slapped her story on top of the tottering heap before returning to her place, cheeks flushed with fury.

'Psst.' I looked up. 'Hey.' It was Tommie Winslow. 'Peter,' he said, 'can I borrow something?'

I nodded warily. After all, I had nothing to lend.

He leant back towards me, his chair balanced on its back legs. 'This,' he said grabbing the piece of paper on which I'd been working. With a smirk of triumph he reduced it to a crumpled fistful and launched it smartly in to the wastepaper bin.

During playtime I wandered around the playground peering into classrooms, checking apparatus, studying the fancy dovecot that gave the school its name. Tommie was on the field playing football. I could feel him watching me, so I tried to look as if I had more important things on my mind whilst listening to the footballers' cries, the hopscotch and the sing-song rhythms of the skipping-rope rhymes:

> *Poor little Alice,*
>   *Berries from a tree,*
>   *Poor little Alice,*
>   *Swimming in the sea.*
>   *Ma's out, pa's out, baby don't cry,*
>   *How many ways must the poor girl die?*

And then I saw Anna-Marie.

Back towards the school was a climbing frame and swings. It was a double swing but the seat of one was missing so the chains hung loose. Anna-Marie, her tatty cardigan now knotted about her waist, was sitting on the other, one foot dragging in the dry dirt.

I was about to run up to her when Tommie appeared and grabbed my arm. 'Do you want to play footie?' he said, pulling me away. 'You can be on my team but you'll have to be goalie.'

Before I could answer we were distracted by a loud voice. This scary-looking woman, a dinner-lady who could just as well have been a dinner-man, was shouting at Anna-Marie. 'Mrs Carpenter says nobody plays on the swing!'

'I'm not playing, Miss Lennox,' said Anna-Marie, shyly investigating a bruise that had appeared at her throat. 'I don't play games.'

'You don't follow rules either,' snapped Miss Lennox. 'Now, off the swing!'

'Why?' asked Anna-Marie. 'I'm not hurting anybody.'

Poor little Alice,
Choking on a cake,
Poor little Alice,
Stepping on a snake.
Ma's out, pa's out, baby don't cry,
How many ways must the poor girl die?

'If you don't get off this swing, I'm going to take you to Mrs Carpenter.'

'Hello, Juliette.' A very pretty young woman with a bundle of dark blonde hair had emerged from a nearby classroom. 'Is there a problem?' The new lady wore a tracksuit and a bright blue bib with 'GA' printed on the front in big white capitals.

A whistle and a pendant hung side by side around her neck flashing in the sun.

Miss Lennox's eyes rolled up and down the younger woman from the top of her curly mop to the toes of her plimsolls. 'No, Miss Pevensie,' she said with a sigh. 'No problem.' She glanced at Anna-Marie. 'Just the Queen of Sheba here doesn't think the rules apply to her.'

'It's a stupid rule, Miss Pevensie,' whined Anna-Marie. 'It's just a swing. It's not like I'm going to kill myself.'

'Come on,' nagged Tommie. 'Are you playing?'

'No,' I said. 'I'm going to help Anna-Marie.'

'No, you're not!' he said. 'I am!'

'Oh, look, Miss Pevensie,' said Anna-Marie as she saw us coming, 'it's Tweedledum and Tweedlethick.' She looked at us as if we were a pair of brown blobs floating in her semolina.

Miss Pevensie puffed out her cheeks. 'Lordy, Anna-Marie,' she said, 'why don't you do us all a favour,' as she spoke she seized a fistful of the hair on the top of her head, 'and get off the swing?'

Anna-Marie sighed and slid to the ground. 'Okay, Miss Pevensie,' she said, and then, 'Well, Miss Lennox, you'd better get me to the old ... dear before I change my mind.' The skipping-ropers stopped to watch as Anna-Marie marched across the playground towards the school building, Miss Lennox spluttering in her wake. Some of the older girls, including Melanie Finch, laughed or hissed at her as she passed.

'Anna-Marie,' I said, 'I—'

'And you two,' she snapped, 'can bog off!'

Poor little Alice,
Skating on the ice.
Poor little Alice,

Careless with a knife.
Ma's out, pa's out, baby don't cry,
How many ways must the poor girl die?

Tommie Winslow was much friendlier after lunch. I didn't know why. He lent me his felt tips and showed me, to Melanie's annoyance, the answers to the maths.

'Well, Winnie,' said Mr Gale, 'Peter's done very well on his multiplication.' Tommie nodded. 'And now I can ... I can ... I can re*tire* with satisfaction. I'll tell you what though,' he said slapping Tommie hard on the shoulder, 'why don't you accompany me to the big ol' blackboard and explain it to the rest of the class?' Tommie didn't move. 'Stage fright? Not to worry, Winnie my boy, pack yourself off to Mrs Carpenter and explain it all to her instead.'

'Please, Sir.'

'*Please*, Sir. *Please*, Sir,' repeated Mr Gale, veins throbbing on his temples. 'Listen, boy,' he snarled, 'I am *not* paid enough to put up with your silly games. Don't take me for a fool, boy! D'you hear me? Don't take me for a fool!' Tommie nodded, his thick-rimmed glasses filled with fear. 'Maybe fifteen minutes at home-time every day this week will make my point for me.'

Tommie's face collapsed. 'A week?'

'Oh, and, Lambchop,' continued Mr Gale with a smile, 'if you don't understand, ask *me*. That's my job. What would I do all day if Winnie were to start teaching the class? That makes sense, doesn't it?' I nodded. 'Fine, fine,' he said. 'Glad to get that cleared up.

'Now, *kids*, why don't you get out your folders and finish off your river poems? And if you've finished your poems you can ... How about a poster for the summer fair? Or something.

'Winnie, take young Lambchop here down to the office

and ask Mrs Ingalls to give him a topic folder of his very own. Wha'd'you say? Splendid.

'Put your hand down, Smelanie. You sound like a gerbil.'

Poor little Alice,
Tripping on a wire,
Poor little Alice,
Playing by the fire.
Ma's out, pa's out, baby don't cry,
How many ways must the poor girl die?

Tommie led me from the classroom to the playground and into a small space between the bins behind the generator.

'Won't we get in trouble?'

Tommie shook his head. 'What do you think of him?'

'Mr Gale?' I said. 'I don't know. He gets really angry.'

'I think he might be mad,' whispered Tommie. 'Once, I was off ill for three days and he read my note to the class. It said that I'd been sick and … stuff. Who would do that? Well, everybody laughed and … Well, some of the girls called me … Well, stuff for weeks. He thought it was funny,' said Tommie. 'My dad says I should stand up for myself.'

'Are you friends with Anna-Marie?'

'Oh, yes,' said Tommie. 'I thought *you* might be friends with her. That's why I didn't like you.'

'*I* thought I was friends with her.'

Tommie frowned. 'Did Anna-Marie ever ask you who your favourite Roller was?'

'Yes.'

'Oh … What did you say?'

'Woody.'

Tommie laughed. 'Ha,' he said. 'It's Les. You see, apart from me, Anna-Marie isn't really friends with anyone.'

Back in the classroom, Tommie returned to his seat but shot straight back up again, letting out a yelp. Mr Gale rushed to him and placed an arm around his shoulder. 'What on earth's wrong?' Tommie flinched as he removed a drawing pin from his behind. 'Oh, my Lord!' exclaimed Mr Gale. 'Whoever's responsible for this heinous crime? Speak now or forever hold your penis.' Nobody even looked up from their work. 'Oh, well, Winnie,' said Mr Gale, a big grin on his face, 'it looks like we may never get to the *bottom* of it.'

Tommie turned to me. 'See?' he mouthed. 'Mad!'

My name is Peter Lambert. I am aged ten years old. 'Lambchop.' *I was nine years old the night my father died.* 'Lambchop!' *Or ten. I don't remember—*

'Lambchop!' Mr Gale was scowling over my shoulder, his large fingers squeezing creases into my work. 'It's not much to show for a whole—'

I grabbed the crumpled paper from his hands and tore it into strips. Melanie gasped and everybody else stared at me like *I* was mad.

Mr Gale looked startled. 'Perhaps,' he said, nodding towards the pale-eyed children whose table stood apart from the rest beneath the window, 'we should put you with the special-learners.'

I slipped the shreds of torn paper into my pocket.

9

At the end of the day Tommie was in his detention and, still upset from Anna-Marie at lunchtime, I was pleased to find Kat waiting for me, lurking with her back to the crowd of mothers standing by the gate. She seemed relieved to see me and took me quickly by the hand but it was already too late. This one woman had turned round as Kat called my name and was staring at her open-mouthed. I recognised her right away. It was that fat lady from the Lodge.

'Well, bless my soul!' she cried.

Kat was about to speak when I squeezed *her* hand as hard as I could, you know, before she broke the rules of the game. I was just in time.

'I'm sorry,' she mumbled to the fat lady and we scurried off like two blind mice.

There was no pavement on the main road, so, hand in hand, we pressed back against the cushion of the hedgerow as vehicles passed. It was warm and we breathed the scent of honeysuckle and other sweet summer smells. Kat took a deep breath, sighed and began pointing out the boundaries between the different farms.

'Isn't it beautiful, Peter?' she said. 'Wasn't it right to come here?' And then, 'Oh, my goodness! Look!' In the distance, maybe half a mile away, there was that man again, the one I told you about, in the middle of a field turning from one direction to another. Kat stopped and stared. She bit her lip and trembled. 'I haven't seen him in years.'

'Who is he?'

'That,' said Kat, 'is the Scarecrow Man.'

★

Mr Waterberry, the school caretaker, came from the village to do the garden. He was blind in one eye with thin grey hair but as tall and as strong as a bear. He pushed an ancient mower through the blistery heat and drank water from the outside tap as sweat tumbled down his wiry chest. 'No one's been in that garden in ages,' he rasped. 'You should've called me years ago.'

'We keep ourselves to ourselves,' said Kat.

Mr Waterberry tilted his head and nodded before saying, 'I know you, m'love, don't I? This is Margaret Goodwin's cottage. You're her girl.'

'Well, you're making excellent progress,' said Kat (meaning the garden).

'It's not a lie,' she explained when he'd gone. 'It's like telling a story. Not everything has to be true but that doesn't make it a lie. We don't want to tell any lies,' said Kat, 'but we don't necessarily want to tell the whole truth.'

She called the cottage our sanctuary. And she was right. Being in Amberley changed everything. But sometimes I'd forget where I was and call her 'Mum' or 'Mummy'. She'd smile and shake her head. 'You can call me Kat,' she'd say, 'with a "K".' And it was nice to pretend. Sometimes pretending was better than when things were real.

She seemed happy and, before long, it was like we'd been there forever. And I think I would've been happy too but for the gloomy, green drape that I passed each night when I went to bed and every morning on my way to breakfast.

'I'll tell you what,' said Kat as if she, like me, had been thinking about something completely different, 'why don't I show you where I used to make magic?'

Magic? I nodded. Well, that was more like it.

I followed her out of the cottage and across the gravel drive to this big shed all nestled beneath the trees. She twisted a squeaky padlock and inserted a key. I couldn't help noticing, as the door squealed on its hinges and Kat encouraged me to peer in, that the bedroom keys had not yet been returned to the brass ring.

'I haven't been in here for a while,' she confessed. The small window was thick with grime and the inside hung with shadows like sides of beef in a butcher's shop. 'There certainly used to be a light in here,' she continued, fumbling around in the darkness. 'Ah, here it is.'

I took a nervous step forward as the bulb glowed and all was revealed.

'This,' said Kat, 'is my workshop. This is where I used to make magic.'

But it didn't look very magical. There were just cardboard boxes everywhere, some sealed, others splitting at the corners or overflowing with magazines; a Union Jack hat sat on the head of a shop mannequin; an old record player and dusty black records in and out of their sleeves; a guitar with no strings; a rusting bicycle; an old paddling pool hung like an elephant skin on the wall; a toy pram still wrapped in polythene; cushions spilling their guts and enough tools to build an Ark.

The walls were lined with shelves and the shelves packed with sculptures, carvings from wood and stone. Some were just weird shapes, all curves and angles, others were of people or animals. One was of a mother and a baby and, although they were sort of naked, when I bent down to see it I thought of those statues of Mary and Jesus they sometimes have in churches.

'I always wanted a little girl,' murmured Kat. 'What do you think?'

'Did you make these?' I was amazed. 'They're really good.'

'No,' she said laughing, 'no they're not, really. But thank you, anyway.' She kind of curtsied and then glanced around. 'Do you know, Peter,' she said breathing deep on the dusty air, 'some shepherd boy only stumbled across the Dead Sea Scrolls because they'd been hidden in the middle of nowhere rather than at the back of my workshop where they would have lain undiscovered 'til the end of—'

'How is it magic?'

She smiled. 'Come on,' she said. 'I've got something to show you.'

In the middle of the shed—I mean the workshop—was a workbench, and in the middle of the workbench, surrounded by chisels and sketch books was something: something big hidden beneath a crumpled, white, paint-spattered sheet.

'Do you want to see it?'

I nodded and, gripping it tightly with both hands, she slowly tugged the sheet away.

It was a piece of wood. But that's like saying *Tiswas* is a TV show and only making it sound like *Nationwide* because you haven't mentioned all the running around and buckets of water and stuff like that. It was a chunk, a slice of rough, knotted tree trunk, as big as an armchair and looking as if it had been wrenched from the very heart of the fiercest monster in the woods.

'Now,' said Kat, 'shall I tell you how to make a beautiful

sculpture? First of all you go into the woods, deep into the woods, and you spend the best part of a *week* finding just the right piece of wood, a special piece of wood.' Her hand caressed the rough bark just like it was Kitty's silky coat. '*This* piece of wood. Then you get your tools: a hammer, of course, and a chisel, good quality ones, nothing cheap, and then, very gently and very carefully, you remove *ev*erything that isn't ... beautiful.'

'What'll it be?'

'What'll it be?' she whispered as if she didn't even know herself. 'It'll be ... whatever it wants to be. You see, Peter, it's separate from me: like I'm standing on a beach, perched on my toes, and its flotsam on the horizon. I just sharpen my blade,' and she picked up a chisel, holding it in the palm of her hand, admiring the curved handle, 'sharpen my wits and let them dance across the grain, like ... like sparks in a fire. I don't make. In fact, I take away and what I, what the chisel takes away is just as vital as what we leave behind. What's just wood, Peter, and what's something more? Do you see what I mean? What do we take and what do we leave? And what's the difference? The wood,' she said, 'the wood tells us the difference.'

'You see, when I'm working—and yes, it *is* work—I close my eyes.' And she did so, scrunching them up tight. 'They're not always the best guide as to what I should do. Sculpture, any art really, is based on trust, you see, on love even. And I don't mean trust or love like in films or TV. I mean on, I don't know, a deeper level, a connection between two, well, souls that's nearly ... nearly physical, that can't be broken, that can hardly be dented by anything but, well ... death. I trust my hands and I trust the wood: that we're not going to mess up. We're a team, the wood and I, a partnership, almost like a ... like a marriage. And yet, do you know, sometimes, well, I worry that, like the hammer,' she picked it up and held it tight, 'and the chisel,

I'm just a tool and we're all being … wielded by the sculpture within.

'So I close my eyes tightly, like this, and my hands move this way or that way as the grain tells them.' She ran the head of the hammer and the blade of the chisel over the rough terrain of the wood. 'I picture myself in the garden of the cottage: this cottage. There's a little girl there, her hair's like … like fire, chasing butterflies, her hands all curious. She falls and she cries,' Kat let out a little cry herself, 'but I don't rush to comfort her. Children require discipline, you know. She'll find no answers here; no explanations; no justifications. I love my child … I mean I love you, Peter,' she opened her eyes and smiled at me, 'no matter how … unruly, in a way that I could never love anybody else's but spare the whip, they say, and spoil the child. Where it would be … tardy, you should make it punctual; where it would be lazy you must apply its fingers to labour without pity. But the unruly child will follow its own rules and keep nobody's time but its own.

'But, you see, Peter, the wood will make her wise. Can you see that? If I trust, if I plug away, cut away long enough, keep calm, do not be concerned—and if I get concerned, stop being concerned—the truth is in here somewhere. Like a midwife, I draw the sculpture from the wood, with my hammer and chisel as, well, forceps. Like Eostre, I take the day by the heels and drag it, hot and steaming, out of the twilight. The truth, when it comes, may be no bigger than a bookend and that will be fine.' She smiled, murmuring, 'Yes, that will be fine.' Her eyes were open now and gazing at me as if I *was* the truth. 'Do you know what I mean?'

I nodded.

I didn't really know what she was talking about.

•

We returned to the cottage and I sat at the kitchen table with my orange maths book pretending to learn my times tables. Kat announced that she was 'popping out' to the church to take some of the wild flowers she'd rescued from the blades of Mr Waterberry's mower. As soon as the front door clicked behind her I counted to exactly sixty fidgety seconds before bounding up the stairs, dragging back the green curtain and revealing the secret door. I seized and pulled at the handle just as I'd done a hundred times before. It was still locked. I pulled and pushed at it again and again until eventually I sank onto the tiny chair and wondered what lay behind.

'Peter,' said my father, smiling, 'have you seen this trick?' He moved to the opposite side of the table and drew back the chair. As he sat he took two paper shapes, a red square and a blue circle, from the pile before me. His tongue licked each shape.

And I smiled because, well, I had a trick of my own. The real me couldn't remember what but the memory-me was bubbling, rattling around on the hob trying to keep his lid on. It was like the world's best secret: like an adult's secret, forever just out of view.

Only this one was mine.

My father pressed the red square to the forefinger of his right hand and the blue circle to the forefinger of his left. He placed each gum-shaped finger on the edge of the table with the rest of his fingers hidden beneath.

I stifled a giggle and he smiled again. I felt a bit bad because he thought I was excited by *his* trick. He didn't know about mine. Not yet. I held the secret in my head where it scorched like a piece of toast. I could hear it tempting me to tell it, a best friend whispering in my ear, 'Go on, go on.' I was impatient for the trick to be revealed, to have my cleverness applauded, to taste success as rich and spicy as the hot ginger cake fresh from the oven but I knew I mustn't tell.

It would ruin the surprise.

'Two little butterflies sitting on the wall,' sang my father. 'One named Peter,' he winked at me, wiggling the broad finger of one hand. 'One named Paul,' he wiggled the finger of the other. Then, with a wave of his right hand, he cried, 'Fly away, Peter!'

His finger returned to the surface of the table and the red square had disappeared. I gasped. 'Fly away, Paul!' he cried, repeating the movement with his left hand. When it returned the blue circle too had vanished.

His eyes smiled.

'That's …That's magic.'

'No,' he said a little sadly. He revealed the rest of his fingers and there were the coloured shapes, the red square and the blue circle, just where they'd always been. He'd changed fingers. 'It's a trick,' he said, and then, 'Look at the mess you've made with that glue, Peter.'

Upstairs the Hoover died.

And then—

Kat had been gone an hour. By the time she returned I was back at the kitchen table, twisting and retwisting Action Man into warlike shapes and trying to smile as if the world was a simple, uncomplicated place full of doors which were always unlocked. She stared at me, her eyes like shadows, as if she couldn't quite remember who I was. And then, when she did remember, she said that she was going to lie down for a while and that I should go outside to, 'play or something.'

I sat awhile longer, twisting Action Man's arms and legs

back and forth, back and forth only to look down and discover that one by one I'd pulled them free of his body. The
kitchen clock ticked, the fridge shuddered again and having
tipped Action Man's sad remains onto the bed of pink roses in
the bin, I crept to my bedroom to find the Robin Hood set
Kat had tugged from under my bed. The green felt hat with
the feather was way too small and babyish for me so, instead, I
wrapped my school tie around my head and slipped the bow
over my shoulder. The skipping rope, a perfect lasso—not that
Robin Hood really had a lasso—was missing.

In the kitchen I slapped syrup and jam onto slices of bread
and made a fierce face at my reflection in the butter knife. And
then I trudged out into the dry afternoon woods to play.

Or something.

10

Of course, Robin Hood wasn't really bothered about having anyone to play with either. Apart from his Merry Men I mean. But when my father died the friends I did have at my old school began to keep away from me like I had some kind of *dead-fatheritis*. They were mostly nice to me because the teachers told them to but in their eyes I was different now, as if I'd visited some alien world—like those children who went on their holidays to Spain—but not one that anyone wanted a postcard from: a world where death was something more than the way bad guys met their ends on TV. It was something real. So I would sit on my own and leave them to their games of chase and *Doctor Who* or *Mission: Impossible*. If someone did invite me to join in I'd pretend I hadn't heard or I'd scream at them 'til they went away and told the teacher:

'Miss. Peter's screaming again, Miss.'

A wood pigeon rattled its way through the treetops and I fired all my three arrows, straight and true—'sh-p, sh-p, sh-p'—but there was no twang in the bow and they fell well short of their target. I collected them back and then began spraying the high branches with pebbles. The bird flew away unharmed so I dug into my knapsack and fed my hunger with syrup and strawberry jam.

I didn't know whether to call Anna-Marie a friend or not. I certainly hadn't decided whether to tell her about that curtain and the secret door. Anyway, she'd been ignoring me since that thing on the school playground. Whenever I'd seen her on the way to or from school she'd speeded up or slowed down so that I could never quite catch her. As I rambled between the trees I thought about Maid Marion locked away in her dingy cell by her wicked uncle. And then I couldn't remember for sure if Maid Marion did have a wicked uncle or if I was thinking of somebody else.

Anyway, I decided I would storm the evil sheriff's castle and slice in two any fool who stood in my way and then I would climb the tower steps and tear back the heavy curtain that concealed the beautiful maiden's cell and then I would gaze upon her long blonde hair and big ears, my heart spinning as I took her in my arms and listened for her soft greeting:

'What took you so long, bog-breath?'

I came upon this tree which had uprooted to make a bridge across the river. I picked up a big branch, nearly as long as I was tall, and gripped it between my two fists, swinging it from side to side, preparing to challenge any stranger who might wish to pass over the water. But it was too heavy and, after nearly toppling into the bubbling stream a couple of times, I leant it against a nearby tree (it was too good a stick to just throw away) and practised my kung-fu. I knew that if I was attacked I could defend myself by using the strength of my opponent as a weapon. I wasn't quite sure how that would work but the man on the television looked quite weedy too so it was possible at least. I stood guard for five whole minutes but, when no one did try to cross the bridge, I got bored, collected my hefty stick and went on my way.

And then I stopped.

I was delighted—and quite surprised—to find that I had come right to the very gates of King John's castle nestled among the trees. I was so surprised to find it there that I couldn't help glancing around to see if there was something else nearby to explain its sudden appearance. It was made of concrete, about the size of Kat's Mini Minor with six or eight sides like one of those shapes in Mr Gale's maths box. Two oblong holes stared back at me making it look a bit like King Richard's helmet. And, from inside, I could hear this voice. It sounded like someone reading the news on the radio:

Hyde Park, summer, 1942.
   Couples supine, leave their curves on the grass,
   'What super-power would you have?' she asks. 'To see through walls?
   To fly?'
   'The power to learn by my mistakes,' I reply.

I crept around the castle walls, each step as dusty as the dry earth, and on the far side discovered steps leading down to a narrow gap through which I could enter.
   If I chose to.
   Above the entrance was a handwritten cardboard sign, saying: DANGER—DO NOT ENTER! Usually that would've been enough. Usually I could just have turned around, still curious maybe but otherwise happy. In the last few days, though, I'd already discovered too many mysterious places and thought too much about the secrets they hid. If I just walk away now, I thought, I'll explode.

We join the queue: Will Hay. The Goose Steps Out.
   Her fingers soft on mine: 'Keep yourself safe,' she says.
'Promise?'

'There's only two kinds of soldier,' I say, lest she forget.
'Those who have died and those who haven't died yet.'

As the poem continued—it was definitely a poem because it rhymed at the end—I took down the *Danger* notice and folded it into my pocket. (I thought it would look good on the front of my scrapbook). I went down step by step and slid through the opening. All the brightness of the day had been squeezed out of the light that dripped into the musty cave through its slender eye-holes. Still dazzled by the afternoon it took a moment to make the most of the gloom. Perched on the concrete shelf that ran around the inside of the block was a pale, middle-aged man, vaguely familiar, his hair fading to grey. Beside him were a Thermos flask and, on a folded red napkin, a half-eaten pork pie. In his right hand a pen and on his lap a pad of paper covered with writing. The dim light tip-toed across the page. His eyes were closed as he spoke aloud, his fingers tracing the words like a blind man:

'A May wedding,' she dreams, 'with bridesmaids in silk,
'Rose petals scattered, the bells unruly.
  'A honeymoon in Brighton: on the esplanade, hand in hand.
  'You should come,' she says. 'To the wedding, I mean. You'd like him.'

Suddenly the man's voice coughed and spluttered like an engine and his body went all stiff. A silent heartbeat followed before his eyes snapped open to discover me standing in the shadows.

'Goodness me!' he cried, his hand shooting to his chest. 'Well, who the … ?' At first I thought he might faint but, as his fingers and the palm of his hand massaged his heart, he drew several deep, shuddery breaths and sighed. He peered at me through the windows of his glasses. 'I was doing it again, wasn't I?' he said. 'Out loud?'

I nodded.

'Oh, oh, oh,' cried the man, placing pen and paper on the shelf beside him, 'what on earth must you think of me. "Unhand me, grey-beard loon!" you cry. Loony old man? Sat in pillbox? Reciting poetry?' He cupped a hand to his ear. 'Yes, yes, that's them: the men in the white coats are on their way. "Old man? Pillbox, you say? Poetry?" they cry. "Lock him away, lock him away." What's that? A dungeon? "Oh, yes, but only the deepest, darkest dungeon you've got. And once you've locked that door," ' he instructed, ' "good and tight," ' jabbing his finger at the air, ' "take that key and send it all the way to Timbuktoo. Oh, yes, that's the only ..." ' He glanced at me. 'I'm sorry,' he said softly. 'Am I scaring you?' And then he tried to smile, I think, although his face didn't seem to have had much practice.

I shook my head.

'You can relax,' he said. 'I'm really not mad. At least, I don't believe myself so. The jury is divided, of course. And I, perhaps, am not the soundest judge of the matter.' He reached for his flask, fingers trembling, and unscrewed the cap, looking me up and down as he did so. 'My goodness, Norman,' he said, looking at me but like he was talking to someone else, 'we've got a quiet one here.' He followed my puzzled eyes as they roamed the inside of his hiding place. 'It's a pillbox,' he said. 'They built them during the war to repel the Germans.' He made a gun shape with his fingers and fired two imaginary shots. 'And what about you? Red Indian?'

Red Indian? What did that mean?

'Well, then I'm confused,' he said frowning, and he tapped

79

the side of his head reminding me of the school tie knotted about my own.

Oh. 'Robin Hood.'

'Robin Hood?' He slapped his forehead. 'Robin Hood. Of course.' And then he laughed, a powdery, throaty sound. 'Indeed, what would the proud warriors of the Apache nation be doing with ties wrapped around their heads? What a thought! Robin Hood and his Merry Men, however, rarely wore anything else.'

Chuckling, the man poured liquid from his flask into a cup. It was thick and brown.

'Oh,' I said as a penny dropped. Not a new penny but one of those big old clunky ones. 'You're the Scarecrow Man.'

He looked startled for a moment and then laughed again. 'Yes,' he said. 'Hello. I've heard that appellation before. It makes a kind of sense, I suppose: "a tattered coat upon a stick." It's a fair description. I couldn't quibble.'

Maybe I shouldn't have said it, but, 'Out in the fields,' I went. 'That's what they call you: Anna-Marie and my … and Kat. I've seen you in the fields.'

'Well …'

'You're always looking for something.'

'Ah,' he said. 'Very observant. *Tres, tres* observant, young man. Looks like the lad's got you bang to rights, Norman. It's always the quiet ones.' And he slapped his forehead again as he told himself off: 'You've got to watch out for the quiet ones.' He adjusted his glasses with his forefinger and peered at me. 'I can see,' he said, 'that an explanation is called for, a *mea culpa* in fact. Well, Senor Torquemada, you see, I am a writer. Well, a poet. Of sorts. There you squeezed it out of me. Like a, you know, a tube of toothpaste. Although,' he muttered nodding at the creased cardboard poking from my pocket, 'I can only pray that my poetry is more convincing than my sign writing.'

'Why?' I said. 'Why do you write? I mean what are you looking for?' I meant when he was out in the fields.

'Aha,' he said, removing his glasses. 'Do you know those almost sound like two different questions?' And he jammed his thumb and forefinger together over eyes squeezed tight, all the way to the bridge of his nose. He tugged the tail of his shirt free of his belt and used it to wipe the lenses of his glasses. As he did so, he mumbled: 'Sometimes I have to pinch myself to be sure I'm not dreaming.' And then more clearly, 'I'm not looking for any more than anyone else. Just answers, I think. Explanations, maybe. Justifications,' as if he were sorting through a box. He squinted at his glasses before replacing them on his nose. 'Words perhaps; perhaps inspiration.'

'Kat says, "Never answer," ' I said.

'Well, then,' he said, peering at me, 'I'm afraid we might not get on.' His thin fingers sifted through his peppercorn hair. 'Who's Kat anyway?'

'She doesn't want people knowing our business,' I said quickly, and then I blushed.

The man coughed with laughter. 'Well, that,' he said, 'is an attitude that I could much more readily get behind. What's your name?'

When I told him, he said, 'Well, it's good to meet you, Peter. I'm Norman—Norman Kirrin—and what I'm look-ing for—'

'Like the shop,' I said.

'Yes, yes,' he snapped, 'just like the shop but, to return to your question, what I'm looking for is forgiveness. You know what that's like, don't you? Everybody makes choices; every-body make mistakes. Sometimes we act when we should have done nothing; sometimes we do nothing when we should have …Well, you get the picture. And it doesn't matter whether

81

they, our mistakes, are big or small, or whether they are well-intentioned or naïve or driven by malice. The most innocuous mistake can have the gravest repercussions. I made a mistake once, thirty-odd years ago, tiny one. I've been searching for forgiveness pretty much ever since.'

'Who from?'

'Who from?' he laughed. 'Norman, who from? From me, of course. Me, myself and I. I have always found that the hardest thing to do is to forgive oneself. Quite rightly so, wouldn't you agree?'

'What mistake?'

'Well,' he said, 'let me go so far as to say that it was tiny,' and he squeezed his thumb and forefinger together to show just how tiny his mistake had been. 'So tiny. I failed to find the correct combination of words. That's all. And, as a result, Peter, lives were ruined. My own, yes, but … also others'. Anyway, that's what I'm searching for in the fields. That's what I search for from the moment I get up until the moment I fall asleep at my desk: the correct combination of words.

'You see, Peter—can I call you Peter?—I should have acted. I should have made a gesture. I should have offered an alternative, an option, for alternatives were available. With that gesture I could have changed the world or, at least, my little corner of it. Have you never had a day like that?' And then he shook his head. 'Of course not. Why would you? How old are you anyway? Eight?'

Ten. I was ten.

'Ten? And you're asking me why I write? "Why does the old man write?" you ask. "The old man in the pillbox: why does he write?" And it's a good question, I suspect, but "Why does he *choose* to write?" That should be your question: Why do I choose to write?'

He sipped from the rim of the Thermos cap, his lips all

puckery, and then a bite from his pork pie. 'Do you choose to write, Norman?' he wondered, brushing pastry crumbs from his red sweater. 'I mean, any more than you choose to respire? Of course, of course. Of course, it's a choice. Don't be so precious. I am not helpless, Peter. It's not an addiction. It is within my power to resist—not everything is—but I choose not to. I choose the infernal cry of the alarm clock; I choose to rise before the sun and drag my shuffling corpse to a desk; I choose to face the acres of Antarctic white and to leave my mark as I trudge across them like Robert Falcon Scott.'

And then he gasped, his eyes wide. 'Oh, Norman, Norman,' he cried, 'putting on quite a show for the lad, aren't you?' He made fists and thumped them on his legs. 'God indeed. You're boring yourself. Robert Falcon Scott? If only that were true.'

He sat in silence for a moment although his lips kept moving. Then he looked up, again seeming startled by my presence. 'Oh, Peter,' he groaned, 'Peter who is also beginning to take on the appearance of a frozen wasteland, you must forgive me. I don't usually get to speak at such length, at least not with such a passive audience. You must forgive me the odd ramble. I must admit that the experience is making me quite lightheaded.' He smacked his lips together.

'So, you want to know why I write, do you?' His voice was soft and then suddenly loud, angry: 'The nerve of it. Why, you may as well ask why Romeo declares his love or Lear his madness or Hamlet his dilemma. You may as well ask a drowning man why he screams for help. Of course, he has a choice not to. He has a choice as to whether he keeps mum and lets the tide wash over him in steady waves or whether life is too precious, too brief to be sacrificed so readily just for fear of alarming the sunbathers on the beach.

'What's the alternative, Peter? Now that would be *my* question: what would I do if I couldn't write?' He nodded. 'Yes, that's it. What kind of existence would that be? Could I be content? Or would I be forced to wander the streets accosting strangers and yelling in their ears until they bleed? Or perhaps I would simply stand in the fields screaming till my lungs split: you know, scaring the crows.'

He finished his pork pie and drained the last of his tea. His hand struggled to rescrew the cap to his flask. There was sweat on his forehead.

'I ... It's my teatime,' I said.

He nodded. 'Of course,' he said. 'Teatime, yes, you're quite right. I too must ... Listen, Peter,' he said, polishing the thighs of his trousers with the palms of his hand, 'before you go, I would be most grateful if you wouldn't tell anyone about,' he indicated the cramped insides of the pillbox, 'my little hide-away.'

'Like a secret?'

'Well, no. Not a secret exactly. That would make me sound far too glamorous. James Bond does secrets; I do ... privacy. I do—'

'But how do you find secrets out?'

'Ouch!' he cried, and covered his ears but he was laughing. 'So, you do have some passion lurking behind that docile exterior. Glad to hear it. Well, my first recommendation, Peter, would be that you put that branch down before someone gets hurt.'

I lowered the branch, pointing its jagged end to the floor.

'Good. And my second piece of advice is subterfuge; subterfuge in nearly all circumstances.'

'Subter ... ?'

'Be sneaky, my friend.' With the cup of his hand the man, Norman, began scooping up the crumbs of his meal into a neat pyramid before folding them into the red napkin. 'But also,' he continued, 'upon reflection, be careful. Secrets are usually secrets for a reason. For instance, what is it you wish to find out?'

When I didn't answer he glanced up at me. 'I see,' he said. 'A secret shared is a secret diluted, of course, and why would you share such a thing with the oddball in the pillbox when he has merely bared his soul? Well, Peter, if I were you, which, of course, I am not, I would proceed with caution. If you're lucky this secret of yours, once revealed, will simply crumble and drift away into nothingness. If you are unlucky, however ...'

11

One Sunday, I was at the kitchen table gobbling cornflakes, listening to Stewpot on *Junior Choice*, when, 'You'll give yourself indigestion.' It was Anna-Marie stepping in at the back door. She wore a dark green dress to just above her knees with white lace trimmings and a pattern of little white flowers, drawn tight to her waist. Her hair was tied with a green elastic band into a long ponytail. On her feet she wore white socks and shiny, white sandals.

Oh. And Tommie was there too, hovering in the doorway. He was wearing a T-shirt.

Kat, at the sink arranging pink roses in a red painted jar, turned round and smiled. Anna-Marie tilted her head and watched as Kat stepped towards her, extending her hand and saying, 'Hello. It's the famous Anna-Marie. Nice to see you again.' Anna-Marie's clear blue eyes stared at Kat's hand. 'We've met before, of course, but …' Stewpot began to play *Morningtown Ride*. 'I'm Peter's Aunt.'

Anna-Marie turned off the radio with a pop. 'I know who you are,' she said, and Kat flashed me this funny look. 'This is Tommie,' went on Anna-Marie. 'Say "hello", Tommie.'

'Hello.'

'I just wanted to say I'm sorry about your window, Mrs ... ?'

'Kat. You must call me Kat.'

'With a "K",' I said.

'... Kat, but I didn't know anybody *lived* here.'

'Oh well, not to worry. We keep ourselves to ourselves.'

'So Peter tells me,' said Anna-Marie. She picked up a piece of toast from the breakfast table, tore off a corner with her thin fingers and popped it in to her mouth. 'After all, everybody needs secrets, don't they?'

Kat's eyes met Anna-Marie's. 'Pretty much everybody,' she said.

Anna-Marie laughed. 'Oh, you don't need to worry, Kat,' she said. 'When I know a secret, I take it to the grave, don't I, Tommie?'

Tommie, pulling at the frayed edge of his T-shirt sleeve, shrugged.

'Okay,' said Kat. 'Thank you, Anna-Marie. But—'

'You can relax, Kat. Grown-ups pretty much believe what they want,' she chewed, 'and that's pretty much what you tell them.' She swallowed. 'Anything else is just too much hard work.'

'Well, thank you then,' said Kat.

'You know, Kat,' said Anna-Marie, 'I think Peter's very lucky to have an aunt like you.'

'Thank you.'

'I wouldn't say it if I didn't mean it.'

'I believe you. Thank you.'

'What lovely flowers,' said Anna-Marie. 'I prefer yellow myself.'

Kat sighed and smiled. 'Me too,' she said.

I finished my cornflakes with a slurp.

'Speak of the Devil,' said Anna-Marie. 'Honestly, Kat, how

do you put up with this chatterbox all day long?' And then everybody laughed at me. So then I knew that everything was all right.

Anna-Marie led Tommie and me into the lane, the morning sun turning the dusty pebbles white. Kitty came out to say goodbye and allowed Anna-Marie to tickle her chin and stroke her long black back.

'Now,' said Anna-Marie, 'if we walk down the lane, where will we come to first?'

Tommie, delighted to have been asked, frowned and considered the question. 'First off,' he said, 'there's the field with the ponies on the right; second, there's the pylons; then there's,' he screwed up his face, 'oh, the Pigeon House. And then the wood-yard.'

'What are the pylons?'

'Electric pylons,' said Tommie wide-eyed. 'They're dead spooky at night, aren't they, Anna-Marie? My dad says they glow!'

Anna-Marie punched Tommie on the shoulder. He blinked but didn't say a word.

'As *I* was going to say,' said Anna-Marie, 'we could walk up to the wood-yard. We go by the pylons, then we can see if they glow or—'

'No!' said Tommie. 'They glow at ni—' Anna-Marie raised her hand again and Tommie took a deep breath. 'Good idea,' he said, and so, together, we headed off down Everlasting Lane.

'What's the Pigeon House?' I asked.

Tommie glanced at Anna-Marie. When she didn't say anything he blurted out: 'It's this big farmhouse, isn't it, Anna-Marie? And the farmer's got a really big ... erm ...'

'Loft.'

'That's right,' said Tommie, 'loft. Anyway, it's massive and there are literally millions of pigeons.' Tommie sniggered. 'It smells like a poo factory,' he said. 'My dad says—'

Anna-Marie cuffed him across the back of the head. 'Don't say "literally".'

Anna-Marie, Tommie and I walked side by side between the high banks and the tall trees of Everlasting Lane. My skin began to tingle and I began to feel as if we were standing still and that it was the lane, not us, which was moving.

We came to a small paddock with horses. Tommie talked about football whilst Anna-Marie fed grass to a white pony and stroked its round nose. We went onto the pylons. Of course it was too bright to tell whether or not they glowed in the dark, but they shone, all cold and metally, in the midday sun.

We walked on. This was not a single lane but many, disappearing around many bends. A rambling, tangling tale, a rustle in the hedgerow, just out of view: a journey without a destination.

At the Pigeon House we watched the birds flapping around, their wings making a foul-smelly breeze that made our eyes water. Later we passed a cottage tucked deep into the greenery that bordered the lane. It leaned to one side as if a strong wind had been at it or, perhaps, as if it'd simply given up the bother of standing straight.

'Who lives there?' I asked.

'That's Mr Merridew's house,' said Tommie with a shudder.

It reminded me of that poem; you know the one about 'the crooked man who walked a crooked mile'. I wondered if this was his crooked cottage.

'Who's Mr Merridew?'

'No one,' said Anna-Marie.

Everlasting Lane opened up before us like a storybook,

pages coloured with green and gold. And like any story that your heart knows, that has thrilled you or lulled you drowsy-eyed and heavy with sleep, it's hard to believe there was ever a time when it was new and strange, when you had to pay attention or risk losing your way among the twists and turns.

'Peter.' Whilst, unlike most stories I knew, Everlasting Lane didn't always follow a predictable path, 'Peter?' it always seemed to know which way I wanted to go even if I didn't know my—

'Ouch!' I yelped as Anna-Marie flicked my ear with her long finger.

'What's wrong with you?' hissed Anna-Marie. 'I'm talking. Don't you ever listen? I'm trying to warn you.'

'Warn me? What about?'

We'd walked all morning long and now we had come to a wood-yard. Through the trees I could see all the buildings but as it was Sunday there was no buzz of saws or conversation. Anna-Marie and Tommie had slowed down and were peering nervously ahead.

'We've got to watch out for the Beast.'

'The what?'

'The Beast of Everlasting Lane,' said Tommie. 'There's this dog. A watch-dog.'

'What does it watch?'

'What does it watch?' sneered Anna-Marie. 'It watches you, of course. And, whilst it's watching you, it's wondering what a chunk of your backside's going to—'

But it was too late. Ahead of us I saw a shape parting from the shadows. And as it shed its dark coat I could see that it was a dog: black and short and very, very ugly. It was snarl-ing and sneering, its jaws dripping with spit. As soon as I saw it my whole body started trembling. At first I thought I was even too scared to run away but as the animal began to bark, great chokey grunts, my limbs stiffened and I found myself edging back from the two rows of shiny, jagged teeth clashing together like knives and forks in search of supper.

'Do we run?' I whispered but there was no answer. I looked back to find that Tommie and Anna-Marie had already retreated as far as the trees that lined the Lane, where they stood flapping their hands to say that I should get a move on if I didn't want to end up a dog's dinner. And then, together, they turned and plunged into the woods.

'Hey ...' but they'd already gone. I took a quick breath, the barks of outrage beginning to nip at my ankles, before following them, hardly wanting to be left behind.

There was something frightful about those woods: but it wasn't the trees, threatening though they were. It was the shadows squeezed between them. The sunlight filtered its way through the thick canopy, but couldn't spare us the crushing gloom. At first it seemed the only sounds were our stumbling footsteps, Tommie's huffing and puffing, and Anna-Marie's curses whenever a branch scratched her arm or a root, nestling in one of those little pools of darkness, stubbed her toe.

'Are you scared?' puffed Tommie.

'No,' I lied.

'Don't be fooled,' warned Anna-Marie. 'Some of the trees can be a bit ... vicious.'

'What?'

'Just some of them,' she said. 'Some of the older ones.'

But she was only joking. Surely.

'Do you have any idea, Peter, how old these trees are? *Hundreds* of years. Thousands, for all I know. Anything'll develop a personality if it lives long enough,' said Anna-Marie. She paused a moment to adjust her sock. 'Even you.'

In the deepest part I couldn't take two easy steps together. Here the dark was liquid, like wading through ink. I began to hear the sounds of the wood and my imagination gave claws and teeth to every rustle and every creak. The darkness grew deeper still.

'Are *you* scared?'

'Oh, shut up!'

The sounds of the woods continued to follow us as we pushed on deeper and deeper towards the river and, once or twice, I thought I caught sight of evil eyes watching us pass, gleaming from behind the thick undergrowth.

Anna-Marie and Tommie ploughed on as the path dwindled and nettles grew ever thicker. But I managed to find every foothold and every branch that had ever expressed an interest in crippling a child or blinding him. Slipping and stumbling, I must've looked like Frank Spencer.

Up ahead a crack of light appeared like a gap in a door. We slid between the trees and prised the door open. Pushing aside the last branches and reaching the riverbank was like reaching the top of Everest. And then we were safe on a sunlit path beside a sunlit river. It was like the first drop of rain after a long hot summer.

But the sound of rapid movement in the woods, somewhere between the trees the way we had just come, hadn't stopped and grew suddenly closer. We heard the sound of panting and pearls of saliva falling in the dry undergrowth.

'The Beast!' cried Tommie.

A scream was welling up inside me about to explode, as I pictured muscles wriggling like rodents beneath a glossy hide and ivory teeth snatching sunlight from the air.

The breathless old man who finally staggered from the bushes onto the path with his gnarly walking stick in one hand and a cigarette burning between the bony fingers of the other was, I thought, a lot less terrifying than the creature my imagination had created. His black suit was interwoven with green thread, the seams loose and frayed; whilst the jacket was fastened the middle button was missing. The hair on his head was thin whilst his moustache, thick and grey, was stained yellow and on his chin a sprinkling of bristles. The glasses he wore across his nose were shiny and round, his eyes twice their real size.

He wheezed with laughter at our startled faces, revealing two rows of teeth like garlic, and wiped sweat from his brow, and his hands on his trousers. 'Ah,' he finally managed to say, ' 'tis the lovely Anna-Marie. I thought I saw you from afar. And how,' he enquired, still gasping for breath, 'are you today?'

'Very well, thank you,' said Anna-Marie taking the hand he offered and curtsying. 'This is Peter,' she said. 'Peter, this is Mr Merridew.' I offered the old man my hand and he eyed it suspiciously.

'I won't,' he said. 'If you don't mind.'

'How are you, Mr Merridew?' asked Anna-Marie.

'Neither better nor worse, my dear, than any other day.' His eyes bulged with curiosity in my direction. 'And where are you bound?'

'Oh,' she said, 'nowhere in particular.'

'Then,' he said licking his dry lips, his mouth the murky entrance to some underworld cavern, 'come to my parlour for some milk or, perhaps, some tea.'

I almost wished it had been the Beast and his glistening jaws which had burst forth from between the trees. This strange old man and his invitation filled me with dread. How could we, as children, say no? Adults were in charge. It was a rule so powerful that it might as well have been magic. Thankfully, Anna-Marie had powers of her own.

'I can't speak for Piggy Malone and Charley Farley,' she

said, 'but I've got literally a million … Well, not literally, but a lot of things to get done. Perhaps we could come next weekend.'

'Ah,' said Mr Merridew his thin smile flickering. 'What a shame.'

He wished us good day but then stood watching as we shuffled off along the path, leering through his goggly glasses. The river was straight and so we could feel his gaze warming the backs of our necks as we walked nervously along. Until, at last, the path turned with the flow of the water and the old man's grim shape finally disappeared behind the river bend.

Tommie collapsed on the riverbank, laughing. Anna-Marie sighed, releasing the green band from her ponytail and slipping it onto her slender wrist. She tipped her head upwards to face the sky. Her fingers ran through her golden hair, pushing it to the top of her head and letting it fall, rolling down upon her shoulders. She repeated the motion, her feet turning step by step, allowing the sun to—

'What's up with you, bog-breath?'

'Nothing.'

'Frankly, you get more peculiar by the minute,' muttered Anna-Marie. 'So,' she said, smoothing her dress under her bottom and sitting among the daisies on the riverbank, 'what do you think of our friend, Mr Merridew?'

'I don't know,' I said. 'He's all right, I suppose.' I wasn't going to admit to anything else.

'Tommie-Titmus here is afraid of him.'

'No, I'm not,' protested Tommie.

'What does he do?' I asked.

'What do you mean?' snapped Anna-Marie. 'What do you mean: what does he *do*?'

'Well, what does he do for a job?'

'Oh, that,' said Anna-Marie. 'Well, he used to be some kind

of scientist I think but he doesn't really do anything now. He says he's lapsed.'

'Lapsed?'

'Yes. He says it's all bunk. Science I mean. He says it's religion for atheists.'

'Atheists?'

'Yes, you twit. It means people who don't believe in God.'

'Well, I know but—'

'Well, that's what he says.' She thought about it for a moment. 'But I don't think he means it. Not literally. It's,' and she cleared her throat, 'poetic licence.'

That seemed a strange thing to say. I knew you needed a licence for a TV and a dog and stuff but—

Anna-Marie sighed. 'It means,' she said, 'that you can say things that aren't true.'

'You should always tell the truth,' I said, but I was confused. My mum had said I should always tell the truth but then Kat had said it was best not to say anything at all. Or was it the other way round?

'But that's real life, isn't it?' Anna-Marie went on. 'That's quite different. It's like in a story. In a story you can say any kind of stuff you like.'

I frowned. Kat had said something similar but I wasn't sure.

'Let me explain something to you, little boy,' said Anna-Marie. 'In a story I could say my dad was Evel Knievel and you could say you lived with the Loch Ness Monster and no one would bat an eyelid.

'You could even say you knew a girl called Anna-Marie who was very pretty and very smart and for all the man-in-the-street knows you've completely made me up. Mind you,' she said, picking her nose, 'considering you've made me sound so dull he might wonder why you'd bothered.' She examined her bogey before flicking it into a nearby bush. She began plucking daisies from the riverbank and arranging them in rows upon the grass. 'The point is, in a story you can make everything better.'

'But why would Peter just make stuff up?' said Tommie. 'Why would he do that?'

'Who knows?' said Anna-Marie. 'Who can explain the workings of an unstable mind? Anyway, don't tell anyone what I said about Mr Merridew. Promise. It's supposed to be some kind of secret.'

'I know a secret,' I said.

'What is it?' asked Tommie.

'How marvellous for you,' yawned Anna-Marie and, 'It's not going to be a very well kept one by the sounds of it.' She returned to her daisies, splitting stalks with the blade of her fingernail and weaving them with quick fingers. 'Perhaps you should look up "secret" in a—'

'It's real,' I insisted. She wasn't taking me seriously.

'All right. All right,' said Anna-Marie. 'Keep your pants on.'

'There's this room,' I said, 'in the cottage. A secret room—'

'A secret room?'

The daisy chain hung suspended between Anna-Marie's open hands. For a moment I thought it was the flowers rather than my news which had caused her to stop.

Tommie's eyes had lit up. 'Why's it a secret?' he asked.

'I don't know,' I said, 'but it's hidden behind this curtain and it's always locked.'

'Wow,' said Tommie. 'I wonder what's inside.'

'Oh, give me strength,' said Anna-Marie. 'Don't you start. Did it even occur to lemon-head here to ask Kat about it?'

'No, I—'

'But, if you don't even have the nerve to ask your—'

'But it is a secret room,' I insisted. 'At Kat's cottage. It's behind this big, green curtain.' Anna-Marie's eyelids flickered with boredom and she put a hand over her mouth as if smothering a yawn. Why wouldn't she take me seriously? She was always treating me like I was some kind of idiot. Actually, when you thought about it, she always treated most people like they were some kind of idiot.

'But, if you haven't even asked about it … What do you expect? I'm sure there's a perfectly logical—'

'But,' said Tommie, a curious light gleaming in his lenses, 'what if it is a secret room? What if there's a—?'

'What if there's a what?' snapped Anna-Marie. 'This isn't Enid Blyton, you know, and it's not a production of the *Children's Film Foundation*. You're not about to have an adventure. If it wasn't for me looking out for the pair of you, you'd be a danger to yourselves and others.' She resumed her threading and I waited nervously as her fingers turned and spun like needles, and the chain between them grew and grew. The afternoon was awash with summer swirling all the way up from the river to the tops of the trees and beyond.

'Why don't you get a hair-grip?' said Tommie. 'I saw them do this on *Columbo*.' He mimed a twisting motion as he spoke. 'You kind of loop it like this—'

'Thank you, Miss Marple,' interrupted Anna-Marie. She turned to me. 'Why don't you just get the key?'

'I don't know where it is.'

Anna-Marie clicked her tongue and nibbled her lip. 'Well,' she said finally, laying her daisies on the ground in a zig-zaggy pattern and giving an exasperated sigh, 'I suppose we'll just have to see what we can do about that, won't we?'

12

'Greetings, Earthlings!' said Kat one afternoon from the up-stairs window. *That* upstairs window. 'It's the three musketeers! All for one, one for all, etcetera!' She was always saying that kind of thing but Anna-Marie and Tommie didn't seem to mind. As we sat on the lawn, soaking in sunshine, she would ask after their mothers, were they enjoying the warm weather, were they going away this summer. Tommie and Anna-Marie liked Kat and chatted happily.

'I'm just popping up to the church, Peter,' she said. 'Will you be all right for an hour?'

'Don't worry, Kat,' said Anna-Marie. 'We'll keep an eye on him.'

' 'Bye, Mrs Lambert,' said Tommie.

Kat tut-tutted, pretending to be cross. 'You can call me Kat,' and we all chimed in, 'with a "K".' She laughed. 'I'll see you in an hour then. No more than two.' She shut the upstairs win-dow: the upstairs window on the left, the window to the left of my bedroom, the window with pink curtains and the strip of cardboard filling the broken pane.

The front door slammed and then a hiccup as Kat's rusty little car came to life and struggled its way out of the drive.

Anna-Marie had been lazing backwards propped up on

her elbows but as the sound of Kat's motor faded she snapped straight up. 'Right,' she said, 'now how are we going to get into this room?'

Tommie had also sprung to attention. 'We need a key.'

I was laid on my tummy, scratching a moat around an immovable stone. 'But Kat's hidden the key,' I protested, turning to squint at my companions.

'Let's think about this logically,' said Anna-Marie. 'Why do you say she's hidden the key?'

'It's not on her key-ring.'

'But does she know you know about the secret room?'

'I don't think so.'

'Well, know so, Peter. Has she done or said anything that makes you think she knows you know about the secret room?'

I thought hard. 'No.'

'Then why,' asked Anna-Marie, 'would she hide the key? Tommie, where does your mum keep her keys?'

'On the hooks in the kitchen.'

'Mine too. Come on.'

They leapt to their feet and raced across the garden into the kitchen. I rose and followed them. 'But we haven't got a—'

Anna-Marie and Tommie were stood staring at the back of the kitchen door, grinning at my stupidity.

'Oh, Peter,' said Anna-Marie as she examined the row of keys. I'd never even seen them before, 'do you realise that if we doubled your brain cells we could have a very small game of conkers.'

Well, that was hardly fair. They only knew there was a secret room because of me. It wasn't like I went round investigating the backs of doors.

'Honestly,' muttered Anna-Marie. 'It's almost like she wants you to find it.'

The keys jingled as her finger traced along the row. She

stopped when she reached the only key that wasn't labelled, lifted it from its hook and smiled. 'Of course,' she said. 'Can you imagine any circumstances in which someone would label a key: *Secret Room*?' She was just like someone out of *The Famous*—

But they were already bounding their way upstairs. As I trudged up behind them I could already hear Anna-Marie dragging back the heavy curtain and Tommie gasping: 'It's true. There is a secret room.'

'Maybe,' said Anna-Marie, 'or maybe there's just a door behind a curtain and an odd little boy,' she glanced at me as I stepped onto the landing, 'with an over-active imagination.'

'But, Anna-Marie—'

'Hush your whining, Peter,' said Anna-Marie. 'Let me think.' She studied the door peering at the hinge and then the lock. She reached out and touched it, placing first the pad of her finger and then the palm of her hand against it as if testing the temperature.

The only sound was our breathing. Anna-Marie put the key in the lock and turned it. I suddenly felt all hot and cold at the same time. 'Maybe we shouldn't.'

'Oh, dear,' said Anna-Marie as the lock clicked. 'Have you got the collywobbles?'

I shook my head but didn't move.

'All right,' said Anna-Marie with a sigh, 'before we go in, let's say for argument's sake that this is a secret door to a secret room. What is a secret?' Her hair was almost white by the light that shone through the landing window. 'What's it for?'

'A secret,' said Tommie, 'is something that somebody knows that they don't want somebody else to know. So they keep it a secret.'

'Good,' said Anna-Marie. 'So, what is it that Kat doesn't

want Peter to know? What are the sorts of things that people keep secret? What are the things that people don't want other people to know?'

'Well,' said Tommie, 'say sometimes a person might have done something like committed a crime or stolen a lot of money and they don't want the police to know about it or they'd go to jail.'

Anna-Marie looked doubtful. 'Are you telling me you think Kat is one of the Great Train Robbers?'

'No, I—'

Anna-Marie groaned and pressed two fingers against her forehead. 'Let's say for the time being that Kat doesn't exactly look like the master criminal type. No, there must be some other reason why she doesn't want Peter to know about this room.'

'Oh,' said Tommie, 'in films they sometimes have secrets like documents that they don't want the enemies to get hold of. They have a big stamp that has "Top Secret" on it.'

'Well, what sort of secrets are they?'

'Like where their missiles are based or it might be a secret code.'

'Again, Tommie, I don't think Kat's the type of person who has missiles.'

'Well, I know, but—'

'Look around you,' said Anna-Marie. So we did. 'It's 1976. It's Amberley. It's not Nazi Germany.'

'All right,' said Tommie, thought wriggling across his brow like a caterpillar. 'Well, a secret is like another word for what's true, isn't it?'

'Go on.'

'And if people don't know the secret,' gasped Tommie, 'then what they think they know is a lie.'

Anna-Marie stared at Tommie. 'You know, that's very

smart,' she said. Tommie smiled. 'For a moron,' and his smile disappeared. 'So, Peter, do you want to know the truth?'

Well, that wasn't even a fair question. Of course I did. This, under my own roof, this was like cheating.

'Peter?'

Because Kat and I did have a secret, of course, but not from each other. Except she did have a secret, didn't she? So, what did I have?

'Peter!'

Of course I wanted to know. I was entitled. 'Ouch.'

'I'll do it again if you don't get a move on.'

'She'll kill me,' I whispered, and Anna-Marie and Tommie laughed but, of course, they didn't know her like I did.

Anna-Marie tutted and reached over my shoulder. 'When Kat's away ...' She pushed the door open and we looked inside.

'Oh,' said Anna-Marie. 'Wow,' but my breath caught in my throat like a large peanut. Scared to talk, scared to breathe, scared to be there at all, it was like stepping into Wonderland but on the wrong side of the looking glass, like we were re-flections, noses pressed against the glass, peering through.

It was empty. The room I mean. I mean it was empty of people. That was the first thing I noticed. The second thing I noticed was that it was twice the size of my room. *Twice* the size! But at least my room didn't have pink walls, and shelves crowded with stuffed toys and glassy-eyed dolls. There were bats and balls too, and cubes with letters, cubes with numbers, all mixed up. There were books: story books, picture books, you know, all over the place. And boxes, toy boxes, pushed up against the walls and, to one side, a rocking horse, shining as if it had been dipped in syrup, a red bridle gripped between its teeth. I could guess who'd made it, of course, working away in her magic workshop, removing the unbeautiful.

'It's a nursery,' said Tommie.

'It's a nursery,' copied Anna-Marie like he was stupid. 'Well done, Magnus.'

She investigated a family of framed photographs. 'Is this your dad?' she said, and then, laughing, 'Is this you?' It'd been taken at this fair when I was four years old and showed me with a monkey (a real live one) in my arms. I remembered it from the mantelpiece at home. It was my mother's favourite. Anna-Marie picked up a silver frame. 'And what about this one?' I hadn't even noticed it at first. It was the same picture as that one above the fireplace in the lounge downstairs but without the torn corner. The mysterious person sat alongside my mother and father was revealed. 'Look at your hair,' said Anna-Marie peering at it with a grin. 'The barber did a grand job that day.'

A clock marked time with thick wooden clicks, winding like string through the toys and games, not so much passing but unravelling. And between each click we heard the silent pulse like that moment between heartbeats when you're little better than dead.

The curtains were open and the room was bright. I noticed the cardboard square that still covered the broken pane. What workman would you call to fix a window in a secret room? But my eyes were drawn to the cot, its pink sheets turned down and laying on its pillow the skipping rope, nearly new. Beside the cot was a small chair, the twin of the one that sat on the landing protecting the green curtain, and on the chair a book of nursery rhymes, a bookmark poking from the pages. Above the cot hung a mobile of bright colours—butterflies— waiting to spin.

And on the wall behind it, in a frame, a name embroidered: 'Alice'.

'Curiouser and curiouser,' muttered Anna-Marie.

They were wrong though. Anna-Marie and Tommie I

mean. It wasn't a nursery. I mean it wasn't just a nursery. It was more like a museum.

'Well,' said Anna-Marie, 'it looks like Kat has more than one secret, eh, Peter?' She walked to a shelf and stroked the hair of one of the dolls. 'So,' she said, looking around, examining the toys and games like a detective, 'who's Alice?'

'Wow,' said Tommie. 'This is great.' He knelt beside the rocking horse, caressing its smooth haunches, moving it back and forth, letting the chain upon its bridle ring. 'My dad used to ride.'

'This must be where Kat sits,' murmured Anna-Marie. She picked up the book of nursery rhymes from the chair and flicked through it.

'Be careful,' I gasped. 'She'll know.'

Anna-Marie returned the book just like she'd found it, her fingers lingering a moment on the cover before they withdrew. She looked at the cot, trying to solve the mystery.

Between the cot and Kat's chair stood a cabinet and on the cabinet there was this small box. Anna-Marie picked up the box between her thumb and forefinger, and examined it before—click!—lifting the lid. When she returned the box to the table, I could see that it was lined with little mirrors each bearing the reflection of a tiny ballerina. Anna-Marie found a key inside the box and put it into the hole, turning it with a soft clicking sound. A melody of gentle chimes trickled out filling the room with light as the ballerina turned.

'Oh,' said Anna-Marie, and she began to sing but so softly, so gently, that she was barely singing at all.

Baby, sleep, my baby girl, Dimpled cheek, a single curl,
Music box of gold and pearl, Baby, sleep, my baby girl.

Daddy's gone, away to war, The beating drum, the bugle call.
The pounding gun, the cannons' roar, Close your eyes and cry no
more.

The music box is tightly wound, The seasons turn the world
around.
Dreams that fade, are seldom found, Stir you not, nor make a
sound.

Baby, sleep, my baby girl, Dimpled cheek, a single curl,
Music box of gold and pearl, Baby, sleep, my baby girl.

The tune ended. But we carried on listening to the silence as if it hadn't.

'So,' went Anna-Marie again as she removed the key and returned it to the box, gently lowering the lid, 'who's Alice?'

'Of course,' said Tommie, 'there is another reason why somebody might keep a secret.'

'What other reason?'

'Well, it's like when my mum and dad were getting a divorce and they didn't tell me for ages and—'

'Get to the point, Tommie.'

'Well, when my mum brought me here they said it was just for a holiday and—'

'Quicker.'

'Well, my dad said it was for my own good.'

Anna-Marie turned to look at him. She'd turned pale. I mean even paler than usual, her freckles standing out like they were sprinkled in a bowl of milk. 'I hadn't thought of that,' she said biting her lip. 'Maybe we've got this the wrong way round.'

'What?' I said. 'What do you mean?'

'Well, because we thought Kat must be keeping this room a secret to protect herself.'

'So?'

'Well, what if she was keeping this room a secret ... to protect you.'

'But what? What do you mean? Protect me from what?'

Anna-Marie's eyes stared into mine. Suddenly I felt like I was standing alone somewhere far away on the shore of two huge, blue lakes emptying themselves into an ocean of worry. 'From the truth,' she said. And then she looked away. 'But there's something else,' she murmured, 'this hasn't just sprung into existence since—'

And then we heard it: the spluttering engine, tyres on gravel, the squeak of the handbrake. We spilled onto the landing. Kitty, sitting just outside the room, eyed us accusingly. Anna-Marie peered through the landing window. 'She's coming! Quick!'

I checked the room to make sure we hadn't left any sign of our visit before closing the door as gently as I could.

'Let's go in your room,' hissed Tommie.

'Oh, God!' I said. 'I've got the key!'

We shot downstairs at full pelt. We didn't have time to be quiet about it. Bouncing off the wall at the bottom of the stairs, I could hear Kat outside the front door wrestling with keys of her own. Down the hall. The front door was opening. Into the kitchen. I slipped, the key clattering to the floor.

'What are you lot up to?' She sounded cross. She always was when she'd been to the church.

I grabbed the key—

'Nothing!'

—Key on the hook—

'Where are you?' A flash of anger in her voice. Even Anna-Marie looked surprised.

—We sat down.

'Oh, there you are,' said Kat marching into the kitchen. 'What's all the running about for?' She slammed her handbag onto the counter and spun to face us.

'Sorry, Kat,' said Anna-Marie, smiling like an angel. 'We were just playing.'

'Well,' said Kat with a sigh, 'not like that, please.'

'Sorry, Kat,' I said.

'Sorry, Mrs … Kat.'

'Are there any biscuits?'

Kat joined us at the table as we drank squash and unwrapped jammy dodgers. 'There's something happening here,' she said, 'and I'm not sure I like it.' Kitty strode into the kitchen and went straight to her. 'Hello, my darling!' went Kat, gazing into her eyes. 'You'll tell me what they've been up to, won't you?'

I shrugged and smiled, whilst my friends drained their glasses and, crumbs still on their lips, departed: Anna-Marie to do her history and Tommie to forge a note for getting out of games. I was left to face Kat alone.

'So,' she said, 'what have you really been up to?'

I was staring at her wondering why she'd torn my face from that picture.

'Nothing,' I said. 'We just went for a walk.'

'Oh, yes? A walk?' She picked up the glasses and took them to the sink. 'And where did you go exactly?'

'Just along the river,' I knew I had to distract her somehow, thinking quickly, 'down to the hospital?'

'Hospital? What hospital?'

'Well, there's this hospital.' I stretched out every word like an elastic band all tight and ready to ping. 'It's where Anna-Marie and I go. And Tommie. It's a big red building; an old building. You know. It's called the Lodge, I think. You go under the road and—'

There was a smash. One of the glasses slipped from her fingers and shattered across the floor. I jumped to my feet but Kat—I mean my mother—had already stepped over the splinters and grabbed my wrist. Her face was all twisted out of shape.

'Peter,' she went, 'you are not to go there again! Do you hear me? Haven't those people … ?' My wrist began to hurt. 'Promise me you won't go there again. Promise.'

And so I promised—crossed my heart. 'But why?'

She slowly relaxed her grip.

'It's for your own good,' she said.

13

'We are here,' said Anna-Marie, eyes glinting, 'to talk about Alice.'

'What about Alice?' said Tommie.

'Well, I've been thinking about her.' That wasn't a surprise at all. I'd been thinking about little else myself. 'And what I think,' she said, 'is that we should find out who she is.'

I hadn't been surprised to find Anna-Marie waiting for Tommie and me at the end of school, sucking in her cheeks and nibbling strands of hair. But I had been surprised when she'd led us to *The Copper Kettle*, this small café in the village. *The Copper Kettle* was a place for grown-ups: the knives and forks were polished and gleaming, and there were paper doilies on every surface. The waitress shook her hair and gave us such a look I wasn't sure we'd be allowed to stay but she smiled quickly enough when Anna-Marie waved a one pound note and requested: 'Two Tizers, please, and a pot of tea for one.'

I felt very grown-up even though my feet barely touched the floor. 'Peter.' I glanced around at the lacy, flowery decorations, and was particularly curious about the young man with the long hair sat at the table next to us. 'Peter.' He was wearing a green jacket, a bit like a soldier, and smoking cigarette after cigarette after cigarette making the whole room hazy and writing in red on a large pad of blue—

'Peter!'

'What?'

'Are you listening to any of this? It's for your benefit, you know.'

'Why?' I asked.

'What do you mean: why?'

'Why do we have to find out who she is?'

'Because,' said Anna-Marie, 'it might be important.'

'But I don't think Kat would—'

'Oh, it's too late to worry about that, Peter. You've already broken into Alice's room, haven't you? You've already poked your nose into things that don't concern you.'

'But you—'

'Never mind about that. The cat's out of the bag as they say.'

'But you said it was for my own good.'

'And now I'm saying that *this* is for your own good. Frankly, Peter,' she waved her hand to whisk away some of the cigarette smoke which had drifted in her direction, 'you are alarmingly slow on the uptake.'

'So,' said Tommie, leaning forward, pushing his thick spectacles as far up his nose as they would go and pulling a stubby pencil from his pocket, 'how are we going to find out about Alice? We haven't got much to go on.' He unfolded one of the paper napkins and wrote *Alice* at the top. He underlined it twice.

The waitress arrived with our drinks and a plate of biscuits. As she placed our order on the table, Anna-Marie said, 'Excuse me, are you Alice?'

The waitress frowned and shook her head. 'No, m'love.'

'Oh. Does Alice work another day then?'

'There's no Alice, m'love. Sorry.'

'No,' said Anna-Marie. 'I'm sorry. I've been misinformed.'

'Not to worry, m'love.'

Anna-Marie grinned to herself as she lifted the lid of her silver teapot and peered in. 'You're right: we haven't got much to go on,' she said, 'but we can ask questions. For instance, we already know she doesn't work at *The Copper Kettle*. Besides we have our imaginations.' She took a teaspoon and stirred her leaves without touching the sides. 'Or at least we have my imagination and you, Tommie,' she said, 'you have your napkin.'

'Okay,' said Tommie. He slowly wrote *Copper Kettle* and put a big cross next to it. He gave his Tizer a triumphant slurp.

'But why?' I said. 'Why do you want to know?'

'Stop whining,' said Anna-Marie. She held her tea-strainer over the top of her cup and poured. 'Have you never heard of knowledge for knowledge's sake?' Well, of course I hadn't. 'For starters,' she said addressing Tommie, 'there are no Alices here and we know there aren't any at school, not even in the infants.' Tommie wrote *School* and *X*. 'But that's not a surprise,' she continued when he'd finished, 'Alice is probably a grown-up by—'

'But how do you know?' I interrupted crossly. Even I could see that if we were going to investigate Alice building by building Tommie would need a much bigger napkin. 'And how do you know she's still here?' I meant still in the village.

'Call it a sixth sense,' said Anna-Marie. Having added milk and a spoonful of sugar she raised her cup. 'Besides, nobody ever really leaves Amberley.' She sipped at her tea, her pinkie curling outwards. 'And some of the toys in the nursery could be twenty years old—'

'Not all of them,' said Tommie.

'—so it seems to me quite likely that we are talking about a young woman. She's probably quite pretty and almost certainly

111

very intelligent. She won't work in one of those boring jobs,' she said leaning forward and adding with a whisper, 'certainly not waitressing. She couldn't stand it.' She returned her cup to its saucer with a rattle.

'Well, what is she then?'

'If you ask me she's probably a teacher.'

A teacher? But why … ? And then I smiled to myself. 'A good one?' I said.

'Exactly,' said Anna-Marie and blew a hole through the sunlit steam rising from her cup. 'You read my mind,' and, well, I had a funny feeling that I almost had.

'Well, what about the teachers?' said Tommie. 'At school I mean.'

'It's Mrs Carpenter,' I said with a gasp. 'I bet it's Mrs Carpenter.'

'Are you not listening? I said a *good* teacher. Besides I happen to know that Mrs Carpenter's first name is Sybil.'

'Sybil?' said Tommie. His snigger turned into a cough as he breathed in a mixture of Tizer and the fumes billowing from the next table.

I reached out for a garibaldi but Anna-Marie slapped my hand away. 'They come with the tea,' she hissed. 'If you want biscuits you need to develop more adult tastes.'

'How do you know?' spluttered Tommie, raising his glasses to wipe a smoky tear from his eye. 'How do you know her name's Sybil?'

Anna-Marie shrugged. 'I make it my business to know all the teachers' names and there's not an Alice amongst them.'

'All right then,' said Tommie. He drummed his pencil for a moment. 'What about Miss Pevensie then? She's not even a proper teacher yet. I'll bet you don't know her name. It might be Alice.'

Anna-Marie shook her head. 'You are so unobservant.

Haven't you noticed her necklace? It's got a big "J" on it. J for Julie or Jane or—'

'Jennifer,' and we all J for jumped. It was that man from the next table. We turned to look at him and he blushed.

'Excuse me?' said Anna-Marie.

'Oh,' he said, 'I'm sorry. I didn't mean to … Jennifer, Miss Pevensie, is a friend of mine. At college. She … I'm sorry. I couldn't help … I didn't mean to …'

Anna-Marie smiled at him and then at that pad he'd been writing on. 'What are you doing?' she asked.

The man kind of moved his right arm, tilting the pad away from us as he did so, so that it lay across the blue paper in front of him. 'I'm erm … I'm writing a story.'

'A story?' cried Anna-Marie gripping the edge of the table. 'I used to write stories.' She leant forward as if she hoped to see some of his words escaping like little red ants from under his sleeve. 'What's it about? Can I see?'

The man stretched his fingers out until they, his entire palm and arm were spread across the paper. 'It's about a girl I know,' he said.

'A girl? What's her name?'

'Well … I don't know yet. I haven't decided.'

'My name's Anna-Marie. Anna-Marie Liddell. Why don't you call the girl Anna-Marie?'

The man smiled. 'I could,' he said. 'Thank you. That's a very pretty name.'

'I know,' said Anna-Marie. 'What's your name?'

'It's Craig. I—'

'Grey?'

'No, C-raig. I—'

'Oh, Craig. Are you a published writer, Craig?'

'Well, no. I—'

'Have you heard of Frances Hodgson Burnett?'

'Well, I've heard—'

'Are you going to be a teacher?'

The man, Craig, laughed. 'Christ! No. I'm a student but I'm studying English. I guess I wouldn't mind being—'

'Why does anybody write stories?' said Tommie with a snort, slouching in his chair. 'They make us write them at school. It's stupid.'

Anna-Marie introduced us: 'This is Tommie. He can't help it: he's an idiot. This is Peter. He's an idiot too but at least he's quiet.'

'Well,' said Craig nodding at us both, 'it is kind of stupid. But it's a lot of fun too. It's almost like being in another world. The more you write the more you feel that that world is real. Not this one.' He lit a cigarette and flapped at the smoke hoping to waft it away from us. He apologised again.

'So you're like an alien,' said Tommie with a grin.

'Well, it sometimes feels like that, yes,' went Craig running his yellow fingers through his long hair, 'but it's even better than that. Imagine if you've made a mistake or done something wrong in the real world; like something you really regret. Say, you've done something stupid or you've hurt someone or someone's feelings. When you go back to this world,' and he patted the pile of paper in front of him like you'd pat a dog on the head, 'you can have another go: make things better; make people better, and not just for a little while but forever. You can even make yourself better. You can do things right,' he said. 'You can make amends. You can—'

'Avoid the consequences,' said Anna-Marie.

Craig hesitated. 'Well,' he said, 'you can but try. I mean the real world, this world,' he gestured with his free arm all around *The Copper Kettle* and then again to include the whole wide world, 'is where the real stuff happens and the real consequences, but in a story there don't have to be any consequences at all.' And he smiled at us as if he really believed that was true.

'But don't you ever get confused?' said Anna-Marie. 'I mean, between this world, the real world, and the world you write about?'

'That's another good question' he said. 'Sometimes it's like you're dreaming when you're really awake.'

'If the other world is so nice,' said Tommie with a smirk, 'why bother living in this one?'

'That's an easy one,' said the man quickly adding, 'but interesting too. The food's better here,' and Anna-Marie smiled at him as if *he* was the child. He cleared his throat. 'Why don't you write stories any more?'

Anna-Marie blinked. 'I'm sorry?' like she hadn't understood the question.

'Well, you said you used to write stories. I was wondering why you don't write them any more.'

Anna-Marie shrugged. 'If you want to write about your feelings you can't ever quite find the right words,' she said, 'because feelings and words are quite different. It's like trying to write a piece of music about the smell of flowers. It's like translating one language into another. It's the difference between a picture of a tiger,' she said, 'and a tiger. Don't you think?'

'Well,' said the man nodding, 'I do now.'

'I mean a story is nothing like real life,' said Anna-Marie. 'Real life is all jumbled up and complicated but a story makes it all sound nice and easy. I don't think it's easy at all. Do you?'

The man shook his head. 'No,' he said. 'Not easy at all.'

'The girl in your story,' said Anna-Marie, 'how will you decide what she's like?'

'Well, I suppose there are lots of ways but I usually think about people I know and—'

'Like Miss Pevensie?'

The man blushed again. 'Well, there's lots of different ways—'

'Say I was writing a story—'

'But you said—'

'Thank you, Tommie. Say I decided to write a story about a girl called Alice.'

'Like Lewis Carroll.'

Anna-Marie smiled. 'If you like, but she's a teacher. How could I find out about what she's like?'

'Well, you could use your imagination, of course, like you said, or sometimes just watch people, but if you wanted to be very thorough you could maybe talk to the teachers at school and find out about their jobs or Miss Pevensie or how about your headmaster—'

'Mistress.'

'Sorry. Mistress.'

'Yes,' said Anna-Marie. 'Well, in fact I'm not sure she'd welcome the attention.'

The man laughed. 'Okay then. Well, how about asking someone up at the college. They might be able to give you some good ideas. And it's a beautiful campus. Maybe Alice could have done her teacher training there.'

Anna-Marie's eyes were as bright as a smile. 'That's an excellent idea,' she said. 'I'm sure that's what she did. In fact,' she continued, turning to Tommie and me, 'we know someone who used to work at the College.' She glanced at her watch and said to the man, 'It's been very nice to meet you but I'm afraid I have to go now. I have my ballet lesson.'

'Ballet?' I said. I couldn't believe it. I'd have been less surprised if she'd told me she was moving to the moon. 'I didn't know you did ballet.'

'Frankly,' said Anna-Marie, 'if that was the only thing you

didn't know, we'd all be in a lot of trouble.' She offered her hand to the man and he took her fingers between his thumb and forefinger as if he'd never shaken hands before.

When we stood to leave, Anna-Marie slipping a ten pee piece beneath her saucer, I took a quick glance to see what the young man had been writing. I only managed to make out the first sentence at the top of the page before he blocked my view with his arm. It said: *We are here to talk about Alice* in red ink and he'd underlined Alice twice.

'Who do we know who used to work at the college?' asked Tommie. He'd forgotten the napkin he'd been writing on, so I scrunched it into my pocket for safe keeping. And then I sneaked the ten pee piece to go in my money box. After all, that ring wasn't going to buy itself.

'Mr Merridew,' said Anna-Marie and Tommie scowled as if he'd just been presented with a plateful of cabbage for his birthday tea. 'We'll go tomorrow after school. And don't be late.'

But by then, of course, Tommie was dead.

14

Well, not really.

It's called poetic licence: it means I can say stuff that isn't true.

But you should've seen your face.

'Very droll,' said Anna-Marie.

It'd been ages since we'd promised to visit Mr Merridew but there'd always been something better to do: talking, exploring, dangling our toes in the river. Even homework seemed more appealing. But now we were—

'Peter?'

'What?'

'Get on with it. Tell me what happened to Tommie. What did you do,' said Anna-Marie, 'to my best friend?'

That hurt: the 'best friend' bit I mean.

'It wasn't me,' I protested. 'I—'

'Just get on with it,' snapped Anna-Marie. 'Just tell me what happened in your own words.'

So, this is what really happened.

Thwack!

'That's a six!' cried Mr Gale as he sent the little red cricket ball shooting high into the cloudless sky. It hung for a moment, like a lost balloon surrounded by blue, before plummeting to meet the earth in one of the fields beyond the school fence. 'That's the way to do it,' Mr Gale congratulated himself in the voice of Mr Punch. And, to the boys gathered around him: 'I don't want to see any of this,' and he wiggled the bat like a sickly bird, his face all puckery, his lip quivery as if he were about to burst into tears, 'like some … some … some great *nancy* boy. You've got to really *whack* it!' and he swung the bat about his head like a mad-man lumberjack.

'Right,' he said, considering the scrawny boys stood shaking in shorts and vest, 'who's up first?' and the tough, sporty boys, 'You,' the ones with chests and no— 'Wakey-wakey, Lambchop. Front and centre.'

Of course. And so I reluctantly joined Mr Gale at the stump, praying it would soon be over.

'Righty-ho,' he said. 'Now, before we start, erm, Winnie, would you be so good as to fetch that last ball for us? Good lad. Mrs Carpenter'll only take it out of my pocket money.'

Tommie had been lurking on the edge of the group, tummy trembling beneath his tight vest, as far as he could from Mr Gale. Any further and he might as well have joined Miss Pevensie and the girls for rounders. Tommie usually faked a letter from his mum or 'twisted' his ankle during playtime or 'developed' heat stroke. The sick note he'd given in that morning, however, was so covered in blotches of blue ink that he was quickly found out.

'My dad says he doesn't care what happens to me at school,' said Tommie. 'And he was brilliant at cricket.'

He didn't look at all sorry at being sent to collect the ball. After all, if he dragged his feet enough, it might take up half the lesson. He lumbered off, making passing snails look like James Hunt.

Mr Gale handed me the bat before grabbing my fingers and forcing then into the correct positions. He told me not to move a muscle and walked off tossing the ball up into the air. He caught it each time, stroking it lovingly like that man with the cat in James Bond. He turned to me with a huge grin. 'Ready?' he asked with his eyebrows, caressing the ball one more time, winding his arm back like a spring and releasing it in my direction.

It sped towards me at about a thousand, million miles an hour, like a shiny red round Concorde growing as it flew, filling my eyes. A moment before this leather bullet ripped my head from my shoulders I tightened my grip upon the bat and threw it bravely towards the ball and my body (less bravely) to the ground. The ball looped over my head and landed with a thump. From where I lay, I could see Tommie huffing and puffing over the fence that lined the edge of the school grounds. After two or three attempts, he swung his chubby leg over the top and plopped down into the field beyond.

Having avoided impact, pain and injury I considered my first attempt at cricket to be a success but not Mr Gale. 'Oh, *Lamb*chop!' he cried, hands clutched to his head as if he *had* been hit by the ball. 'That was pa*thetic*, you big woofter! "I'm free!" ' he squealed. 'You're like the guy in that show,' he said, stepping like a dancer, flapping his hand at the wrist and blowing kisses. "I'm free, Mr Humphries! I'm free!"

'Now,' he said, 'this time,' glowering, 'watch!'

He seized the bat in his right hand and swung it back and forth whilst tossing the ball up in the air with his left, a little higher each time, watching it fall with a careful eye. When he got it just right, he tossed the ball upwards one final time, his tossing hand quickly joining its partner on the handle of the bat and swinging it powerfully into contact with the falling sphere.

Thwack!

'Another six!' he cried as the ball flew high into the air. 'I could've played for England, y'know. I could've played for Yorkshire if I'd wanted. I just got ...' he hesitated, 'got ...' following the direction of his shot, 'got distrac ...' One raised eyebrow traced the slow flight of the ball over the school field, over the school fence, towards the field beyond.

'Oh, no,' he mumbled. 'Oh, no!' and then, 'Tommie!' his voice raised. 'Tommie! Tommie! Oh, for Christ's sake, look up, you stupid ... Tommie-fucking-Wins—'

Pok!

And poor old Tommie went down like a concertina.

Mr Gale handed me the bat. 'Nice shot,' he said. 'Shame about the skull fracture.'

The afternoon passed in a blur (as it must've done for Tommie too): adults running, an ambulance with flashing lights, and flustery attempts at first aid. Mrs Ingalls appeared. And then Miss Lennox. Then Mrs Ingalls disappeared and Mr Waterberry appeared. Miss Lennox disappeared to be replaced by that student teacher, that man's friend, Miss Pevensie. It was kind of fun to see so many adults running around, as Anna-Marie said later, 'like blue-arsed chickens.'

Eventually we all ended up back in class reading 'in absolute silence' whilst Miss Lennox patrolled the room, slapping a twelve inch ruler into the palm of her hand. Nobody was really reading—nobody apart from Melanie—but everyone was silent. When Mr Gale entered the room in the company of Mrs Carpenter dressed in black, there was no need to cough or tap on the board for attention.

'I have come to reassure you all,' said Mrs Carpenter, 'that I have just heard from the hospital that Thomas Winslow,' her voice all high and flutey, 'despite his best efforts to convince the doctors otherwise, has sustained only a mild concussion as a result of this morning's,' she looked at me, 'incident.

'In tomorrow's assembly, we will thank God both that Thomas has been delivered from a potentially serious ... potentially fatal ... injury *and* that none of his classmates are currently,' she looked at me again, I wasn't sure why, 'sitting in a police cell awaiting a charge of either grievous bodily harm or manslaughter.'

Mr Gale was looking at the floor. And then, very quietly, he said: 'Well, Mrs Carpenter, it wasn't really Peter's *fault* ... It was just a ... a ... a *terr*ible accident.'

The classroom turned cold. 'Really, Mr Gale?' said Mrs Carpenter. 'You gave me the distinct impression that Peter Lambert was wielding the bat.'

Mr Gale's eyes tip-toed over the upturned faces of his class. His face coloured as he cleared his throat. 'Well, I think what I meant to say was that Peter was holding the bat immediately after the ... the ... the incident.'

'Peter,' snapped Mrs Carpenter, 'is that your recollection?' I wasn't completely sure what she meant but half nodded anyway. 'Then, Peter, perhaps you can tell me who *was* holding the bat when the incident actually occurred.'

All eyes turned to Mr Gale.

He spoke softly. 'It was me, Mrs Carpenter.'

Mrs Carpenter looked at Mr Gale with no surprise whatsoever. 'Well, then, Mr Gale,' she said, 'we'd best meet for a little chat in my office once you have dismissed your class. Yes?'

'Yes, Mrs Carpenter. Sorry, Mrs Carpenter.'

Once the headmistress had left, Mr Gale fiddled with the piles on his desk, his face blushing like a great pink rose. 'Well,' he murmured, 'I think we've all learnt a valuable lesson today.'

And, as he stood there looking so serious and sad, unable to look us in the eye, I thought, well, maybe he has.

Anyway, that's what I told Anna-Marie. But as I was telling her I couldn't help feeling guilty. After all, I had held the weapon in my hand, the grip still warm, the thwack of bat and ball still tingling in my fingers. I mean, I couldn't see how I could be held to blame for someone else's crime but I felt responsible for Tommie anyway. But then even if it had been my fault it wasn't like I could have done anything to change it. It'd already happened, you see, and, whatever I did, I couldn't go back. And I couldn't avoid the, you know, the consequences; not like I'd avoided that cricket ball.

'My dad used to listen to cricket on the radio,' said Anna-Marie as we approached the cottage Tommie shared with his mum. 'But I never liked it. Watching cricket is like watching paint dry. Watching paint dry, by comparison, is, in fact, a pastime filled with excitement and fraught with danger. Mind you,' she concluded as she thumped on the door, 'cricket was fraught with danger for Tommie.'

I laughed. At least it seemed that Anna-Marie didn't blame me for what had happened.

'Now, you know how Tommie's dad doesn't live with his mum?' she whispered as she continued to pummel the knocker even though we could already hear feet stomping towards us on the other side.

'Yes.'

Pummel—pummel.

'You're about to find out why.'

The door swung open and the largest woman I had ever seen squeezed her way into the frame. Mrs Winslow was the kind of woman who had to turn sideways to leave her own house.

Where other people had a waist, Mrs Winslow had a bulge that prevented her from tying the loose cords of her apron behind her back. A black wig slid back and forth upon the surface of her scalp and two little eyes, pressed like blue raisins into the sweaty pink folds of her face, stared at us with hatred.

'Good afternoon, Mrs Winslow,' said Anna-Marie pleasantly. 'Can Tommie come out?'

Mrs Winslow's brow dripped with sweat, her voice with anger: 'After what this lout did, it's a wonder he'll ever walk again.'

'Now, now, Mrs Winslow,' said Anna-Marie, 'Peter's explained everything to me and I can assure you that it was nothing to do with him. Besides, you should look on the bright side.'

'What?'

'Peter was telling me,' lied Anna-Marie, 'about a boy at his old school who got hit on the head by a cricket ball and all his hair fell out. That would be the worst thing of all.' She turned to me. 'That would be the worst thing that could happen, wouldn't it, Peter? I mean,' she continued as Mrs Winslow's face grew darker, 'you'd have to wear one of those awful wig things. Can you imagine, Mrs Winslow? People would stare at you and laugh. Well, people can be so cruel, can't they? Anyway, I digress: when *will* Tommie be allowed out?'

'Why you little ...' spluttered Mrs Winslow. 'If you think I would ... Just you wait until—'

'Keep your hair on,' said Anna-Marie. 'You seem to be having trouble finishing sentences, Mrs W. You haven't had a cricket ball-related incident of your own,' she enquired, tapping her finger on her forehead, 'have you?'

The door slammed in our faces, generating enough of a gust to send us back a step.

'Told you,' said Anna-Marie.

●

We kept to the shadowed side of the lane where the ancient trees linked their arms forming high green arches, but even here the leaves, a rich Englishy green, allowed the sun to sparkle through.

'What do you think Mr Merridew will tell us about Alice?' I said. To be honest I didn't see how he could tell us anything useful about Alice at all but I thought it would make Anna-Marie happy to think I did.

'I don't know, do I?' she said taking a bite from the apple she had hidden in the pocket of her dungarees. 'That's what we're going to find out.'

'Anyway,' I said, 'I thought he was a scientist.'

'But he used to work at the college. Like a teacher,' said Anna-Marie. 'Now he's—'

The Beast.

What I mean is, we'd turned this corner and come face to face with the Beast of Everlasting Lane, close enough to smell its breath and see its steaming nostrils, its gleaming teeth. The dog was just as surprised but that didn't stop an evil smile from curling its lip. We began to back away, trying to look all casual, but my heart was beating like a hammer on a fencepost as the Beast's eyes followed each terrified step.

Perhaps we'd be safe. I was beginning to think we might be until it took its first step towards us. I nearly fainted. It snorted. It sneered. It sniggered. It took a second step and we jumped. Both of us.

'What do we do?'

'Don't show him you're afraid,' said Anna-Marie. 'He can smell fear.'

Well, I thought, he won't have much problem smelling m—

It took another step towards us and we screamed.

And then we turned.

And then we ran.

And then we screamed again.

And the faster we ran, the louder we screamed. And we ran very fast indeed, our feet pounding the road. Anna-Marie and her long legs were soon out in front. I glanced back and saw only jaws: bloody-pink gums gaining on us, teeth shining. The lane zipped beneath our feet; the black Beast slobbering in pursuit, muscles pumping, rasping, gasping as if a tiny man was drowning in its ugly throat.

I screamed again and, with a determined burst of scaredy-catness, overtook Anna-Marie. And charged straight into Mr Merridew. I hit the ground with a thump. Anna-Marie fell on top of me with a bump.

Mr Merridew chuckled.

In his right hand the old man held his long walking stick and, twisting it like a sword, he stepped over our tangled bodies to face the Beast of Everlasting Lane.

The Beast, which had paused to enjoy our crash, raised a puzzled eyebrow as the old man, stick swishing from side to side, drew closer. He snarled. Mr Merridew I mean. The dog snarled right back. Not to be outdone, Mr Merridew began to growl. So did the dog. When Mr Merridew began to bark it wasn't a surprise when the Beast answered even more ferociously.

And then, with astonishing speed, Mr Merridew thrust his stick deep into the dog's open mouth. The dog crunched the stick between powerful jaws but the man twisted, turning his weapon in neck-breaking directions, forcing the dog to follow. The dog's eyes bulged and its heavy body flipped from side to side. Blood began to ooze from the sides of his mouth.

The old man laughed.

The movement of the stick got faster and faster until it and the dog went all blurry. Sweat sprayed from the dog's thick, black body and a mad panic crept into its eyes. With a great wave of his hand, the old man threw both stick and dog down the lane. The dog, now whining like a pup, flew through the air and slammed onto the road, the stick clattering to the ground beside it. It must be dead, I thought, the Beast, but no, its heavy sides were still rising and falling. Mr Merridew approached cautiously and, retrieving his stick, prodded the body. The animal flinched, its eyes spinning in its head.

'We should call a vet,' said Anna-Marie.

'Nonsense,' said Mr Merridew. 'The animal is in pain. I suspect a rib has punctured its lung. It is my responsibility. I must put it out of its misery.'

'But—'

'Any veterinary would do the same,' said Mr Merridew with a wave of his hand. 'Ninety per cent of a vet's work is merely finishing off what nature has started. Anyway, there is no time. We must act now to avoid unnecessary suffering.'

Mr Merridew removed his jacket, folded and handed it to me—it smelt of old smoke—and then his tie. He whistled through his teeth, glancing about and rolling his sleeves as if about to put oil in his car. He took hold of his stick, like a club, testing its weight. The dog could see him coming, its shiny eyes rolling with terror. The man lifted the stick above his head where it hung suspended for one heart breaking moment. And then it descended.

With a crunch.

A crunch.

Crunch.

We stared, Anna-Marie and I, horrified, but also hypnotised like it was a swinging watch. Crunch. It seemed to go on and on. Crunch. I flinched with each thud of the heavy stick. Crunch. And I could feel my face burning. Crunch.

Anna-Marie's face colourless. Crunch. Her blue eyes wide; her body stiff. Crunch.

The old man's expression was determined but … Crunch … calm as if he was struggling … Crunch … as if he was struggling with a knotted shoelace. Crunch. He paused only to wipe the sweat from his brow. Crunch. To adjust his grip. Crunch. Or his angle of attack. Crunch. The violence was like a machine, all springs and cables. Crunch. Extreme and cold. Crunch. The steady rhythm made it all seem nearly normal. Crunch.

I felt sick. Crunch. I wanted to be sick. Crunch. And yet I couldn't completely … Crunch … completely look away. Crunch. Such violence was nearly beautiful. No, no, not beautiful. It was ugly. The mirror reflection of beautiful: exactly the same and exactly the opposite.

Finally it was over and Mr Merridew sank panting to his knees beside the body. He pressed two fingers against what was left of the creature's throat and looked away, humming as if trying to identify a distant tune. He looked up at us and smiled.

'It's dead,' he said.

Anna-Marie was staring at her feet. A large blob of blood, as dark and round as an old penny, had fallen on the strap of her white sandal. 'Dead,' she repeated. She bent down to wipe the blood away with her finger. It left a pink smear.

'He'll not bother you again,' laughed Mr Merridew. And then, noticing our faces, he cried, 'Life is transitory! It has no intrinsic value; the life of a dog, doubly so. You are simply indulging in the sentimentality typical of youth.' He took his tie from me, wrapped it around his throat and tied a knot. 'I dare say,' he went on, 'that you would rather I had had you turn your backs or sent you home.

'Well, I do not believe in indulging the sentimentality of children. It is an unnatural state and particularly nauseating when applied to animals. If you wish to be treated like children then you should return to the playground whence you came.'

His tie straight, he took his jacket from me, shaking it twice and glaring at me as if the creases were my fault. 'Not so very long ago,' he continued, 'you would by now have been groomed for a life in the chimneys or domestic service and quite rightly so. Why should children expect special favours from the universe only on account of their age?' He pushed his arms into his tatty jacket. 'The opposite of experience is not innocence, it is ignorance. Ignorance should not merit special treatment and it merits none from me.

'The arrogance of children!' he declared. 'You believe that the universe exists solely for your benefit, and yet you do not have the wit to accept one iota of the responsibility that would be your due if that were actually the case.' He suddenly looked directly at me. 'You think I am a bad man, Peter.'

'No,' I protested weakly.

'You do not think I am a good man!'

'No, well, I ...'

He laughed at my embarrassment. 'There is no difference,' he said. And then, 'Now, how about that milk?'

15

I hadn't seen Mr Merridew's cottage close up before. It was built of red bricks, many of which were crumbling to sand beneath the weight of the clumsy, black slate roof. Now that I'd met him, there was no mistaking the crooked man's crooked home. He led us up the crooked path and opened the door. But I hesitated on the crooked doorstep.

Anna-Marie laughed at the look on my face, and whispered, 'You're scared of him, just like Tommie-Titmus.'

So I went in, but only to show Anna-Marie that I was braver. And because she pushed me. But I noticed how her own foot hovered just a moment before itself stepping in to that miserable hallway.

And I didn't blame it either because the house was even odder inside than out: floorboards bare and wallpaper hanging down in flaps. Rubble and rubbish lay on every surface in a grim, smothery gloom. 'I have an aversion,' explained Mr Merridew, 'to the light.' I tried smiling behind the old man's back and got a sharp poke in the ribs from Anna-Marie.

The furniture in the living room was old and worn and smelt of damp woodland. Anything not already broken looked ready to break. Books tottered on tables and shelves. There was dust everywhere. There were no photographs.

Anna-Marie and I sat down on an old sofa, the cushions bruising our bottoms, and Mr Merridew sat opposite us in a high-backed armchair. A fire, in spite of the heat outside, roared in the grate. For some minutes the old man stared at us through his small, round glasses, with a mysterious smile on his face.

He produced a packet of cigarettes. I stared as his long fingers prised a cigarette free, and then swallowed with horror as he turned and offered the packet in our direction. I couldn't have been more shocked if he'd offered me a shrunken head. Anna-Marie said, 'No, thank you,' and the old man chuckled as a bright flame wrapped around the end of his cigarette. He sucked until his skin stuck to the shape of his skull. He noticed me looking at him and smiled, exhaust fumes gushing from between his yellowy teeth.

'Biscuits?' he asked. 'Milk?'

'Yes, please,' we said, and he laughed at our politeness.

Whilst he was gone, I nudged Anna-Marie and sucked in my cheeks, leering through the small round frames that I'd made with my fingers. But she ignored me, turning her gaze to the burning blaze of the fireplace.

The biscuits, when they arrived, were soft and stale, as if they'd sat too long on a sunlit windowsill as if such a thing existed in that gloomy place. The milk too tasted a little funny as if it'd been stood alongside the biscuits soaking up the sun. Mr Merridew prodded the fire with a poker, just as he'd poked the body of the Beast with his stick, before settling with a creak into his armchair.

'What did you mean,' asked Anna-Marie, placing, after the slightest sip, her glass on the floor at her feet, 'before, when you said there was no difference if Peter thought you were a good man or a bad man?' I was surprised. She was supposed to be asking about Alice.

131

'Ah!' exclaimed Mr Merridew. 'An excellent question.' He turned to look at me with graveyard eyes. 'I will tell you, Peter,' he said, 'it has been my pleasure to watch Anna-Marie grow over several years. Why, do you remember what an uncouth child you were when first we met?' He drew smoke from his cigarette. 'I seem to remember,' he murmured, 'a blue dress with, I think, a white ribbon in your hair. *Imperious Prima*, indeed. Am I correct?'

Anna-Marie smiled but said nothing.

Mr Merridew shook his head, suddenly waking. 'Where was I? Where was I? Ah, yes. Well, to answer your question, I would firstly say that I might simply have meant that Peter's opinion is of no importance, either to me or to the universe at large. Secondly, I probably meant that bad and good, good and evil are meaningless terms: they are simply human descriptions of actions or behaviour that have no bearing on whether the actions or behaviour have any ethical content whatsoever. In brief, although the *con*cepts certainly exist there are no such things as good or bad in a Godless universe. There are merely shades of moral ambiguity.'

I sneaked a glance at Anna-Marie. She was staring at Mr Merridew as she'd done earlier when she'd watched him beat the dog to death. I nudged her once and then twice again to get her attention. She seemed surprised to see me.

'I kill a dog,' continued Mr Merridew, 'and Peter thinks I am a bad man, but I spare a dog pain and he might think me good. But, of course, I injured the dog so I *am* a bad man, but I was protecting children so perhaps I *am* good.' The room was so warm that I was beginning to feel a bit suffocated. 'In conclusion,' said Mr Merridew, 'perhaps all I meant is that Peter should not leap so quickly to his ... conclusions.'

'If it really doesn't matter,' said Anna-Marie, 'you could tell the police what you ... what happened.'

Mr Merridew sniffed. 'I can't see what would be gained by such an action.'

'Well,' said Anna-Marie, 'you'd be telling the truth.'

'The truth?' asked Mr Merridew. 'Truth, as you know, is in the eye of the beholder. I tell the truth *ergo* I am a good man. But if you don't want to hear the truth *ergo* I am a bad man. Is it still the truth?'

'But it depends on you, doesn't it?' said Anna-Marie. 'Whether you mean to be cruel or kind.'

'What are my good intentions worth if they result in unhappiness for Peter? Who is to judge? Peter? You? From where do you derive the authority to convict or acquit? Only those with the self-righteous morality of children would dare to pass judgement based on such absolutes.' He looked at me, his eyes cold dark craters. 'You are so cock-sure that you are right and I am wrong, yet without God neither even exists. There is only chaos.'

'No,' protested Anna-Marie. 'The world isn't like that. There are consequences. You're a scientist. You have laws—'

'*Was* a scientist,' snapped Mr Merridew with a sharp flick of his hand. 'Was. Until I grew sick of the halls of academia bulging with myopic fools: passing their laws, sacrificing their principles as if you could simply trap chaos behind the bars of a chart; just as historians dress cavemen in suits of clothes and call it civilisation. Yes, perhaps if you look with your eyes closed,' said Mr Merridew, 'and if your scope is sufficiently narrow you might discern order in anything; but open them wide and you will see only chaos.'

'But if that's true,' said Anna-Marie, 'what's the point in even living?'

He chuckled.

'Perhaps,' he said, 'I lack the courage of my convictions. But, if life is meaningless then death is also. It is not superior to life. It matters not if I live or die or if I have never lived; that is not, in itself, reason to proceed from one state to the next.'

'But what about the dog?'

'The dog,' he said slowly, 'was in pain. Life may or may not be pointless, but life in pain is intolerable; certainly when compared to death free of pain. Don't you agree?'

Mr Merridew didn't talk like any other grown-up I'd ever met. He didn't pretend that everything was all right. I felt I was being shown something dreadful, like a stone being lifted to reveal all the wriggling creatures underneath. His words were even more brutal than the death of the Beast. As I sat and listened his voice became quicksand and I had to fight to keep all the hope from being sucked out of me.

'But being alive *is* better than being dead,' protested Anna-Marie. 'Surely.'

'Is it? And how do you know?'

'Well,' said Anna-Marie, 'say there's this girl: Alice.'

Alice? At last!

'A friend of yours?'

'Yes,' without a pause. 'She went to the college. Did you know her?'

Mr Merridew shrugged. 'If I ever did, I have already forgotten. My very point.'

'But she doesn't want to just live like nobody's even noticed. Nobody wants that.'

'My dear, I suppose you would have me reassure you and pat you on the head and say that we live on in the memories of others. Pah! Nonsense!'

'But what about in books, say?' said Anna-Marie. 'We met this man, didn't we, Peter? And he said when you make up people and things they do in books and stories it is like they could last forever. You can make them real. I mean in the books and the people who read—'

'Anna-Marie,' said Mr Merridew, and he leant forward to take her hands from her lap and hold them between his own like a sandwich, 'I *do* understand,' and he kind of looked at me as he said it. 'Your determination is nothing if not endearing but this girl—this Alice—is no different from you or I or ... or anyone else. It gives me no pleasure to crush you like this bar the satisfaction of telling you the truth—'

'But you said truth was—'

He silenced her with another wave of his hand.

'I suggest, my dear, that you visit the graveyard for a more realistic perspective.'

'The graveyard?'

'You will find it littered with corpses any of whom may have imagined they had some claim to renown. Who tends to them now?' cried the old man. 'Who fashions the carpenter's coffin? Who digs the gravedigger's grave? There is nothing: nothing after; nothing before. Eternity after eternity, eons of vacuum, of nothingness, interrupted only by the briefest flash of sentient consciousness.'

'But that's what it's about!' pleaded Anna-Marie. 'Surely! That flash! Isn't that what makes the emptiness bearable?'

'No,' said Mr Merridew darkly, releasing her hand. 'The emptiness makes the flash intolerable.'

'Well,' said Anna-Marie, 'I can't speak for Peter, but I *would* rather be alive than dead even if there isn't a God. I like the world how it is: when the sun comes up in the morning, and the wind. I like watching the butterflies. You know, and when it snows. That's why people believe in magic. That's why people hope tomorrow will be better than yesterday.'

Mr Merridew sighed, irritated I thought.

As I sat there I began to remember the world outside: the sun on the lane, the leaves and the cracked old branches. It was all such a long way from that dreadful little room in that dreadful cottage. It was like when you suddenly remember a dream you had the night before and you start trying to remember all the bits that you hadn't even realised you'd forgotten. My eyes looked into the fire crackling in the grate. I so missed the light. It had all but ceased to exist since we'd been trapped in Mr Merridew's home.

Anna-Marie sat straight-backed and cleared her throat. 'Thank you for the milk, Mr Merridew,' she said. 'It was very kind but I think we'd better go now.' My limbs felt so heavy I couldn't move. 'Come on, Peter,' said Anna-Marie, 'it's time to go home.' My head was swimming and my eyes struggled to stay open. 'Thank you for the milk, Mr Merridew,' said Anna-Marie again. 'Peter, come *on!*'

We left the house. Leaving the darkness, I was so dazzled by the sudden burst of summer's afternoon that it took me a moment to realise that Anna-Marie hadn't turned towards home at all but back down the lane, back towards the woodyard, back towards the Beast.

'Where are we going?' I said, struggling to keep up with her long strides.

'*We're* not going anywhere,' she said. 'For all I care you can just toddle off home like a good boy.'

'But I don't want to go home,' I lied.

You see, Everlasting Lane was different than it was before. The air was still now like a heavy cloak and the birds were silent. But I don't think Anna-Marie even noticed. She was walking as fast as she could and she didn't slow down or even turn to look as she passed the body of the Beast, a steady pool of blood oozing from beneath its still body.

'Are you going to the end?'

She gave an irritated sigh.

'Anna-Marie?'

The lane was twisting and turning now, wriggling like the Beast beneath the blows of Mr Merridew's stick. As we rounded each bend we held our breaths as if we were bound to find out the truth but each time all we could see was another bend up ahead and then another and another.

'What if there isn't an end?' I said.

'Everything has an end, Peter,' sighed Anna-Marie. 'Didn't you listen to a word Mr Merridew said?'

I shuddered. 'Yes, but ...'

And then we finally turned a corner and stopped in amazement. But it wasn't the end: it was something worse. Anna-Marie swore and then she said, 'Go on, Peter. Make yourself useful. You choose.'

Right in front of us Everlasting Lane did something neither of us had expected or even imagined possible. It split in two. One fork turned to the left and the other, of course, to the right. I hesitated. Why did *I* have to decide? Anna-Marie stood waiting, tapping her foot and I stood there until I wished I could just tear myself down the middle and send half each hopping off in different directions. If only that was possible.

'I could go one way,' I said, 'and you could go the other.'

But I didn't want to go alone and I don't think she did either. And, anyway, that didn't even solve the problem. You see, we could go down one but we couldn't go down both. I mean, not at the same time. Not together. It was one or the other: like a choice. And if we went down one, say, we went down the right hand one, then we might never know what we might've seen down the left hand one. And if we went down the right hand one then all the things we saw and thought about would be different from what we would've seen and thought if we'd gone down the left hand one. Or the other way round.

'Well?'

It kind of made your head all swimmy.

'Peter,' said Anna-Marie crossly, 'which way?'

'I don't know,' I said. And then, 'I want to go home.'

And so we walked back home in silence. You see, I'd been scared that whichever one I chose would be the wrong one and that I wouldn't even know; not even if the one I chose seemed like it had been the right one because, when you thought about it, I would never know for sure. And then—

'Oh, Peter, bog off!'

And she didn't talk to me again for a week.

16

If I'd squinted I could have just about imagined that, despite her scrawny face, it was Anna-Marie, not her mother, who cowered in the kitchen doorway of their cottage peering at me with bitter blue eyes. Anna-Marie had never invited me into her home. It was wintry cold and I could see dirty plates piled high in the kitchen sink. A peculiar sweet smell rose from the grimy rugs which laid a path through their house.

Mrs Liddell, yet to speak, raised her broomstick a second time and pounded again on the ceiling. In answer I could hear a flurry of footsteps overhead.

'What is it?' came the crabby response. 'What is it?'

I concentrated all my attention on the only picture hung on the hallway wall: a man, tall and stocky, embraced his wife and tiny daughter, and all three smiled as if they didn't know how to stop.

A door slammed and Anna-Marie's white socks and sandals appeared at the top of the stairs. 'I told you: I don't want to …!' they roared as they stomped their way down. 'Peter?' I looked up into Anna-Marie's horrified eyes. 'I told you,' she said, 'bog off!'

•

But even Anna-Marie couldn't stay mad at me forever. For-giveness arrived as I left the school gates on the last day before the half term holidays in the shape of a stone. 'Ouch!' Right between the shoulder blades. A small stone, yes, but, well, even so. A second pebble clipped my ear. 'Hey, stupid,' shouted Anna-Marie just to make clear that these missiles were meant to be friendly, 'wait for me!'

I waited.

'Listen,' said Anna-Marie, seizing me by the arm and pulling me along the grass verge, 'you're not going home yet, okay?'

'Why?'

'I've got a job for you: that's why. Come on,' and she was off, towards the church. I had to trot to keep up. 'I've been thinking about Kat,' she announced. 'Why is she always bring-ing flowers up here? What does she do at the church? Does she ever come to church on Sundays?'

I shook my head. 'No.'

'That's what I mean. She's not really the Christian-type. She's nice enough but in a normal way. Nice to talk to I mean.'

I shrugged.

'Heavens-to-Betsy, Peter, without me you'd end up in the soup with the rest of the veg. I mean there must be a reason.'

She meant all that stuff about consequences again, but what if there wasn't any reason? Surely, sometimes things just hap-pened. Sometimes people just took flowers to churches, didn't they?

'I want to know about the nursery,' went on Anna-Marie, 'and Alice and I would like you, if it's not too much trouble, to have a look round and see what you can find.'

'But what am I looking for?'

'Clues, of course.'

'What sort of clues?'

'What sort of clues?' she repeated in that voice she did that always made me sound like a twit. 'If I knew that I'd find them myself.'

'But why the graveyard?'

'Crikey, Peter, have you forgotten every word Mr Merridew said?'

Forgotten? Of course I hadn't. Not a thing. Even my dreams had been riddled with Mr Merridew's words. Try as I might I couldn't quite put the stone he'd lifted back into place; I couldn't quite keep those squirmy, twisty worms out of my brain.

'But what are you doing?' I said. 'Aren't you looking for clues too?'

'I'm busy,' she answered and again began to walk off.

I was struggling to keep up with her. 'But *where* are you going?'

'To the church hall.'

'Why?'

'Are you being sponsored?' asked Anna-Marie. 'Ten pee for every idiotic question. If you must know,' she sighed, 'I'm going for my ballet lesson.'

Looking both ways, we crossed the road, out of the cool shadows into the warm sun. As we walked along, I dragged my hand over the railings of a fence enjoying the ripples in my fingers.

'What's ballet like?'

'It stinks!' said Anna-Marie.

'Why do you go, then?'

'Don't you ever get fed up poking your nose into other people's business?' I shook my head. 'My mother makes me. I mean, you're the expert when it comes to doing everything your mother says.'

Well, I didn't know what that was supposed to mean.

'Can I watch?' I said.

Anna-Marie looked appalled. 'Can you watch? No!'

'Why not?'

'I told you,' she said. 'It's stupid. It stinks. Besides Miss Drew would probably have a spasm.'

A dozen or so girls, too young for school, stood on one side of the church hall door, protected by their mothers. Half as many girls, including Melanie Finch, had already walked up from Dovecot and were gathered to the other side chattering in a bunch. Anna-Marie stood alone. The Dovecot girls, falling silent, swapped shifty glances and stared at their shoes. Anna-Marie ignored them right back.

And then, 'Hello, Peter,' said Melanie smiling. 'How's Tommie?' One or two of her friends giggled. 'Are you coming to ballet?' and they all exploded into laughter.

Anna-Marie winced. And I didn't feel very comfortable either. Here's why:

'Woah!' Mr Gale had exclaimed, waving his hand in front of his nose. 'Who let that one off? Crikey, that's ripe! Was that one of yours, Smelanie?' Melanie, busy designing her fourth poster for the school fair, didn't say anything. 'Ha, ha,' said Mr Gale. 'Only joking!'

Melanie's ears burned so redly that I could see little whispers of steam escaping. She reached into her pencil case. She had drawn this picture of a fortune-teller and needed a yellow to do the gleam in the gypsy's eyes as they peered into the crystal ball. Melanie's pencil case was a wonderful, decorated thing, all loops and twirls and pictures of kittens and rabbits, and all the work of Melanie and her fine blue cartridge pen. But that day I spotted a new doodle: a love-heart shape with 'MF for PL' written inside.

It made me feel kind of odd. I only half understood what

it meant. Melanie spent more of her time chasing me in the playground and hitting me than anything that might deserve a love-heart. I discovered, however, to my surprise, that I wasn't completely unhappy about it—whatever 'it' was. And my heart went kind of pitter-pat with a chuckle in my tummy whenever I thought about it. I mean about her.

I mean Melanie.

As soon as I'd seen the pencil case she'd pulled it from our table and tucked it into her lap. Her felt-tipped pen squeaked across the paper and Melanie's ears grew so red they were purple. I scraped my chair backwards afraid that her head might shoot off and swallow the entire room in embarrassment.

Later on, when I was putting my reading book in my drawer I found an envelope. I recognised Melanie's handwriting straight away. I looked up to see her watching and this time we both blushed. And at lunchtime, when we all played chase, she caught me and hit me harder than ever before.

'Hey, hey, hey,' said Anna-Marie punching my arm. The ballet girls had begun to shove their way through the now open doors. 'Planet Earth to Peter: what are you thinking about?'

'Nothing.'

'Oh, wow!' said Anna-Marie as she pushed her way crossly through the crowd. 'Sorry I missed that.' Just before she entered the hall she turned to face me. 'Get on with it!' she hissed. 'Just the main part. Don't go beyond the oak tree.'

'Why?'

She looked exasperated. 'Just because. Now, get on with it! I'll meet you here in half an hour.'

As the last girls shuffled their way into the village hall I turned away and headed for the graveyard. I really didn't know what I was supposed to be looking for so I wandered lost among the headstones. Many of the graves were decorated with flowers: bluebells, big bushy chrysanthemums, tulips tied with ribbons; wreathes of daisies and buttercups; pink roses in a painted glass—

'Kitty!' I cried. 'What are you doing here?'

She lay on the low stone wall, watching me with arched eyebrows, and gave a loud meow. She didn't seem surprised to see me and allowed me a tickle behind her ear. Then she slid to the ground and swaggered homewards. She didn't even look back.

Alone again I poked my head around the corner of the church. The road was deserted. The girls had entered and the doors had been shut. I darted from the pavement and hid behind a tree, emerging a moment later to creep around the outside of the building. I sneaked along the pavement, hiding in shadows and looking everywhere but my destination: the church hall. I hummed a tune.

I was James Bond.

I rattled the doors. They were locked and the windows were beyond hopping height. The deadly assassin, I continued around the back of the building to where two dustbins stood. Ignoring the smell, I pocketed my Walther PPK, left my satchel on the ground and clambered up. Perched on my toes, I could see over the window ledge and, using the sleeve of my black tuxedo, I cleared a porthole through the slime and grime. The window, bordered by its blistering frame made the room like a painting: lit by the dusty afternoon sun slicing across the room and the wide brush strokes polishing the halos that shone around the assembled girls.

Wooden chairs and tables had been pushed and stacked to one side, and the would-be ballerinas were bouncing on their toes and heels in the middle of the room. They wore leotards and tutus like a tin of Quality Street. Their teacher, Miss Drew, stood tall amongst them in a flowery dress, hair tied into a grey bun and glasses hung on her huge chest. She organised her troops with a powerful, high-pitched voice.

'Swans,' she commanded, 'a semi-circular loop around the perimeter of the hall.' She twirled her finger in the air like a baton. 'The *edge* of the hall. Yes, you too, Emily. Sugar Plums, would you ...I know you're a Sugar Plum, Alison ...Would you construct a straight line to the front of the room.' Her finger drew maps of this arrangement and she waited as various girls tip-toed into position. 'A *straight* line. Would Miss Pevensie call that straight, Jessica? I thought not. Now, where is Anna-Marie? ... Lorraine! Just put it away, Lorraine! I don't care where you found it, just put it away! ... Fine, dear, you *tell* your mother! ...Anna-Marie in the middle.'

With her hair tied back and stretching her scalp, I hadn't spotted Anna-Marie at first, but there she was, moving into the centre of the room. And there she waited, calm among the itching, scratching, nose-picking rabble. She had one foot placed in front of the other and her hands behind her back. She was elegant like a cat; her eyes closed as if asleep.

The light-shade sent its shadow revolving across the room, whilst the afternoon sun burst silently through the dusty windows. But it was not so much the sun as the effect of its light that grabbed my attention: the room glowed like coloured oils, dazzling and bright; the surface both smooth and rough to the touch.

Miss Drew waited until a shadowy silence had fallen upon her class before sitting, upright, at the piano. Her bayonet-eye jabbed at the dancers one final time as she counted: 'One, two, three, four. One, two ...'

Goodness me, that piano was out of tune: a milk float full of broken spanners crashing into the room. I covered my ears and, watching the fat little girls shuffling around the room, I wanted to cover my eyes. The more skilful threw legs in the air; others waved their arms about as if greeting distant friends.

In this sea of confusion, Anna-Marie was a desert island of golden beaches and gentle palms. Her arms crossed upon her chest, her hands resting on opposite shoulders, she began to nod as if accepting that some never-ending argument had been settled, finally and beyond doubt, to the agreement of all. Her face wore the expression of a child wandering through dreams, at one with a universe that could not be questioned. As chaos crashed and clashed around her in a clockwise direction, she began to move: slowly, carefully, and with a startling grace. It wasn't ballet but she danced with a weightlessness beyond the other girls bumping into one another like a waddle of drunken ducklings.

The music became less alarming as Miss Drew found her rhythm. She didn't do much in the way of actual teaching, barely looking up from her piano keys. Her pleasure came, I thought, only from her music. And as she began to mix trickling ripples with booming waves of sound, her dancers might just as well have been playing hopscotch.

The speed increased, Miss Drew punching the keys, and Anna-Marie responded. Her arms rose into the air, swaying in some heavenly breeze. She stepped backwards and forwards, each step simple and precise like the insides of a watch. Her head tilted back as if meeting the golden light of the sky. I was enchanted: my eyes, my mouth, my heart wide open.

And then something strange happened. Among all the rough material, as quavers bickered with crotchets like some playground fight-fight-fight and the chords quarrelled trying to hack each other from behind, Miss Drew began to weave notes of golden silk. As hammer hammered on wire, soft and loud, and churning bass notes drove her on, the music became, I don't know, bigger somehow. Important. It began to stir feelings, and memories too, like Wellingtoned feet stirring banks of autumn leaves, making me sad and happy at the same time: memories of my father, and thoughts of my mother.

I don't know how. After all, it was only music.

The other girls, dumpy little trolls, disappeared, and, whilst Miss Drew, I imagined, performed for cheering crowds at the Albert Hall, Anna-Marie danced for an audience of one. A secret melody took her by surprise, capturing her, and now she moved like sorcery, the prisoner of some silver spell that led her on in the dance. Her soul shone like eyes as her feet moved across the floor like Miss Drew's fingers dancing across the keys.

My porthole became a microscope. I didn't know whether Miss Drew was aware of Anna-Marie, perhaps not, but I saw everything. Everything: the demerara freckles on her shoulders; the fine hairs on her arms; the mole behind her ear; the dimples in her knees; the bruise on her neck, a blue-black island in a milky sea. She leapt and, for an instant, gravity released her from its grip. She climbed and conquered the space about her.

And I thought of what Anna-Marie had said: 'Your grip on reality seems so tenuous.' No, no, not that. I mean all that stuff about tigers and the smell of flowers; and I wondered if maybe she was wrong because this dance was about something other than dancing. Something more. It was about, I don't know, hope. About sadness too, yes, but about the hope, like she'd said to Mr Merridew, that tomorrow would be better than yesterday. Her dance told its story as clearly as if her feet tripped across a page, like Norman's white wasteland, her toes dipped in ink; or painted a picture so real that the tiger threatened to tear free of the canvas and sink its cavernous jaws into her pale skin.

And then something else happened. Until that moment,

Alice, the real Alice, had seemed to me only like a distant dream, a thought unthought, a memory forgotten, but to Anna-Marie she had become something more, something real and solid. I knew it was true because she no longer danced alone: twin dancers like reflections in a looking glass; everything opposite, everything the same. Two tiny ballerinas like Christmas fairies. Two swans fixed to the surface of the lake, but who was real and who the reflection?

What a thing to see: colour, real colour, light, white light, the way the light fell upon the spinning sisters, shape and motion, with everything that wasn't beautiful removed. Anna-Marie's headband had fallen away and the afternoon sun set her hair on fire, and ablaze, in that penetrating light, I saw her revealed.

I was ashamed to see her so.

I wanted it to stop.

I wanted the light to burn my eyes.

Finally, as Miss Drew crashed into a final chord, Anna-Marie collapsed alone in the centre of the room. As the dying notes shook the walls setting the old joists and beams trembling, the other girls reappeared still shuffling around the room like two dozen blind mice. Having circled the room about fifty times, they were tired and, as Miss Drew briskly dismissed them, they shambled out, leaving Anna-Marie in the middle of the room, her chest and shoulders heaving.

Miss Drew got to her feet and, fingers trembling, began shuffling sheet music into a leather brief case.

'Anna-Marie?'

Anna-Marie looked up. Strands of hair sparkled sticking to the sweat that coated her forehead.

'Yes, Miss Drew?'

'Very nice, dear, but next time I fear we should try some actual ballet, don't you?'

Anna-Marie smiled like a saint.

'Yes, Miss Drew.'

And from that day on when I dream, if I dream, I don't dream of Mr Merridew and things best kept beneath stones; I dream of Anna-Marie and Alice, locked together, spiralling like constellations across the night sky, scattering silver in their wake.

17

This one day I came home from school and was shoving my bag into the understairs cupboard when the telephone rang. I jumped as if someone had lit a firework in my back pocket. Most times Kat left it unplugged—'It's not as if anyone even knows who we are'—but she'd also been searching for the part-time work that, she said, was all that lay between us and 'the poor house'. It seemed like she'd forgotten to unplug it after her last thumb through the *Yellow Pages*.

The ringing continued as I stepped into the kitchen and even as I kicked off my shoes. I was about to go and face the telephone squatting alone on its little table when I heard Kat trotting down the stairs. I was about to call out but she'd already reached the receiver and lifted it with a loud click.

'Hello,' she said. 'Amberley 49312,' and then, 'Oh, Doctor Todd, it's you.' She sounded kind of funny when she said it, like her collar was done up too tight. 'Yes, Clive, of course … Have you? No, it's not been ringing this end …Yes, I will. I'll get the line checked. Of course …Yes, I did get them. Of course. They were lovely. They are lovely …Yes, they're right here,' and she waved vaguely in the direction of the empty telephone table. 'A lovely scent. It was very thoughtful of you, Doctor … Clive, but you really … No, you really shouldn't've …' Kat took a shuddery kind of breath and listened for a moment before swapping the receiver from one hand to the other and folding her hair back behind her ear. She started listening again. 'I do appreciate everything, Clive, of course I do, but as I've said before it's Peter.

'I can only … Yes, but I can only … One thing at a time. I'm sure you understand …

'No, he's fine, I think. Well, you know Peter: he doesn't say much. But I don't think he remembers … Dangerous? What do you …? Of course not. No, nothing like that … Of course I will. Yes, of course, if there's any … Yes. Look, I'd better go. He could be home any minute, but, Clive, please no more roses. Promise me … Please promise … Okay, I promise I'll call if you'll promise no more flowers …

'Yes, well, goodbye, then. Goodbye.'

The silence that remained, once she'd hung up the phone, throbbed. I stepped into the hallway as she wrapped the cable twice around her knuckle. 'I'm not sure why we even need a phone,' she muttered as she yanked it from the socket. She looked up startled to see me standing there before brushing past me on her way to the kitchen.

Even though the phone had been silenced, I struggled to pull my eyes away.

Why was Doctor Todd even calling us?

Anyway that's what I was thinking about, sat on a clump of grass by the cemetery wall, when Anna-Marie came out of the church hall and waved.

'Hi.'

'Hello,' I said. 'How was it?'

Anna-Marie wrinkled her nose and shrugged. 'All right,

I suppose,' she said. I tried to say something else but nothing would come. She laughed, her school shirt sticky with sweat.

'Good afternoon, children.' The vicar, squinting through his glasses, those funny glasses with two halves, was striding along the path towards us, the top of his pink head shining in the sun. I recognised him from school assemblies. 'Isn't it hot?' he cried. And then, 'Are you waiting for someone?'

'I've just had my ballet lesson.'

'A-ha,' said the vicar as if this wasn't quite good enough. He was about to enquire further when Anna-Marie's tight grip pulled us out of view around the back of the church and into the graveyard.

'Well,' she said, 'did you find anything?'

I told her how I had searched the graveyard up and down and inside out for clues but found nothing.

'I wonder,' she said, muttering, 'Well, if you want something doing ...' Tucking her P.E. bag under her arm, she folded back the dry grass that camouflaged the nearest headstone. 'The problem,' she accepted, 'is that you only know the clues you're looking for when you find them. It's like in the books.' She examined the faded words. 'Nobody even realises a clue is a clue until about twenty pages after they've first seen it, as sure as "i" comes before "e".' She moved among the graves. 'Except after "c" of course.'

Anna-Marie didn't worry too much about the graves or the memories of the people within. 'Honestly, Peter, you can take that look off your face. They're past caring. It's not the dead ones you want to worry about. When I'm dead and gone,' she went, 'you can leave me at the back of the church hall with the bins. Better still, chop me up and feed me to the ducks. Mind you, I'm pretty sure ducks are vegetarian.' She read each inscription with interest but thought they were silly.

'Of course they're going to *miss* them,' she sneered. 'That's hardly stunning information. It's a waste of good stone,' she snapped, like she was daring God to interrupt. 'They might at least have put on something useful: the bus timetable, for instance, or how many miles it is to London.'

I stepped more cautiously. No grave ever had opened up under my feet; no worm-eaten hand ever had stretched out to drag me beneath the earth, and I knew those things were just stories. But I didn't dare think they never happened at all. However small the chances of being sucked down into the hidden world of the dead, such things, if they did happen, were unlikely to end happily.

I was relieved though to find that many graves were marked by huge stone slabs making sure that the ghosts beneath stayed safely underground. Their words, the headstones', were worn away by winters and summers, like great, grey flags of victory. Death, they said, always wins. And the big old graves didn't attract the flowers and baubles of the newer ones. Perhaps the newer pretty graves, I thought, explained the lack of flowers on the bleak older ones.

I thought of the man who'd carved those letters generations ago. It was a small village and probably he'd've known the dead. Unless his heart was harder than the stone he must have glanced up at the sun or into the blue sky or, at least, listened to the crickets in the grass or the birds in the trees. Perhaps his mind was on his breakfast or a note from a pretty girl. Surely, as he worked the stone, hammer and chisel, deep and straight, his mind would have marvelled to think that one day they, and their message, would have faded so. I found myself wondering who in turn had carved *his* headstone. Who digs the gravedigger's grave? That's what Mr Merridew had said. I don't know why it made me shudder.

I thought of my father's grave and wondered whether he

was lonely with no one visiting or arranging flowers for him. I hoped he understood.

'We thought we knew all about Kat's secrets,' said Anna-Marie. 'But we didn't know about the nursery and we don't know about the church: that's not a coincidence.'

'We're like the Famous Five or something.'

'What on earth are you wittering on about?'

'We could be the Famous Five. You could be George—she's a girl—and I could be ... Well, I can't remember the boys but I—'

'This isn't a game, you idiot.' And before I could avoid them, Anna-Marie's long fingers reached out, pinched and twisted my ear sinking me slowly to my knees. 'This is a real mystery. Can't you tell the difference? Besides,' she said, finally releasing her grip, 'I don't play games. Honestly, it's no wonder you couldn't find any clues on your own.

'Alice wouldn't take any of your nonsense, you know,' said Anna-Marie.

'Alice?' Rubbing my sore ear. 'Why?'

'Why?' Anna-Marie snorted. 'She'd be far too busy.' She knelt before one of the graves and began to rearrange some purple flowers, tired and dry in a silver vase.

'Busy doing what?'

'I told you before,' tutted Anna-Marie. 'She's a teacher. She works in this really big school, probably in London—or maybe Edinburgh—but all the children absolutely adore her. Her lessons are always so entertaining and the children learn so much they think their brains will burst with it but they don't mind. And all the parents, when they come and see her on parents' evening, bring flowers and stuff. She's the best teacher the school's ever had but she doesn't let it go to her head. She works hard that's why she's so good.'

Anna-Marie had now removed the thin flowers from the

vase and laid them before her across the grave, the purple separated from the brown, the near-living from the definitely dead.

'But how do you know?' I said. 'About Alice, I mean.'

'Most of all she loves her own children, of course,' she said, 'and her husband. He's a farmer and he—'

'A farmer?' I said. 'In London?'

'Sssh. He works all day on the land and he's big and strong and quiet and everyday he brings her a cup of tea and two biscuits when she gets up. Chocolate ones. And then she gets up and gets up her children. She's got three boys, and a daughter who's just as beautiful as she is.'

Anna-Marie returned the flowers to the vase and, having completed her task, she sat back and admired her handiwork. And then she went on: 'At weekends she's got this pony— Alice I mean—and she takes all the children to the stables and they ride around in circles one after the other and the horses swishing their tails and what-not. And after that they feed them apples and then she takes them all home to see her husband whose been tending the farm. And she cooks them all roast chicken with roast potatoes and veg and Yorkshire puddings.'

The graveyard was quiet but for the soft chortling of the birds, muffled by the warmth of the afternoon. A truck chundered to a halt with a load of barrels for *The White Hart*. I sat down beside Anna-Marie and listened to her soft voice.

'And they live in this big farmhouse with two cars and two televisions—'

I couldn't help laughing. '*Two* televisions'? I couldn't help wondering if she wasn't just making this all up.

'Yes,' said Anna-Marie, 'why not?' getting to her feet. 'Two televisions.' Brushing herself down. 'And one of them in colour. And in the evening we'll sit and listen to the Bay City Rollers and maybe watch something funny on *both* our televisions until it's time for bed.' She stretched and looked about her, fingers tumbling through her hair. 'And then we'll all kiss and cuddle good night and we'll go on a seaside holiday once a year and then the same thing happens all over again the next day and …

'Oh!'

'What?'

Anna-Marie had stopped talking and was absolutely still—headstone still—staring across the graveyard.

'What?' I said again. 'What is it?'

'Do you remember,' she said slowly, 'that day I came to your cottage: when Kat was putting flowers in a painted glass jar?'

It seemed a strange question, but, 'Yes.' Vaguely.

'It was red. I noticed it because I made something similar myself in school.' I smiled blankly. 'Well,' growled Anna-Marie, 'it's now sitting on that grave over there.'

Oh, that jar. I could see it now. It did look like the kind of thing that a child would make. It was pretty in an arts-and-crafty kind of way with—

'Oh, for goodness' sake,' snapped Anna-Marie pushing me out of her way. 'Now's not the time.'

We crept between the graves towards the jar until, less than ten feet away, we caught sight of someone kneeling. She had her back to us but the rust-coloured hair was unmistakable. Anna-Marie and I dipped behind the headstones to lie among the nettles and dandelions. Kat was undisturbed by our movement, her attention devoted only to the grave before her.

We could hear her voice talking in gentle tones: half to herself and half to … No, she was singing.

He'll return, one summer's eve, When sun is low, behind the trees. He'll sit you down upon his knee, His voice is soft, he'll sing to thee.

Baby sleep, my baby girl, Dimpled cheek, a single curl,
Music box of gold and pearl, Baby, sleep, my baby girl.

She was arranging flowers—pink roses—in the red jar that now rested in her lap. It was then I noticed that we weren't the only ones spying on Kat. Butterflies: all around the graveyard, fluttering in the breeze, falling like blossom. I saw them watching. It was like a weight on my chest and I could hardly breathe.

The singing faded away and we peered out to see Kat struggling to her feet. I would have rushed to help if Anna-Marie's grip hadn't reminded me of what we were up to. This, after all, was subter ... being sneaky. We waited until we heard the clunk of a car door, Kat's engine whine into life and then a whole minute or more to be safe. I got up, brushed down the grass stains and crept out of our hiding place. As I approached the grave a butterfly came to rest on the rim of the red vase and moved its wings in a slow wave.

'Peter.' It was Anna-Marie. I turned around. She was still on the ground but sat up, her arms wrapped about her knees. She shook her head. 'No, Peter. I don't want to know.'

And then I got that feeling. You know that feeling you get when someone walks over your grave. Well, I got it right then. It was kind of funny when you thought about it, what with all the graves Anna-Marie and I had actually trampled over.

'It's all right,' I said.

'No, Peter! Please don't.'

But I'd already picked up the red jar and was examining it with interest, although I didn't really know what I was looking for. And then a sudden hand grasped my shoulder.

'Ha!' cried the vicar. 'I knew you two were up to no good!'

The jar slipped gently through my fingers. It fell, turning, reflecting unexpected patterns of light. It took ages to fall and crash upon the ground, but still quicker than my attempts to catch it. We, the vicar and I, watched as the vase shattered into large blades of glass and splinters of dust, exploding in slow motion. The red shards were vivid like my mother's eyes.

'Why you little vandal!' The vicar's grip tightened. 'You deliberately broke that vase! Have you no shame? I've been watching the pair of you marching over the graves like you own the place. Rearranging flowers! Spying on people! Have you no respect?'

I began to protest but the vicar was too busy shaking his spare fist at Anna-Marie as she escaped over the low, stone wall.

'Come on, Murphy!' she yelled from the pavement.

'Don't think you can run, young lady. I know you. Anna-Marie Liddell. Oh, yes, I know all about you and I'll be speaking to Mrs Carpenter about this, don't you worry!'

He was so agitated that he barely noticed me wriggling and pulling against his tight grip, dragging him with me. And then I tripped, falling as fast and as slow as the red vase. As I did so I glanced in the direction of the other part of the graveyard, you know, beyond the oak tree and saw this jar perched on one of the graves. It was blue with daisies. It looked like the kind of thing a child would make: pretty in an arts and crafty kind of—

And then I saw the grave. The grave where the red vase had sat. The grave where Kat had knelt as the butterflies had watched. And then I saw what was written there.

And I read every word.

And then I scrambled to my feet and followed Anna-Marie as fast as I could, scraping my leg as I clambered over the uneven wall.

And we ran, ignoring both the vicar's bellowing and the green cross code. Anna-Marie managed to stay ahead all the way along the Nancarrow Road until I caught up with her resting against the sign that read Everlasting Lane. She was clutching her sides, swallowing lungfuls of air when she could.

And then she said, 'Well, did you see it?'

'Yes,' before I could even think of anything else to say.

'Well, what did it say? Whose grave is it?'

But all I could think of was Anna-Marie dancing. And Alice. Spinning round and round. Reflections of each other. But who was right-handed and who was left? Who was leading the dance and who following?

'My grandma,' I said.

'What?'

'It's my grandmother.'

Anna-Marie took a deep breath. And then she laughed. Like a mad person.

'It's not funny,' I said. 'He's going to tell Mrs Carpenter.'

But she wouldn't stop laughing. She laughed until tears rolled down her cheeks. And then the laughter stopped but the tears kept on going.

And when I asked her why she wouldn't even tell me.

'After all,' she said, 'you know all about secrets.'

But she was wrong. Anna-Marie I mean, when she said I knew all about secrets. I didn't know anything about secrets. Not really. All I knew was that a secret was like a big sack over your head and so dark that you couldn't see anything. And when you did finally manage to poke a couple of eye-holes all you really found out was that there was another big sack over the first sack.

But I did know someone who knew about secrets.

18

The pillbox was deserted—although a new handwritten sign warned that *Trespassers will be persecuted*—so I made my way back to Amberley and pressed my face against the big window at *Kirrins'* cupping my hands to keep the sunlight out. The elder Mr Kirrin stood behind his counter like the troll beneath the bridge ready to eat the three Billy-Goats Gruff. And there, down between the aisles, at the back of the shop I could see Kat's ring winking at me.

To the side of the shop, a wooden gate had been propped open with broken plant pots and sacks of horse-stuff, and through it was an alleyway running down to the back of the building. I slipped down the narrow tunnel and found myself in a backyard cluttered with everything the Kirrin brothers had ever given up trying to sell: broken ladders, rusting tools, rotting vegetables and a large metal drum containing the black ashes of crates and packing boxes.

Here was another door and a small window through which I could peep. Norman was sat at a round table, head in hands, a pencil drumming on the top of his thin hair and before him blank sheets of frozen snow. I scanned the rest of the room but he was alone. I tapped on the glass but as hard as my fingers worked Norman remained still. Perhaps I should have gone.

He had told me how much he valued being private and I wasn't at all sure that I'd be welcome. But I also knew that I had questions and no one, not even Anna-Marie, had come close to pointing me in the direction of the answers.

So I cleared my throat and called out whilst the palms of both hands pummelled the glass between us. Norman fell from his daydream with a start. He stared at me for a moment, eyelids blinking, before he recognised me and leapt to his feet.

'Good Lord, Peter, was that you?' he cried as the back door swung open. 'What on earth is wrong? I thought Greg must be murdering someone over the price of a cabbage. Here. Come in.'

From the shop, I heard the other Mr Kirrin's voice: 'Norman! Norman, I've told you: for God's sake keep the hysteria down 'til closing. We can do without you scaring off the customers?'

'Sorry, Greg. I erm ... I burnt my hand on the kettle,' called Norman. 'Won't happen again.' And then, 'No, no, it's all right,' he reassured me as I glanced in the direction of the shop-door. 'Greg knows better than to disturb me mid-flow. Besides, we'll keep our voices *sotto voce*. I mean quiet. And if we turn the radio on,' he did so, 'he'll think we're *The Archers*.'

Taking my arm, his grip firm, Norman escorted me into the kitchen. He lifted rather than pulled out the chair next to where he'd been sitting and waited until, 'Right,' I'd taken my place, 'what's your poison? No, no, I mean what do you want to drink? Don't look so worried. Look, I know, we'll start with a glass of water.' He handed me a tissue, his gesture suggesting that I should dry my eyes. 'We'll work up to the harder stuff,' he murmured, 'if needs be.'

I sipped the water, warm from the tap, from a chipped mug, whilst Mr Kirrin squeaked back and forth across the kitchen floorboards muttering to himself and stealing a peek at me every now and then. Eventually, when I'd stopped shaking he took his own chair and sat down. He took up a pencil and began to sharpen it, unpeeling it like an apple as he waited for me to speak.

But I didn't

In the end he said, 'So, to what do I owe this unexpected— though by no means unwelcome—interruption?' He squinted through his spectacles down his pencil-sharp nose. 'How is the search going? Have you uncovered your secret yet?'

I nodded and took another sip of water.

'Really? Excellent.' He put down his pencil. 'Ah, but I can see by your face that it isn't excellent at all.' He retrieved his pencil and, without ever taking his eyes from my face, began to draw great looping patterns on the empty paper in front of him. 'Well, can you tell me anything?' I hesitated. 'Whilst you mull that over,' he said, 'let me just say that I think you and I have established a ... a connection. Perhaps you're too young to appreciate how rare that is. But, Norman, what an assumption! Perhaps, of course, it's not rare at all for a young man like Peter. But, believe me,' he murmured his doodles growing ever more complicated, 'it is a singularly uncommon experience for me. Perhaps it isn't—'

'There was this secret room in the cottage.'

He put down his pencil again. 'Really? How exciting. And have you found out what's in it?'

I nodded again, unsure as to how much I should tell him.

'Listen, Peter, rest assured I don't want you to tell me anything you're not comfortable—'

'It's a nursery,' I said. 'A little girl called Alice used to live in it. But I don't know why it was a secret. Kat kept it locked and there was this big curtain across it. Anyway, we—that's Anna-Marie, Tommie and me—we found the key and we went in and it was this nursery and so we wanted ... Well, Anna-Marie wanted to find out who Alice was so we asked the waitress at the café but she didn't know and neither did this man in the café who was writing about us and there's this man Mr Merridew and he said that life was pointless and we might as well be dead or something but then we went to the graveyard and Kat was there and there was this vase and it got broken, although it wasn't our fault, and the vicar is going to tell Mrs Carpenter about it and Anna-Marie won't tell me—'

'Woah, woah!' cried Norman laughing. 'Hold your horses, Peter. Goodness me, when you get started ... Well, you remind me of someone not a million miles from you right now. I told you we'd made a connection, didn't I? See, Norman, see. I told you: Peter is one of us.' He smiled to himself and tore the page on which he had been scribbling from its pad with a dramatic rip. 'Well,' he said, 'you've certainly been busy. But clarify one thing for me, I'm confused, have you discovered the secret or not?'

I shook my head. 'Every time we find out a secret it's like there's another one.'

'Ah, I see. 'Twas ever thus.' Norman bounced his pencil thoughtfully against the palm of one hand. 'Tell me, Peter, bear with me a moment, but have you ever encountered a game called *Consequences?*' I nodded. Well, I'd *heard* of it. 'Okay,' he said. 'Let's have a go,' and tore the clean page from his note-book. 'Now, you write a name at the top of this piece of paper and then you fold it over so that I can't see it.'

He handed me the pencil and my spare hand hovering over the paper so that he couldn't see, I wrote *Anna-Marie*. I folded over the page as instructed.

'Left-handed, eh?' said Norman. 'Good for you. Now, I write *met* and add a name.' He did so. 'And now I fold it over again and give it back to you and you write *in* and add the name of a place.'

I wrote *in Everlasting Lane,* folded it over and handed it back.

'My turn,' said Mr Kirrin. 'Now I write *He said* followed by something that he said.' Once he'd finished writing he returned the paper to me and I wrote *She said* ...

'I can see you've got the hang of it.'

... a secret is like another word for what's true.

'Splendid. And finally I write *And the consequence was,*' and he completed the sentence with, you know, an exclamation mark at the end. 'And when we read it out we find: *Anna-Marie met Peter in Everlasting Lane. He said, "I have a secret." She said, "A secret is like another word ... for what's ..."* ' Mr Kirrin read to the end before crushing the paper in his hands and popping it into my empty mug. It sat there like a crumpled egg in an egg-cup. 'Anyway,' he said, 'I think you get the point ...' I must have looked unsure. 'Well, the point is that everything has a consequence. You cannot act—you can't even avoid acting—without causing other things to happen.' He took his pencil. It balanced on the palm of his hand. 'What happens if I drop the pencil?'

'It'll fall?'

He turned his palm upside down and the pencil fell to the floor. He leant forward to pick it up. Now he held it in both his fists, his thumbs meeting at the halfway point.

'Another easy one: what'll happen if I push up with my thumbs and pull down with my hands? That's right: get the cogs turning.'

'It'll break?'

The pencil broke with a sharp snap.

'And now a hard one: what will happen if I leave my two pencil halves side by side here on the table?'

'Nothing?'

'Maybe,' he said. 'Maybe but you can never be sure.'

I looked at the two half-pencils. 'What will they do?'

'They might ...' He hesitated. 'I can see I might have stretched this particular metaphor to a breaking point of its own. What I'm trying to say is that sometimes we can predict consequences and sometimes we cannot.'

I must have looked doubtful.

He sighed. 'Look, Peter, you have a choice. Well, you have two choices. Two options, if you will. One: you can forget all about secrets. If you can drive them all to the back of your mind, or, preferably, out of your mind altogether, then do so. Or, two, if you can't forget, then you must go on, unpicking each secret until you get to the heart. Until you discover the truth. What do you think?'

'But you said—'

'I know, I know. You're quite right,' he said. 'I say a lot of things, but ...' and then he muttered, 'Oh, Norman, you're skating on thin ice here. Why should Peter listen to you? Why should he learn from your mistakes? Why should you, Peter? Listen, do you remember when we first met and I told you a little about my secret?'

I did.

'Then let me tell you a little more. When I was a young man I was in the army. I wasn't alone, of course. There was a war on after all. I knew a girl and I loved her very much. She loved me too, I think, but she didn't want to marry a soldier. Why should she? It was a terrible time. It must be hard for you to imagine what it was like. When you watch the movies, well, you always know how it's going to end, don't you? Of course you do. We emerge victorious. Hurrah! Hitler's defeated. Mussolini too: strung up on a lamppost. And, what's his name, the Japanese fellow: Hirohito.

'But what was it like then? Have you ever wondered? We didn't have the comfort of knowing how it would end. It wasn't like that. Wouldn't we all have liked to shriek at the silver screen, "Come on, Mr Projectionist! Skip to the last reel! Let's find out how this nightmare ends!" It wasn't like that to live through, Peter—like the films is what I'm trying to say. We didn't know what people know today. We didn't know it was going to be all right. We didn't know we were going to win. Or even that it was ever going to end, no matter what Mr Churchill said. Let me tell you, Peter, that kind of life,' he said, 'that kind of existence, well, it leaves its mark.'

Norman removed his glasses and buffed them on the corner of his sleeve. Without his spectacles his eyes seemed larger, the opposite of Mr Merridew, but they were kind eyes surrounded by a flurry of tiny wrinkles.

'You were in the army, Norman. North Africa and Italy. Do you remember?' he said in that way that made me feel like I wasn't really there. 'Remember?' he exclaimed. 'I can still taste the sand between my teeth.' He picked at them as if he'd been eating raspberries. 'Oh, and the heat,' he went on. 'Each day, Peter, someone would wake us up and we'd polish our rifles and whatever else we had to do for King and Country and we would go out to face the world. And each morning as you looked out on the desert or across a valley you wondered whether you'd still be alive to see that same sun go down or whether you'd be … I knew a lot of men, Peter, decent men from all over the country: Merseyside, London ('All right, Guv'nor?'), Geordies, Scotland who died in places they'd barely heard of. Imagine that: six years of going to bed never knowing what tomorrow would bring.'

I had never heard anyone talk about the war like that. Certainly my dad had never spoken about it. It all seemed such a long time ago and yet here I was talking to someone who had lived through it, with memories so sharp that to him it must've seemed like yesterday. And then I thought about my father. It must've been the same for him, of course: getting up in the morning, going to work, even as he lay there dying the war, the whole war, must have been in the back of his mind— and maybe not so far back. And as he stood there washing his car or, later, lying in bed gasping for breath listening to me running around in the garden taking pot-shots at German trees, what must he have thought?

'Difficult times, Norman,' muttered Mr Kirrin. 'Dreadful times. Greg,' he said, nodding in the direction of the shop, 'was in the RAF. Very dashing he was, with a glorious,' he rubbed his thumb and forefinger together twirling an imaginary, 'handlebar moustache. Me: I was in the army: eighth army to be precise.' He shot to his feet, snapping to attention and saluting, cast on the opposite wall, his own thin shadow: 'Kirrin, Norman, 70th Infantry Division, Sah! Africa and Italy,' and then he laughed. 'Your face, Peter, says it all. No,' he reclaimed his seat shaking his head wearily, 'I wasn't much of a soldier then either.'

For a whole minute Norman sat with his forehead resting on the back of his right hand. I took the opportunity to rescue the crunched ball of paper from the mug and sneak it into the pocket of my shorts. When he continued speaking his voice was, at first, a mumble: 'Her name was Lois,' he said. 'What can I say about Lois? There's nothing to say except that she was … extraordinarily light. I used to tell her she could fly if only she'd flap her wings hard enough. But she never would try. I don't know why. She never would indulge … She looked like Deanna Durbin, you know? The movie star? Well, of course not. But anyway, she wanted … stability.' He laughed. 'Didn't we all? And I wanted … her. And peace. To me the two … the two concepts … were inextricably linked,' and he entwined his fingers like a church roof. And then he said:

What matter the decades turned to dust?
Twenty, thirty, forty years a sparkle in your eye.
Kisses preserved and pressed like leaves in the soft cement of time,
Our wanton lips together dance like sun upon the Serpentine.
  Ma vie sans tu est finie.
  She laughs. What did Horace say, Winnie?

And then he laughed again. And then he stopped short. 'Do you understand the word "wanton"?' I shook my head. 'It's probably for the best,' he said with a thin smile.

  'Anyway, I asked Lois to marry me—I proposed—Hyde Park, 1942:

And Eros, melancholy-drunk, somewhat lop-sided,
Peppers Hyde Park with missiles misguided.

  'But she declined the offer. She'd met a man—a butcher, as I recall—who for reasons unknown ... Perhaps it was just one of those jobs we couldn't do without. Butchery! How out of place that would've seemed on the battlefield. Perhaps even in the face of the oncoming Nazi hordes we couldn't do without the great British banger feeding and fortifying the generations. Lord preserve us,' his voice had begun to climb, 'from having to face the day without six inches of pig fat and gristle shoved into an intestinal sock,' climbing like a schoolboy up a tree. ' "The rest of you," says good old Mr Churchill, "are expendable as long as the young ladies of Blighty are getting a regular diet of good old British saus ..." ' Norman, blushing, stopped and looked at me. He certainly didn't sound like *The Archers* now. 'I apologise, Peter,' he muttered. 'You are witness to levels of cheap innuendo that would disgrace the business end of a seaside postcard.

  'My point is, and I feel, Norman, that you must hurry to

address your point before young Peter is as old and meaning-less as you are, is this: Lois had a secret and it was my failure to discover the truth of her secret that threw her towards the faithless arms of the butcher. And that is why I would encourage you to persist in your endeavours. Half a secret, half the truth, is no better than no truth at all and where would we be, Peter, without the truth?'

'But ...' I waited.

'Go on. Go on. I know you can do it.'

'That thing you said about never knowing whether you'd be alive or dead at the end of the day ...'

'Yes. Yes.'

'Isn't that always true? I mean, when I woke up this morn-ing I didn't know whether I'd even be alive at lunchtime. I mean, not really. We don't even really know whether we'll be alive at bedtime, do we?'

Norman Kirrin shook his head. 'You're right, Peter,' he said. 'We don't know. Not really.'

The afternoon sun grazed my head as I walked back to Ever-lasting Lane, its gaze finding me even beneath the shelter of the trees.

I unscrunched the ball of paper which I had taken from Norman's kitchen. It read:

Anna-Marie met Peter in Everlasting Lane.
    He said: 'I have a secret.'
    She said: 'A secret is like another word for what's true.'
    And the consequence was: Peter had to choose!

But choose what? Mr Kirrin hadn't been as much help as I'd hoped.

As I approached the cottage I could see Anna-Marie perched on the wall waiting for me, her hand sliding along Kitty's silky back. She looked up but said nothing, occasionally flicking her hair from her eyes as I approached. Eventually I stood before her and prepared myself for the usual—

'Peter,' she said softly, 'I need your help.'

I hadn't expected that at all. 'What?'

She glanced back at the cottage. 'I've been up all night,' she whispered. 'I knew there was something about the nursery that didn't make any sense. I mean apart from the fact that it existed at all.'

'What?' I didn't know what she meant.

Anna-Marie growled. 'Look, Peter, it's like I said: that nursery didn't spring into existence the moment you and Kat arrived, did it? I mean you've only lived here five minutes.'

'But—'

'Oh, give me strength.' She stood and seized the lapels of my T-shirt, pulling the collar tight around my neck. 'Do I look like an idiot? You're not talking to Tommie, you know. That nursery must have been there when the old lady, Mrs Whatnot, Mrs Goodwin her name was, the nursery was there when she lived there. Yes?'

I nodded. Ever so slightly. I didn't want to encourage her if I could help it.

'And then I thought but that doesn't make any sense either because Kat's still keeping it a secret from *you*, isn't she?'

I—

'Isn't she, Peter?'

'Yes.'

'And then she was next to your Grandma's grave. So, what

I want to know is why is Kat protecting you from some old woman's secret?'

'I think,' I said, and cleared my throat, 'I think she was my grandma: Mrs What-not.'

'I beg your pardon.' Anna-Marie's fingers had released my collar and were trying to rub the tired shadows from her eyes. 'Who? What are you talking about?'

'The old woman,' I said. 'I think she was—'

Anna-Marie slapped her forehead with the open palm of her hand. 'Your Grandma. Of course. It's so obvious. Now we're getting somewhere.'

'And I lived here when I was little.'

'You lived here? Why didn't you tell me, Peter? That's a clue. A really important—'

'But you said no one even recognises a clue until twenty pages after they've seen it.'

'That,' said Anna-Marie, 'is no excuse.'

PART III

Who Digs the Gravedigger's Grave?

19

We were sat on the riverbank opposite the Lodge. It was early Sunday morning, the day before we went back to school, and a lazy morning mist hung over the nettles and the tall meadows, yellows, blues and reds sprinkled on top. Anna-Marie and I had settled beneath the branches of the great tree. I overturned a piece of bark, still damp with dew, and watched the woodlice scatter for cover. Ants marched backwards and forwards along a branch, bits of leaf or twig balanced on their shoulders, an everlasting stream pushing upwards like the man in that story forever pushing his boulder up a mountain.

I sat beside Anna-Marie, her thin leg close to mine, listening to the rattle of the leaves, the birdsong and the busyness of the insects. We held our breaths and watched a family of wild rabbits appear on the Lodge's golden lawn, nervous and sniffing the warm air. Time drifted like smoke across the morning, nature unfolding before us, and we watched in wonder as ...

Well, actually we got bored and began unwrapping and stuffing ourselves with sandwiches.

Anna-Marie was saying something about the Bay City Rollers and how much Alice liked them but I wasn't really listening. It was like I had all these things in my head squeezed together like Mr Gale's class on the story carpet, all shoving and snapping at each other and saying: 'Think about me! Think about me!' and my voice like Mr Gale's saying, 'Pipe down, squids, or we'll never get this bloody story finished.'

It was funny because thoughts are just like words really—words in your head—but bigger somehow. And I had such a lot of thoughts to think about that I didn't really want to think about. It didn't seem fair that Anna-Marie's talking was forcing me to keep everything in my head, so I said, 'What do you think she'll do when she finds out about the vase?'

'What?' said Anna-Marie crossly. 'Who?'

'Mrs Carpenter!'

'Oh, that,' said Anna-Marie belching cheese and onion. 'I don't know, do I. She can't do anything to me, can she. I'm leaving in a few weeks anyway. And I'll be glad too—horrible little place.'

'But why don't you like it?' I asked. 'School I mean. I thought you were clever.'

'Cleverer than you anyway,' she said with a sigh, nibbling the rim of her Jaffa cake. 'Look, Peter, it's got nothing to do with what I like. The school, that is the teachers, Mrs Carpenter: they don't like *me*. Except Mr Gale. He's all right. It's like I told you before: kids do stupid things because they never think about the consequences; adults hardly do anything because that's all they think about. Mr Gale's a bit of both. He makes school more interesting.'

'But Tommie says Mr Gale's mad,' I said. 'He could've killed Tommie. Sometimes he's like a big kid.'

'That's what I mean,' she said with a yawn. 'Anyway, schools are for sheep.'

'Sheep?'

'Of course, mutton-head.' She popped the centre of her Jaffa cake into her mouth like one of those aspirins my mum used to take whenever her leg was bothering her. 'If there was a school in the whole of England that taught children any-thing worth knowing they'd bolt the doors quicker than you could recite your two times table. By which I mean,' she added under her breath, 'within the hour.'

'But why doesn't Mrs Carpenter like you?'

Anna-Marie gazed over the river to the Lodge. The patients had not yet been assembled and the lawn sparkled with dew like stars on the greenest of nights. 'Because I'm *too* clever.'

'Like a swot? But teachers do like swots.'

Mind you, I thought, Mr Gale didn't like Melanie much and her handwriting was just like a grown-up's. I decided not to mention this, what with an invitation to Melanie's birthday party hidden pink and perfumed between the pages of my scrapbook.

Anna-Marie frowned as I ground a fistful of crisps into crumbs and sprinkled them into my sandwich. 'Look, the main reason Mrs Carpenter doesn't like me,' she explained, 'is because I'm like that boy in *The Emperor's New Clothes* who realises the emperor's naked.'

'Mrs Carpenter?' I sniggered, a dribble of Cresta escaping my nose. 'Naked?'

'Now, listen, little boy, you know how Santa Claus is just a man in a suit, don't you?'

I—

'Well, you do now. Anyway, he's not magic. He's just a man in a Santa hat and a Santa beard. Wearing a peaked cap doesn't make you Donny Osmond, does it? I mean, how does he fly around the world in one night? Santa I mean. It's not even possible.'

'But it's magic,' I protested. 'It could be magic.'

'Oh, Peter,' she said, 'there's no such thing.'

'But you—'

'Hush! Now, take Mrs Carpenter. Every Christmas she and

our friend the vicar ask all the children what Santa's bringing them. Why? There's no Santa, so why? The woman's either a liar or a fool and, whilst I'm quite prepared to believe she's a fool, I strongly suspect that she's just a ferocious liar. And, when they ask you and you say, "Nothing, Miss, because Santa doesn't exist," and all the infants start crying and then they get angry and send you to the office and call your mum to come down and get her all upset …

'Well, that's when I realised that teachers aren't teachers at all. They're not special or intelligent or even particularly good at teaching. They're just people,' said Anna-Marie, 'wearing teachers' hats and teachers' beards.'

'What?'

'Look, Peter, can't you see? Teachers teach you facts. It's their job. Facts are nice and simple and uncomplicated and don't cause anybody any problems. They're just the bits that join up what you understand. Understand?'

I nodded. I really had no idea what she was talking about.

'What teachers don't like, because they don't understand it, is knowledge. It's beyond them, frankly. If you know stuff, if you understand stuff, then the facts will take care of themselves. They don't want you understanding stuff they barely understand themselves. It's the difference between a "what-question" and a "why-question". Ask a teacher, "What King?" or "What Queen?" and they're quite happy. They're on solid ground. Start asking them, "Why?" and see how long it is before their faces change colour.'

'I—'

'Have you ever done a jigsaw?'

'Y—'

'Facts are like jigsaw pieces. You know, how they're always scattered across the carpet, disappearing up the Hoover. That's facts. But understanding is what happens when you start putting the pieces together and you start seeing the joins: "Oh, this fact goes with this fact. And the pair of them join up with this bit over here." ' Anna-Marie's thin fingers mimed the making of a puzzle. 'And then, gradually,' she went on, 'you begin to see the picture—not necessarily the whole picture; I don't think anybody can see everything—but a bit of it. It's like the Lodge,' and she nodded towards the sturdy red walls and shimmering windows. 'You start off with a pile of bricks and glass but if you put them together properly, you end up with a building. Somewhere people can live and be safe. Anyway, then you begin to get the idea that all these facts aren't on their own. They aren't separate. Everything joins together. And the teachers don't like that because most of them are barely aware of it themselves.'

'I—'

'Well, intelligence is like how well you can do the jigsaw, but it's not about how well you do it or how well you fit the pieces together. It's how well you can do it when there are pieces missing. Intelligence is about using the pieces you do have to work out the pieces you don't have: the picture and the shape and everything.

'Now, take Alice: in this hand I have a nice bit of Alice-shaped jigsaw, and in this hand a nice Kat-shaped bit but when you try to join them,' Anna-Marie's face shone with frustration as she attempted to wrestle the two imaginary puzzle pieces together, 'they just won't fit. But hang on a mo', here comes knuckle-head Peter with his last minute revelation regarding the old woman who lived in the shoe.' She reached forward and stole a third pretend section from my lap and waved it in the air like an invisible trophy. 'Hurrah, because Grandma fits in between the two and when they're together,' she admired her handiwork with a satisfied smile, 'things begin to make sense.'

Her smile faded as she laid, like a daisy chain, the completed puzzle on the ground beside her. 'The only thing we don't know,' she murmured, 'is where the Peter-shaped piece goes.

'The thing is, lots of people think they're smart because they have lots of pieces. Teachers are like that but they have no idea how to work out what the missing pieces are.

'Do you know what I mean?'

'I—'

'Oh, spare me, Peter,' groaned Anna-Marie. 'Anyway,' she said, '*that's* why teachers don't like me.'

'Because they're like Father Christmas?'

'Exactly.'

'Because they have beards?'

'No, you moron. Because I don't believe in them either. And that *is* a fact.'

I couldn't think of anything to say. I bit on my sandwich and chewed hoping that silence would encourage more wildlife to emerge from the shadows and take Anna-Marie's mind off jigsaws and Father Christmases before she could start all over again.

I scanned the twisted trees, studied their cruel expressions for ... for something. I don't know what. And then I dug deep into the spaces between: the shadows, the remains of the night: for whatever remains in the dark when the night has gone. I tried to imagine the world that lay within. I had always thought it must be very different from my own and that was why it wasn't in any book or on any television show and why no grown-up, except perhaps Mr Merridew, had ever tried to explain it or even mentioned it in passing.

But what was most frightening was that I wasn't one hundred per cent sure any more that this strange, unknown world was actually any different from my own at all. Something was telling me that these two worlds were, in fact, one and the same, like two sides of the same mirror or, as Anna-Marie might've put it, two perfectly fitting pieces from the same puzzle. I was scared by how little I knew about things; about how few puzzle pieces I had. And whatever pieces I did have didn't seem to fit together at all no matter what she said. What pieces were missing? How many of them were there?

And what was that moving towards us now?

Pushing its way through the nettles.

Rustling the leaves.

Grunting.

Fangs?

Gasping.

Fur?

Faster and faster.

A ghostly bark?

My heart set my whole body throbbing as, to my horror, the shape, burst into the clearing, revealing its true form.

'I thought you might be here,' said the shape breathing hard.

'Tommie!' exclaimed Anna-Marie, leaping to her feet and clapping her hands. And then, 'What are you doing here, you toe-rag? You're supposed to be in bed.'

'I climbed out the bedroom window,' said Tommie with a big grin. 'She thinks I'm asleep. Ooh, is anybody eating those? I'm starving. I haven't eaten since breakfast.'

Tommie sat and began to tell us, through mouthfuls of crisp, his adventures since the cricket ball hit his head. As he told the story, I wanted to laugh out loud. One minute he was never going to walk again; the next, he was unhurt but fooling the doctors and nurses into believing he was at death's door. It was hard to know what was true—probably none of it.

But Anna-Marie was fascinated.

Tommie's biggest complaint was that Mr Gale hadn't been sacked and that he was expected to go back into his class as if nothing had happened. But his anger was slightly lessened by Mrs Carpenter having insisted Mr Gale visit Tommie at home. Tommie bloomed with pleasure as he described how Mr Gale, shame-faced, had stood in his mother's parlour and promised, promised, promised that he would, 'Never do anything so … so … so *reck*less again.'

'I thought he was going to cry,' said Tommie. 'It was brilliant. And the best thing of all,' he went, 'is my dad's going to take me on a special trip tomorrow. He says he wouldn't do it if he didn't have to.' He giggled with glee. 'Hey, Peter,' he slapped my arm, 'I'm going to miss a*nother* day off school.'

'Well,' said Anna-Marie, 'I'm sure we're all relieved that you didn't get brain damage. On the plus side, it must have been a great relief to your parents to have the existence of a brain confirmed. Just think: if it hadn't been for Mr Gale we might never've known for sure.'

And then she smiled.

And so did Tommie.

So I said, 'The Beast is dead.' I didn't even try to stop myself.

'What? How?'

Anna-Marie's smile vanished. 'I don't want to talk about it.'

'Tell me. What happened?' and Tommie wouldn't give up, going on and on about it until, reluctantly, Anna-Marie began to describe our afternoon with Mr Merridew. As she told the story her face deflated like a punctured balloon but Tommie's grew red with anger. He winced with each crunch of Mr Merridew's stick. He was no fan of the Beast but by the time Anna-Marie finished his fists were clenched in fury. 'Why would he do that?' he said. 'We should call the police.'

'You're too scared,' I blurted out. 'Anna-Marie said you're

scared of him. Mr Merridew I mean. Didn't you, Anna-Marie? She said you were Tommie-Titmus.'

'I'm not scared of him,' protested Tommie. 'You are.'

'I'm not. You are.'

'Oh, shut up!' Anna-Marie looked at us both with disgust. 'You two morons clearly haven't been paying attention. If you really don't think he's scary, you obviously haven't been listening. Or maybe you just don't understand. That's probably it.

'But they *are* scary, Tommie—not Mr Merridew—but the things he says. They scare me.' Tommie's mouth fell open, his tongue speckled with crisp crumbs. 'What if he's right?' she said. 'Maybe you haven't thought about that. What if it doesn't matter whether we live or die? Maybe we aren't any more important than ants. And close your mouth: I don't want to see the inner workings of your lunch, thank you very much.'

Tommie closed his mouth and swallowed. 'That's stupid,' he said, meaning what she'd said about Mr Merridew but his voice was kind of shaky.

'Oh,' growled Anna-Marie. 'What would you know about it anyway?'

'Well, what about the Beast?'

Anna-Marie bristled. 'It was only a dog, Peter.'

'Well,' I said, 'Kitty's only a cat. My dad said that animals are people too.'

'Goodness me,' said Anna-Marie. 'Why does everybody's dad have an opinion? Listen, Peter, the dog was in pain. Mr Merridew put it out of its misery. Don't you—'

'Well, I don't want him putting me out of my misery,' said Tommie. 'I don't want him to kill me just because I'm in pain.'

'Well, funnily enough,' said Anna-Marie, 'I want to kill you because you are a pain. Listen,' she said, 'you know, that old poem ... I mean, nursery rhyme: *The Grand Old Duke of York*?'

'He had ten thousand men!' I said.

'That's right. He marched them up to the top of the hill—'

'And he marched them down again,' said Tommie.

'Well, done,' said Anna-Marie. 'Congratulations. You know it. When I want a recital, I'll know who to call. Now, what happens next?'

'Well,' said Tommie, 'when they were up they were up.'

'Okay,' said Anna-Marie. 'Have you ever wondered, what if that's all they do? They march up to the top of the hill and they march down again. And then they march to the top of the hill and they march down again: like that, over and over again, forever. What would that be like?'

'It'd be boring.'

'Why would they do that?'

'Because they're people and that's what people do, isn't it?' said Anna-Marie. 'That's what people's lives are like. They get up and go to school, come home and go to bed, get up and go to school, come home and go to bed.'

'That's not all they do,' protested Tommie.

'It's all *you* do,' muttered Anna-Marie. 'But how would they feel? The ten thousand men, I mean.'

'They'd be bored,' said Tommie, and I nodded.

'No,' groaned Anna-Marie. 'No, they wouldn't. I mean maybe they wouldn't. Maybe, once they realised, if they re-alised, that it was all pointless, once they realised that they were going to go up and down that hill forever, maybe then they'd be happy. It wouldn't matter if they were up or down or half way up, they'd be happy.'

'Happy? Why?'

'Because they're safe. Life's never going to surprise them and they won't ever be worried or frightened or scared. It's predictable. It's pointless: that's the point. Maybe you can't even be happy until you realise how pointless everything is.'

She growled at our blank expressions. 'All right,' she said, 'you know how Jack and Jill went up the—?'

'But—'

'What?'

'But,' I cleared my throat, 'if that's true ...'

'Yes? What?'

'Then why *aren't* we happy?'

Anna-Marie stared at me. 'Oh, shut up!'

I noticed again the procession of ants before me: shoulders sagging, stumbling over the rough edges of the branch, forever upwards, forever downwards: the ten thousand men. I leant over and began to press down on them with my thumb, one by one.

Anna-Marie gasped. 'What do you think you're doing?'

'Putting them out of their misery.'

Anna-Marie got to her feet. 'That's it!' she said. 'I've had enough of you two. I'm going to find somebody intelligent to talk to; somebody who doesn't speak to you with a mouth full of crisps or stare at you like a moron.' Tommie and I glanced at each other uneasily as she collected together her sandwich wrapper and crisp bag. 'How lucky we are,' she said, 'to live in Amberley. After all, every village in England should have an idiot of its own, and we,' she concluded, 'have two.'

Tommie and I sat in silence watching Anna-Marie stomp off in to the woods. I looked at Tommie and Tommie looked at me. We had been left alone together exactly as neither of us wanted it. But we had to make the best of things. At times like this there were only two real possibilities: football or—

'Let's play war,' said Tommie.

20

Private Tom 'Winston' Winslow stroked his granite jaw with fingers so scabby they could barely feel the three days of stubble, just as his cucumber-cool mind was barely aware of the three nights that had passed since he'd last slept. At his feet, I, his loyal companion, Private Pete 'Lambchop' Lambert, bent low, ear to the ground. Deep behind enemy lines, hidden from the pop-pop-pop of the guns beneath a canopy of leaves, the last two survivors of the Amberley First Regiment, we took stock of our position.

'A patrol: ten men,' I whispered, 'half hour back.' I listened again. 'Make that twenty-five minutes.'

Winslow shouldered his rifle. 'No rest for the wicked.'

'There's plenty of worms out there,' I said springing to my feet, 'for us early birds.'

Many stories emerge from the chaos and carnage of human conflict, just as flowers bloom amidst the rubble, fully petalled, once the storm has departed. Here is one such tale, a tribute to the exploits of extraordinary men who fought for Britain in extraordinary times with pride and patriotism flowing freely in their veins; men who wrote the word 'courage' in the ever-present shadow of *Monte Cassino*—in letters of blood—for we waged our war with ruthless efficiency and efficient ruthlessness—

'No, that's wrong.'

'What?'

'The Germans were ruthless and efficient. We, the British, we were brave and ... erm ... resourceful.'

'Oh.'

—they waged their war with brave resourcefulness and resourceful braveness.

It didn't sound as good.

I asked Tommie whether his dad had ever told him about the war. He gave me a funny kind of look. 'People who go to war,' he said, 'never talk about it.'

We moved on: every nerve, every muscle alert to our surroundings.

'What's your position?' I hissed into my walkie-talkie. 'Over.'

'I'm deep in enemy territory,' replied Winslow. 'Over. Ouch! Watch your rifle!'

'You're standing too close.'

'Over.'

'What?'

'You're supposed to say "over",' he said. 'Over.'

'I *know*,' I said. 'Over.'

'From here,' whispered Winslow, 'we can make our way to those trees and, from there, follow the line of the river up and over those crags. Dozy old Jerry'll never see us coming. We'll give 'im a bloody nose.'

'Just the two of us?' I growled. 'You're crazy. You'll get us both killed.'

'Nah,' sneered Winslow. 'Your average Jerry couldn't 'it Marble Arch with an 'Owitzer. When you've been at it as long as I 'ave, you get to know which bullets 'ave got your details attached.'

'What do you mean? I've been here as long as you have.'

'Listen, Lambchop, if you've lost your belly, I'll go it alone.'

'Hey, I haven't lost my belly!'

'Okay, calm down,' said Winslow. 'Don't lose your head!'

'There's nothing wrong with my head! I haven't lost my head *or* my belly. Don't worry about my head! Worry about your own!'

The rumble of a thick Italian river ran close by but no bird sang in that blood-stained valley. We flicked from tree to tree like tricks of the light, soundless, our fingers petting cold steel. And then we froze. Moving within a clearing less than thirty feet from where we stood, the unmistakable grey of Nazi uniforms, and the casual chatter of the enemy: their strange, metallic tongues carried easily in the still air.

'Ach, schweinhund!'

'Gott in himmel.'

'Jawohl!'

Winslow smiled. 'This is sweet,' he said. 'They're too busy tucking into sauerkraut and schnitzel. They'll never see us coming. We'll spread 'em on a slice of good ol' British toast!'

'It could be a trap. We should take a turn around the park just in case it's a nasty Nazi trick. If we're not careful we could get clobbered.'

'There's only two kinds of men on a battle field,' muttered Tommie, 'those who are dead,' he cocked his rifle, ready for action, 'and those who aren't dead yet.'

Closer, closer, we crept upon our quarry until we could hear each other's heartbeats echoing like kettledrums. The German troops continued to chatter, little suspecting that for them the war, and not only the war, would soon be over.

'Himmel.'

'Schnell!'

'Manchmal, wenn ich denke, dass sie offen sind, meine Augen sind geschlossen.'

I held up a silent hand and mouthed: 'On three: one ...'

'Aaargh!' roared Tommie as he burst into the clearing, his gun low, spraying the Germans with bullets.

'Two ...'

'Na-na-na-na-na-na-na-na!' he screamed. 'Take that, Fritzy!'

'Three!' I shouted leaping from a tree-stump, my bayonet slicing Nazi head from Nazi neck. 'K-pow! K-pow! K-pow!' I roared as one, two, three German soldiers enjoyed an unexpected breakfast of Italian dirt.

It was over in seconds. Only the commanding officer remained: a pitiful creature, a quivering wreck of fear and cowardice, his face pale and his eyes as scared as saucers. In faltering English he begged for his life.

Winslow walked up to the cowering figure, indifferent to his pleas.

'So, Hauptmann Gale, we meet again,' he murmured. 'Vera Lynne always said we would.'

The German officer ceased his babbling and looked at Winslow with curiosity. 'You?' he said. 'But you're ...'

'You know him, Tommie?'

'I should say I do,' said Winslow. 'The Captain, here, and I have crossed paths (or should I say *swords*) before.' He gently touched the side of his head. 'I didn't get this old war wound in a game of cricket, eh, Herr Hauptmann?'

The German put his hands together as if in prayer. 'Gott in Himmel,' he said. 'Private Vinslow, if I had only known. I beg you for mercy!'

'Mercy?' laughed Tommie. 'Mercy? Ha! There's no mercy for you here, Mr Gale.'

189

He fired once—a single bullet—straight through the skull of the repentant Hun: a perfect round hole through which, briefly, a glimpse of blue sky could be seen as the body fell forwards with a thump.

Tommie lowered his rifle. 'That was fun,' he said.

★

Mademoiselle Marianne Le Dell of the French Resistance, golden tresses falling from beneath her beret, marched briskly along the lane to her rendezvous with Monsieur Merdeux. Merdeux had promised her secret intelligence of invaluable assistance to the war effort. Right now, however, her sixth sense was tingling. Like a gazelle sensing the lion on its trail she knew she was not alone. She took courage from her own fortitude and from the silver revolver, concealed beneath her petticoat, with which she was wont to ruthlessly despatch the Bosch. 'Halt!' I stumbled out of the trees onto the road. 'Who goes there?'

'Mon Dieu!' gasped Mademoiselle Le Dell.

I pointed my gun at her. 'Marianne,' I said, 'we have come to save you.'

Tommie and I had long suspected that Monsieur Merdeux was nothing but a Nazi stooge and whilst we knew that Marianne was both brave and resourceful (and resourceful and brave), we had sworn to prevent her from walking into a fiendish—

'What the hell are you doing?' enquired Mademoiselle Le Dell in flawless English. 'Creeping up on me!'

'I ... I ... There might be somebody following you.'

'There *is* somebody following me,' said Anna-Marie.

'I mean it might be a madman.'

'It *is* a madman. Why are you pointing that stick at me?'

'It's not a stick,' I protested, lowering my gun. 'It's a … It's a rifle.'

'It's a bloody stick!'

'In fact,' said Private Winslow, emerging from the brush, 'it's a Lee-Enfield rifle—number four, mark one.'

'I might've known,' sighed Mademoiselle Le Dell. 'There's always two Ronnies.'

'We finks you's walking into a trap, miss,' said Tommie, 'dahn the dog and toad.'

'That's *frog* and toad, you berk.'

'Mr Merridew's a collaborator,' said Tommie.

'You might be in danger,' I said.

'You'll be in danger if I have to stand around listening to this hogwash for very much longer!' snapped Mademoiselle Le Dell.

'Oh, come on, Anna-Marie,' said Tommie. 'It's only a game.'

'Well,' said Marianne, 'I do not play games. Now, bog off and leave me alone!'

With that she walked off, her heels clicking on the surface of *La Petite Route Éternelle*. And, as she departed, leaving a whiff of Gauloises and a waft of Chanel no. 5, I heard her muttering to herself:

'Imbéciles.'

★

We rested awhile, basking in the warm Italian sun, shadows striping our faces, but our rest was disturbed by the sound of footsteps. Somebody was walking … no, stumbling through the undergrowth. Winslow put a stubby finger to his lips. We waited, rifles cocked, breath bated, for the sound to pass.

'Someone's up to no good,' muttered Tommie. 'Come on, let's follow.'

We moved more skillfully than our quarry: sometimes side by side, sometimes separating leaving the mysterious figure at some point between us. I looked around. Our pursuit was taking us far deeper and far darker into the woods than I had ever come before. The trees here were wild and twisted, struggling free of the earth rather than simply growing from it. As we moved through the dirt and dust, down towards the very lowest point, I noticed how the forest turned its back on the light leaving the darkness undisturbed.

Tommie and I met on a narrow ridge overlooking a dark clearing where the sound had come to a halt. I heard a gust of wind and the high branches going clickety-clack, like God was Hoovering the trees, and then as we began scrambling down towards the pit, approaching the clearing, the unmistakable sound of panic.

As before we burst from the undergrowth with a yell. But there were no Germans here, just a single soldier in British uniform. The man was on his hands and knees with his back to us, scrabbling around in the leaves and undergrowth. He seemed unaware of our presence so Tommie walked up to him: 'What's up, chum?'

I could see now that, in his arms, the soldier held the body of a girl or woman, her flesh shiny like the white skin of a hard-boiled egg; hair matted against her cheek; blood: some crusty, some moist and jelly. The whole image is printed in my mind like a photograph on silver plate.

The soldier had turned his head quickly to see who had spoken, and, as he did so, I stared. You see, it was my daddy. Not as I remember him at home but like he looked in that photograph on the telly: young and handsome. He looked at us with pleading in his eyes.

'Oh, Peter,' he said, his voice hoarse like gravel, 'you'll be the death of me.' And then, 'Anyway, do you want your cake now,' he said, 'or will you save it for later?'

'This isn't any fun,' I said.

'Oh, I know,' said Tommie as we trudged back towards the lane, 'we could be Americans. We could parachute into occupied France.'

'No.' It was stupid being on the same side.

'All right. You can be the Jerry and I'll be the British.'

'No,' I said. 'I don't want to be a Jerry.' I felt close to tears and not like playing anything. I walked off down the lane, tossing my branch into the trees. Tommie ran after me, still carrying his own stick like a rifle.

'Well, be a Jap, then,' he panted, drawing level. 'I'm never the Jap. My dad says the Japs were worse than the Germans.'

'Anna-Marie's right. I don't want to play your stupid games.'

Tommie's mouth twitched with fury. 'They're not stupid,' he said. He pushed my arm. 'They're not stupid: *you're* stupid.' I shrugged him off and carried on walking. He tried to trip me from behind but missed. 'You're an imbecile,' said Tommie. 'Anna-Marie says it. You're always staring at her like a retard.'

I stopped, blushing with embarrassment. 'Well, you're a bog brush! Anna-Marie says so.'

We paused a moment devising new insults. 'You're a bird-brain,' spat Tommie, 'and your mother's a loony. That's what my mum says.'

'Well, *your* mother's a fat, old trout!' I shouted. 'Anna-Marie says so.' The tears that were threatening to come were as much from rage as from hurt. 'And you're always talking about your dad but he never even comes to see you or anything.'

Blood flooded Tommie's face and he flew at me with chubby pink fists. The list of rude names grew longer but I was too busy defending myself from his wild punches to take much notice.

Tommie was a better fighter than me. Much better. He was chunky and determined. He kept bending one of his legs round one of mine so as to pull me into the dirt. I held onto him and found myself hopping and jumping to avoid his stocky leg. At the same time he delivered dozens of tiny punches to my tummy. I fell backwards and bruised my bottom. I tried to get back to my feet but my knees scraped on gravel as Tommie kicked me. I grabbed his T-shirt. It tore loudly. His glasses flew from his face, somersaulting through the air. Tommie loomed over me, his lip quivering, his nose running.

He helped me up.

'Thanks.'

He punched me in the stomach.

And then everything went dizzy. My head kind of throbbed, flashing hot and cold. Black clouds clustered around me and the world splintered like the red vase. I watched from behind the trees as I threw myself at Tommie, my arms twirling like a broken windmill. He backed away, his stupid fat face bubbling blindly with surprise. I saw myself step towards him, seizing his gun and wrestling it from his hands. The cracked bark blistered my palms as his grip weakened. I pulled and tugged, grunting and screaming until his fingers failed and his fists split open. I took his rifle and pushed it into his tubby guts. From a distance I watched as his legs surrendered and he fell backwards, dust and gravel flying up around him as he landed on the road.

He couldn't fight me. He couldn't defeat me. I was like the Incredible Hulk.

I felt my hands rising above my head, and then when I looked down I saw my own reflection fall across his discarded glasses: stick raised, face quivering in anger.

'No.'

I dropped the stick with a clatter.

I breathed hard until my head stopped being so swimmy

and the trees stopped swaying and the ground felt and looked like ground rather than, well, porridge.

I retrieved Tommie's glasses and checked the lenses for scratches before placing them lopsidedly on his ears. 'Why can't you leave me alone?' I said, sitting down beside him and wrapping my arms about my head. 'You wouldn't fight if Anna-Marie was here.'

The afternoon had moved on since I'd last been aware of it. The sun had begun its slow descent and the air was a little cooler. I studied my knees. They didn't look as bad as they felt. I glanced around at Tommie. He was looking at me, his glasses as stable as Mr Merridew's cottage. His T-shirt was torn to the bellybutton and his face, arms and legs were covered with small scratches. His hair, wild and untidy, was just like normal.

'Do you want to go back by the river?' he said.

I sniffed. 'Okay,' and we helped each other to our feet.

We didn't talk as we walked back along the riverbank. Only when we approached the trees that backed onto Kat's garden did Tommie say: 'Let's sit down for a while.'

We removed our shoes and socks and dangled our feet in the river. It was cold.

'As cold as the Russian front,' said Private Winslow.

I splashed water on my wounded knees. Tommie picked up a stone and tossed it into the river. It made a satisfying plonk.

'What do you think of Anna-Marie?' he asked.

'She's all right,' I said carefully. 'Why? What do you think of her?'

'She's all right.'

'Yes,' I agreed. 'She's okay.'

The sun eased itself down, an inch closer to the horizon, just brushing the tops of the trees.

'I mean,' said Tommie, 'she goes on a bit.'

'Oh, yes,' I agreed. 'But she's okay.'

'Yeah, she's okay,' said Tommie, 'for a girl.'

Another stone—another plonk.

'Yeah.'

'Girls are wet,' said Tommie.

'Yeah, they're wet,' I agreed, though neither of us believed it.

We hung our feet in the river and the cool water refreshed our toes.

'Anna-Marie's nice though, isn't she?'

'Yes,' I said, and our hearts melted.

21

'I would like to speak to you both about a recent ... incident.'

Mrs Carpenter placed her elbows on the edge of her desk and rested her chin in the nest of her fingers. Behind her glasses thick eyelids rolled back and forth over ice-cold eyes. Her tongue moistened her thin lips. She swallowed and a shudder slid down her throat. The clock on the wall behind me ticked. And then ticked again.

Anna-Marie and I were stood wilting beneath the skylight, beneath the glare of the headmistress' eyes. My own eyes avoided hers only to meet themselves in the polished surface of the desk. Anna-Marie's gaze was fixed on her own reflection in the gleaming glass of the trophy cabinet, a tooth digging into her lower lip. The face and hands of the clock were reflected in a gallery of old photos hung on the wall.

Mrs Carpenter hissed, her fingers uncoiling. Sitting beside her, the Reverend Potter, pink and plump, looked us up and down whilst his handkerchief dabbed the skin of sweat that glistened on his smooth, shiny head and rosy cheeks.

'I am surprised,' said Mrs Carpenter, sliding open a drawer, 'that anyone—even you, Anna-Marie—could take this matter so lightly.' From the drawer she took a leather strap. 'Even you cannot have imagined that Peter could get away with this.' She laid and then straightened the strap on the desk. 'I don't think you fully appreciate the magnitude of his actions.' Her eyes flashed. 'Explain yourself. Justify yourself. Answer me.'

The vicar sneezed, his nose buried deep in his hankie.

'But it was an accident,' said Anna-Marie, her voice all funny. 'We didn't do anything wrong. I mean, yes, Peter's careless—'

'Careless? Do you imagine the family of the deceased will forgive him quite so easily?'

'Well, I ...'

'Then answer the question,' muttered the vicar, 'for God's sake, child. Have you no idea of the example you set this boy, trampling through a graveyard—a holy place, mind—as if it's your own personal playground?' He waggled his finger in Anna-Marie's face. 'No regard for the dead. No ... No respect for God. What on earth did you—?'

'So, *that's* it,' cried Mrs Carpenter. 'Of course.' She picked up the strap and slapped it against the desk-top. We all jumped. The vicar's jowls wobbled. 'We've been here before, I think,' she scowled. 'I dare say, Robert, that you remember Anna-Marie's little ... outburst during Christmas assembly. No Father Christmas, indeed! It's hard to know which is worse: corrupting minors, desecrating graveyards or denigrating the name of the Lord.' Her voice trembled. 'Now, Anna-Marie, right now, in front of Peter, take back your foul lies.'

'But ... What lies?'

'If I may interject, Sybil,' said the Reverend Potter, 'this is my, ah, chosen specialist subject, so to speak. And an easy one at that.' He leant forward and fixed me in the eye. 'Peter,' he said, 'we—Mrs Carpenter and I—are well aware of this girl's opinions. And believe me, whatever she has been telling you, there *is* a God.'

And he leant back. Satisfied.

'But I didn't—'

'So, Peter,' said Mrs Carpenter with a slithery smile, 'that must put your mind at rest. You mustn't let,' she waved her hand casually, 'someone else tell you what to think. You have a choice to make, Peter, but be sure you make the right one.'

My shirt had begun to stick to my back; my hair to my forehead.

Anna-Marie sparkled with sweat. The heavy heat rising from the vicar mixed with the stink of fresh polish making it hard to breathe. Only Mrs Carpenter seemed comfortable. My head ached as I tried to turn the backwards clock into a time I could tell. If only I had a watch. It was the day of Melanie's party and if this went on much longer—

'So tell me, Peter—no, don't look at her—reassure me that your faith is intact. Tell me now.'

'You can't ...' started Anna-Marie, and Mrs Carpenter raised her eyebrows. 'I mean,' she mumbled, 'you can't just make Peter say what you want.'

'But I dare say,' said Mrs Carpenter, 'that it's fine for you to do the same. Isn't that just *typical*. You know, I really did think that after last Christmas' ... debacle we had seen the end of these silly games.'

'I don't play games,' whispered Anna-Marie.

'Neither,' said Mrs Carpenter, 'do I.'

Anna-Marie didn't say anything for a moment. In the re-flection I could see that her eyelids were closed but that be-hind them her eyeballs were spinning like dirty laundry. 'You always,' she started softly, opening her eyes, 'and the teachers too, in assembly, I mean, you talk about God and Jesus but you never,' she took a deep breath, 'I mean you never prove it. We, I mean I, well, we're supposed to just believe it and, well, if we're not sure we're not supposed to say or we'll get told off or something.' She looked from the vicar to Mrs Carpenter and back again.

'Well,' smiled the reverend Potter, 'if you have some doubts, my dear, perhaps this is the perfect opportunity to address them. If it's proof you want …' He chuckled and leant towards the book sat on the edge of Mrs Carpenter's desk. 'The Bible tells us.' He patted the book like a puppy. 'It's all the proof a Christian needs.'

'But, well, for instance,' said Anna-Marie, 'the Bible says God made the universe in six days, doesn't it, and the teachers, well, most of them, say, it took millions of years.'

'Oh.' The vicar chuckled again. 'Is that what this is all about? Well, my dear, the Bible is an allegory. An all-e-gory is a story that's a bit made up but …' He caught the frown that flickered across Anna-Marie's forehead and cleared his throat. 'Well, the Bible is an *allegory* about how people came to be here and our relationship with God. It's not meant to be taken literally. Literally means …' but he coughed and changed his mind.

'Well,' said Anna-Marie, 'Mrs Carpenter always says the Bible's the word of God.'

'Oh, yes. Yes, indeed, but God didn't sit down and write it like,' the vicar mimed God with a God-sized pencil, ' "In the beginning was the word and the word was …" No, no. The Bible was written by men … simple men. God in*spired* them to write the Bible. A God of infinite love filled their hearts with—'

'But people thought it was true, didn't they? In the olden days.'

'Well, of course it's *true*, girl!' snapped Mrs Carpenter.

But, 'You're right,' agreed the vicar. 'Before Charles Darwin and men of that ilk, many people thought it was *lite*rally—'

'But then they were wrong, all those people, weren't they? I mean literally.'

Anna-Marie's frown now flickered across the vicar's brow. 'Well,' he said, 'you see,' plucking at the creases in his trousers, 'the people in olden days didn't know as much about the world and the universe as we do today. They didn't understand telephones or televisions or anything like that. The Bible was written in a way that they would understand.'

'Oh,' said Anna-Marie, 'so the word of God isn't supposed to be taken literally?'

'What? No, no. I mean it's, it's …' The vicar slid a finger between the frayed edge of his dog collar and his pale throat. And then he sneezed getting his hankie in place just in time. 'I can see,' he said once he'd recovered, 'that you are a dreadfully confused—'

'And what about blind people or mad people?' insisted Anna-Marie. 'And why does God *take* someone's dad? A child's dad, say? And what about all those miracle things? And what about all those children with the little arms and legs?'

'How dare you!' barked Mrs Carpenter. 'Is this the kind of thing you say to Peter?' They all turned to look at me as if they'd forgotten I was there. I'd nearly forgotten I was there myself. 'Anyway,' snapped Mrs Carpenter, 'Peter can't avoid the consequences of his actions,' and then she smiled, 'any more, my dear, than you can avoid the repercussions of your own.

'Go on, Robert,' sighed Mrs Carpenter, her voice uncurling its coils. 'Put an end to this nonsense.'

'Erm …' The vicar's fingers drummed on the desktop like a nervous typist. 'What do you … ?'

'Tell her!'

'Now, Sybil, it's very hard—'

'Go on, go on.'

'Well, Anna-Marie, the Bible does tell us that the only

way to … to …' The vicar sneezed again, his nose exploding into his hankie. '… the only way to Heaven is through Jesus. But you can change,' he said quickly. 'God has given you that power: free will.'

'But what about my dad? Will he be in Heaven?'

'Well, erm, if he believes in Jesus, then yes.'

'And I'll be in Hell.'

'Well—'

'But … But won't my dad mind?'

'Won't … ?' The vicar's fingers knotted and unknotted as he considered, his left eye twitching. 'Well, I'm not sure—'

'I mean whilst he's all happy with Jesus and God.'

'Well, I … I suppose God will probably make him forget about you or something.'

'But isn't that horrible? You said about infinite love.'

The room went deadly quiet. Do you remember when I told you about Mr Merridew's funny little cottage and how it looked like it might collapse at any minute? Well, that's just what the vicar looked like: like all his foundations had crumbled away and the next gust of wind would reduce him to a big, fleshy pile of bricks.

Mrs Carpenter was staring at him, her mouth open. Anna-Marie could see it too. She stepped forward. 'Isn't it like you've only got one foot in the real world?' she said, placing the tips of her fingers on Mrs Carpenter's knuckle. 'Isn't it like somebody who thinks they're awake when, really, they're dreaming? But if you never wake up,' her blue eyes shone, 'you'll never know you were sleeping.'

Mrs Carpenter slowly withdrew her hand from Anna-Marie's touch.

'How dare you!' she hissed. 'How … dare … you!' The sun splashed light upon the lenses of her glasses, her eyes filling with fire. 'Your destination is not in doubt. I am confident,' she spluttered, fingering the crisp stitching of the leather strap, 'that Lucifer is already sharpening his pitchfork.'

'Now, Sybil ...'

'But I'm ... I'm not a bad person,' said Anna-Marie.

'Ha!' cried Mrs Carpenter. 'God may not be so magnanimous.'

'Well,' said the vicar, '*I'd* say that you're clearly a very compassionate—though very confused—little girl.' Mrs Carpenter snorted like a pig. 'Young lady,' he sighed, 'anyone *so* strongly opposed to our faith has a faith just as strong and yet yours is sorely misplaced. You might as well have faith in God as in nothing.'

'I know Jesus is true and that God is real. For me, if I suffer, I *know* there's a reason even if the reason is a mystery. For you there's no mystery, no reason, but still you suffer and your suffering is meaningless.'

'How can you live, child?' spluttered Mrs Carpenter. 'How can you bear a life so ... devoid of meaning?'

'Look at the world,' pleaded the Reverend Potter. 'Jesus lived nearly two thousand years ago and never travelled more than a few miles from where he was born. And yet, here we are talking about Him today. Do you really think He was made up? How could that possibly be true?'

'Nonetheless,' muttered Mrs Carpenter, 'I am afraid we have listened to this infernal drivel long enough. I have never in all my years been spoken to in such a hateful manner. It's amusing how you ... *a*theists,' dabbing her lips with the word as if it were a dirty dishcloth, 'are so consumed by hatred of God considering how adamantly you insist He does not exist.'

'Look at poor Peter,' said the Reverend Potter nervously. 'We've sent him off to sleep with all our chatter.'

I didn't say anything. I knew that if this went on much longer I would be late for Melanie's party. I was afraid that any contribution I made—not that I had any to make—would only make it longer still.

'Your problem, my dear,' went on Mrs Carpenter, 'is that you simply lack the courage to believe. Even now, having had all your questions answered, you would rather deny the Lord than admit you are wrong.'

'But you haven't answered them,' cried Anna-Marie in frustration. 'You haven't answered them at all: the miracles, the babies. We didn't mean to break the vase. It was the grave. We just wanted to—'

'It's always sad when people die, my dear,' said the vicar, 'particularly a child when they've barely had a chance to live, but, well, it's complicated. I wouldn't expect a child to—'

'What?'

'I said, I wouldn't expect a child—'

'It was me,' interrupted Anna-Marie. 'It was all my fault. The vase I mean.'

'Really?' Mrs Carpenter looked up. 'Are you sure?' Her smile unfolded like a tablecloth. 'But Peter's guilt seems—'

'It was me,' said Anna-Marie again. 'I mean it was my idea.'

I wanted to protest. I mean I tried to. But, well, it was Melanie's party and she—Anna-Marie—well, she wouldn't even look at me.

'At last, perhaps we are getting somewhere,' said Mrs Carpenter rising and marching to the office door. She swung it open, the blast of cool air making me dizzy. Returning to her desk the headmistress shouted: 'Caroline, would you call Mrs Liddell and have her come to school right away. Tell her it's urgent.

'And fetch Mr Gale to come here at once.'

She turned to Anna-Marie. 'What an obnoxious child you are,' she said. 'I don't doubt that you think you are very clever: standing here debating with the vicar like a ... like an adult but your … *games* will have their own … ramifications. As reluctant as I am to resort to this,' her thumb lovingly traced the harsh curve of the leather strap, 'it is, sometimes the only satisfactory deterrent to this kind of …

'After all, Anna-Marie, if you wish to be treated like an adult, then you must be prepared for punishments that fit your misdemeanours, don't you think?'

Anna-Marie's top teeth clamped down on her lower lip; her eyes set like stone; a rod of steel ran through her, and she said, very softly: 'Yes.'

Mr Gale barged in looking flustered and sick. 'Mrs Carpenter?'

'Take Peter to collect his belongings from the cloakroom and off the school premises.'

'What about Anna-Marie?'

'Anna-Marie must learn to suffer the consequences of her crimes.'

'Crimes, Mrs Carpenter? To be fair—'

'And when I *want* your opinion, Mr Gale, I will ask for it.' As she leant forwards, resting on the flinty squares of her raw, red knuckles her face shifted and collapsed in on itself. But it was the same old mask that turned to face my teacher. 'Go!'

Mr Gale stood guard as I collected my bag from the cloakroom and gathered my stuff. We walked from the classroom and across the hall to the exit. I jumped from my skin when he turned and said: 'Going to Melanie's party tonight?'

How did he know?

He escorted me to the main doors past Mrs Carpenter's office. At that very moment we heard a slap and a muffled cry as if through gritted teeth. Mr Gale glanced at his watch and laid his hand on my shoulder.

'Peter,' he said, 'you really are a … a … a gutless cunt, aren't you?'

I wanted to say something, something to defend myself, but my tongue wouldn't let me. You see, it knew, like I knew, that he was right.

You see, I never answered the question: did I believe? In God, I mean. And, well, I don't know, but if Anna-Marie was right and there's no God: well, when there's hurricanes and floods and disabled babies and stuff like that, who are you supposed to get angry with?

22

Leaving Dovecot behind me, I trotted through the village and left into Fugler Lane, which, turning quickly to gravel and dust, led me upwards and out of the valley. Every step of my shoe slapped on the ground like a leather strap on naked ...

I hadn't told Kat about the party, of course—I suspected it wasn't the kind of thing she meant when she said we should 'keep ourselves to ourselves'—so I was still in my uniform and the fierce sun soon made my collar tight and my shirt as hot and sticky as it had been in Mrs Carpenter's office. My pace began to drag, my satchel cutting deep into my shoulder, until I began to feel like one of those ants sagging beneath the weight of a twig: an Anna-Marie-shaped twig stretched across my shoulders like a bad feeling, just waiting for God's great pink thumb to descend from the sky.

But I shrugged off the weight as best I could. After all, when you thought about it, it wasn't really my fault that Anna-Marie had been so rude to Mrs Carpenter and the vicar, was it? Not really. If they'd only asked me what had happened with the vase I could've told them. It was only an accident after all. It was Anna-Marie who had started going on about God and stuff like that. I hadn't even known what she was talking about.

Who would argue with a vicar about God and stuff? It didn't make any sense.

As the road straightened out, I glanced across at the fields draped over the hilltops. From up there it was hard to believe there wasn't some kind of fountain high up in the hills, pumping out field after field until they flooded the land as far as I could see. Of course, usually they'd be all different shades of green and maybe yellow but that day, that summer they were all brown, dry and crispy like pie crust. I looked down to the village sparkling like gold at the bottom of a clear, glassy pool. I could see the church too, its spire like a rocket, the high street, the little cottages scattered like pebbles and, of course, the school where Anna-Marie was ... where Anna-Marie was.

I could hear this little voice in my head: 'What do you mean you didn't wait for her? You went to Melanie's party? Who would do that?' It sounded a lot like Tommie Winslow but there was no point going back now, I told him. Not really. Whatever punishment Mrs Carpenter had chosen, it would be over by now and Anna-Marie on her way home. I mean even if I'd turned around that minute, that very minute, by the time I got back to school she'd already be gone.

Probably.

Besides it would be just as rude to accept an invitation to a party and then not go, wouldn't it? For all I knew I might be the only guest and it wouldn't be much of a party for Melanie if her only guest didn't turn up, would it? And Anna-Marie, of course, when you thought about it, was much tougher than Melanie anyway. I mean Mr Gale had read us this story once and this dog died and Melanie's eyes had got all watery on the story-carpet until Mr Gale snapped at her to pull herself together, 'For God's sake,' because 'It's only a story.' I mean Anna-Marie hadn't even cared when the Beast died. And that was real.

And it wasn't like it was even the first time that Anna-Marie had got the strap at school. Tommie had told me that. After all she was 'bad news.' She'd said it herself.

Ahead of me, Finches' Farm—the farmhouse itself and all the sheds and barns—rose into view, nestled in an orange burst of late afternoon. The farmyard was cluttered with wood, rusting metal, planks and tubes, bales of wire, random wheels, like the dismantled remains of some fancy machine. And the smell, the stink, as if some fairy-tale giant had been left slowly rotting to death in this empty barn, was so wet and heavy the still, warm air was smothered by it.

I stood alone, just a little dot, in the middle of the road to the farmhouse as it whipped away to the left. Fine for a truck or a tractor but for me another half hour's walk. In the distance, the faint tremors of a party: like hens cackling and dogs barking and the Bay City Rollers singing.

So I wasn't the only guest after all. But it was still best that I go.

When you thought about it.

So I ploughed straight across the field, chest high through the withered crops.

Ten minutes later the farmhouse door gaped open drooling with the high-pitched squeal of children. I hesitated a moment before stepping softly onto the welcome mat. The insides of the Finches' farmhouse were all over the place as if several buildings and rooms, not to mention the furniture, had been shoved together by that dead giant I told you about before, but at its heart was a kitchen, and a stove burning as if it'd been lit a hundred years ago and never allowed to die, separated from the living room only by the tassels of a large and ancient rug. The homely stink of dogs kept the stench of the farmyard at bay but whatever tangle of dogs usually stampeded from room to room had today retreated to cower in safe, shadowy corners well away from the many-headed monster of girls that now filled the farmhouse.

Because, whilst I wasn't the only guest, I was the only boy.

Every corner was crammed with girls: either gathered in gossipy groups or dancing alone or splitting off into pairs, one sobbing and the other, an arm about her friend's shoulder, throwing daggers at a third until the sobber sobbed herself dry and the pair limped back to the dancing as another couple removed themselves and the scene repeated.

Oh, and I was the only person still wearing their school uniform. Everybody else, each girl, was dressed in clothes that made them look about five years older than they had in assembly that morning and their faces were all smeared in powders and creams so thick you could've stuck teaspoons in and stirred without touching the sides.

And, as I stepped into the room, the moment spun on the edge of silence as every head twisted to look at me. And then a swell and a burst of laughter knocked me backwards and the monster on the living room rug teetered gleefully in its tiny party shoes.

They were like hens in a chicken coop: snap, cackle and pop.

But then, there at the centre of all the giggling silliness, I saw Melanie. Her lips and her nails were painted a shiny pink and a red ribbon sat in her dark hair. When she saw me her cheeks glowed and, for an instant, her eyelashes dropped to the floor before she rushed up and grabbed me.

'Mummy—Mum—this is Peter,' she cried, pinching me by the elbow towards a pink smock stretched over the big behind of a woman, arms buried bubble-deep in the sink. But there was something about that pink smock that made me uneasy.

And, when she turned around and smiled, I found it very hard to keep breathing. You see, she was that woman from the Lodge: the one who recognised Kat on that first day of school. She was short, no taller than me, plump like a ripe fruit, with a pale face and Melanie's pretty pink lips. When she caught me staring—perhaps I stared a little longer than I should—she winked.

'Oh, Peter, m'love,' she cried, and her soapy hands clasped mine. 'I was *so* pleased when Mel said you was coming. Ooh, and look how smart you are.' She meant because I was still in my school uniform. 'Let me get that for you,' and she slipped my bag from my shoulder. 'Mind, you're so late, we was fretting you weren't coming after all.' And then, 'Oh, Peter!' now rubbing *Fairy* soft suds into my cheeks, her smile a lipsticky flash of amusement. 'You know, you're very familiar, aren't you? Have we met before?'

I lurked, back to the wall, in the shadows of the party, peering in at the strange dancing creatures and casually looking at the family photographs that cluttered the sideboards and shelves. I could feel my face glowing like headlights on a flying saucer. Every now and again one of the girls would grin in my direction but, if I tried to smile back, my face got all hot and cardboardy and out of place like it wasn't my face at all but like some stranger's face stuck on with glue. The music rattled around my ears like ball-bearings in a tumble drier. My big, clumsy feet tried to shuffle in time and I tried to move my arms in rhythm but it was like all the bits weren't even connected to the rest of me any more, just pieces of the wrong puzzle all jammed in together.

Anna-Marie wouldn't've had any time or patience for this party, I thought. I pictured her in tatty plimsolls and a grubby frock; I could even see her grumpy scowl. Anna-Marie would never cake her face or have any time for all the giggly gossip or high-pitched nonsense. She was so very different from them.

If you wanted to think about it.

Which I didn't.

And then I saw this one photograph which made me gasp. It was one of those old photos. No, not black-and-white-old. Not that old. It was coloured but all soft and blurry, slowly fading away with the summer. And it, the photograph, made me think of this story my dad once told me about these burglars who would break into people's houses but instead of taking all their jewellery and stuff they would only rearrange their furniture. It seemed a kind of funny thing to do, which is why I remember it, so that when you came down in the morning you'd trip over the rug because it hadn't been there before and when you went to find your favourite chair by the window it was by the door instead. Anyway, that was kind of like what the photograph was doing inside my head: rearranging the furniture so that nothing was in the right place any more.

I recognised Melanie straight away, of course, even though she was only a little girl. Even then she was pretty enough to turn you into sand. I couldn't miss the black-jack hair and her lips all strawberry-red like those hard boiled sweets on Mr Kirrin's high shelf. And, of course, I recognised the little boy too, the Pinky-Perky puppet waving from his hand, even though I was too little to remember. I mean I recognised his face from the bathroom mirror and the silver tap in the school cloakroom, upside down in spoons and the reflection in my mother's eyes. It was like seeing yourself for the first time but knowing, just knowing that it's you and that that's your mouth and your nose. And you know they're your eyes even though you've only ever seen them from the wrong side before.

We were sat together, in the picture, Melanie and me, in that paddling pool. You know, the one that was hanging in Kat's workshop like a big, blue rubber skin. And there behind us was the cottage, Kat's cottage, my cottage and, over there, my willow tree. And there with us was Kat: smiling at us, smiling at the camera. And it was like I was in there with them, like I was inside the little silver frame, and I could laugh at all the splashing and feel the warm sun and hear the willow leaves ripple like the pages of a book.

But it was funny to see Kat in that picture: funny because she was almost as fat as Melanie's mum. I mean her face wasn't so fat but her big flowery frock, like that sheet in the workshop covering something secret, was draped all the way over and her big belly looked like it was about to pop. It was like one of those dresses ladies sometimes wear when they're going to have a—

'She was my best friend, you know.'

A big dark shadow had loomed up behind my reflection in the photo glass like the Loch Ness Monster. And I felt Mrs Finch's hand on my shoulder, her meaty fingers slowly flexing. 'Peas in a pod, we were,' she said. 'The Giggling Gerties they used to call us. You probably want to know what happened.' I shook my head. Well, I wasn't sure whether I wanted to know or not. 'One day,' she went on, 'I went down to the cottage to see her just as usual and she'd gone. It was her mum opened the door. I says, "People just don't up and go," and her mum says, "Well, then, how come that's just what they've done?"' Mrs Finch's fist turned me round to face her and she looked at me like a judge: 'What do you have to say for yourself?' her eyes whispered. 'How do you plead?' like I was the guilty one. But it was as if I was swallowing this big slice of birthday cake in my throat.

'Mel says you live with your aunt,' said Mrs Finch. 'Was that who I saw you with at school? She looks just like your mum, doesn't she?'

I tried but I couldn't say anything, could I? I only coughed and spluttered. I mean, what would you have said?

Melanie shared her mother's pretty face and rosy lips but her skinny shape and dark skin she got from her father. He was sat at the over-laden kitchen table, a shotgun laid across his lap, fuelling and refuelling his pipe and sweeping a suspicious eye over the intruders. From his large feet, cooling in a bowl of water, to the sweat on his brow he was made of the un-ploughed earth, of the crops he raised, of the seasons that turn the world.

Mrs Finch began organising party games, strutting up and down like a German General and barking instructions but it wasn't until Mr Finch rose from his place and stood there stiff like the village green War Memorial that the snort-ing and sniggering quietened down enough for games to begin.

We sat in a big circle flinging brightly wrapped parcels from lap to lap. And then we stood in a circle and, this time, when the music stopped, we had to stand as still as statues. I won, my arms and legs like stone, whilst the girls pulled faces and, if they thought they could get away with it, pinched their neighbours. And then another circle and we played a game of *Truth or Dare* which went well enough until Mel-anie twirled the bottle and it pointed at me like an angry teacher.

'Peter?' It was Charlotte Blackett, a girl with glasses and bunches from the second year. 'Do you love Melanie?'

Mrs Finch performed a pantomime 'Ooh' of surprise and clutched a hand to her heavy bosoms as my cheeks bulged with all the crimsons of the world and the room began to spin just like the bottle had.

And then Lizzie March said: 'Or Anna-Marie?'

'Ugh,' groaned Cheryl Sawyer. 'Anna-Marie smells like cabbage.'

'That's because she never washes,' said Sarah Randall.

'Now, now, girls,' said Melanie's mother, 'it's not like Anna-Marie can help being a bit … different,' and everybody laughed. 'Now, who's hungry?' and everybody cheered.

At the head of the table sat Mr Finch. Next to him sat Melanie and, at Melanie's insistence, I sat next to her. We were sur-rounded by plate after plate of sandwiches: ham on one side, cheese on the other, egg and cress in the middle. Crisps and snacks were spread before us and pineapple chunks, cheese and sausages lost in forests of cocktail sticks. Glasses, cups and tumblers were filled to the brim from large jugs of squash. Mrs Finch drew a loud chair to the table and squeezed herself in so that she was facing me, her eyes bright and nosey. Mr Finch was watching me too, eyeing me like a crow, his mind turning over like dry earth.

'Who's the lad?' he asked, speaking for the first time.

'Why you daft old soak,' said his wife, picking a ham sand-wich from the pile and folding it between her shiny lips, 'it's Peter. From Mel's class. Remember?' And then again, 'Remember?' like a sandwich with double filling.

Mr Finch's hooded eyes blinked for a moment before: 'Oh, aye,' they were suddenly lit from within. He tapped his pipe on the tabletop. 'This is the lad, is 'e? The one you saw? Peter, is it?'

'Aye,' said his wife, sandwich churning inside her cheek. 'Mel's sweet on him.'

I glanced at Melanie who broke from a delicate corner of cheese and tomato to smile, her sweet lips quivering by the warmth of the stove.

'D'you know, girls,' said Mrs Finch, addressing the whole table, 'not so long ago I thought I saw an old friend of mine— Karen Goodwin, as was—not so long ago out of school but when I spoke to her … Well, she walked on as if she didn't know me at all. Now why would she do that?' Her big eyes were like keys unlocking all my secrets. 'Still,' she said, 'I must've been mistaken, I'm sure.'

'As I say,' said Mr Finch with a gravelly groan, 'best go see her 'stead of sitting up here chundering on.'

'No!' declared Melanie's mum. 'No!' dabbing the corners of her breadcrumb lips with a napkin. And then, huffing softly: 'She knows where to find me.'

Mr Finch shook his head, a slow swaying movement like a cathedral bell. 'Pride,' he muttered, and a crooked smile slyly split the top of his face from the bottom. 'Pride comes afore a—'

'Pride, is it?' cried his wife slapping the table. 'Am I too proud now? Too proud to crawl? Aye, and suppose I am. Too proud to beg? What of it? Why, you …' She turned her eyes from his slopey grin. 'It's like … It's like … It's like that Anna-Marie. That's exactly what it's like.'

'Oh, aye?' Her husband scanned the group. 'Is she here? Annie, you here?'

'Anna-Marie and Peter had to go and see Mrs Carpenter today,' chirped Melanie. 'Didn't you, Peter? What did you do?'

'Nothing,' I squeaked.

'No!' cried Mrs Finch as if her husband were stupid; and loud enough to get the attention of everyone at the table. 'Course she's not here, you daft so-and-so. After what happened? You'll be wanting that head of yours examined, m'love.

Turning up here at all hours as if she could make herself a new life just by talking about it. You know, rub it out and start over.'

'Wouldn't be the first to try, mind,' said Mr Finch solemnly.

'She took that funny turn, don't you remember? Anna-Marie I mean.'

'Course I remember,' murmured Mr Finch.

'Now, girls,' Mrs Finch said, 'this isn't for your ears so …' and she flapped her hands for them to look away before turning back to her husband. 'It's Anna-Marie I'm talking about,' she hissed, slapping Mr Finch's shoulder, her voice really no quieter than before. 'You remember. Well, I *say* funny turn. It made *us* laugh.'

'Made *you* laugh.'

'Aye,' said Mrs Finch. The party guests chewed in silence, ears twitching like radar. 'At first. Scrawny little creature she was, sat at table, right here, stomping her feet, refusing to go, saying how she was Mel's best friend. But after a while …Well,' she turned to share her story with her daughter's friends, 'it was scary. She wants me to be her mummy, she says, and Ben here to be her daddy and she wants to—'

'Hush now,' muttered Mr Finch, striking a match, eyes glancing at Melanie's guests.

'Well, all I'm saying is maybe it's not just her *dad* they should've locked—'

'Hush now!' His voice was firm. He pressed the lighted match to the barrel of his pipe. 'No need for that.'

'Well, all I'm saying is stay away when you're not wanted.' Mrs Finch curled another sandwich into her mouth although her lips were tight and wiry. 'Peter!' she cried suddenly. 'Why, you haven't touched a crumb.'

And then Mr Finch's finger was waggling at me, his face cracking with his big, broken-toothed grin. 'Look at him! Look at him!' he cried. 'He's sat there staring like the Scarecrow

Man.' Mrs Finch flinched and her frown curled into a question mark. 'Aye,' said her husband with a nod, 'top field, up by Suicide Tree.'

'Makes my skin crawl,' muttered Melanie's mother with a shudder. 'Gives me the shimmies.'

Mr Finch picked up his shotgun and took aim, firing two imaginary shots—K'bm! K'bm!—in the direction of his wife's fat bottom. He leant forward and pinched the flesh of her arm 'til it trembled. 'Oh, he's harmless enough.'

The table fell into a rowdy clutter of chattering and clattering as plate after plate was cleared and teeth chomped and chewed, and cheeks bulged with handful after handful of sweet and savoury. Hands, mouths and stomachs were all stuffed to bursting until completely satisfied.

'Melanie,' asked Michelle Carr, 'did Anna-Marie really used to be your best friend?' She asked it in a sing-songy kind of nasty way.

Melanie blushed and Mrs Finch asked sternly, 'What of it, young lady?' her spine straight and prickly. 'Friends come and go, don't they, Peter?'

'They'll be wanting their cake,' growled Mr Finch, bitter smoke billowing from between his teeth.

With much scraping of chairs and, ''Scuse me, m'loves,' Mrs Finch left the table and made her way to the pantry door, returning a moment later carrying the cake to the table like it was a Persian prince with a crown of candles, ten candles, placed evenly around the edge. Mr Finch produced a taper, burning bright, and took it to them one by one. The individual flames flickered and, once all were lit, a golden glow bathed Melanie's face.

Everybody sang.

Melanie blew and the flames went out one by one. Mrs Finch wielded a knife as long as her arm and sliced chunks from the cake, leaving the mark of her meaty prints on each piece. Her red lips sucked the crumbs from her fingers as she wiped the blade clean on the corner of her apron. Mr Finch stood and bent low to his daughter and kissed her on the throat just below her jaw: a daddy's kiss full of sweat, stubble, love and bad breath.

'Speaking of friends,' said Mrs Finch, smiling slyly, 'I think Peter might know another old friend of yours, Mel.'

'Who?'

'Oh, you was very young. You used to call him Pinky-Perky-Peter.'

Melanie frowned but then her eyes caught sparks and glowed like the tobacco in her father's pipe. She smiled. 'Pinky-Perky-Peter,' she said as if repeating a dream. And then she turned those sparkling eyes to mine.

'A little tyke he was,' said Mrs Finch with a chuckle. 'Always up to no good.'

'Seems lad's picking up bit of colour,' remarked Mr Finch his expression unchanging.

'Aye,' said Mrs Finch. 'It'll be all that party food.'

'Look at him,' went on Melanie's father with a dry laugh, his long fingers snapping in my face. 'Look at him. He's away with faeries. His mother'll think you've not been feeding him.'

'Lives with his aunt, they say. Isn't that right, Peter?' and then under her breath, 'supposedly.'

'Good Lord, woman!' barked Mr Finch like an angry tractor. 'Go and see her, I say!' He rapped his pipe three times on the table. 'Or ask her blasted mother what happened!'

The audience fell silent, their eyes startled wide reflecting the flickering candles.

Mrs Finch's finger tucked a loose curl back behind her ears. Her eyes toyed with me. 'She says she'll never tell.'

23

'Now,' cried Mrs Finch, raising her voice and poking as big a chunk of cake as would fit into her fat face, 'it's time for *Hide and Seek*!' She clapped like a performing seal and everybody leapt to their feet.

As Rebecca Blackett, Charlotte's twin, counted from one to ten I slipped through the door and out into the farmyard whilst everybody else squealed and went in search of nooks and cubby-holes, wardrobes and shadows.

'Here I come, ready or not.'

It was twilight and I breathed deep, the air wet and spicy with dung. I looked around for a secure hiding place: the best hiding place. You see, I didn't want to be found. By which I mean I didn't even want to be sought. I wanted to disappear altogether.

Beside a paddock in which Melanie's pony, Goldilocks, grey in the sooty fading light, trotted back and forth with a pleasing clippertyclop, I found some bales of hay and drew myself into as tight a space as I could manage, my nose tickling. I held my breath.

'Hello, Peter.'

It was Melanie. She squashed in beside me, so that together we filled just as small a space as I had on my own. She smelt flowery, her hair in my face making my nose twitch even more, her soft hand slipping into mine. Her head turned slightly so that her velvety pink lips touched mine. To the side Goldilocks' droppings were shovelled into a single wet pile. I could hear Melanie breathing through her nose, and taste sweet and savoury on her breath.

'Pinky-Perky-Peter,' she sighed.

I could hear where flies had buried their eggs with a pl-pl-pl-plpl in the mountain of dung, and sense their wriggling white babies burrowing towards the centre of the heap. Melanie's little tongue was in my mouth like a strawberry.

And then, 'Peter.'

Melanie's lips parted from mine with a syrupy slurp.

Anna-Marie was stood before us, her face pale like the rising moon. I wriggled free of Melanie's arms and struggled to my feet. Even in the twilight I could see something new in Anna-Marie's face, something I hadn't seen before.

'Nice tie,' she said looking at my school uniform. 'I didn't know it was fancy dress,' but there was no feeling in the way she said it.

I don't know if Melanie called out or if somebody else saw what had happened but before long everybody had gathered to stare at Anna-Marie in the farmyard. They were just like a jury on that show *Crown Court* which is always on when you're off school with a tummy bug, all scowling before they even knew what she was supposed to have done, but Anna-Marie didn't move or speak.

At the centre of the mob Mrs Finch's face steamed with anger as Melanie wept into her chest. 'You're a ghoul,' she wailed at the visitor. 'You're not welcome 'ere. 'Ow many times ... ?' Melanie's friends swarmed about her, patting her back and condemning the criminal with poisonous gasps. Their feet stomped with outrage; their eyes shone with delight.

Mr Finch emerged from the farmhouse and the group separated to let him through. 'Go easy on the lass,' he said. This is what daddies do, I thought. He approached Anna-Marie and laid his hand, as big as a field, on her shoulder. 'She's done no wrong.' Sometimes we all need a daddy just to sort things out.

'No wrong?' spluttered his wife. 'No wrong? I can't believe my ... *This* is your daughter, you old fool, sobbing in my arms.'

Anna-Marie tilted and rested her head against the man's chest. He touched her hair gently. 'You'd best be gone, m'love,' he whispered, his voice soft as earth. Their eyes met for a moment before Anna-Marie turned and disappeared into the shadows.

'Well, thank goodness for that!' exclaimed Mrs Finch.

'Are you her friend, lad?'

'Yes.'

He looked at me with sad eyes. 'Aye, then,' he said, 'you'd best go with her, eh?'

And I knew he was right. I'd deserted her once, I couldn't do it again.

It was properly dark by the time I reached Everlasting Lane. I saw Anna-Marie waiting for me beneath the glow of a lamp-post at the top of the path that led down towards the river, but again she turned into darkness as soon as I drew close. I followed the rustle of her feet through the undergrowth.

By the time I found her she was stood on the riverbank, her sandals and socks had been removed and lay beside the cold, dark water. She told me to sit down and had me tug off my own socks and shoes and roll up the bottoms of my trousers.

I couldn't believe how freezing the water was. The only light was provided by the moon, so silver it was almost blue.

I was just beginning to wonder where I'd left my school bag when Anna-Marie said, 'How was the party?'

'How did you know?'

Anna-Marie shrugged. 'Oh, Peter, do you think nothing ever happened before you came here? It's her birthday. She always has a party. I went once. How's her dad?'

'Okay.'

'You know, once when I was there they let me ride on the pony. Goldilocks. It was great.'

'Melanie loves me,' I said.

'Sure,' said Anna-Marie. 'She loves everybody for a while. Without wanting to spit in your cornflakes, she was in love with Tommie for six weeks when she could barely stand to look at him. Melanie's problem,' she said, 'is she's not prepared to forsake a little love.'

'What happened?' I meant about Mrs Carpenter and that.

Anna-Marie told me to swirl my foot in the water. I could hear her sucking in her cheeks and turned to see her biting her lower lip, frowning at the stars.

'What was your dad like?' she said.

Black shapes swooped back and forth in the field before us. The bells of the church began to sound the hour. They seemed to go on and on.

I cleared my throat. I told her that he was tall, that sometimes he was a bit tubby in the tummy; that he had a moustache except when he didn't. I told her that he'd worked for someone but I didn't know who or what he did. I told her that he'd been in the war and that sometimes he could be noisy and funny and at other times he would be quiet and—

'No, Peter. I mean, what was he *like*?'

When I had chicken pox once the spots were so scratchy I

couldn't sleep and lay in bed, crying. My dad sat with me and told me a story about a man who shot his own foot off thinking it was the hand of a ghost. That was a bit scary, so then he told me a funny story from the war about a chicken and a German soldier. Then he told me not to worry about sleeping. He said, 'Sometimes you only think you're awake when in fact you're dreaming,' but he stayed with me, dabbing ointment on my spots, until I drifted out of this world into another.

Anna-Marie nodded. 'Yes,' she said. 'That is kind,' and then she was silent again.

I turned again to face her. I couldn't really see her face, just the sparkle of her tears. 'What about your dad?' I said.

'Don't look at me,' she said, so I turned around again. 'What about your mum?' she said. 'Do you love her?'

It was strange to hear her say 'mum' like that, but I nodded. 'Yes.'

'You love her better since you came here.'

'Yes.'

It was funny because I didn't really know what she meant. I mean about whether I loved her—my mum—more since I'd come to Amberley. I was confused. But then I realised that Anna-Marie knew that Kat was my mother. And then I realised that she'd always known; I mean nearly as long as I had. And that was all right. I didn't mind her knowing, but—

'How did you know?'

'Oh, Peter,' she sighed, 'it's as plain as that stubby, fat thing in the middle of your face.'

'Don't tell Tommie,' I said.

'Tommie?' She laughed. 'You're joking, aren't you? His brain can barely contain the football results without dribbling down the sides. But,' she said, 'what was she like before? Kat I mean. Your mum.'

'I don't know.'

I was too embarrassed to say anything else, you see, because the really funny thing was that I'd kind of forgotten. I mean that Kat was my mum. I don't really know why. I guess I'd just kind of wanted to forget. It's like I said before, sometimes pretending is better than when things were real.

'*My* mother,' said Anna-Marie making the word sound inedible, 'is a nightmare. A complete nightmare.' She began to copy her mother's gloomy voice: '"Anna-Marie, do this. Anna-Marie, do that. Tidy this, clean that, polish this, scrub that." Frankly, my mother is a pain in the ... backside.'

And then I suddenly realised why, well, why she wasn't sitting down.

But, 'What about your dad?' I said.

'Melanie's dad was always nice to me,' said Anna-Marie. 'He used to show me how to milk the cows and things like that. I didn't even want to go home sometimes.'

'What about *your* dad?'

I turned my head to see Anna-Marie gazing deep down into the muddy water in search of a lost ring, seeing the shine but not the ring itself. She told me to swirl my foot again and for a moment the water cleared. I looked up. Her eyes were filled with tears. A shiver passed from the river and twinkled its way up my spine.

'The problem with you, Peter,' she said, 'is that sometimes you're watching *Blue Peter* when everybody else is watching *Magpie.*'

'What?' I didn't really know what she meant.

And then she said,

> '*Alice*
> *Daughter, sister, mother, friend*
> *Child of the pure unclouded brow*
> *And dreaming eyes of wonder!*

Though time be fleet, and I and thou
Are half a life asunder.
R.I.P.'

speaking slowly, from memory, as if she was carving the words with her voice.

They were the words from the gravestone. Alice's gravestone. I could remember nearly all of them myself even though I'd only seen them for a second.

'Why didn't you tell me?' she said.

'I …You said you didn't want to know.'

'I suppose,' she sighed. And then, 'But it's true, isn't it?' she said. 'Mr Merridew was right. I mean it didn't even have any dates on it.' She meant the gravestone. She was right. I didn't know much about graves but I remembered the dates from my father's headstone: so precise like rules that can't be broken. 'It's like she died without even being born.'

'What?'

'What would that be like,' wondered Anna-Marie, 'if you'd never been born?'

I turned again to look at her. She looked kind of funny like a, well, a little girl. I mean that's silly, I know. She *was* a little girl, of course: younger than I am now. I'd just never really noticed before.

'What? I don't know.'

She'd always seemed so much older.

She shrugged. 'Well, what about other people? What about me and Tommie? You *were* born, so do you think we'd miss you if you hadn't been? And what about your mum? I mean if you were supposed to be born, but weren't, wouldn't you leave a hole?'

'I don't …A hole?'

'For people who would have known you. I wonder if

226

people can tell there's someone missing. Do you know what I mean?'

The funny thing was I did. I knew exactly what she meant. It was just like the secret room. It'd looked like a nursery but it hadn't felt like one. It had been more like a picture of one. There was no memory of a child at play; no ripples in the air caused by long ago games. The dolls and stuffed animals were nameless and unloved. Had that cot ever been slept in? Had the mobile ever turned, turned, turned so slowly sending tired eyes to sleep? It wasn't a room of ghosts, but of ghosts of ghosts, of shadows of shadows: of absence, of nothing, of less than nothing.

'Which is worse,' wondered Anna-Marie, 'living, knowing you're going to die, or never living at all?'

'What?' Which was *worse*? Neither filled me with glee. 'If you never lived,' I insisted, 'you wouldn't know any different.'

'I wonder,' said Anna-Marie.

And she was right to wonder. That's what I think. It's like Norman said: who isn't kept awake at night dreaming of the things they should've done but didn't, of the chances they missed that they should have taken, of the things that needed to be said but weren't? How is that different from a life un-lived: a life without love, without friendship, without touch? What might have been said that went unsaid? What might have been done that went undone?

They're like pale ghosts of ghosts who never cry, never lie, never shout, never shiver; that gaze in the broken mirror aching for all this: for joy, pleasure, love, affection, trust, truth, friendship, for everything they've been denied. And do we miss them? Do we miss their presence? Do we notice their absence? No, because they're only dreams: echoes without sound, smoke without fire, consequences without events. And yet, something of them remains, for sometimes when I'm dreaming I think I'm awake; and although my eyes are closed I believe them open.

The best I could manage was a kind of grunt.

A breeze lapped at the edges of the leaves. I watched the ducks and ducklings and the wide Vs they left in their wake. Two fat teardrops were rolling down Anna-Marie's cheeks. Her blue hair shimmered, snot bubbling in her left nostril.

I was so confused. I had no idea what to say but, 'It's all right,' I said. 'It's summer and—'

'Oh, Peter, grow up!' She snorted loudly and the snot disappeared. 'Nothing lasts forever,' she sighed drawing the back of her hand across the space between her mouth and nose. 'The summer won't last forever. The lane doesn't last forever.'

'It might.'

'Oh, Peter,' said Anna-Marie, her voice sounding sad and tired, 'you're such a baby.' And then she said: 'What are you most scared of?'

'Nothing.'

'Don't be stupid,' she sighed. 'What are you scared of?'

I glanced at the trees and their darkness. I couldn't admit to being scared of them, could I? I didn't want to own up to anything I might regret.

'I'm scared that Kat will decide she doesn't want me around and no one will care about me,' I said. 'What about you?'

Anna-Marie stood in silence a long time, staring blindly, her long fingers playing her hair. When she finally spoke it was so soft I had to ask her to say it again.

'Everything,' she said. 'The future. Everything.'

I was stunned. Everything? 'What do you mean?' Every thing? That was a lot to be scared of. 'The future?' I'd never really thought about the future or things that might happen tomorrow or the day after and certainly not what might happen next year or the year after that. Of course I knew things changed. That was why we'd come to Amberley. That's what consequences were all about but it seemed there was enough going on now without—

'It's like Alice,' sniffed Anna-Marie. 'Now that we know who she is, doesn't it make you sad? Think about all the things she might've done. Think about all the ...'

What did that mean: 'Now that we know who she is'? What did we know?

'I'm just scared of what's going to happen,' went on Anna-Marie. 'Not people dying and stuff. Not really. I don't think I'd care if my mum died. Not particularly. And I'm not scared of dying myself, whatever Mrs Carpenter says. I'm more scared of what's going to happen if I don't. I mean the future, when I have to grow up and everything. I mean, going to Second-ary School and everything. Sometimes I think ... Sometimes I know my life's just going to be horrible and that I'm going to be horrible. And the worst thing is that I can't do anything about it. I'm just going to watch it all happen like I'm a char-acter in *Crossroads* or something.

'I don't know why,' said Anna-Marie answering the ques-tion I was too stupid to ask. 'I feel like a parcel under the Christmas tree on New Year's Day, just sitting there waiting: waiting, waiting, waiting for a Christmas that's already gone. But I'm scared too, not knowing what will happen once I'm opened. Do you know what I mean?'

I didn't.

'I knew you would,' said Anna-Marie. 'I mean, everything's just ... crap. I don't mean to be like I am but I can't help it. It's like there's somebody else who makes me do things or say things. It's like the stuff I say to you and Tommie: it's like somebody else says it. I always want to be nasty to people. I don't know why.'

'Tommie likes you,' I said.

'I know,' said Anna-Marie. 'He's my best friend.'

'But you're always nasty to him.'

'I said: I don't know.'

'I like you.'

'I know,' said Anna-Marie. 'I just wish I did.'

But then I had an idea. 'What about the fair?' I said. 'You could go to the fortune-teller. There's going to be one. Melanie's drawn about fifty posters. I mean if you want to know about the future.'

'Good grief, Peter!' she cried. 'What are you … ? That's all mumbo-jumbo. Besides, after all this, Mrs Carpenter and everything, my mum's not going to let me go to the fair in a month of Sundays. Not that that's going to keep me awake at nights.'

I stood up, my feet numb from the cold river, and hobbled towards Anna-Marie. I closed my eyes and leaned up towards her to kiss her cool, wet cheek. But before I could she slapped me hard once—twice—three times on the side of the head. My ear echoed and throbbed. 'Don't you dare,' she said, adding under her breath, 'Creep!' We stood for a long time in silence. My thoughts were unsettled like the stars on the moving water. Occasionally Anna-Marie would sniff—she was close but the sound seemed to come from a distance, a distance beyond the river, beyond the trees, beyond the fields and villages. It was as if she were drifting away from me. And each time she sniffed I was reminded that I had failed. I didn't know how and I didn't know what I could have done to change it. But I knew that I had failed.

But I still wanted to do something—anything—to make her feel better, so I sat down sideways so that I could see her and told her what Mrs Finch had said.

Anna-Marie was quiet for the longest time after I'd finished, and then she said, 'Tell me again what Melanie's mum said about Karen's mum. The bit about how she never told her what happened.'

I didn't know why that bit was particularly interesting but I told it again, repeating Mrs Finch's words just as I remembered them.

Anna-Marie nodded, the smile on her lips as soft as the night sky.

'What?'

And then she shook her head. 'Peter,' she said, 'what are the chances, do you think, that you are the stupidest boy on the planet?'

I was about to complain but then I didn't. After all, when you thought about it, the chances were probably quite high.

We wandered back towards the cottages. A small car had pulled up outside Tommie's and Tommie, sitting in the back seat, waved and leapt about when he saw us.

'Hi!' he shouted. He wriggled his way over the passenger seat. 'Wow, you two are up late! Dad! Dad, come and see Anna-Marie!'

A short man, flabby like a deflated balloon, with thin hair dragged across his scalp got out of the car. He stared at us.

Tommie ran round to him, seizing his hand. 'Come on, Dad.'

The man shook his hand free. 'Don't grab me,' he said. His voice came through his nose. 'I've told you before not to grab me.'

'You remember Anna-Marie,' said Tommie, 'don't you? Oh, and this is Peter.' He was wearing a little brown cap saying 'zoo'. The letters were made with a snake and two octopuses.

'Hello, Mr Winslow,' said Anna-Marie.

The man sighed and grunted, but he didn't come out from behind the car.

'Guess where we've been,' said Tommie.

Anna-Marie glanced at his cap. 'I don't know,' she said. 'Some kind of museum?'

'No: the zoo!' cried Tommie. 'It was brilliant. We saw the tigers, didn't we, Dad? Real live tigers!'

'Here's your bag,' grunted Tommie's father. 'I'm going now.'

Tommie looked disappointed. 'But, Dad,' he cried, 'are you going to say "hello" to mum? You promised.'

The little man's moustache twitched. 'Don't whine at me,' he said. 'I've told you before about whining.'

'Sorry, Dad,' said Tommie. He went to kiss his father on the cheek.

'And you can cut that out for starters,' said the man backing away. 'I've told you before about all that stuff.' The man dumped Tommie's small bag on the pavement outside his front gate. As he did so, Tommie smiled. 'My dad,' he whispered.

Anna-Marie nodded and smiled.

With a grinding of gears the car lurched into life and departed. As it did so, Tommie's front door flew open and Mrs Winslow squeezed into view. Before Tommie could bid us goodnight he was grabbed by the collar and sucked into the house like the last gulp of water down the drain.

I turned to Anna-Marie and saw her blue-moon face. 'At least he's got a dad,' she said.

Anna-Marie was right of course. I mean about not being allowed to go to the school fair. On top of that, Mrs Carpenter told her that she had to stand outside her office, nose to the wall, 'every minute of every playtime,' until the end of term, and demanded that she be escorted by her mother to and from school each day. And Mrs Liddell made a prison of her daughter's bedroom, banning her from going out up to and including the fair. Tommie and I would meet each Saturday morning and look up at our friend's window to see her golden hair glowing at the top of her tower and her blue eyes haunting us.

24

We, Tommie and me, couldn't bear to see her watching us, Anna-Marie I mean, from her bedroom window, so we would hide beneath the branches of the willow tree. We could escape the morning heat and the leaves touched the ground providing a curtain, a perfect camouflage, behind which we could sit and talk.

'There's something funny happening,' declared Tommie. As the days had passed he had grown increasingly convinced that there was more to Anna-Marie's imprisonment than just a broken vase. He adjusted his glasses and frowned to show that he didn't mean 'funny-funny'. 'Think about all the things that have happened,' he said. 'We discovered the secret room; *you* broke that vase; Anna-Marie got punished.' He showed me the piece of paper on which he'd listed these events and the chewed pencil with which he planned to list others.

'You got hit on the head.'

'Yes,' said Tommie snapping his fingers, and writing it down. 'Before that, Mr Gale shouted at me in class. Do you remember? That was your first day at school.' I couldn't believe that Mr Gale had never shouted at Tommie before that. And I wasn't sure that that was the kind of thing he thought it was anyway. 'What I mean,' he insisted, 'is that it can't all be coincidence.'

Well, of course, it wasn't coincidence. Even I knew that. It was like Anna-Marie's jigsaw—

'But,' said Tommie, 'it's like every time we're about to discover what's happening something distracts us.'

'Oh, what about the butterflies?'

'Butterflies? What butterflies? What are you talking about?' Beneath the leaves of the willow his face looked all green.

'What? Sorry, I—'

'You're not even listening,' he snapped. 'I'm trying to solve the mystery and you're … Listen, there must be something that has caused all this to happen.' He ran his fingers through his dark, curly hair. 'What about when Mr Merridew killed the Beast?'

Kitty, purring like a radio signal, slipped beneath the willow's branches, her smooth fur sliding between us.

'What about it?' I didn't want to think about *that*. The heat of the day began to seep through the branches, dripping sweat between my neck and collar. It was the day of the school fair and—

'Tommie! Peter!' We barely heard the first hoarse whisper of our names. 'Tommie! Peter! Oi, cloth-ears, up here!'

We scrabbled out from under the willow tree like mice in the pantry and looked up to find Anna-Marie leaning out of her bedroom window, a big grin dangling between her ears. With her long hair hanging downwards she looked like Rapunzel.

'Are you all right?' I asked, as quietly-loudly as I could.

'Keep the noise down. My mum's having a nap; she's not dead.' Then she laughed. 'Honestly, Peter, you're such a cretin. Are you two going to the fair?'

We shrugged. We hadn't decided.

But then Tommie said, 'I'll get you something.'

Damn.

'I'm going to go to the fortune-teller,' I said.

Anna-Marie shrugged. 'Please yourself.'

Damn.

And then she laughed again. It was quite a difference from the night of the party. She must've seen my confusion. 'Oh, and another thing,' she said, as if it explained everything, 'I know how to find out about Alice.'

Oh no. Why didn't I want to hear that?

'How?' asked Tommie although I'd been wishing he wouldn't.

Anna-Marie began to hum like a ghost and waved her hands in the air like a conjuror. 'I predict,' she said, 'I predict a journey to the Lodge.'

'Why?' asked Tommie. No amount of wishing seemed to shut him up.

'Because there's someone there that will be able to tell Peter what happened to his sister.'

Sister? What was that supposed to mean? But Anna-Marie had already pulled her window to a close.

By the time Tommie and I arrived at the school fair it was bubbling like soup. The air was rich with laughter and raised voices: there were children dressed loudly for the *Fancy Dress Competition*, eating candyfloss; the old men from *The White Hart* sipping beer and picking at all the good in the world; and music, the kind that sounds like it's turned with a handle, and all of it basting in a hot summer's afternoon of bric-a-brac stalls and food on a stick and lucky dips and slides and swings.

'People don't do that though, do they?'

'Do what?'

'Beat a dog to death I mean. I mean who would do that?'

I couldn't believe he was going on about *that* again. 'But Mr Merridew—'

'Not even Mr Merridew,' said Tommie. He drew his pencil, folded his paper into the palm of his hand and prepared to write. 'Tell me what he said again.'

I didn't want to think about that. I was still trying to understand what Anna-Marie had meant about my sister. I didn't have a sister. Did she mean Alice? But—

'Peter. Concentrate.' It was Tommie again. He was waving his piece of paper in my face. 'Tell me what Mr Merridew said.'

I tried to remember, forcing my mind back inside that dreadful cottage, watching the shadows on the wall. 'He said—I didn't understand everything—but he said if there was a cow and it was big close up and small in the distance that maybe it wasn't the same cow.'

Tommie looked confused, pencil suspended in mid-air. 'Why would he say that?'

'I don't know,' I said. 'Or maybe it was that the cow *was* the same cow whether you were close up or a long way away. Maybe that's what he meant.' I must've told Tommie this a thousand times.

'That still sounds like a load of rubbish to me.'

'He said children shouldn't judge people.'

Tommie's confusion tied a complicated knot between his eyes. 'Why would he say *that*?'

'Nothing means anything.'

'What?'

'He said nothing meant anything and we might as well be dead ... Apart from when we're alive.'

'What? Stop it. That's stupid.'

'There's only chaos.'

'Stop it, Peter,' cried Tommie. 'Shut up! He didn't say that! He didn't!'

Then something new occurred to me: 'Anna-Marie believed him.'

But there couldn't only be chaos, could there? I mean if that was true, then you wouldn't have to worry about consequences at all because nothing you did would matter. And if that was true, then you couldn't do anything wrong or anything right. And then you wouldn't have to apologise or feel guilty for anything. But if Alice *was* my sister, then—

'Anna-Marie's right about you,' muttered Tommie, his teeth working the end of his pencil like it was a *Curly Wurly*. 'She's stuck in her room and all you're doing is muttering to yourself. I'm doing all the work,' he complained. 'You're just staring into space.'

What I wanted to say was that he couldn't just write things down when they didn't mean anything. It wasn't all coincidence. Something caused something else to happen but that didn't make it mysterious. That's just what happens. Tommie got hit on the head but that was just an accident and Mr Gale was really sorry. And I dropped the vase and that was an accident too. It slipped out of my hands when the vicar jumped up on me. It was like Anna-Marie's puzzle: everything did seem to fit together because that's what everything does. It didn't mean something just because Tommie wanted it to.

I said, 'You're just being silly.'

'If I'm so silly,' said Tommie crossly, 'then why is Anna-Marie locked in her room and not you?'

'I don't know,' I said. I was lying, of course, but that didn't make it like a clue.

We'd come to a line of children waiting to throw sponges at Mr Gale—*'five pence a throw'*—our teacher kneeling behind a wooden screen with his head poking through. On the screen was painted the body of a schoolboy with short trousers and a blue knotted tie, on his head a schoolboy cap. He looked like that man—Terry Someone—who does *My Bruvver* on the telly. Tommie was delighted and quickly forgot about mysteries and coincidences as he joined the queue, rolling a ten pence piece impatiently between his fingers, until swapping it for two sopping sponges.

'Ah!' exclaimed Mr Gale, 'it's Winnie the Winslow boy and his demon googlie.'

Tommie, muttering to himself, wound and then unwound his first shot with so much anger that it flew about a mile wide of Mr Gale's broad grin. The teacher roared with laughter. Tommie scowled with concentration as he again took aim. 'I'm glad to see you've recovered,' said Mr Gale, 'even if your sense of direction is still piss-poor.' Eyes blazing, Tommie failed to concentrate at all and his second throw missed its target by an even greater distance. 'That's it,' laughed Mr Gale, 'practice makes perfect.'

'Give me two more,' demanded Tommie.

'I'm sorry,' said the money-taking lady, 'you'll have to go to the back of the—'

'It's all right, Joan,' laughed Mr Gale, 'let him have another crack whilst he's doing so well. I'll make a cricketer of him yet.'

Tommie sent sponges three and four flying with even greater determination but no greater success than the first two. Mr Gale laughed and teased Tommie to new levels of failure. 'Keep 'em coming!' he yelled. 'It's all in a good cause.'

This time, much to Tommie's annoyance, the lady refused to sell him any more sponges until he'd, 'made sure there isn't something more worthwhile to spend your money on.'

'You'll never bowl for England!' yelled Mr Gale.

With my encouragement and Mr Gale's taunts in our ears we wandered off between the up and down of the merry-go-round and the belching beer tents and the flies buzzing lazily around the bottoms of donkeys as they carried toddlers back and forth. The donkeys I mean. Not the flies.

'If nothing's happened,' said Tommie, 'why do you think Anna-Marie is being punished? Don't you think that's mysterious?'

I groaned. You see, he was wrong. It wasn't a mystery; it was just a story and a story wasn't the same as a mystery at all. Really a story is just consequences: consequence following on consequence like those domino things they're always doing on *Record Breakers*, clickety-clack with Roy Castle tap-dancing in the background and playing the most instruments in the world ever. Just because Tommie didn't understand everything he thought it was a mystery but it wasn't a mystery because somebody *knew* the answers; like somebody knew whether Alice really was my sister or not. To somebody it wasn't a mystery at all just like some of the things *I* knew—like where I hid my scrapbook or the things I put in it—would be a mystery to someone else.

Unless I told them.

And maybe the worst thing we could do was solve a mystery, because Alice was a mystery and a mystery was just another word for a secret and a secret was just another word for the truth and when we solved it, when it wasn't a mystery any more, all we'd have left was the truth. Or maybe nothing.

'Nothing?' Tommie stared at me open mouthed. 'What do you mean?'

'Nothing.'

'I think you're mad,' he said. 'You're just mumbling to

yourself and … Don't you care? When Anna-Marie gets out I'm going to tell her you just daydreamed the whole time.'

'I'm sorry, Tommie,' I said, and I meant it. 'I *was* listening,' but I prayed he wouldn't test me.

We came upon a stall where you could win a goldfish—*Genuine Goldfish* said the sign—by throwing a big hoop around a little glass bowl. We stood at the back of the crowd and watched the man demonstrate over and over again. It looked so easy.

'I'm going to win a goldfish,' I said. I didn't tell Tommie that, just in case there wasn't a real fortune-teller, this would be my gift for Anna-Marie. I didn't want him copying me.

'That'll be ten pee for three throws, young sir,' grinned the stall-holder, his grey teeth were like two rows of broken stones in a graveyard. 'Best of British.'

As soon as I held the first hoop I could tell that it was a trinket compared to the fish bowls staring back at me like the crew of Apollo thirteen. I mean with their big space-man helmets on and stuff. Despite the encouragement of the man with the bad teeth ('So close, sooo close …You're nearly there … One of the best so far') I was soon thirty pence down and beginning to realise how hard it was. I'd taken a handful of coins from my piggy-bank, from my 'ring-money' and was heartbroken to lose it so easily.

'Never mind, my young friends,' said the man when, after another twenty pence of failure, I hung up my hoop. 'Wisdom isn't free but at fifty new pence it is at least reasonably priced.' That was easier for an adult to believe than a ten year old. 'However,' he said to cheer us up, 'before you go, how about this?' He dipped his fingers into one of the bowls, pulled out a wriggling goldfish and popped it, to our amazement, into his mouth, giving it a satisfied chew. Our nervous laughter turned to horror as he revealed the goldfish remains reduced to paste between his ugly teeth.

'They don't 'alf tickle on the way down,' he said with a laugh.

Tommie found a stall selling tiny, tinny necklaces and bracelets. He picked up one after another and examined them like he was Sherlock Holmes as the woman behind the bench reassured him that each one was better than the last. What a fool! I almost laughed when I pictured his miserable face as I shared the words of the fortune-teller with Anna-Marie. The future: that was the biggest mystery, the biggest secret of all. And when I'd explained all the mysteries of the world until there were no mysteries and no secrets left, wouldn't Tommie's list of mysteries look like, well, a scrap of paper?

And then I saw Melanie. She looked beautiful, a princess with flowers woven into in her hair.

'Hello, Melanie,' I said.

'Pinky-Perky-Poof,' she said to the delight of her friends.

The crowd grew and grew until it was impossible for us to take more than two steps together before bumping into someone ('Sorry') or someone bumping into us ('Grunt'). Bits and pieces of conversation mixed with nursery rhymes and mingled with babies crying and old women laughing. And the noise kept growing until we pushed our fingers deep into our ears. In the end we found a gap between the canvases of Mrs Twist's *Guess the Weight of the Cake* and Kirrins' *How Many Wine Gums in the Jar?* stalls. Greg Kirrin, pink belly peeping out between the buttons of his shirt, glowered at me as we slipped past but I didn't see Norman anywhere at all. We emerged from the shadows to find the stalls on the other side were dark and shabby with black flaps drawn across the entrances, but at least this side of the fair was softer on the ear, the air was cooler and there were fewer, if any, people wandering around.

And then I saw this sign: *Madame Vérité—Fortunes Told* just like I'd hoped. Tommie snorted. 'My dad says that kind of stuff's all a rip-off,' he sniffed.

But he was the one who kept going on about mysteries and secrets. The future: the biggest secret of all, a secret that no one knew the answer to. Now that was a proper mystery.

'I'm going to get Anna-Marie a proper present,' he grumbled, stomping off in disgust.

What a fool!

I lifted the flap and peered inside.

Madame Vérité was sat hunched at an old school-table and dressed just like a gypsy from one of those stories: an old shawl, like a tablecloth with tassels, was wrapped about her and the tent trembled with darkness and candlelight.

'Cross my palm with silver,' she said in a croaky voice.

I didn't have any silver but I nervously uncurled and handed over my pound note: a whole pound, yes, but worth every penny, and she was happy to take it, fold it three or four times and pop it into this tin with a slot cut in the top like my Pinky-Perky money-box. There was a veil across her mouth and the shawl was pulled so far over her head that I could barely see her face, only shadows and the quick flickery flash of big gold earrings and a shiny pendant, like a capital J.

And then she said, 'It's Peter, isn't it?' which was kind of funny and sort of magical because she didn't even know my ... But then I thought: Capital J? Why would Madame Vérité be wearing a pendant with a capital J? Madame Vérité didn't even start with a J. But then neither, I thought as the so-called fortune-teller pulled back her shawl and lowered her veil, did disappointment.

'I was hoping,' said Miss Pevensie with a smile, 'that I might run in to you today.'

But I wasn't smiling: I was cross. I mean she always seemed very nice and everything but, after all, she was only a teacher. In fact, she wasn't even a proper teacher yet. In fact, she was no more a real-life fortune-teller than Mr Gale was a real-life schoolboy.

I should have known.

'Sorry,' she said. 'Blame it on the PTA.'

'Can you really tell the future?' I said. I'd had a headful of questions: about Anna-Marie and about—

She shook her head. 'No.'

'Oh.' I wasn't even surprised. 'Well, what about the past, then?' Maybe she could tell me whether Alice—

'No,' she said, 'but let's see if I can't tell you what's happening now.'

Now? Now? That didn't sound like a whole pound's worth. I rather thought I could do that for myself.

She waved for me to sit down on the stool that faced her.

I sat and she said, 'Give me your hand.' Miss Pevensie stretched out my palm and studied it, tracing the wrinkles with her finger. 'Your life-line is very long,' she said.

'Is that my life-line?'

'I think so. But they're all very long so I don't think you have anything to worry about.'

'It's like Everlasting Lane,' I said, watching it wriggle off into the distance.

'Oh,' she said. 'Do you think so? Well, I suppose it could be.'

She slipped some blue cards from under her gown and removed the elastic band holding them together. The cards were covered in red writing. She began to shuffle them badly.

'You've got to ask me a question,' she said.

'Where did you get those cards?'

'No,' she said. 'Try something more, I don't know, magical.'

I thought about it and then I said: 'Who digs the grave-digger's grave?'

Miss Pevensie looked a little surprised. 'Well,' she said, 'that is an interesting question.' She held out the blue cards in a fan. 'Pick one.'

I took a card and cupped it in my hands hiding it, trying to read it in the dark.

'No,' said Miss Pevensie, 'it's okay to show me. It's not like a card trick. Well, not exactly. I can't guess what you've got. You're going to have to show me.' She took my card and held it beside the candle. 'I'm supposed to read it to you,' she said.

'Is it like a story?'

'Sort of,' she said, 'but it's more like a riddle.'

'Like a joke,' I said. 'Like a knock-knock joke.'

She smiled, you know, that smile that grown-ups do when you've got something wrong but they don't want to say so. Some teachers do it all the time. 'Now,' she said, and put on this funny voice like Norman reading his poem: 'Who digs the gravedigger's grave?'

And then, squinting by the flickering light, she read aloud:

A ship sets sail: its purpose, a return to where it started,
A child chosen as a guide to oceans yet uncharted.
The ocean rests upon its bed: fat, content, indifferent,
Whilst chaos turns your little boat from harbour dim and distant.

I stared at her in amazement. I had no idea what she was talking about.

'Did that, erm, answer your question?' she said.

I think she knew the answer to that but when I didn't say

anything she puffed out her cheeks, took my hand and opened up my palm before me. 'Look closer.'

'It's all wrinkled,' I said.

Dark and light continued to ripple around the tent, shadows scurrying across Miss Pevensie's face like mice, but I tried to ignore their spooky tricks and concentrate on the book which the teacher—the so-called teacher—now pulled from beneath her robes: a small book but thick like the Bible I'd seen on Mrs Carpenter's desk.

She shuffled the pack again. 'Let me try one,' she said. 'Who puts the words upon the page?' She pulled a card from the pack and said, 'Every page is similar but,' and then she coughed. 'Sorry,' she said. 'I forgot who I was supposed to be.' She cleared her throat and started again in her best hocus-pocus voice:

> Every page is similar but every page unique,
> And each turns independent t'wards the ending that you seek.
> Upon each page, upon each life, the Author's words are gold,
> A single page asunder would leave the tale untold.

I wrinkled my nose. Again I had no idea what she was talking about and wished, wished, wished I'd saved my money. Suddenly it didn't seem quite so likely that I would get to enjoy Tommie's look of shame as I *Top Trumped* his piddly necklace. Maybe you couldn't buy wisdom after all. Even for a whole pound.

Miss Pevensie passed me the book. 'Look closer.'

I flicked through the pages. 'Some of it's missing,' I said. And then I said, 'Where did you get them?' I pointed. 'The cards, I mean.'

'What? Oh, these.' She examined the pack. 'A friend did them for me. They were supposed to be funny.'

'Is that the man from *The Copper Kettle*?'

She didn't seem to know what I was talking about but then she said, 'His name's Craig. Do you know him?'

I nodded. 'Yes,' I said. 'He was talking to me; me and Anna-Marie. Didn't he tell you?'

'I don't think so,' said Miss Pevensie. 'What did he say?'

'He said you were his friend.'

She smiled. 'That's right,' she said. 'He's in the room next to mine at college. What else did he say?'

'He said … Well, he said that you could—like in a book— he said you could avoid the consequences. Like if you'd done something wrong.'

'Oh.'

'Is that true?' I said.

Miss Pevensie smiled. She shook her head. 'No,' she said. 'No, that's not true at all.' Then from beneath her robes, she drew a mirror, just like the one Kat kept on her dressing table. She peered into it. 'Let's have one more go, shall we? Your turn to ask a question.'

I looked at the mirror. 'What's the opposite of reflection?' I said.

'Let's find out,' she said optimistically. 'Pick a card.'

I did and handed it to her. Again she held it close to the candle but then sighed. 'Lordy,' she said. 'Whoever thought red ink, blue card and candlelight would be a good combination, eh, Peter? He'd've been better off writing them in Braille. Listen, would you mind if I … ?'

No, I didn't mind.

She stood and went to the entrance, pulling back the flap and a large slab of daylight crashed into the tent. She spent several minutes wedging the heavy material behind the tent pole and then she took off her shawl and slipped off her robe. Underneath she was wearing jeans and a T-shirt just like a proper person. I mean, not like a fortune-teller. Or a teacher.

She sat down and ran her fingers back through her hair leaving some of it pushed up into the air. She was very pretty. 'That's better,' she said. 'A little less mystical, perhaps, but ... Anyway, where were we? Oh, yes: Peter, your question again?'

I cleared my throat. 'What's the opposite of reflection?'

You must look deeper than the glass to find the truth obscure,
'Tis not the consequences of our deeds alone which we endure.
You see the world you choose to see within the mirror's frame,
But tales you tell with your left hand will seldom seem the same.

Well, I couldn't see what was wrong with being left-handed.

'Look,' Miss Pevensie turned the mirror towards me, 'your face is pressed against the glass.'

'It's broken,' I said. All the cracks made me look like an old man.

'Look closer,' said Miss Pevensie pushing the broken mirror towards me. 'Open your eyes. What do you see?'

The sudden daylight had dazzled me but I looked deep into the mirror until my eyes were crossed. 'It's me,' I said. 'I'm the opposite of my reflection.' I stared at her. I felt very strange and a bit frightened although I didn't know why. 'What does it mean?' I said.

'It means ...' Miss Pevensie looked unsure, puffing out her cheeks again and scanning the red ink for clues. 'Look, Peter, the universe is full of things: things and things that happen and some things that don't. And sometimes things mean something but, sometimes, some things, well, they don't really mean anything at all.'

'But it does,' I said. 'It does.' I knew what it meant. 'It means I have to find the secret about Alice.'

'Sometimes, Peter, secrets are secrets for a reason,' said Miss Pevensie. And then, with a sigh, she folded the card and tucked it into her jeans pocket. 'I think you were right, Peter. It's like you said: it's just a joke.' And then, 'Knock-knock,' she said.

'Who's there?'

'Oh,' she seemed startled but then she said, 'Well, it's like *I* said, Peter: sometimes it's best not to know.'

I burst out of the tent, dizzy with confusion, and ran straight into the middle of Miss Drew and the Amberley Ballet Group. Parents tut-tutted as I fought my way free of pink taffeta. All around me stalls were being folded away and their contents packed into boxes.

I chased after Tommie as fast as I could.

25

'How's my favourite boy?' asked Kat, hugging me from behind whilst I sat at the kitchen table, making me jump about a mile and a half. She planted a loud, wet kiss under my ear.

It was a hot afternoon and she'd been locked in her workshop all morning, suddenly appearing with a grin like she'd won the pools and humming along to the radio.

'What are you doing?' she asked.

Well, she could tell what I was doing just by looking, couldn't she? With Tommie at his dad's and Anna-Marie spending her last day in solitary confinement, I'd settled down to stick Tommie's latest list into my scrapbook and to write about some of the things that had happened. I'd even written down all those things Miss Pevensie had said—as much as I could remember: it'd taken ages. So, anyway, I had my book spread open on the table and bits of paper and a tub of glue with a gunky glue-stick poking out the top and Kat made a joke of peering over my shoulder. I had to keep skidding my book around the table and covering it over like that man at *The Copper Kettle*. It was sort of funny at first but I was glad when she gave up.

'What do you keep in there, Peter?' she asked tapping me on the head with her knuckle. I wanted to say it was a secret but even that was a kind of secret. She wasn't the only one with secrets, you know. 'I wish you'd let me see,' she said, and then grabbed the top piece of paper waving away my hand as I tried to take it back. She squinted at what I'd written, her face all puzzled. 'I can't even read your writing,' she said. That was because I kind of wrote everything backwards like in a mirror (but that was a secret too).

She handed me back the paper but pretending like she was going to tug it away again. She looked a little sad as she said, 'I wish I knew what went on in that head of yours,' before clapping twice and, 'Anyway,' smiling again, 'where's the Dynamic Duo? I haven't seen Anna-Marie in ages.' I told her I was on my own. I hadn't told her anything about Anna-Marie's punishment obviously.

'Marvellous,' she cried. 'I'll put the kettle on and we can have a catch-up. You can tell me everything you've been up to.' She went to the sink to fill the kettle, spoon tea-leaves into the pot and arrange cup, saucer and spoon. 'Or maybe you want to ask me something.'

Well, I wanted to ask about Alice. Of course I did. But how could I? Everything I knew I knew because of, well, you know, subterfuge, just like Norman said. What would Kat say if she found out? Well, that much I didn't want to find out. If Alice was my sister, then why had no one ever said anything about her? It was this big secret and I wasn't supposed to know and I certainly wasn't supposed to be going around trying to find out.

So, instead I said, 'Will you tell me about Dad?'

She turned around to look at me. 'I might,' she said, slipping a hand into her front pocket. 'That would depend on what you wanted to know.' Standing with the kitchen window behind her, her hair shone like copper.

'I don't know,' I said. 'Just talk about him.'

'Well, okay. Let's see.' She folded her arms, the tip of her tongue touching her top lip. 'He was an amazing man your father,' she said. 'Have you heard the expression: still waters run deep? Well, it means that he was calm on the surface but, well, underneath … He never talked about the war. He would never say what he'd seen or what he'd done.'

'Did you ask him?'

'Why, when it caused him so much pain? But it made him the man he was. I suppose I thought I had a whole lifetime to find out but, well …

'He was a good looking man your dad—dashing—everybody said so. He had a bearing. Do you know what I mean by that? It means like he had a presence.' She poured me an orange squash, filling the glass with shiny water from the tap. It tasted sweet and syrupy. 'It's hard to explain,' she went on. 'It was the war, I suppose, all that marching up and down and parades and whatever. He never lost it. Even when he was …

'Are you sure you want to hear this?'

'Yes.'

'Well, he wasn't just good looking either; he was clever too. It's not always easy to tell the people who are genuinely clever from people who just surround themselves with cleverness. But I always knew with your dad: you could see it in his eyes.'

Kat's own eyes grew smoky as she remembered my father, memories billowing and merging with the steam erupting from the kettle. She turned her back to me and unplugged the kettle before pouring the hot silver water. 'After the things he'd seen in the war it,' she said, gently shaking the tea-pot and gazing out of the window to the garden, 'it made him a better man, I think. He was a brave man. He wouldn't talk about the war. He wouldn't even talk about his dreams and I know he dreamt about it. How could he not? Maybe you have to see the worse things, the worse things people can do before you can forgive. When you've seen real cruelty maybe, maybe it puts, I don't know, foolishness into perspective. But I was never like that, I'm afraid. I couldn't forgive,' she looked at me over her shoulder, her eyes suddenly sharp, 'indifference,' before returning to pouring her tea.

Kat took a tissue from the box on the windowsill and blew her nose. She brought her tea to the table, and biscuits, those mint ones with their own tin-foil wrappers, and the tissues scrunched under her arm. I noticed that her eyes were red, but not in an angry way. She sat down and studied her hands.

'Sometimes I have such wonderful dreams,' she said, 'you, your dad … All of us together. Sometimes the shock of waking up is … But then, I guess, if I didn't wake up I'd never've known I was dreaming. I dream he's still alive, just sitting in an empty chair and we talk … I forget he's supposed to be dead, you see, and it's the most natural thing in the world,' and as she spoke it really was like he was there, 'and we talk about things and we talk about you,' listening to what Kat was saying, nodding like he used to and pinching my ear when I wasn't looking, 'the family, the future. We were so happy here.' And then she smiled like it was all a bit silly. 'But then you can do anything in dreams, can't you?' she said. 'Be anything. It's like there's never any—'

'Consequences,' I said taking her by surprise. 'Maybe that's how you tell the difference. I mean between dreams and when you're awake. In dreams there aren't any consequences.'

'Well, I suppose so,' murmured Kat, 'but it's all very well talking about consequences—I mean consequences in real life—as if you can always tell what they're going to be. Yes, sometimes it's like, I don't know, sure, you push a button and a bell rings but other times you can push a button and a bomb goes off, you know, kaboom!,' her hands opened like an explosion, 'blowing everything to kingdom come. It's not like you ever even know which button is which.'

She blew away the steam before taking a sip of her dark brown tea.

'But if we were so happy ... I mean, do you know why we left Amberley?'

She didn't say anything for such a long time that I thought she can't've heard me, but then she said: 'Phew, what a question. Are you sure you wouldn't rather know where babies come from or something like that?' but she was only joking. 'Are you sorry we left?'

I shrugged.

'You're just like your dad, Peter. Did you know that? Still waters. You just sit there and listen, digging elephant traps for people, and they rabbit on, ten to the dozen, all the things they should probably keep to themselves.' She reached out and patted me gently on the arm and then left her hand there a moment longer like she was just touching me to make sure I was real. Then she took her hand away and wrapped it back around her tea-cup.

'You had everything here, Peter,' she said. 'Who couldn't love living here? You had a lovely home and parents who adored you. You even had a mad grandmother who thought the sun shone out of your tiny—'

'So, why did we leave?'

Kat hesitated just a moment before, 'Sometimes,' she said, handing me a biscuit and unwrapping one for herself, 'things happen.'

'Like consequences,' I said.

'Since when did you start worrying about consequences, Peter?' she said. 'Oh, Lord, it's Pinky and Perky all over again.' She bit into the biscuit leaving the shape of her teeth in the soft chocolate coating. 'But, yes, I suppose you're right. But then you shouldn't cry about the past. That's what everyone says. Well, maybe you can cry just a little bit but it's spilt milk, they say. And all you can really do is mop it up and start again.' As she spoke she squeezed the tin-foil into a tiny ball and popped it on the table. 'And, I don't know, buy more milk and not make the same mistakes next time.' She took a tissue from the box and sniffed.

I didn't think that she'd really answered my question.

'But why did I come back here?' I asked.

'Don't you like it here?'

I nodded although really I wasn't sure how much I did like Amberley. It seemed such a strange place. I don't know what my face looked like but suddenly Kat leant forward, her eyes glowing like light-bulbs.

'Go on,' she said, excited, just like a kid. 'What have you been up to? What have you found? What have you seen?'

It was almost like she wanted me to tell her. I pushed my whole biscuit into my mouth and made a face that said: 'Like what?'

'I don't know,' she said. 'When I was your age we used to go up and down all day long, looking in every hedge for things we shouldn't know about. What about you? You can tell me anything, you know.'

Except I couldn't, could I? 'No,' I said. 'Nothing.'

She seemed disappointed. 'Perhaps you're not looking hard enough,' she said. 'There's secrets under every bush round here. Some of them are right under your nose. Sometimes you just have to lift the stones,' I couldn't help thinking about Mr Merridew's stones, 'stones that are staring you right in the face to find something ... really interesting.'

Like I said, it was almost like she wanted me to tell her.

'Well, anyway,' went on Kat, 'I'll tell you why I brought you back to Amberley, shall I?' I nodded. 'There are three things you can do in life, Peter, when you're faced with … problems.'

'What?'

'You can stand your ground and look them in the eye,' and she stared fiercely at her imaginary problem, poking it in the face with her sharp nail. I nodded again. 'You can walk away.' I nodded a third time. 'Or you can run,' she said, 'as fast as you can.'

'What did you do?' I asked.

'Oh, I ran,' she laughed. 'I ran away from here,' and she glanced around at the yellow walls and the brown cupboards, 'and then I ran straight back. That's why we ended up back here. Listen, do you remember when you used to run to your room and hide? At the old house? Well, Amberley is *my* room and Everlasting Lane is my sheets. This cottage is my blanket. Do you understand?'

And I nodded again. I really did understand. And then I said, 'Why is it called Everlasting Lane?' I'd asked her once before but she'd never really answered that either.

She looked surprised. 'Haven't you worked it out yet? Why do you think? Remember what I told you before: a name is important …' She meant it like a clue.

I screwed up my forehead like a tin-foil wrapper but it was like long multiplication; a sum I couldn't answer.

'Can I tell you a story?' she said, and settled back in her chair like one of those people off *Jackanory*. She cleared her throat. 'Are you sitting comfortably etc.? Well, once, when I was a little girl, my mother, your grandmother, took me on a trip to see some aunt or uncle or something. We went on a train. I remember it was really boring shunting through all these little stations and everything. But then we came to one station and I was just staring out of the window, minding my own business, and there was this pole or post, you know, quite wide, supporting the roof over the station and behind it was this brick wall and there was this man walking along the platform and as he was walking along he passed behind the post but, and this was the thing that caught my attention, he didn't come out the other side.' I gasped. 'Just like that,' she said. 'And it was like he'd disappeared. And then another man, coming from the other direction, did the same thing: he just passed behind the post and poof he was gone.'

'Where were they going?'

'Well, I didn't know. And then another man, a completely different man, just appeared from behind the pole and walked off down the platform. It was the strangest thing. It was as if he'd come out of nowhere. Well, you can imagine. I started pulling at my mother's coat and saying what I'd seen but she was reading one of those trashy books she always read and she was all: "Kat, stop it! Stop it! Karen Angela Goodwin, I'm talking to you!" ' And Kat flapped her hands about just like my mum used to do.

'Anyway,' Kat went on, 'at last, and it probably wasn't even more than a minute or two, the train started to pull out and I could see what was behind the post.'

'What?' I said. 'What was it?'

'It was the entrance to the gents' toilets,' and then she laughed. 'What I mean, Peter, is that I knew it must be something like that; that there was some kind of explanation like a hidden door or ... something. I wasn't *that* little but,' she said, 'for just a minute it was nice to think that maybe the world was a little bit different to what it normally was; a little more magical. Because that's what magic is, isn't it? It's a mystery. It's just what we call something that we don't know or understand like I didn't know what was going on behind the post because I couldn't see.'

'Like a secret,' I said.

Kat shrugged. 'Yes, I suppose.' But that didn't make any sense. I must've looked awfully confused because she said, 'What's wrong?'

'Well,' I said, 'you said magic was like a mystery. Well, a mystery is like a secret and a secret is just another word for the truth so then magic must be true.'

'Well,' she said, and her eyes twinkled like Melanie's birthday candles, 'I suppose it must be.'

'I thought it was all pretend.'

Kat was startled. 'Of course not. Aren't you alive? How magical is that? Haven't you ever seen a ... a butterfly? Haven't you seen a sunrise or a sunset? Peter, magic is all around you all the time, every day. Not just you but everybody. And, if you don't think it's magic, well, maybe you're setting your sights too high.'

She shook her head. 'No, magic's real enough. Look, think about the name: Everlasting Lane. It's just a lane, just a road and in some places it's barely even that, but you make it so much more. You, Peter. That's not boring or mundane or whatever the opposite of magic is. That's real. Only children can do that. When you get to my age nothing seems possible any more. You're stuck. The idea that you can just change your name and ... That's absurd. But you did it. You made me better than I was. Without you nothing would be possible.

'People don't just change their names, change their lives. I mean they can try but it's not going to work unless someone else believes them. Adults never believe—well, hardly any— but you did. I mean I envy you, Peter. I really do. You just close your eyes—and sometimes you don't even do that—and you're somewhere else entirely. You're some*one* else entirely and all that stuff that worries the rest of us, keeps us awake at nights, well, it doesn't matter to you at all. If that's not magic, I don't know what is.

'Look,' said Kat, 'do you remember this?' and she took two of the tin-foil wrappers that she'd rolled like thin sausages. She wrapped one around a finger on each hand like rings. 'Daddy used to do it.'

'I remember,' I said.

She seemed surprised but said, 'Okay, now watch carefully,' and then she did that rhyme. 'Two little butterflies sitting on a wall,' and as she sang it she wriggled her butterfly fingers in time, 'One named Peter, one named Paul. Fly away, Peter,' and her right hand fluttered up into the air like it was flying before returning to its perch on the table's edge. 'Fly away, Paul,' and her left hand too soared and swooped retaking its place alongside Peter. Both fingers were now naked, their rings gone.

'It's just a trick,' I said. 'You've swapped fingers.'

Slowly, slowly Kat revealed the rest of her hands, placing them out-stretched either side of her tea-cup. The rings were nowhere to be seen.

I felt my eyes grow big. 'That's … Is that magic?'

Kat smiled. 'Maybe,' she said, 'or maybe it's just a better trick.'

26

'People don't like it though,' Kat said as she collected the little silver balls and sausages of foil and popped them into her empty tea-cup. 'They have to give it a name or let somebody else give it a name for them. A name like 'God' maybe or 'Allah' or whatever but as soon as you give it a name you make it small. That's what I think. You take away the wonder and the mystery. You're saying, like, this *isn't* so special because some old man with a beard made it. And once you think you've solved the mystery it turns to dust anyway. It all depends on where you're standing.'

'Like cows,' I said.

'If you like,' said Kat. 'Sometimes mysteries are better left unexplained. They're only interesting because they *are* mysteries.'

'Sometimes,' I said, 'it all seems like a dream.'

Kat smiled. 'Real world, dream world. It's like I said: sometimes it's hard to tell the difference. You've heard the expression, 'he's not all there,' haven't you?' I nodded. 'Well, it's a bit like that. Those people aren't mad, they're just not *all there*. They're half here and half somewhere else. But they live a life, a complete life, just like you and me, only half of it's lived here; the other half somewhere else. The mistake so called *sane* people make is to think the part that's not here isn't anywhere. It is. And who's to say that that somewhere isn't just as important as here.

'It's like you, Peter: sometimes I look at you and you're like ... Where do you go when you're not here, Peter?'

I blinked. I didn't know what to say.

'What I meant to say,' said Kat, 'was how Christians and people like that are the same: they're only half here. Of course, they don't see it. They don't think *their* reality is any less real than ours. In fact, they probably think theirs is *more* real, and they don't suffer for a lack of reality any more than a, I don't know, a badger suffers for the lack of the latest David Cassidy album.'

'That sounds a bit like Mrs Carpenter,' I said. 'She believes in God, but she's cross all the time.'

'It's not enough for some people,' said Kat nodding, 'living for living's sake. They give it a name like "God". But you have to pity those people not resent them. After all, "God" is just another word for "Help!" He's a way of hiding the truth, hiding the madness, but it's a bit like trying to hide World War Two.

'You see, it's all random, it's all chance; beauty, ugliness, pain and suffering, whatever. It's all chaos, but that doesn't mean you shouldn't revel in beauty and recoil from the rest.'

She stood up and took her cup and my glass to the sink. I was worried that the conversation might be over so I said, 'What's your biggest secret?' I made it sound just a normal question.

Kat sighed. It wasn't a little sigh either but a sigh like rolling a boulder up a mountain. 'How much I love you,' she said, 'in spite of everything.'

Well, I wasn't sure about that. I thought about Alice and the secret room and, well, everything. I didn't think she was telling me the truth at all.

'I'll tell you what,' said Kat. 'Come to the workshop. I've got something to show you.'

The workshop was just like it'd been when I'd first seen it: all boxes and junk. The only new thing was a large light on a stand glaring at the object—Kat's sculpture—beneath its canvas sheet. It looked like a mountain, one side in daylight, the other washed in night time.

'This is why I was smiling,' said Kat. 'I've finished it,' and she gripped the corner of the sheet. 'Do you want to see?'

Of course I did.

She took the sheet, and my breath, away.

'It's … It's so,' being a boy, I didn't want to say, 'beautiful,' but once I had I knew that no other word would have done.

It was a wing, a butterfly's wing, emerging from the heart of the rough, knotted slice of tree trunk as if from a cocoon, or uncurling like a petal beneath the rising sun, so fine you could dry tears with it. I looked at it and felt a thrill in my heart. I couldn't believe *she* had made this.

'It's,' I didn't know what to say, 'really good.'

You know how a television show is sort of 3-D even though the screen is flat? It was like that. Although it wasn't alive and it didn't move, although it was carved from a single piece of wood it was like life, movement and colour. It captured a moment of time, a moment of time when magic was possible, like a reflection in a flowing river.

'Why do you like them so much?'

'What? Like what?'

'Butterflies,' I said. I'd always wanted to ask her.

Kat looked puzzled for a moment but not in a bad way. It was like she was thinking how to answer. And then she said, 'It's like I was saying before about when I was a little girl. I always wanted to believe in ... something, I suppose. Something magical. And butterflies, well, how could the universe just roll the dice and come up with something so beautiful. I mean, what are the chances, Peter?'

I didn't know.

'I think we're all of us, most of us, like caterpillars. You know, we just eat and crawl along and hope we're not going to get finished off by the first available sparrow. But, if we're lucky, we get a second chance. Do you know what I mean? I mean, we can change. If we're lucky, really lucky, we can be butterflies.'

'You mean like when we die.'

'No, no. I mean when we're alive. It's—'

'It's like laughing your head off,' I said, 'but not literally.'

'Yes,' she said. And then she laughed. 'Something like that. I mean, some people are caterpillars their whole life. They can't help it: they're just born that way. But other people, people like your dad, maybe ... Whatever he went through in his life—how ever horrible it must've been—it changed him. But it changed him for the better.'

'What about me?' I said.

'Oh, you're like me,' she said. 'You're a caterpillar. But what'll it be like when you get a second chance? Think what it'll be like to fly.'

'Do people get second chances?'

Kat hesitated. And then she said, 'Have you ever wondered what would have happened if your dad had been killed in the war? Millions were. You wouldn't be here because he wouldn't be here. What if *I'd* never been born? You just wouldn't exist.'

'But I do exist.'

'Because dad was lucky. Millions weren't. You were lucky. You got your chance: your first chance.'

'But I *do* exist. So, even if I didn't exist I'd exist somehow, wouldn't I?'

'Oh, sweet, I don't know about that. I don't see how. Do you have any idea how many people *don't* exist. If everybody who'd never been born still existed somewhere? How many ways in which the world might be different?'

'Well, maybe that's where the people who aren't all there go the rest of the time.'

Kat smiled. 'That's a nice thought. It's nice to think that they've got company. But listen, Peter, we can't change stuff that's happened,' she said, gently touching the wing of her creation. 'It's not like writing a story where you can have as many goes as you like to get it right. You can't just put in the things you want, like in your scrapbook, and leave out the things you don't want …

'Imagine you had a jewel,' she said. 'Oh, the most precious jewel in the world. And somebody stole it from you; just took it away. Maybe they didn't even mean to take it. Say, it was a joke or a game, but once the jewel had gone—'

'But you could go to the person who stole it,' I interrupted. 'I mean, if it wasn't on purpose, then they might give it back.'

'But it got broken, Peter. Shattered into a billion pieces.'

'Well, maybe they could stick it back—'

'Not this jewel, Peter. No.'

'Well, then,' I didn't know what to say, 'maybe there's nothing—'

'But they could say sorry, Peter.'

'Well, yes, but you still wouldn't get it back—'

'No, but I … but you could see that the person was sad too and that they knew how sad they'd made you and that would help, wouldn't it? But imagine if they didn't even care. Not one bit. They couldn't even be bothered to remember what they'd done. Wouldn't that make you sad, Peter? Wouldn't that be the saddest thing in the world?

'Why would someone do that, Peter? Can you think? Why would someone not explain why they did something?' She was speaking quickly, her words tumbling into each other like circus clowns. 'And even if they couldn't answer or explain or … justify what they'd done,' she cried, 'wouldn't they at least say sorry?' with fire in her eyes. 'Wouldn't they at least admit that they'd been wrong?' It was like when she was talking about her sculpture. 'Why wouldn't they say that, Peter?'

'Maybe they're mean,' I said, 'or cruel or—'

'Cruel is only the beginning, Peter. Cruel is only the first word in the dictionary.

'If you'd done something, Peter, something wrong, you'd tell me, wouldn't you?'

I nodded.

'Anything at all? I mean, even if you thought it'd make me angry,' she seized my hand, squeezed it tight, 'if you had to choose between doing the right thing or the wrong thing?'

'Yes,' I said, but my voice was kind of squeaky when I said it. Pinky and Perky squeaky. Would it be easy to know what was the right thing and what was wrong?

'And if it made me very sad, this thing, would you be sorry?'

'Yes,' I said. Of course.

'Well,' and she hesitated, 'is there anything you want to tell me about? Right now?'

But I could hardly think where to start: I thought about the vase but that wasn't really my fault, and I thought about the Beast and the secret room and each of them made my face blaze in shame.

'No,' I said.

'You're such a tease, do you know that, Peter.' Her voice

was cracking like that broken mirror. 'There's only one thing I ever wanted from you. Just one thing. But you never …You don't even …'

'What is it?' I said. 'What is it?'

'See? You don't even remember.'

'You know, Peter, the greatest loss, the hardest loss to accept, is the loss of something you never had: something that you thought was yours, something so close you could touch it and hold it. And then to have it just ripped away as if it was never there. Do you know what I mean?'

Kat stood for a moment, as still as her sculpture, before taking the edge of the canvas and drawing it back over the butterfly. 'I'm sorry,' she said, 'about what I said earlier. I mean, when I said how loving you was my biggest secret. I mean, I'm sorry I kept it a secret for so long.'

And I said, 'I love you too.'

I would have done anything for her. Anything. Except that's only what I thought because when it came to it and I had to choose, I didn't do the right thing for her at all. I mean she was important and Alice was important too, they both were, but it was too late for them, and when it came to it there was someone else, someone just as important that I could still help.

If you see what I mean.

Kat put her hand on my head and ruffled my hair. 'What am I going to do with you, blue-eyes?' she said.

I smiled too and said, 'We could ask Mummy.'

And then she gave me the funniest look. It was like I'd farted or something.

27

So, anyway, I decided I was going to do something nice for Kat. You remember that ring I told you about? I'd been saving my pocket money all term long and, after she'd shown me the butterfly sculpture and told me about my dad and everything, I couldn't think about anything else but buying it for her. So this one morning I clambered out of bed, put on my school uniform as quickly as I could and didn't even stop to have my *Rice Krispies* or wait for Anna-Marie and Tommie to walk to school.

But when I got to *Kirrins'*: disaster!

A note written on a torn flap of cardboard had been hung on the inside of the glass door: *Gone out! Back in fifteen!* Fifteen? Fifteen what? Fifteen seconds? Fifteen hours?

I placed my school-bag and my piggybank on the ground and began to bang on the door, politely at first but then louder and louder until I was unleashing tiny, little fists of fury. There was no point, of course. The sign was quite clear: GONE OUT! But I banged anyway until the glass rattled and the frame shook, not because I thought it would change anything but because, well, it was all I could do.

But then I looked up to see Norman, Norman Kirrin, frail and pale, blinking at me through the glass. He reached up quickly and then down shoving back the bolts and opening the door, saying, 'Peter, Peter, where's the fire?' and glancing from one side to the other as if checking that I wasn't the first in a long queue sneaking all the way back to Buckingham Lane. And then he wrapped his arms around me and stroked my hair until, as my fury began to pass, whispering, 'Calm down, Peter,' and, 'It's all right.'

As my trembling faded he said, 'Tell me, Peter, do you never read signs or is it just their content you ignore?' but he didn't sound unkind. 'My brother's out,' he said, 'apparently. And I was just out for a walk myself ...'

But he placed his hand on my shoulder and led me into the shop. Once inside he pulled open a can of fizzy drink and pushed it into my hand. I took a deep drink and burped back the bubbles. Chuckling, Norman returned to the door and re-bolted it before pulling down this blind so that we couldn't be seen. He shuffled behind the counter and rung up the cost of the drink. When the till's little drawer popped open he dropped a few pennies in.

'I have learnt to my chagrin,' he explained, 'that Greg is mightily fastidious in his totting up.' He looked me up and down. It was kind of as if I was someone in disguise that he only half recognised. 'So,' he said, 'to what do I owe the pleasure, and it always is a pleasure, Peter, of your visit?'

I thrust my piggybank at him. 'I want to buy—'

But he held up his hand. 'Peter, before you go any further,' he said, 'I have what you might call a small confession to make. You see, I hate to admit it to you, Peter,' he murmured, scratching his jaw all peppery with stubble, 'you of all people but I'm ... Well, I'm not really supposed to serve. Greg doesn't like it.'

'I only want one thing,' I said.

'Well,' he twitched, 'I suppose, as it's you,' and then gave a little smile. 'I'm a bit rusty,' clapping his hands together, 'but in the tradition of this proud nation of shopkeepers,' he placed his knuckles on the counter and struck a pose before saying in this London accent: 'What can I do you for?'

I grinned before turning and rushing to the back of the shop. I was suddenly filled with terror that the ring—that precious ring—would have gone, snapped up by some passing millionairess, her fat fingers already crusty with jewellery. But, no, it was there just like always. I grabbed it, relieved but a little disappointed at how light it felt, and carried it back to Norman. He looked surprised as I tipped it into his open palm.

'Is this it?' he said. 'Are you sure?' I nodded. 'This is what all the banging and yelling was for?' Again I nodded. He held it up to the light, squinting, and then moved his glasses kind of back and forth as he examined it. 'Well, Peter,' he said at last, 'I quite understand.' He nodded wisely. 'It's a very fine piece. What Greg is playing at leaving such a valuable accoutrement at the back of the shop with the toys and games, I can't imagine.' And then he smiled. 'That'll be fifty new pences,' he said, as he dropped the ring into a tiny bag.

'Doesn't it come with a box?'

'Erm, I'm sorry, Peter. I strongly suspect that it doesn't.' He smiled again. 'But this little bag, although it may seem like paper to you and me,' he leant towards me and whispered, 'is in fact spun from the finest Moroccan silk. Okay?'

Absolutely. I popped open the cork that was stuck in the pig's tummy and gently shook until the right money had rattled into my hand. I handed it over. Fifty pence wasn't nearly as much as I'd thought.

'So,' said Norman as he pushed the big buttons on the till, 'how's it going in the world of secrets?'

Well, I just stared at him, didn't I? I didn't know what to say. What could I say? What would you have said? I didn't want to know about secrets anymore. I didn't even want to think about secrets. And, well, it was like what Miss Pevensie'd said: sometimes secrets are secrets for a reason.

He stared right back as if he was listening, as if I was actually telling him everything with just the look on my face. Eventually he nodded. 'I see,' he said. 'So, is that it?' He pushed the till drawer to a close, my money still in his hand. 'Is that the end of the matter?'

I nodded. And then I smiled. I mean I really tried to smile.

'I wonder,' said Norman. 'Listen, Peter,' he placed my coins on the counter and slid them slowly back towards me, 'before we conclude out transaction, I wonder if … You see, I am of the persuasion that believes, as an article of faith, in fact, that, on occasion, it's perhaps hard to tell whether you've actually really solved a problem or whether you've simply managed to convince yourself, erroneously, that it wasn't such a very big problem in the first place.' He sighed and ran his hand through his thin grey hair. 'Do you know what I mean?'

I didn't say anything. I did know what he meant. Of course I did. I just wasn't sure I wanted to. My smile was beginning to hurt a bit, like my face was about to break.

'Tell me, Peter, did I ever tell you about Lois? No, no, don't worry. I know full well I did. But I didn't … I didn't go into the detail, did I? No, Norman, not the nitty-gritty, you didn't. And, well, I wouldn't now, but … I don't want you to make a mistake. You need to be sure that you can just pack everything back in the box, your … box of secrets, and that it won't … explode in your face.'

'But I need to—'

'No, no,' he said waving his hand. 'Hush. Listen, Peter, I wouldn't … I'd be failing in my responsibilities as … a friend? We are friends aren't we, Peter?' I nodded. Of course. 'As a human being even if I just … I don't know what you've found out. It's not … I wouldn't expect you to tell me … I'm not asking but … If you can spare me five minutes, I'd like to …' And then he looked at me as if he'd asked me a question and was waiting for an answer, but before I could—

'The last time I saw her was in Hyde Park in London. Nineteen-forty-two. I think I may have told you. I asked her to marry me. I mean I didn't know anything about … anything. But it wouldn't've bothered me, I swear. I swear to you, Peter. I wanted to be with her and her to be with me, do you understand?

'But she turned me down. Flat. Pancake-flat. And what could I do? I tried again, of course. And again and again. You tried, Norman, you can't deny that. Again and again. Lord, I tried to find the combination of words, the right combination that would make the difference, that would help her make that choice, to my mind the right choice, but, of course, in retrospect she may have felt that …

And she smiles, feet planted firmly on spring's fertile ground,
Whilst I have one foot in winter all the year round.

'Because what I haven't told you yet and what I didn't know at the time was that Lois was pregnant. With all due respect, Peter, I will leave the birds and bees to others more qualified and move swiftly on. Suffice to say, when the butcher's family found out, the mother, the fearsome matriarch, appropriately bacon-faced, stepped in. There's this thing called … called an abortion. It means that if a lady gets, well, pregnant and doesn't want to be the doctors can take the baby away.'

'Didn't she want a baby?'

'Oh, Peter, it was a different world then. You can't imagine. It was a terrible thing to have a baby without being married. Sometimes the lady's parents might throw her out on the street. Sometimes they'd send her away to get rid of it.'

'Get rid of it?'

'Well, the butchers were scandalised. They couldn't abide any kind of scandal, so they insisted Lois have an abortion. And Lois, bless her, was only too willing to please which, I suppose, was pretty much her problem in the first place. The problem was, Peter, that abortions were, well, illegal. You know what 'illegal' means, don't you?'

'It means you can go to prison.'

'Exactly,' said Norman. 'Any doctor who performed an abortion could go to prison. But there was something called a backstreet abortionist … Certain men or, indeed, women who circumvented the … But not all of *them* knew what they were doing. When Lois had her abortion, the man—the man in Leeds, of all places—well, anyway, the man who did it made such a mess that she … Well, she …' He made a funny noise like a sob. He pulled a scraggy old hanky from his pocket, buried his nose in it and blew. 'I'm sorry, Peter,' he said. 'Her mother, Lois' mother, collected her from the train. Her coat, Lois' coat, was soaked with blood. Swimming in blood. She was in such pain … I …'

Norman was shaking, his hands squeezing the handker-chief dry. He took a deep breath, almost a gasp, almost a cry, and thumped his chest. I thought he might be about to faint but instead he fiercely gripped the edge of the counter and looked at me, his eyes sticking to me like beach tar.

'Because it's love, Peter. It's love and it doesn't matter what the person you love has done. You should forgive. No!' he barked. 'Not 'should'. You *will* forgive because you have no choice. If it's love, Peter, then you have no choice. The good Lord in all his infinite generosity denies you that.'

'But I thought … Don't you have to choose?'

'Yes!' he cried. 'Yes, of course you have to choose. But you have to choose when a choice is presented and sometimes …'

Well, there isn't always a choice to be made. Sometimes there's a choice and sometimes, well, the choice is out of your hands. The trick, you tell him, Norman, yes, the real trick, is to know the difference. What I'm trying to say, in my round-about way, ha, my merry-go-round way, is that it's not just the consequences of your own choices which you have to endure.'

I wanted to go. I needed to go. Mr Gale would be reading the register and scowling when I didn't answer my name but then maybe Norman was right and, sometimes, like he said, you don't really have a choice even when you think you do.

'Well, in the end I gave up, of course,' said Norman. 'We're back in Hyde Park now by the way. That was the choice I made: to give up. That was my failure. How noble I was. "So, marry your butcher," I said. "Marry the sausage-man." What else could I say? I don't know, but I should have … I should have persisted. I didn't know … I should have slung her over my shoulder and carried her off, caveman-style, shouldn't I?' He shook his head. 'No,' he said. 'No, of course I shouldn't. You're right. Such an act would've been philistine but, in retrospect, maybe …' He blew his nose again, a big raspberry blow. 'When one has a choice one shouldn't be … timid.'

Norman sighed. He pressed down on the till and—cha-ching!—rung up fifty pence. He scooped my money across the counter into his other hand and dropped them in. I smiled with relief, seized the little bag and shoved it down deep into my pocket. Now all I needed was to the right moment to—

But, 'Remember, Peter,' said Norman, 'it's not just the things you do. Sometimes it's the things you don't do, the things you know you should've done. When you get to my age, Peter, when you reach this lofty summit, you'll regret the things you didn't do, not the things you did.'

28

'A brilliant pass by Lambert.' I pumped the ball goalwards. 'Straight to Lambert's feet. He's only got the goalie to beat.' A cheer rose in the crowd's throat but, as I prepared to shoot, I was battered from behind by a concrete bollard called Tommie. 'A shocking tackle by Chopper Winslow!' I fell to the ground crippled, clutching my leg.

Team-mates rushed to my assistance, the commentator raged and the referee reached for his reddest card. Meanwhile, United's burly centre back stood with his hands on his hips. 'Peter,' he spat, 'you're such a poof. I hardly touched you,' as I attempted to rub his footprint from my shin. He offered his arm and I hauled myself to my feet.

And retaliated.

'And Lambert's hit Winslow!' gasped the commentator, shocked at the mayhem unfolding on the pitch. The crowd squealed like apes. 'They're wrestling now. What will the referee do?'

The whistle blew like a banshee and the referee yelled, 'Hello, Mungo. Hello, Midge. What are you two bozos up to?'

We sat up, startled. Wembley, the twin towers and a hundred thousand screaming fans blurred and faded. It took me a moment to remember where I was and another to locate—

'Anna-Marie!' exclaimed Tommie.

She was free at last but the expression on her face was grim. She pointed at me. 'You!' she said. 'Kitchen!' she said. 'Now!'

At the kitchen table, Anna-Marie cradled her orange squash, wiping condensation from the rim. Her hair was loose and dry; her skin even paler than usual; the tinny necklace Tommie had bought her at the fair hanging around her neck.

'So,' she said, placing her glass on the table, 'are you ready for your trip to the Lodge, then.'

It wasn't a question.

'Why?'

'I told you, mutton-head,' she said. 'I think there's someone there you might want to see.'

'But who?'

Anna-Marie's face rippled with annoyance. 'Honestly, Peter, don't you remember Mrs Finch's ghost story?'

Ghost story? I couldn't remember ... What was that supposed to mean?

'Didn't you even listen to what you were telling me?' she went on.

'But ghosts aren't real,' protested Tommie.

'Well, we'll just see about that, won't we,' she said, emptying her glass with a confident slurp, 'at the Lodge.'

'But we're always going to the Lodge.'

'You've not been inside before.'

Inside? I shook my head. I wasn't sure it was such a—

'Good idea,' said Tommie.

Typical.

•

Leaving Everlasting Lane we crossed the main Nancarrow Road and turned down towards the Lodge. This side road was all gravel and dust and fell with a steep curve towards the river. Very quickly I lost sense of the road behind us. Here the thick trees and bushes muffled everything but the birds and our own stony footsteps. It was calm and peaceful.

'What if someone catches us?'

'We're just visiting.'

That reminded me of that thing you have to say in *Monopoly* when you drive past the jail but you're not actually in jail.

'You haven't even told us who we're going to see.' I had this funny jittery feeling in my tummy. Not ha-ha funny but like I was going to be sick.

'Shut up!' said Anna-Marie. 'It's for your own good.'

She sounded just like Kat when she said that and that reminded me of how Kat had said that that was exactly why I shouldn't go to the Lodge. I hoped I was wrong but I had a horrible feeling that whatever it was Kat wanted me to stay away from and whatever it was Anna-Marie wanted me to go and see might be the same thing. Then I wondered why their advice was so different.

And then I wondered who was right.

The trees grew deeper and darker as we approached the back of the Lodge. I mean the front of course. Its red brick and haphazardy walls were so familiar and I felt a shiver of pleasure when I remembered that first time I'd seen it with Anna-Marie when Tommie had been at his dad's. On this side of the river though we were blocked by thick bushes.

Peering through the leaves, I saw Miss Pevensie, that teacher from school who was pretending to be the fortune-teller. Her frizzy blonde hair was tied back in a bunch and she was pushing at the handlebars of a bicycle in a pink T-shirt and long skirt. Standing upright in the basket on the front of her bike were some thick books and about thirty thin ones like exercise books.

As she approached, a rustling passed through the bushes and trees like a breeze you couldn't feel. Branches cracked and twisted, and trunks seemed to shift in the earth. Leaves, that a moment earlier had seemed too thick and thorny, faded until they were just shades of light revealing a road, a driveway, leading right to the front door of the Lodge. We gasped in wonder. Miss Pevensie mounted her bicycle and passed through the gap. Once through the sole of her sandal scraped her to a halt. We ducked under cover whilst she glanced around as if looking for someone. She didn't see us and after a moment she pushed down hard on her pedal and went on her squeaky way.

Once she'd gone we quickly shuffled through as the leaves and branches started to creak back into shape behind us.

Having admired it so often from afar, we approached the Lodge like it was a church. It was like seeing the page of a storybook made real. The red brick though was older, less shiny than it appeared from the other side of the river. The ivy that clung to the walls made it look older still. Anna-Marie was right after all: there were ghosts here. I could tell. I could see how time had left its footprint in the air like a boot in wet cement.

Anna-Marie approached the big front door and tugged at the handle like it was her own. But it wasn't fooled.

'No, no,' muttered Anna-Marie. 'That's not the one. Come on, there's another one at the side,' which was funny because I didn't remember her ever saying she'd been this close to the Lodge before. She marched off with Tommie and me following to another door, smaller and perhaps more easily tricked. We had to go down some steps to reach it and, again,

Anna-Marie pulled at the brass knob. Again it remained unmoved. Maybe it was like a jail after all. This time, however, like a master thief, stretching on tiptoes, she ran her nimble fingers over the door-frame, and then lifted the mat and then looked under various plant pots. But there was no key.

'Oh well,' said Tommie.

'No,' hissed Anna-Marie seizing his arm. He winced. 'I will *not* be defeated.' She studied the wall that framed the door, tapping the bricks, head cocked to one side, listening. Eventually, 'Aha,' she cried, grinning. She seized the most recently tapped brick and dug her fingers deep into the clay that surrounded it. Her thin fingers wiggled the brick from side to side, slowly prising it from the wall until it came free with a sudden pop leaving a brick-shaped hole. I couldn't help noticing that it wasn't the only one.

Anna-Marie tipped the brick from one hand to the other, testing its weight, before gripping it firmly, shielding her eyes and propelling it against the pane of glass nearest the door handle. The glass shattered and with a few follow-up thrusts the remaining jagged edges were removed. Anna-Marie reached through the hole muttering, 'I will not be defeated.' And then she turned to face us. 'Aha,' she said, 'a key!'

We found ourselves in a kitchen with dark wooden surfaces and a huge white sink. Apart from a few ancient kettles and toasters it appeared abandoned but, at least until Anna-Marie peered into the trembling old fridge—'Yuk!'—clean. Buckets of sun poured through the sealed windows. The air was warm, cosy and curled up like Kitty asleep on my lap.

At least it had been.

'Come on,' said Anna-Marie, taking the handle of the inside door.

'Where to?'

'Well, we didn't come to look at the kitchen.'

'What did we come to look at?'

'It's not a what,' she said with a smile. 'I told you: it's a who.'

'We're going to get in trouble,' I said, 'aren't we?'

Tommie did that clucking like a chicken thing and Anna-Marie's eyes widened. 'Don't worry, poppet,' she said pinching my cheek. 'Listen.' I listened. 'It's as quiet as a graveyard.'

I laughed. A bit. You see, I knew she was trying to be scary.

She led us down a narrow corridor. To one side, high windows welcomed in warm sunlight, to the other we passed three or four doors and pale pictures of fields or oceans. There was dust, deep and crisp and even, on every surface and the air seemed as if it had been undisturbed for so long that the smells of damp didn't know what to do with themselves, cowering beneath the woodwork as we passed. For all her braveness even Anna-Marie flinched at the slightest sound of a gurgled pipe or a squeaked floorboard, and shushed Tommie and me as we tiptoed in silence.

At the far end of the corridor was a wide double door, almost like it was too big for the corridor itself. Anna-Marie grabbed both handles and, with a silent 'Ta-dah,' flung them open. We stepped into a large, and thankfully deserted, room. It was a lounge, I suppose, with a polished floor, chairs and a telly and, to Tommie's delight, a big piano like a grand piano. He went straight to it, lifted the lid and, before Anna-Marie could stop him, hit as many keys as he could.

'Tommie!' she hissed as the deafening, mishmash of notes echoed and faded away. 'We don't want to get thrown out until we're done.'

Now, this was the big room that we could see from the other side of the river. From here, I could look back through the French doors across the lawn, across the river to the point on the opposite bank where, on other days, I might have seen myself squinting with curiosity, wondering if the ghostly face at the window was my reflection or something else. Looking through from this angle, I could see where people had left their fingerprints smudged upon the window. It was odd to be there, on the other side of the mirror, face pressed against the glass.

'Come on,' said Anna-Marie, 'let's look upstairs.'

'What stairs?'

'These stairs.'

To my surprise, although we'd gone back through the same door by which we'd entered we hadn't returned to the narrow corridor but into what seemed to be the entrance hall lurking behind the front door. And there, as Anna-Marie had said, was a flight of stairs. It didn't seem quite right but Anna-Marie was already half way up before Tommie called, 'This isn't right.'

'What's your problem, Tommie?' she snapped. 'You need to relax. Some buildings *do* move about, don't they, Peter?'

'Yes,' I said. 'Some buildings do. I think so.'

I didn't really think that at all but there was no point trying to reason with her when she was in that kind of mood. Besides, I *was* beginning to relax. The Lodge seemed so pure and peaceful. Any ripples I could feel in the air didn't necessarily mean there was someone else in the building. They were only toes wriggling in a stream.

It was a strange place, the Lodge. Walking around it, exploring, was like waking from a dream in the middle of the night. You know the moment when you're not quite sure where you are or who you are, when you still think your dreams are real? When you're lying there wondering where the monsters went? Well, not *that* moment. But you know the next moment when everything falls back into place like the pieces of a jigsaw and you remember who you are and that the monsters are all in your head and that your mum's asleep just across the landing? *That* moment. It was like falling into a warm bath of yourself.

But, it's like, if you have a moment, an instant, any moment, how are you supposed to capture it? It's a bit like trying to catch a butterfly. You can run and cup your hands all you like but when it's gone, it's gone. Your best hope of capturing it, of making that moment last, is to capture it in words, like Norman said or—what's his name?—Craig, not a jar or a net. If you capture it in just the right words, then you can keep it forever. It's better than … What's it called? That yellow stuff they use? Anyway, if not, if you can't capture it, well, it's all pointless anyway and the moment flutters away over the cornfield and into the distance.

Because life is really just a collection of moments. Isn't it? A crowd, a fluttering rabble of butterflies.

29

At the top of the stairs, Anna-Marie, who seemed to know exactly where she was going, turned down another corridor. This one was dark, lit only by cracks of light that sneaked out from behind the edges of the three or four doors that it contained. Anna-Marie was checking the door numbers. She stopped outside the door which had a big silver number four on it. She reached out and turned the handle. The door opened.

'You two wait here,' she said, and slipped into the room. Tommie and I squeezed into the gap and watched her. The room was neat and tidy with two beds, a chair and a desk. There was a little sink against one wall and posters and pictures for decoration. There was a perfumey smell—I mean you could tell it was a lady's room.

Anna-Marie wandered around brushing her hand across the top blanket of one of the beds, rearranging the mugs and spoons on the little tray next to the kettle. There were a few stray biscuit crumbs on the tray and she licked her finger to pick them up and flick them into the wastepaper bin.

She sat down at the desk and began sorting through the contents like a spy in search of secret information, replacing everything just as she found it. Finally, she selected a pen from one of those pots like they make on *Blue Peter*. She studied the nib and, to check that it was in working order, drew a thin line across her finger tip. Then, laying the pen to one side, she took a book—it looked quite new—and opened it slightly, as you do with a new book in a shop, so that you can put it back on the shelf without having to pay for it.

Having treated it so carefully, Tommie and I gasped when, having found the very first page—the one that doesn't really have any writing on it—she tore it from the book. One quick rip.

'Anna-Marie … ?'

'Sssh!'

She replaced the book, reassuring herself that the tear would remain unnoticed, at least until the book was opened, before taking the empty page and writing across it—not much just a few words—before returning the pen to its pot and folding the paper into a small cube. Pushing herself back from the desk she again appeared to be searching, this time finding a little gap between the desktop and the side of the drawers. Her fingers squeezed the square of paper and pushed it into the space, tapping it a couple of times to make sure it was properly wedged. She got up and pushed the chair back into its original position and, with a final glance around the room, closed the door, joining us in the corridor.

'What did you write?' asked Tommie.

'That's for me to know,' said Anna-Marie.

'Well, can we go now?'

'Oh, no,' said Anna-Marie with a shake of her head. 'That was only a diversion. This,' and she pointed to the next door, a big silver five and a name card I couldn't quite read, 'is the one we've come to see.' She tappety-tap-tapped on the door. 'I made enquiries,' she said, 'by telephone,' before cooing, 'Hello.' When there was no answer Anna-Marie reached out with the flat of her hand and pushed against the door, opening it easily.

This room was simple. There were a few shelves but they were empty and the only things hanging from the walls were curtains. There was a bed in one corner and in the other, beside the window, was a chair. And in the chair was an old woman. She looked like a pile of monkey bones bundled into a waxy, wrinkled bag of skin. She was sleeping, her head tipped slightly to one side, her mouth open and sloping, and a bead of dribble trickling down one of the deep trenches in her walnut face. Or maybe she was dead. It was certainly hard to think of her as being real. I mean in the way that I was real or Anna-Marie. Or even Tommie.

But it was funny. Didn't old people surround themselves with souvenirs, just like Tommie had kept that hat from the zoo, to remind themselves of what it was like when they were young and death seemed more like a dream that would never come true? When my father was ill he'd surrounded himself with pictures of me and my mother and other things that he liked, like my first tooth and this little cardigan with pink lace and those butterfly earrings I told you about. He wanted to be close to them so that, I think, if he remembered them well enough when he was alive it would be like he might remember them after he died. Or maybe he thought he could fill himself with so much of what it was to be alive that it would be like he hadn't died at all. The old lady didn't have anything like that but then, I thought, maybe some people didn't want to remember. Or maybe she just wanted to forget.

I was always a bit scared of old people but fascinated too just like I was with vampires and werewolves and other monsters. All those weird creatures who looked like they might be real people but weren't really. They were only reflections of what real people were like. Like that picture of a tiger, I suppose, but one drawn by a four year old with scratchy, dry felt-tips that have had the caps left off.

Anna-Marie stepped up to the chair and bent towards the old woman. 'Hello, Mrs Goodwin,' she said. 'It's Anna-Marie. Anna-Marie Liddell.'

The old woman moved and then her eyes began to fidget around behind her lids. Her head jerked. When her eyes finally blinked open they reminded me a bit of Kat's, grey and smoky, but wet and cloudy like smoke from a fire that's been put out with a tin-bucketful of water.

'Alice?' said the old woman and a glance ricocheted like a pinball between Anna-Marie, Tommie and me: ten thousand points! 'Alice?' Her voice was a froggy-croak, dry like a dusty sand dune.

How did this woman know about Alice?

She—the old woman—reached out and touched Anna-Marie's hand. Her eyes widened further as her spindly fingers traced the ridges of Anna-Marie's knuckles like a blind woman reading that writing that's all lumps and bumps. 'Bless me,' she said. 'You're real.'

'It's me, Mrs Goodwin. It's Anna-Marie. Do you remember? Anna-Marie Liddell.'

Anna-Marie had a lot of smiles and not all of them were very nice: mickey-taking smiles, sarky smiles and smiles when you'd said something stupid. But the smile she smiled now had none of that nasty stuff. It was like an orange with all the pips taken out or a weekend with no homework: just sweetness and kindness.

'Anna-Marie? Is it really? My angel?'

'Yes, Mrs Goodwin. I've brought someone to meet you.'

'Mrs Goodwin?' muttered the old woman. 'Mrs Goodwin?' She laughed like she had sawdust in her throat. 'Nobody calls me that any more, my dear,' she said. 'I'd almost forgotten it was me.' The chair creaked as she shuffled her skinny bottom from side to side. 'They call me Maggie you know, dear. When I was a little girl like you, you see, everybody used to call me Maggie. A name's important, don't you think? The name, or names, you're given; the names you choose. When I was called Maggie,' she said, 'I *was* a Maggie. I *felt* like a Maggie. I used to play in Everlasting Lane and run through the woods like a wild child and up to *Finches*'. Dirty face, dirty hands. And when I was older, you see, I would go up into the fields behind *Cloisters* with,' she chuckled, 'with the boys from the farms.' She just went on and on. It was like listening to the radio. I mean the radio keeps talking whether you're listening or not and she was just the same. 'But when they started calling me Margaret or Mrs Goodwin, you see, or mother, poor Maggie died. They might as well have put me in a brace. It's like being wrapped in chains. It's like being locked away. Such a change,' she murmured. 'Such a change, you'd think I would have noticed it happening. But … no. And now I'm Maggie all over again.'

'Mrs Goodwin?' said Anna-Marie.

' "Would you like a drink, Maggie? Oh, you haven't finished your toast, Maggie. Have you made a mess again, Maggie?" '

'Mrs Goodwin?'

'I sometimes wonder what she would make of me now: little Maggie I mean. Would she think me worthwhile?' The old woman's breath came out of her with a sigh but she looked up at Anna-Marie and grinned like a chimpanzee. 'And how's your mother, dear?' she asked. 'And your father? What a lovely man. And, bless me, who are your friends?'

'This is Tommie,' said Anna-Marie, 'and this,' she tugged my sleeve closer, 'is Peter.'

'Peter?' muttered the old lady, 'Peter?' as if trying to solve a puzzle. And then a strange kind of growl came out of her throat.

'No,' said Anna-Marie, 'it's Peter: your grandson.'

And it was funny because I suddenly remembered once when my mum was taking my dad to hospital and I had to go and play with this little boy next door. We were playing sword fighting. He had a really good sword, it was wooden but it had a proper handle. My sword was only really a cardboard tube and wasn't very good at all, so after a while I went into the kitchen and found this knife with a big handle and a sharp edge. We chased each other round and round the house for ages until I hid behind the sofa and waited to catch him by surprise. He didn't even see me coming and I slashed my weapon through the air like Errol Flynn in that film.

Suddenly he fell to the floor. I could see where there was this thin line across his forehead all the way from one side to the other. And then this flap of skin above his eye began to uncurl and show all his blood and stuff underneath. He, the boy, I can't remember his name, stared at me for a moment, just sitting there like a little statue as the blood began to ooze out and run down his face.

And then he began to scream.

And then his mother came into the room and saw that there'd been an accident and she began to scream too. And the two screams together were like a snake with razor-fangs and a poisoned tail wrapping its coils around the room. And the snake grew longer and stronger until it filled my head and I tried to grab at its throat to squeeze it in to silence.

Because the scream said: 'Peter, this is your fault!'

And, you see, when Anna-Marie said my name and the black holes of the old woman's eyes stared at me and opened up like little mouths with thin grey lips, that's just what my grandma did: scream. Like those two screams together: the little boy and his mother.

Anna-Marie, Tommie and I all stepped backwards startled by the sudden noise, hands clasped to our ears. We took another step back as she began to stand, struggling to pull herself upwards on arms no thicker than Kat's walking stick. She wouldn't stop screaming. I thought my brain was going to burst. She raised her arms, long and thin, and began to wave them at me, trying to hit me. She looked like a featherless ostrich, blind and thrashing around, her beak open and screeching.

Somewhere we could hear or feel doors slamming and people running, summoned by the wailing siren of the old woman's howl.

We turned, of course, and ran: out of the room and stumbled through the shadows of the darkened corridor. We clattered down the stairs but as we reached half way Mrs Finch and her pink overalls appeared blocking our escape. Her face exploded with anger but I couldn't make out her words what with my grandmother's pain still filling my ears. Anna-Marie faltered but only for an instant. She swung her leg high over the banister and spun out into the open air landing with a clunk on the floor below. Tommie's legs weren't as long but he followed her anyway. And I, in turn, flung myself over the rail towards the floor beneath. Pain shot through me as I crashed to the ground but nothing broke and, like my friends, I was too afraid to worry about the grazes on my knees.

Anna-Marie was already at the door and with the sound of other voices and feet rushing in our direction she seized the handle and pulled ferociously. The door opened with a shuddering rattle and we flew through and ran like lunatics forcing our way, scraped and scratched, through the leaves and branches which would no longer separate for us.

The ground raced beneath us, gradually slowing as the shouts and the screams disappeared and we were once again surrounded only by the birds, the bees and the gentle splish-splash of the river. Finally, finally we stopped running, our hands collapsing to our knees as we gasped and wheezed. My heart was jumping and bumping around inside my chest. I felt as if I had a big load of vomit just waiting to burst out of me. Better out than in, my dad used to say, but although my throat was gagging nothing would come until I looked up to see Anna-Marie sat on this tree-stump trembling and watching me with tears in her eyes.

'Oh, Peter,' she said, 'what did you do?'

And then I was sick. Not much but, well, enough.

30

We were sat together, cross-legged, Anna-Marie and me and Tommie, beneath the swelling curves of the willow tree. Early morning sunlight peeked through the canopy, eyes twinkling. The summer breeze made the willow leaves rise and fall like the ribs of a sleeping man. A stronger touch and leaves parted revealing glimpses of the outside world.

The summer term had drifted towards the holidays like a disabled dinghy towards a sunlit beach. The man on the television warned that the weather was turning with thunder and lightning to come. And you could feel it too. You could feel it in the air. You could see it in the sun, burning and sinking beneath the horizon each evening like a great glowing beach ball. It was the last day of term and as her days at Dovecot were coming to an end, puffed out one by one like the candles on Melanie's birthday cake, Anna-Marie had unpeeled like an apple, the skin all gone and only the pale flesh remaining.

Nobody was talking and the silence was big. Too big. As big as the fields and the sky gaping like the top and bottom of an open-air sandwich with me, alone and lonely, standing right in the middle of one of those fields, only the crowless sky to keep me company.

Nobody was talking but we were all thinking: Anna-Marie

nibbled her white lip, her face all droopy and sad, grey curves like tiny moons beneath her eyes; Tommie clutched his football on his lap, picking at the stitching between the leather, occasionally drumming his fingers on its tight surface. I don't know what they were thinking about although I thought I could guess.

Me? I was thinking about a different world. I don't mean like Mars or Saturn or anything. I mean a different world just like this one, with the same trees and the same cottage and Everlasting Lane and Kitty and everything; but a world in which there was a good reason why Mrs Finch wouldn't call Kat and tell her about our visit to the Lodge. Or, even better, a world in which we hadn't gone to the Lodge at all and Anna-Marie had been quite happy to wander up and down the lane, pockets bursting with snacks, chatting about ponies and The Bay City Rollers instead of grandmothers and mysterious girls. But I knew she never could've done that, so, how about a world where I'd never come to Amberley; or a world where I'd never left.

Because it was the last day of term we were allowed to take games or toys. Tommie had brought his football of course but that didn't count because he always did. I'd brought this game called *Mousetrap*. Maybe you know it. It's this funny game where you build a machine that's a mousetrap with slides and chutes and marbles and when you turn the handle all these things happen one after the other until your mouse is trapped in a cage. I used to play it with my dad because some of the bits were a bit fiddly and would fall over and not work properly.

Anna-Marie hadn't brought anything, of course. She didn't play games.

So, it was the last day of term: toys and games and no

uniform and the leavers' assembly and, in my old school, the teacher maybe brought sweets. But nobody was talking.

At least not until Tommie went: 'We could walk the lane to the end.'

'What?' said Anna-Marie and glanced at her watch. 'I don't think the old bag would approve.' She meant Mrs Carpenter, of course.

'Not today,' said Tommie. 'I mean in the holidays. Let's see if it really lasts forever.'

Oh. Well, maybe he hadn't been thinking about Alice after all.

'Don't be stupid,' said Anna-Marie. 'It's only a road. Roads don't last forever.'

'The Romans built a road from London,' said Tommie, 'to ... I think it was Newcastle. My dad says.'

'How far is it from London to Newcastle, dimwit?'

'I don't know.'

'Neither do I,' said Anna-Marie, 'but it's hardly forever, is it?' Tommie shrugged. 'Is it?'

'No,' mumbled Tommie, 'it isn't.'

Could she really be my grandma? That's what I was thinking about now. That old lady with the screaming eyes, I mean. Was she really my grandma? Part of me kept thinking it couldn't be true but the other part, the bigger part, knew it was. When I was looking at her I knew even then, even before she started screaming. Because I could see Kat's face in hers, even though it was so old, like I was looking through broken glass. And I wondered if one day I'd look in a mirror and see my daddy looking back at me.

I hoped so. I'd like that.

Oh, and, of course, she was called Mrs Goodwin which was my grandma's name too.

'Oh, go on, Anna-Marie,' pleaded Tommie. 'It'll be fun. What else is there to do?'

'Yes, Anna-Marie,' I said. 'We won't do it if you're not coming.'

'Fine,' said Anna-Marie. 'Then don't do it.'

'Well, what *are* we going to do?' asked Tommie with an exasperated sigh. 'I mean we've got all summer.' He had begun to toss his ball up in the air, whirling it until it looked like the world going round and around. 'We've got to do something, haven't we, Peter?'

'Stop it,' said Anna-Marie, her voice like a whisper. And then: 'Stop it!' so loudly my ears jumped and Tommie stopped his spinning. 'Don't you understand, you idiots?' she wailed. 'We're children: we don't *do* stuff. Stuff is done *to* us. Haven't you noticed? It's the adults who decide everything. You've been watching too much television, Tommie. Peter's not in Amberley because he chose it: he was brought here whether he liked it or not. You didn't decide your parents shouldn't live together: they decided. You're just two little boys with two little brains.'

'But we do do things,' insisted Tommie, reeling from Anna-Marie's outburst. 'We go down the lane and we go to the pylons and we go to the Lodge ...'

The look on Anna-Marie's face was ugly. 'Of course we *do* things,' she snapped. 'That's all we ever do. But that's not what I meant. What I mean is ... we don't *change* things.' She made a funny noise, half way between a cough and a sob. 'We don't change anything.'

I looked at Tommie. Tommie looked at me.

'I thought we could,' said Anna-Marie. 'I thought if we found out about Alice, then we could change things. Maybe. I thought I could change things.'

'What things?' said Tommie.

'Things!' snapped Anna-Marie. 'Things. What do you mean,' she did her stupid-question voice, 'What things?' She sighed. 'Just things.'

'But what things?'

'I thought,' Anna-Marie took a deep, shuddery breath, her fingers twisting her necklace, Tommie's necklace, looping it around, 'I thought I could change me. I thought I could ... be better. Like Alice.'

'Better?'

'We shouldn't've gone to the Lodge,' I said.

For a moment, from the look on her face, I thought she was going to hit me. Anna-Marie I mean. And I would've let her too. I deserved it. But, instead, her hand stayed in her lap and she said, 'Really?' and then she said, 'Do you think?'

She'd pulled the chain of that necklace tight around her finger; the tip all white but bulging, gasping for blood.

'But we had to, didn't we?' I said.

'What do you mean,' and she put on her idiot-voice again, 'We had to, didn't we?'

I hesitated. Searching for the right words was like searching for pennies in a big, black bag of sand. 'I mean it's like what you said about consequences,' I started. 'You made us go to the Lodge because we knew about Alice. Going to the Lodge was a consequence of that just like us all sitting here like this,' I meant because we were all so miserable, 'is because of going to the Lodge. I mean Kat says that consequences can be bad as well as good: like bombs going off.'

'What do *you* know about consequences, Peter?'

Actually, I was suddenly beginning to think I knew quite a lot: my 'chosen specialist subject' as the vicar might say. 'It's like *you* said: kids don't know about consequences when they do things. They just do them anyway. And when we started trying to find out about Alice we didn't know if it was a good thing or a bad thing. I mean what happened to her and if we hadn't gone to the graveyard and if we hadn't gone to the Lodge then we wouldn't know but we did and now we know that something bad happened and we can't change that, we can't change what we—'

'That's what I mean,' said Anna-Marie. 'We can't change—'

'No,' I said. 'We can't change but that's the point because now we know about the things that happen. Now we know about consequences we can decide what to do because we'll know that there's consequences and we can try to work out what will happen if we do this thing or that thing. It's ...' What I wanted to say was that it was like what Anna-Marie had said about being a good teacher and teaching kids about consequences and that they should think about things before they do them and that if she hadn't insisted maybe we wouldn't've gone to the Lodge and we might never've known and that was a good thing, wasn't it? But I didn't say that. It would've sounded stupid, so, 'It's like something you said,' I said.

'Something?' Anna-Marie laughed. 'Something I said? Something you did, Peter. Something you did.' She reached over and grabbed my knee. 'Peter,' she hissed through her teeth, her fingers like claws, 'what did you do?'

I shook my head. 'I ... I don't know ... I—'

'My dad's dead.'

I looked up at Anna-Marie not quite sure I'd heard what I thought I'd heard. 'What?'

'My dad,' she said again, 'is dead.' She was twisting the necklace round and round her finger until it was pinching her neck.

I glanced at Tommie. He was watching Anna-Marie but I could tell he already knew. I mean, of course he already knew. Everybody knew everything except for me. But even so, this was ...

'What do you mean? When?'

'He hit me with this broom once, you see. A broomstick I mean. He broke it clean in half.' She released the necklace for a moment to mime the breaking of a stick. The chain had left a thin white line about her throat which quickly flooded with dark pink. 'Across my back,' she sniffed, her wrist across her nose she unpicked a tear from the corner of her eye with her thumb. 'I broke his watch, if you must know.' She examined her tear. 'But it was an accident. He didn't mean it,' she said. 'He just got angry, you know, and didn't know how to …

'Oh, it's easy to sit in judgement, Peter. We all make mistakes. You've made a few yourself.'

'But … What happened?'

Anna-Marie looked at me. Tears were running down her cheeks like drizzle down a window pane, snot bubbling in her nose. Again she wiped it away leaving a swipe on her sleeve. 'Peter,' she said, 'do you really have no idea? Do you really have absolutely no idea?' She made a noise like it was supposed to be a laugh but wasn't. It was more like a croak really, like she was being choked. 'The police came. My mother called them and they came and took him away and they put him in a … in a cell and then they decided to put him in … in the Lodge,' she took another deep breath all tattered and torn, her shoulders trembling, 'because he wasn't well and we could go and visit him but when I came home,' she sniffed, 'came home from hospital and my mother took me he wouldn't see us and then,' deep breath, 'after we went home again he went to his room and then,' deep breath, 'he took his shoelaces and tied them to the light and stood on a chair and …

'Oh, Peter,' she cried, 'don't you know anything?'

No. No, I didn't know anything.

'I thought he was in sales,' I said.

I needed to think. I needed to get away and find a willow

of my own. No, I didn't know anything, but I thought that if I could just go somewhere, somewhere else where nobody was talking to me I might be able to start fitting the jigsaw pieces together.

But the funny thing was I'd thought it was only me—I mean me and Kat and Grandma and Dad and Alice—who had a jigsaw. I hadn't realised or at least I hadn't thought that Anna-Marie might have one too. And if Anna-Marie had one, what about Tommie? I glanced across at him, his spectacles all shiny like silver coins. Did he have one? What about his mum and dad? What about Norman Kirrin? Or Mrs Carpenter? The vicar? Surely not. Or maybe … maybe it was all just one big puzzle.

Glancing at her watch, Anna-Marie lifted her bag and hung the strap across her shoulder. 'But the thing is,' she said, getting to her knees, wiping her eyes dry with the back of her hand, 'do you want to know why he died?'

I stared at her, her eyes so cold and blue. I shook my head. No. No, I didn't. Not at all.

'Because, Peter, people don't get second chances,' she said. 'Not really. Not … Not literally. He couldn't undo what he'd done and he couldn't be forgiven any more than … any more than you can.'

And then she was gone.

31

Tommie and I rushed to collect all our bits together; to chase after Anna-Marie as quickly as we could. But we were bumping into each other like a pair of *It's a Knockout* penguins and my *Mousetrap* box fell from my arms, all the pieces higgledy-piggledy across the ground. Tommie was ready to part the long leaves of the willow and laughed to see me scrabbling around on my hands and knees. But then, with a sigh, he bent to help me shove all the bits back the way they'd been.

It'd been so cool beneath the willow that we hadn't thought how warm the morning was even though it wasn't yet nine o'clock. It was too warm to run—all hot and treacly—but, as Tommie and I hefted our bags and stuff onto our shoulders and under our arms, Anna-Marie had already disappeared, so we didn't have much choice if we were going to catch up with her, did we?

As we panted up Everlasting Lane, Tommie shook his head and said, 'She's really cross. Maybe we should leave her alone.'

But I was thinking, was she right? Anna-Marie I mean. When you thought about it, her dad was just like my dad. Not just that he was dead but because he didn't get a second chance either. And I think it was all he wanted, my dad. He didn't want to die. And I know Anna-Marie said we didn't get second chances but she'd been wrong before. She'd been wrong about Alice, hadn't she? And about going to the Lodge too, so maybe she was wrong about this. I was trying to think about something Kat had said.

We didn't catch up with Anna-Marie until the sign at the very top. She was waiting for a gap in the traffic, arms crossed, toe tapping impatiently as the school cars and a big blue bus passed by.

'It's not true,' I said breathlessly as we reached her. I grabbed her arm and said it again: 'It's not true.'

'What?' she spat, spinning round to face me, shaking my hand free. 'What's not true?'

'I mean maybe your dad didn't get a second chance but that doesn't mean nobody does. Some people get stuff like I got an Action-Man helicopter for Christmas once but not everybody did. It's like we're, you know, butterflies—'

'What are you wittering on about, Peter? Tommie,' she pleaded, 'shut him—'

'No, no, listen,' I said. I tried to take her hands in mine but she pulled them away like I had that ring-a-roses plague thing Mr Gale told us about.

'Don't you speak to me—'

'Shut up!' I shouted. 'Just … It's … Let me think … It's important. I …' I took a big breath as I shoved my hand deep into that sand, you know, not real sand but the sand in that black bag I was telling you about. And then I found it: a big shiny penny glinting in my hand. Not a real penny but … Well, you know what I mean.

It was too late.

Anna-Marie was already crossing the big road—the main Nancarrow Road—just managing to skitter out of the way of this big lorry that blared its horn as it roared by. Tommie and me shouted at her to slow down but she wouldn't. So then we had to wait for this tractor—this big, smoky, green tractor with a rattley tin trailer—to go by before we could chase after her again.

We squeezed along the hedges that separated us from the fields where Kat had seen the scarecrow man—I mean Norman—that day, with the hills all crumpled up in the distance like the folds of my blanket. We reached the pavement and passed the *Amberley* sign into the village. This was Rone Lane and all its little tea-pot cottages and creosote fences and low brick walls. I could see a lady outside *The White Hart* standing on a chair and pouring a pan of washing-up water into the hanging baskets. The pavement was all cluttered with children on their way to school, toys and games carried preciously in their arms, school-bags dragging along in the gutter behind them.

Anna-Marie brushed past them all; Tommie and I stumbling along in pursuit taking turns to knock each other into the road.

'Maybe,' I said, 'you don't get second chances,' as we pulled level with Anna-Marie alongside the telephone box. 'Not even like that man in the Bible that Mrs Carpenter always says. Maybe that's not what a second chance even means. You can't change a dead man into a live man. Nobody can do that; not even grown-ups. Maybe not even Jesus.' I was all breathless, what with walking as fast as her. 'But maybe a second chance isn't the chance to make a wrong thing right or a bad thing good,' I went on. 'Maybe a second chance is a chance to do another thing, a new thing that is good or right. But maybe you can't know. Maybe it is a secret. But you can find secrets out like we found out about Alice.'

I didn't know for sure that she was even listening, until she said, 'But—'

I waved her quiet. She was always talking, wasn't she? Now

it was my turn. 'Because Alice was like a mystery,' I said. 'She was like a magical thing that we didn't understand like I don't understand how a fridge can be cold even when it's warm or how the world's spinning about at a million miles an hour but we're all here as if we were—'

'Oh, Peter,' growled Anna-Marie, 'please don't tell me you think fridges are magic.'

'In olden times,' called Tommie jostling along behind us, 'like in caveman times, if you had a fridge they'd think you were magic.'

Yes, I thought. Just like that. Thank you, Tommie.

'It's magic,' I said. 'And magic is true.'

Anna-Marie stopped and turned and, well, you know how sometimes if you go for a walk in the country and sometimes you'll see a field with horses in? There was one in the lane which I told you about. Anyway, sometimes we'd go right up to the fence and Anna-Marie would hold out handfuls of grass and the horses would come gallumphing over and nibble at the ends and then every now and again one of the horses would snort and ripple its nose about. Well, that's pretty much what Anna-Marie sounded like when I said that magic was true: a big, horsey snort like I'd just said the stupidest thing in the world.

And she was off again

'Aaaow!'

It was a funny noise to make, I know, but right then I just wanted to box her ears but I don't mean box them like Muhammed Ali floating like a, well, a butterfly. I mean I wanted to cut them off and put them in a box and then take the box somewhere secret and private well away from her mouth like, maybe, the pill-box where I met Norman Kirrin that first time or deep in the woods. And when I was there I'd open the box and scream at the ears and they'd have to listen and her mouth would be too far away to interrupt.

'But that's what you used to say,' I called after her. 'You used to say it might be magic: the lane. I remember.'

'Used to!' I heard her shout. 'That's the kind of crap kids say!'

I didn't think *Amberley* had ever seen anything like this. Anna-Marie, head down, as she stormed along. Me shouting like I didn't care who heard. I remembered that first day when I'd followed her hop-scotching from square to square and look at her now. How had this happened? What had I said? What was I trying to say? I was trying to make things right but it was like whatever I said came out the wrong way to make Anna-Marie understand.

Tommie and me were running again. We passed the village green and all the little cottages that overlooked it. The grass hadn't seen rain in months and the ducks that had once paddled in the pond had given up and disappeared weeks ago. Anna-Marie had stopped to wait for this car to reverse into the mouth of Fugler Lane. This time I jumped right past her so we were face-to-face.

'But Kat said that magic *is* real,' I protested. 'Listen: a secret is another word for finding out what's true, isn't it?' Tommie was nodding. 'And a secret is just a mystery like in Sherlock Holmes.' It was like he had a bee buzzing about his head he was nodding so much. 'And magic is, well, it's like a mystery that you don't know the answer to but once you find it out what you find out is true.'

It was like that bag of sand again but now it was a big saucepan full of words, all bubbling to the top. Words like 'secret' and 'true' and 'magic' and 'mystery' and, of course, 'consequences' all juggling around in my head and me trying to put them in the right order so that Anna-Marie would understand.

'You know how you ... ? Do you ever pretend things? I mean do you sometimes pretend something is true when it isn't?'

Anna-Marie glanced at Tommie and raised her eyebrows. 'What sort of things do you pretend, Peter?' Her face was all quivery she was so cross.

But it was hard to answer. I couldn't think of anything right then. But maybe that was the thing with pretending. I mean sometimes, if you pretended strongly enough, it was hard to remember what was real and what was only pretend. Sometimes it was better to just forget there was a difference.

'When I play football,' said Tommie, bouncing his ball on the pavement, 'I pretend I'm Martin Chivers.'

'That's right,' I said.

Thank you, Tommie, I thought again. I nearly could've kissed him. Well, not really but, well, you know ...

'My dad says—'

But she was already gone. It was driving me mad. Every time I tried to explain she was always stomping off and not listening to a word I said. But then she would stop and I couldn't get the words in my head to catch up with my mouth. I wanted to say how sometimes I could pretend something so much that it was almost like it was true. And sometimes I could pretend something so much that it was like my dad *was* alive. Just like she did when she said her dad was in sales. And, well, it was like in a story. You know, like cats and dogs and laughing your head off. If you really wanted, then you could make it true if you ... It was like in my scrapbook—

We passed the church just as the bell began to chime: nine times, school time. I saw again that blue vase sat on a distant gravestone—do you remember?—except now I knew whose grave it was and now I knew whose vase and why Anna-Marie had told me not to go to that part of the graveyard.

Here lies Christopher Alan Liddell,
much missed father and husband.

But if I'd seen it that day, would I have understood? If I'd seen it that day in the graveyard, would I have realised? In the distance I could hear the school-bell monitor—ring-a-ding-ding—sounding the end of morning play. The children would be lining up; the teachers opening their registers, pens at the ready. If I'd seen it though, would it have made any difference?

We caught up with Anna-Marie at the school-gate. I grabbed her, feeling her tight waist beneath my fingers, the material of her T-shirt. But before I could think of what to say, she screamed: 'Have you listened to yourself?' and pushed me so hard that I stepped back into the road. 'Good Lord, you're like an infant.' She was crying now. 'Have I wandered into the chimpanzees' tea-party? What are you talking about, Peter?'

'But you said ...' I almost wanted to cry too. I put my head in my hands. I felt like I was running ten laps round the school field with Mr Gale going: 'Come on, Lambchop, get your arse in gear!'

'Don't you remember?' I said. 'When you told me your dad was in sales? I thought it was true. I mean, it *was* true. It was true to me. And it was nice, wasn't it? That someone thought he was alive. And, when you told me that, because I believed it, it must've been like it was true. Even to you. I mean that's why you said it. And if it's like it's true, why isn't it?'

'Because it isn't, Peter! What are you saying? You're saying this means this and that means that as if it's all true but—'

'But ...' I wanted to scream. 'But ...' I really did. Why did everything have to be so hard? 'It *was* true and if I was telling someone about it they'd think it was true too. So to them your dad was alive and they would think he was away on business and they might never even think to themselves: Oh, I wonder if he's dead instead. And to those people it would be true. It *would* be.'

'But it wouldn't be true to me and if it wasn't true to me then it wasn't really true at all, any more than you and your mum ... Like magic: magic isn't true.'

'But Kat said—'

'It doesn't matter what Kat said. Everlasting Lane isn't magic just because—'

'But the magic *is* the name,' I pleaded. 'And the name is true. It's like if you were driving down this road and you saw a sign like Everlasting Lane you'd think, well, that's a funny name and you might start to think about it like at night when you're supposed to be sleeping and about who might live there and are there children or families or something? And then it would be like throwing a match into Mr Finch's cornfield—*whooosh!*—or doing that thing with a magnifying glass, you know? And you'd be thinking, well, what sort of houses do they have in Everlasting Lane? Are they just like normal houses or would they be a bit magic? Because the name is like a magical thing, isn't it? And you might think there was a dog like the Beast and a funny man like Mr Merridew and you might wonder about what the trees would be like and always, always you'd be thinking, well, what's at the end? What's at the end of an everlasting lane? And in the end you'd have to know because otherwise you might never get to sleep again.

'Don't you want to find out?' And then she hit me.

It was funny because, of course, she was always hitting me. And Tommie too. But she'd never *really* hit me before. Not like she did then. My whole ear went kind of numb and echoey.

'I've told you before!' she screamed and there were tears running down her face. 'There's no magic!' she cried. 'Don't you remember what Mr Merridew says? There's only chaos. Nothing means anything. There's no point.' Her face was moving around like a sheet on a windy washing line. She was cross because she didn't believe what I was saying was true.

And then she hit me again.

And then she swung her satchel round until it whacked me in the face.

And then she hit me again.

She was screaming: 'So, what, Peter? I just squeeze my eyes and pretend that my dad is still alive? That he tucks me in at night? I mean I can pretend but pretend doesn't make it happen. You can write it all down in a story but that wouldn't make it true. I mean, even if I did pretend it still wouldn't be true.'

All that time, Anna-Marie carried on hitting me. The last straggling children had stopped to stare. I could just about see their feet as I tried to turn away from the blows. I was bent over, my hands covering my head as punch after punch, slap after slap came down upon me. Every now and again I felt her satchel again. It was like she had a million hands.

I could hear Tommie saying, 'Anna-Marie,' and, 'Anna-Marie,' and, 'Anna-Marie,' in lots of voices—soft and loud—but it didn't make any difference.

'Do you know, Peter,' she was yelling, 'I think you may be the stupidest, stupidest nine year old I've ever met.' Ten! I was—ouch—ten! 'Think about it: don't you think if I could change things about my dad I would? Don't you think I would change about Alice? Yes, I could write a story and maybe if you read it you'd think it was true but—'

But she was getting it all wrong. I wanted to say about that man, that man in *The Copper Kettle,* when he said it was like living in a different world or something. He'd said it was nicer there, hadn't he? Apart from the food, he said. That's what I meant: that she could pretend and it would be better. And, maybe, if she pretended hard enough, it'd be true.

'If you've done something wrong,' she sobbed, 'it stays wrong; it doesn't suddenly get right because you do something else. The things that happen stay happened. You can't change things, Peter. You can't change what happened to Alice, whatever it was. And I can't change what happened to my dad. I miss him but all the pretending in the world isn't going to bring him back.'

And the funny thing was that after a while all the punches, pinches and slaps stopped hurting. Well, not literally. I mean they still hurt but I didn't mind and once you don't mind something then it hurts a lot less than it would do anyway. I thought about that thing, you know, about if there's hurricanes and floods and if your daddy dies, then who are you supposed to get angry with? Well, I thought, if there's no God then perhaps all you really need is someone else who doesn't mind you being angry with them. But then, maybe that's what God is for anyway.

'Listen, Peter, you could walk from one end of Everlasting Lane to the other and back again and it wouldn't make my dad be alive or your dad or Tommie's dad and mum get married again. Everlasting Lane is just a road. It's just a road with a funny name. The name doesn't make it magic. A name is just what something is called.'

All my world was made up of feet and ground. Tommie's dirty scuffed shoes and Anna-Marie's black plimsolls, a flapping sole and thread hanging loose; the dry pavement on which they stood; my bag and the *Mousetrap* box and all the little bits of coloured plastic. And then the rows of shoes stood by the school-gate, staring. And then I saw this other pair of shoes: brown, large and laced-up, shiny.

And then I smelt this smell. This smell that I'd smelt before.

And then the brown, laced-up, shiny shoes said, 'Now, now, young lady, I *think* that's quite enough for one day, don't you? *Quite* enough!'

That voice: I couldn't think where I'd smelt it before.

I turned my head to see Anna-Marie still crying and … Well, I've run out of different ways to say she was walking away again, shuffling through the school-gates.

But that smell. A smell that reminded me of—

'Well, Peter, it looks like I found you *just* in time.' A voice that twisted me like a Chinese burn. 'Peter?' And that smell again except now I remembered where I'd smelt it before. 'Peter!' The smell of a cat. 'Peter!'

A dead cat.

'Ha!' cried Doctor Todd as I looked up. 'At last! Excellent to see you, Peter. *Ex*cellent.' He clapped his hands. 'Well, you *have* been in the wars, haven't you? Anyway,' he said, 'ahem, we've got a bit of catching up to do, I hear, haven't we, eh?'

PART IV

A Picture of a Tiger

32

'That's it,' said Doctor Todd. 'A deep breath … and out. Again … and out. That's it, Peter. Good boy. So, tell me, where are we now?'

'On the swing.' A gentle breeze lifted my hair and the seat creaked as I moved back and forth, the loops of chain cold in my fists.

'The swing? Which swing?'

'The one at school,' I said, squinting across the playing field, brown and thirsty, to the school buildings. I could see Miss Pevensie, hair bunched at the back of her head, pinning pictures to the classroom wall. Otherwise, the building seemed deserted like on a weekend.

'Can you describe it?'

'It's sunny.'

'No. The swing.'

'It's red.'

'Okay, and this is where you come to—'

I shook my head. 'No,' I said, 'we're not allowed to play on it; to sit on it I mean. It's broken.'

'Broken? How is it broken?'

'One of the seats is missing.' I wiped my eyes. The smoke from Doctor Todd's cigar was making them all prickly.

'Oh, I see. There are two seats.'

'No,' I insisted, 'one of them's missing.'

Miss Pevensie had glanced up and seen me. She came to the window and waved. I waved back.

'How long has it been broken?'

I shrugged. 'Always.'

'Of course,' said Doctor Todd. 'I see. So no one sits on the swing? Peter? I said, so no one gets to sit on the swing? Is that right?'

'Anna-Marie does.'

'Anna-Marie? Oh, yes, of course: the young lady with the flying fists. So why does she get to sit on the swing?'

Miss Pevensie was at her classroom door, the one that opened onto the playground, and tugging at the handle.

'It's not like she's going to kill herself,' I said.

'But doesn't she get punished?'

'Who?'

'Anna-Marie.'

'Oh. She doesn't care.'

'I see.'

'Peter.' Miss Pevensie was half-walking, half-running across the field and calling my name. 'Peter.' I slipped guiltily from the swing-seat to stand on the dusty ground still gripping the chains behind me. 'Peter?' It was Doctor Todd now, his voice poking me like a knife. 'Peter? Are you aware that you're waving? Who are you waving at?'

'Miss Pevensie.'

'Who's she? A teacher? At school?'

I nodded. 'She's trying to tell me something.'

Slap! I felt the hot sting of his hand upon my face and blinked in shock.

'Peter,' Doctor Todd smiled at me with his woodland teeth, 'thank goodness. I thought we'd lost you there.' He took his red pen and wrote in his blue notebook. As he did so, he said, 'Look around you.' He had the same notebook as that man Craig from *The Copper Kettle*. 'Do you know where you are now?' He looked up at me. 'I said, do you know where you are now?'

I nodded. 'The lounge.'

'That's right, Peter,' he said. 'Well done. Well done. Now, I want you to tell me who else is in the room with us. Can you do that?'

Of course I could. I turned around. The narrow space between the curtains, drawn against the bright morning, produced a slice of light that cut the sofa in two. They were sat on opposite ends like reflections of each other, clutching identical tissues to their faces, eyes red-raw like devils' eyes. They sobbed as if their tears were a scratchy record, its needle jumping in and out of the dusty groove.

'Mummy,' I said, the inside of my chest echoing to the throb of my heart like Mr Waterberry bashing the school water-tank with his big rubber hammer, 'and Kat.'

'I see,' said Doctor Todd. He scrunched the end of his cigar against the lip of the ashtray and it sat there hanging by a thread of smoke. 'Let's play a game, shall we?' he said suddenly. 'See if you can tell me what I'm holding in my hand?'

'A pen.'

'Good. Can you describe it to me?'

'It's red.'

'Yes. Good. Anything else?'

'It's got a little silver thing to hang in your pocket.'

'That's good. Now, what about this hand?'

'Nothing.'

'That's right. Good. Now, pretend I have two pens. Can you do that?'

Of course I could. That was easy. I did so and watched as he juggled them between his hands.

'Now,' he said, stretching out his palms, 'which is real?'

I raised my hand ready to point but hesitated. It was hard. They looked just the same.

'I see,' said Doctor Todd. Popping both pens into the pocket of his jacket he slipped another cigar from its thin box and lit it sucking thoughtfully on the end like a hungry calf. The tip glowed like a precious red jewel. 'Now, there's no need to be shy, is there? Why don't you come and sit down?' He patted the cushion beside him. 'We've got a few things to talk about, you and I, haven't we? And I want you to tell me everything. Your mother wants you to tell me the truth. Remember?'

I shuffled forwards until I was standing right in front of him. But I didn't sit down.

'I've been looking through your scrapbook,' said Doctor Todd. And he was telling the truth. I could see it sat on his lap beneath the notebook. I could see the corner of the cover poking out with Norman's sign on it: *Trespassers will be Persecuted*. 'I hope you don't mind,' he said. 'It's really the most astonishing piece of work. A*ston*ishing.'

I was about to say that he couldn't've read it. I wrote it all backwards, you see, so that nobody could. But he held up that little mirror and smiled at me with jagged teeth. It was broken—the mirror I mean.

'You've had quite a time it seems,' he said. 'All these adventures. Goodness me! This Mr Merridew: what an extraordinary character. Extra*or*dinary. And this is a gruesome series of pictures,' he went on. '*Very* gruesome. Who is this poor chap?'

'Tommie Winslow.'

'And what's happened in this picture?'

'He's been hit by a ball.'

'Goodness, what a lot of blood. And this one?'

'He's been hit by a stick.'

'And this one?'

'He's been shot.'

'Shot?'

'With arrows.'

'Oh, they're arrows. I see. And who *is* this Tommie Winslow? Is he a friend of yours? You've certainly created a lot of unhappy fates for him. Is he someone you know?'

'He's a friend of Anna-Marie's.'

'Ah, that name again.' He flicked through the pages. 'Ah, yes, here we are: a wholly different set of pictures. My, what an incredible imagination you have. Incredible.

'Tell me, Peter, did anyone ever read you the *Alice in Wonderland* stories when you were younger?'

'My daddy.'

'Ah, I see. Of course. But the interesting thing about *Alice in Wonderland* was that it was all a dream, wasn't it? In fact, you've written it here.' Again he flicked through the pages. 'Ah, yes, *All that Alice-in-Wonderland ...*' and he wrinkled his snout as he mouthed: crap. 'All of it locked away in little Alice's head. It makes you wonder, doesn't it, Peter? I mean the stuff that we lock away in our heads. The trick is to know what's inside our heads and what's outside, isn't it, eh? Can you see the difference? Because,' went on Doctor Todd, 'well, you like to make up stories, don't you?'

I shook my head. I hadn't made up anything. It was all there: Tommie's napkin, the shredded remains of my class work, the game of *Consequences* I'd played with Norman Kirrin. They were all there. And more. Stuck in. And they were all real.

'What I mean is it's more like an impression, a picture of what the real world, your world, is like. It's like—'

'A picture of a tiger.'

'Yes, yes, that's it. In fact, I was just admiring your own

picture. The black and orange stripes. Very vivid. And those jaws. Argh! I could quite feel myself breaking into a sweat.

'And, of course, the story of Alice—I mean *Alice in Wonderland*—was make-believe. A man called Lewis Carroll made it all up but her adventures can seem very real because, like you, he had such a *viv*id imagination. Now, Lewis Carroll was real, of course, but that doesn't mean Alice was real, does it? How could she be? Think about all the strange things that happen. How could it be true?'

'Alice thinks it's true.'

'Ha! She does. You're quite right. But isn't that because she's dreaming? When she wakes up she knows it was all just a silly dream, doesn't she?'

'But ...'

'Yes?'

'But she's not real,' I said, 'so she can't dream, so she can't not know what was real and what wasn't when none of it was.'

Doctor Todd stared at me. 'Exactly.' He cleared his throat. 'Absolutely. But putting that to one side for the moment, I think what I'm trying to say is that there's a line to be drawn between what's real and what's not but, maybe for some people, maybe for you, Peter, it's not always clear exactly where that line should be.'

I frowned. What Doctor Todd didn't understand was that sometimes something that wasn't real could be as real as something that was. *That's* what I'd been trying to say to Anna-Marie, of course. It was like, I don't know, sometimes you're dreaming but you think you're awake.

'Yes,' said Doctor Todd, 'but then you wake up and realise that it was all a dream, don't you? In retrospect. Like *Alice in Wonderland*.'

Well, I thought, sometimes you do. Maybe.

'What I'm trying to do, Peter, is to find the words to help

you understand,' said Doctor Todd. 'Your mother has difficulty ... relating to you, doesn't she, Peter? Have you ever wondered why? All the stuff in your scrapbook: all that stuff about Alice. Haven't you been wondering what happened to Alice? The real Alice I mean. Have you never wondered why your mother feels the way she does?'

'That's why she has a doctor.'

'Oh, Peter,' said Doctor Todd. 'No. I'm not your mother's doctor. I'm yours.'

I blinked in surprise. What did he mean? There wasn't anything wrong with me. Was there?

'Let's talk a little bit about your grandmother, Peter. I understand you paid her a visit the other day.'

I nodded.

'Why did you attack her?'

'I didn't. I ...' If anything she'd attacked me. 'I didn't know who she was,' I said. 'I didn't hurt her.'

'Unfortunately, Peter, that's not strictly true. Not strictly. She doted on you when you were little, of course, like any grandmother would but she could never forgive you for what you did to your mother; for what you did to Alice.'

'She tore me out of that picture.'

'Well, that's right. You can imagine, I think—after all, you have a very *powerful* imagination—how she felt when you turned up out of the blue yesterday and—'

'But I didn't—'

'Now, now, Peter. What I would like you to focus on—really focus on—is the truth.'

'Like a secret?'

'No, Peter, this isn't a secret. Do you remember when I came to visit you at your house,' I nodded, 'and you threw your bowl on the floor? And then you broke that watch I bought you, didn't you?' I nodded again. 'That lovely watch.

And then I understand you hit this poor boy with a cricket ball.' He nodded down at my picture of Tommie. I'd used lots of red for the blood but there hadn't been any blood really. 'And then that poor dog. And the vase, of course, from your sister's grave. And then there was today's little, ahem, altercation at the school gate. Isn't it fair to say, Peter, that sometimes you ... ah ... let your emotions get the better of you? That sometimes you get so cross you forget what you're doing?'

I didn't know what he meant. He had me all confused. It was like he was one of those magicians on TV and his words were like card tricks, pretending to be magic. I didn't hit that cricket ball, did I? It was Mr Gale, I thought, but I couldn't remember for sure. And the Beast? Crunch! That was Crunch! That was Mr Merridew.

'All these incidents,' said Doctor Todd, 'they're not *coinci-dence*, are they?'

No, I wanted to say, they weren't. Even I knew that. They were consequences just like in the game. But I didn't say anything. You see, I wasn't sure what they were consequences of.

'Let's talk about Alice,' said Doctor Todd. 'The real Alice. Tell me what you know about her.'

'She used to live here,' I said. 'She had a nursery.'

'Yes, that's right, she had a nursery but she never lived in it, did she? Do you remember why?'

I shook my head. 'She was my sister.'

'That's right, Peter.' Doctor Todd nodded slowly. 'That's right but Alice was never born, was she? Your mother brought you here to help you remember why. Do you?'

'Mummy had an accident. That's why she has a sore knee.'

'That's right. Well done, Peter. Splendid. But do you remember the accident? Do you remember exactly what happened?'

33

I studied the door, peering at the hinge and then the lock. I reached out and touched it, placing first the pad of my finger and then the palm of my hand against it as if measuring the temperature.

'Where are we now?' asked Doctor Todd.

'Outside the kitchen.'

'Good. Now, in you go.'

The only sound was my breathing. I put the key in the lock and turned it. I felt suddenly hot and cold. I pushed the door open and looked inside. I saw myself sat at the table cutting random shapes, like lop-sided stars, with round-bladed scissors, dollops of glue setting hard on the table-top.

'Now, who's with us?'

'Daddy.'

He was soaking paint brushes, white spirit tinged with pink from the nursery walls. Spicy ginger was rising in the oven; milk was bubbling in the pan. My lips could already taste the creamy ring of chocolate.

'Where's your mother?'

'She's upstairs.'

She was cleaning up after Daddy and his painting, her belly

all swollen with my little sister, her Hoover clickety-clack against the skirting board of the room above.

'How are you feeling?'

'Funny.'

The skipping rope tied clumsily across the top of the stairs. It was only a joke. Would she see it? Would she not? She'd always wanted a little girl.

'Oh, Peter,' said my father, 'you'll be the death of me,' as he picked at the blobs of hardened glue. 'Anyway, do you want your cake now or will you save it for later?'

I stared at Doctor Todd. My mouth was sticky and dry. My tongue rasped over my lips.

'What happened next?'

'She fell.'

'That's right. She fell, didn't she, Peter?'

Yes, she fell. I could see her limbs flying and tumbling like a woman at the circus which was kind of funny because, of course, I didn't see it. I only heard it. Her body like a bag of bones, clumpety-clumpety-clump. And her cry: frightened, yes, but soft like a mouse because there was nothing she could do. And then the clumping came to a final thud, her leg broken, the white bone peeking through the red skin, blood in her lap, and then there was a pause—I giggled at my father's face—and then the screaming started.

'Peter!' My father leaping to his feet. 'What did you do?'

I'd never heard him scared before. My father's face: I'd never seen him scared. Pretend-scared, yes, if I was playing at ghosts or being a monster but not properly-scared. All the way through the war without a graze—Tobruk, Sicily, Rome—but he died right there. Just like Alice. The cancer killed him in the end but really he was already dead. I mean, not really but … Sometimes it's hard to be sure.

I stopped giggling.

'Peter, what's happening?'

And yet he forgave me when my mother never could. Why couldn't she forgive me? It was my fault but ... I didn't know anything about consequences, you see. I'd never even heard of them. 'Peter?' I didn't know things happened in chains. 'Peter!' I thought they happened in bubbles.

I felt Doctor Todd's palm again, sharp on my face. I stared at him. His pen, the real one, tappety-tappety-tappety-tap on the corner of his notebook. The room was full of smoke. I could hear tears flowing but I couldn't tell whose.

'You've reached an age, Peter,' said Doctor Todd, his voice sounding cross, 'when—how can I say this?—you need to grow up. You can't keep hiding from the truth. You can't keep evading responsibility for the things you do. Karen—your mother—has, well ...' His glasses glinted at me and then flashed right through me to the hazy shapes on the sofa. 'You have been terribly over-indulged. *Terribly.*' It was a strange expression—on his face I mean: half anger and half that look Melanie got sometimes when she wanted her story marked now but Mr Gale would only point to the top of the pile. It was like facing an invisible wall you could never climb. 'Isn't it time to take your place in the real world, Peter? To be a real tiger, perhaps, eh? And then, I dare say, you will at once begin to recognise how,' he jabbed his cigar at the air, 'how frustrating your peccadilloes have been.' With white knuckles he ground his cigar into the ashtray 'til the sparks nipped at his fingers.

'But Kat—'

'Kat? Oh yes, ha, the mystical aunt. What a creation! But you realise, don't you, that Kat was ... well, a game? A game,' again he flicked through the scrapbook letting the pages uncurl until he came to the right place, 'yes, a game of the imagination. Your mother, Karen, wanted to help you, both of you, create some distance ... distance from events. Look at the sofa.'

I did so.

'Now,' he said, 'your mother or Kat: who is real?'

But it was hard. Like I said before they looked just the same.

'You remember, don't you, Peter, that there never was a Kat? I mean, there was only your mother. I would be very worried ...'

I did remember. Of course I remembered. Why did everybody think I was such an idiot? But ... But what I wanted to explain to Doctor Todd was that Kat *was* real and that she *was* different to my mother. I mean a different person. She was warm where my mother was cold, she was happy where my mother was sad. She was a mother where my mother—

Doctor Todd's problem was that he was talking like he thought things that weren't real weren't as important as things that were. I suppose a lot of people think that. People like teachers or people on the news maybe. But I think they're wrong in a way because there was a lot of stuff in my head that wasn't real but was really important: like the things I wanted to happen or the things I wished had happened instead of the things that had. They were just as important as the things that did actually happen.

And it was like that when my mum was just my mum and she wasn't very happy but when she pretended—and I pretended too—that she was Kat and then she was happy. I mean she was pretending to be Kat but she wasn't pretending to be happy. That was real. And she was happier being Kat than when she was real because who she was when she was real wasn't who she really was.

Doctor Todd sighed. 'People need to keep what's real and what's not real in separate boxes, clearly labelled. If you get them mixed up, well, that's really not very healthy.'

Now he was talking like it was easy to know what was real and what wasn't but he was wrong about that too. It was like the difference between a trick and magic; like that Peter and Paul thing. Sometimes all you knew was that the lady was sawn in half or the man guessed what card it was or the sun rose in the sky. You didn't know whether it was magic or a trick but maybe it didn't matter. And maybe, even if it did matter, it was up to you to decide anyway.

Because what I think is that some people might think that things that are real and things that are unreal are opposites, you know, like black and white or the different sides of a coin. But I don't think that's true. I think that things, whether they're real or unreal are on the same side of the coin. What's on the other side is nothing, no things, absolutely no things at all.

'I couldn't remember.'

'Remember? Well, memory's a fickle thing, Peter. It doesn't always do the things we'd like it to. You know how hard it is to forget something bad. Well, sometimes it's just as hard to re-member and it doesn't matter how hard we try. Sometimes we want to forget. I suppose it's a bit like all those dreams locked away in Alice's head. Your mind didn't like what it saw so it locked it away: put it all in a secret room and hid the key so that you couldn't find it. That's why we—well, your mother— had the idea to bring you back here: so that you could find the key and open the door.

'It was all too hard for your parents. Can you imagine what it was like, Peter, for them? To live each day with the knowl-edge of what you'd done but you didn't even remember.'

'What do I have to do?' I said. Daddy would've known. That's what daddies are for. I stepped towards my mother. 'I'm … I'm …' I held out my hand to her.

Slowly, slowly she turned to face me and wrapped her arms around me. She placed her face against my tummy until her tears were soaking my T-shirt. I wanted to say sorry. I wanted to say I'm really, really sorry but I didn't know how. The words in my head sounded so stupid. But then I put my hand into my pocket and there was the ring in that little bag. And I thought now is the best time because although it was only a little thing I knew—and I hoped my mummy knew—that it meant something much, much bigger than just a ring. But, just when I was about to take it out of my pocket, Mummy said: 'Oh, Peter, you'll be the death of me ...'

And I said, 'Cake.'

My mother looked up at me. 'I ...What?'

'Do I want it now,' I said, 'or will I save it for later?'

She was staring now. She was trying to smile but looked like she was a little bit scared of me. I felt Doctor Todd's hand on my shoulder. 'I'm sorry, Peter,' he said, 'I think you've rather lost us there.'

But I wasn't really listening any more. You see, once at school, at my old school, I'd seen this film about World War Two. I watched it really closely in case I saw my dad because it wasn't a proper film like *The Great Escape* or something. It was all lots of little films, only a few seconds each. So there was Mr Churchill with his v-sign and his cigar, and men in black and white suits, and then there were all the planes firing their guns and then all those people that the Germans killed with gas and stuff and at the end was the big mushroom bomb. Your head was all dizzy from it and when my mother said that thing about me being the death of her it was the same kind of thing. I saw Anna-Marie on the red swing—'It's not like I'm going to kill myself'—and then at the ballet with all those marks around her neck and then the soldier, my father, in the woods with the girl in his arms—'Will you save it for later?'—

'Peter?' It was like I'd just finished the puzzle, 'Peter?' sat back and seen the whole picture for the first time.

'Anna-Marie,' I said.

324

My mother's smile flickered. 'No,' she corrected, 'it's Mummy.'

'No,' I said. 'It's Anna-Marie. She's in … She's in trouble.'

The red swing—the broken seat.

'Oh, Peter.' Her hands released me. 'After everything …'

'Peter,' said Doctor Todd. He sounded cross. 'I really think you need to focus on what's important here.'

'No,' I said. 'I mean it is important. She … Anna-Marie … She's …'

And the chain growing tighter and tighter.

Doctor Todd grabbed my shoulders and spun me round to face him. I could smell his dead-cat breath all over me. 'You need to pull yourself together.' He was kind of shaking me as he said it. 'What have I been saying?' he said. 'It's time to leave all these little fantasies—'

'But I've got to—'

'I think your duty is to your mother, Peter, not to some *school*girl.'

Do you remember that time that Anna-Marie and I walked down Everlasting Lane and there was that fork in the road? Do you remember how hard it was to choose which way to go? Well, I didn't really decide at all, did I? Well, it was just like that: there were two ways to go and I couldn't go both ways. It was Mummy or Anna-Marie and I couldn't really split myself in two. It was like Norman said, I had to choose.

'And, besides,' said Doctor Todd, 'whatever it is that seems so urgent, well, I'm sure it can wait until—'

But how could I wait?

It's like when there's a fire. You don't say: 'There's a fire. I'd better get out of the house later'. You say: 'I have to get out of the house now', just in case you burn to death. That could happen. I mean that's what I'd say.

And, I mean, well, what would you have done?

34

'If you had to choose,' I demanded, crashing through the kitchen door, piggy-bank stuffed beneath my arm like a rugby ball. 'I mean if you had to choose between the mother and the baby, who would you save?'

Norman Kirrin, sat at his morning table nursing a cup of tea and a pen, looked up at me startled from his thoughts. 'Well, Peter,' he blinked, 'ever the one for the dramatic entrance. I must say—'

'But which is it?' I cried. 'Who would you …? Who would you save?'

Norman stared at me as if I'd just offered him poison. 'How …? Oh, Peter, what a cruel question. How could one even begin—?'

'I know,' I said. 'But if you *had* to choose.'

Norman looked away shaking his head. 'I don't even know,' he said, 'whether the child …'

'But if you *had* to choose!'

'Norman!' It was Greg calling like thunder from the shop. 'I'm warning you! I'm totting up for God's sake! Enough with the bloody hysterics!'

Norman nearly tripped as he clambered from his seat, his

finger hushed against his lips. He seized my sleeve and dragged me across the floor, pushing me into a chair.

Pulling the back door softly shut, his fingers rifled through his thin hair. 'Peter,' he muttered, retaking his place, 'Peter, Peter, why do you ask that? What is it? No human being should have to make that choice.'

I didn't have time for this. I reached out and grabbed his arm. 'Please,' I said. 'Tell me what to do.'

He had tears in his eyes now, his head shaking slowly. 'I'm sorry, Peter,' he said. 'Only you can decide that.'

'But you know.'

He shook his head again. 'It doesn't matter what I know. Only you can decide. But, Peter, when have you ...? Have you ever had to make a choice like that?'

'Yes.' Because he was right: sometimes there wasn't a choice. 'It's today.' But sometimes there was.

Norman's eyes widened. 'Oh, Peter,' he said, 'really?'

I nodded. And I had to make that choice. Because that was it: did I want cake now or would I save it? I mean, save *her*. I wanted to save her, of course. Of course, I wanted to save her, but I wanted—I needed—to save her now.

'And can I ...? What can I do? Can I help?'

And I knew how to do it. 'Yes,' I said. 'It's in the shop.'

He looked unsure, glancing nervously at the door that separated us from his brother. 'In the shop you say.' He stroked his stubbly chin. 'Well ...'

Norman winced as he opened the door with the slightest creak. We peered in. Greg Kirrin was weighing potatoes and tomatoes for a lady with one baby on her hip and another tucked sleeping in the bulge beneath her summer dress. He was tut-tut-tutting about the weather and she, soft with sweat, was nodding in return.

Norman hushed me again as we muffled our steps and entered the shop. I took him by the hand and led him close enough to see Anna-Marie's fairy smiling at us and pointed her out. The fairy which had once seemed so tatty was now glittering in its taffeta frock and was suddenly beautiful, not for what it was but for what it could achieve. Norman didn't hesitate. He seized it in his fist and squeezed it into mine. 'Will this do it?' he hissed.

I nodded: Yes. And I really believed it would. 'I've got money,' I whispered, and offered him my piggybank. 'I've—'

He shook his head. 'No,' he said. 'There's no time. Go now. Don't look—'

'What the bloody hell's going on?'

Greg Kirrin loomed above us. The topping of white hair made him look like a snow-peaked mountain, a mountain in an open necked shirt and a ratty blue jumper like something Kitty had dragged in. The pregnant lady had left and Norman and I had never even heard that little bell ring. 'I said,' boomed the shopkeeper, 'what the bloody hell is going on?'

'I was just serving—'

'Serving?' Greg laughed but not in a funny way. 'Serving is it? You know you're not to serve unless—'

'I know, Greg—I'm sorry—but on this occasion I—'

'So, *now* you're a shopkeeper, eh?' His great tummy rumbled with silent laughter. 'I'll be looking forward to help with the accounts, then, will I? Stocktaking? It's not all standing around in a coat being jolly, you know.'

'I know, Greg. I'm sorry. I was just talking to Peter. He only wants the fairy and I thought—'

'Peter?' He sniffed the word suspiciously. 'First name terms, is it? What's been going on?'

'Look, I've given him my word. I've—'

That same wheezing, unfunny laugh. 'Well, it's always words with you, isn't it, Norman? Bloody poetry. Well, when it comes to this shop, I'm in charge of everything including the words and the only word we have on offer today starts with "n", ends with "o" and rhymes with "no".'

The bigger Mr Kirrin's chunky fingers squeezed into my tiny fist and released the fairy from my grip. Norman leapt forward and seized Greg's arm in both hands but his skinny body seemed to collapse beside the bulk of his brother; his shape shrivelling in the big man's shadow.

'You don't understand,' he whined. 'Greg—'

'It'll be some bloody girl, won't it?' Greg shook himself free of his brother's grip. 'Jesus Christ, look at you, Norman. You're pathetic and now you want to ...' Greg Kirrin stared down at me with a strange expression: angry, yes, but kind of a bit sad too. 'How old are you anyway? Seven? Eight?'

Ten. I was ... I was ten.

'It doesn't bloody matter,' he said, adding, 'and the last thing you want to be doing is listening to the ravings of this bloody lunatic,' as, with one arm, he raised his brother to his feet. 'Anyway, Norman, it's nearly time for your—'

'Greg,' he pleaded, 'it's not about me today. It's about this lad. It's about Peter. We can help him. *You* can help him. Just listen to—'

'All right, all right. Anything to shut you up.' Greg turned to me. His fat, pink face looked down upon me, his forehead mopped in sweat just as it had been the first time I'd met him. 'What is it?' he demanded. His left eyebrow moved upwards by about one metric centimetre and his right downwards by the same amount. 'What's so important?'

I cleared my throat. I said, 'I'd like to buy the fairy,' and pointed to where it nestled in his sweaty palm.

Greg Kirrin looked at me with steely blue eyes. 'The fairies aren't for sale.'

'I've got my piggybank,' I said, and I held it out to him as if begging for more.

His leaden expression weighed down on my hopes like Mr Gale's one kilogramme block. 'The fairies aren't for sale.'

'I might be able to borrow five pounds more,' I said. My mouth was as cracked and dry as the village pond.

'The fairies aren't for sale.'

'Oh, come on, Greg,' interrupted Norman. 'Look at the boy ...'

I dragged my tongue across my lips. 'I could borrow *ten* pounds.' My eyes burnt into the little doll imprisoned behind the pink bars of Greg Kirrin's podgy grip. Her pearl of a face, barely bigger than a tear, stared at me. 'For the blonde one,' I said, 'with the blue eyes and freckles and a wand.'

'The fairies aren't for sale.'

This was all wrong. This wasn't what was supposed to happen, was it? I'd read enough stories and seen enough films. The children were always able to persuade the grown-ups to do what they wanted. That was their magic power. I mean nobody stopped Christopher Robin or Dorothy from the *Wizard of Oz* from doing whatever they wanted, did they? Nobody in stories put up such walls. Stories always ended happily; why wouldn't this one? It was like I had one story in my mind but Mr Kirrin didn't know how it was supposed to end.

Norman had collapsed on the floor, his arms wrapped about his knees, his head nodding like a dandelion. He was moaning softly.

If I'd been older or taller I might have told Greg Kirrin that he was a horrid man with a horrid shop and that I was offering all the money I had in the world and even some that

I didn't have for a little fairy that a friend of mine happened to think looked like her. I wanted to hit him and kick him. Not 'kick' as in a stupid kid's fight kick but a 'kick' like in the films I'd seen: a big, grown-up's kick that would send him to the floor, wriggling in agony. I wanted to rant and rave and tell him that my dad was dead, dead, dead. I wanted to say that I was only a little boy, ten last birthday, and that I felt lost and alone most days. I didn't know where I was or where I belonged or where I might end up. That I'd done things that would never let me sleep. I wanted to shout at him that there were things all around me that I didn't understand: the small, narrow faces that watched me from behind trees; secret rooms; grown-ups, men and women, and the things that they said and the things that they didn't say.

And I wanted to tell him, what I really wanted to tell him, was that in the middle of all this was a girl, tall and blonde who I … who I liked. And who I wanted to buy a fairy for. And if I didn't, well, something terrible was—

'I'll give you all my pocket money 'til Christmas,' I said. 'And this!' I pulled my mother's gift from my pocket, silken purse and all. 'And this ring!'

Greg took the ring from my hand, revolving it between his fingers and examining like Norman had the day he'd sold it to me. 'All that money?' he murmured. 'And the ring? All for the fairy? Well, that's quite an offer.' And the he grinned. 'Unfortunately,' he said, 'the fairies are not for bloody sale,' and he wedged the poor creature back into the display.

The bell above the shop door rang and Mr Kirrin and I turned to see who had entered. It was Mr Merridew. His great yellow teeth smiled broadly.

'Good morning to you, Mr M,' wheezed the shopkeeper. 'Be with you in a tick.' He winked at Mr Merridew and turned back to me. 'Now, will there be anything else, *sir*?'

I stared straight ahead, my top teeth biting deeply into my lower lip.

'Please don't hurry on my account, Gregory,' said Mr Merridew shuffling towards us, stepping around Norman's trembling shape, one curious eyebrow raised. He leered down at me, his mossy green eyes glowing. 'Why, it's ... It's Peter, isn't it?'

I nodded enthusiastically. Perhaps, perhaps ...

'Gregory,' said the old man, 'Gregory, what on earth have you done to cause young Peter such distress? Have you caught the young miscreant pilfering and administered a sound beating?' and he smacked a fist into the palm of his hand causing the end of his walking stick—that walking stick—to wave dangerously close to the fresh eggs.

'No, no, Mr M, nothing like that. It's kids' stuff; that's all it is. He's after one of the fairies. You know the little fairies in the toy display. Well, if I let *one* go ...' He shrugged. 'You know the drill.'

There was a look in Mr Merridew's eye. A gleam. If Mr Kirrin wouldn't listen to me, I thought, then surely he would listen to Mr Merridew. Perhaps, perhaps ... But instead the old man simply laughed, spitting from his quivery lips.

'Here, here,' he said, holding out his hand, clicking his fingers. 'Let me see.'

Reluctantly Mr Kirrin took the fairy from the display and dropped it into his customer's upturned palm. The old man's bulging spectacles studied it closely, a frown growing on his face. 'It seems an odd little item to merit such distress,' he informed Mr Kirrin. 'A cheap ephemeron: nothing more.' He looked up and smiled. 'Its significance must, I therefore suggest, be symbolic. It bears, I believe, a relevance to Peter of which you and I, Gregory, are thus far ignorant.'

'Well,' huffed Greg Kirrin, gazing disapprovingly at his

brother, 'I don't have much time for symbols myself, Mr M. I like things to be what they are. I don't have time for much else.'

'Ah, but you are a practical man, Gregory: a man of business.' Mr Merridew looked at me. 'Peter, I fear, is … something other. Peter, do you have an answer? Can you explain or justify yourself?'

All I said was: 'Anna-Marie.'

He returned to the fairy, stroking her long blonde hair with his old man's fingers, touching her sparkly frock, her lacy wings, a sneaky smile creeping from corner to corner across his lips. 'Indeed?' he muttered. 'Indeed? Well, a passing resemblance, perhaps …

'You imagine, do you, Peter,' he said angrily, 'that by possessing this item you might likewise possess Anna-Marie? Is that it?'

What? No! That wasn't it at all. What was he even talking about?

'Well, if not that, then what?' He mulled this over. I wasn't going to help him. I don't think I could've done even if I'd wanted to. 'Perhaps, then, it is this: this bagatelle represents something to the fair Anna-Marie herself. And you, by acquiring it on her behalf, seek in some way to gain her favour. Is that it?'

I wasn't sure but it sounded closer.

Mr Merridew suddenly roared with laughter. 'Don't you see, Gregory?' he cried. 'Don't you see?' Mr Kirrin shook his head. He didn't see. 'This fairy is not simply a symbol. Oh, no, it is nothing so anodyne. It is something far greater: it is a token!'

The old man laughed again, clutching a nearby shelf for support with one hand, leaning against his stick with the other. Tins rattled and the shelves shook as he struggled to control himself. Mr Kirrin joined in but his great barking bellow came only from his throat. In his eyes I could see him wondering whether Mr Merridew wasn't a little bit mad.

'It is a common mistake, Gregory, to which Peter is victim and one that drove me from my former profession: that old canard that action equals reaction, cause and effect, that order can be defined and that the consequences of our actions can be predicted.

'Tell me, Peter,' and here he grabbed me quite hard just above my elbow, pinching, his stick still held tight between his fingers, 'do you imagine that the events of your life can be ordered like these tins and packets on Mr Kirrin's shelf: a place for everything and everything in its place? Well, think again.' The other hand, the hand which was still gripping the shelf began to tremble. 'Imagine the universe ripping said shelf from the wall.' Both the items on the shelves and Greg Kirrin began to shift about uncomfortably. The shaking got more violent until a tin of pears fell from high on up, crashing to and rolling across the shop floor. 'Ha!' exclaimed Mr Merridew, 'See, Peter, see how easily order is disrupted.'

'Now, now, Mr M,' warned Mr Kirrin lumbering across the floor to retrieve the can, gasping as he bent and glancing nervously at his jiggling stock. Another tin—baked beans—leapt from the top shelf missing his head by no more than the width of a ten pence piece.

'Who can know where each item will fall, Peter? Watch as all your assumptions come crashing to earth with—'

'Mr Merridew!'

The shaking of the shelves stopped immediately and Mr Merridew attempted a bow towards the shop-keeper. 'Apologies, Gregory. Apologies: a perhaps overzealous attempt at a visual demonstration designed to show poor Peter the futility of his efforts.' He cleared his throat. 'I quite forgot myself.'

'Well, be that as it may, Mr M, this is my bread and butter as it were. I'd be obliged if you would save your visual demonstrations for where I can't see them.'

Again the doorbell sounded. We looked up to see Mr Waterberry shuffle in. Norman barely stirred. The school caretaker stared at us with his single eye: me and Mr Merridew; Mr Kirrin stumbling to his feet and the shopkeeper's brother collapsed in the corner like a bag of potatoes.

'Frank!' exclaimed Greg, straightening his spine with some difficulty. 'What a relief! You can't imagine the shenanigans we've had in here this morning.' He bustled off behind the counter. '*Express*,' he said, folding a newspaper, 'and an ounce of the usual?'

The two fell into conversation. Pleased to be away from us, Mr Kirrin continued to glance in our direction every now and again whilst Mr Waterberry read aloud the morning's headlines growling with disbelief and—

'Ouch!'

'Then tell me this, Peter,' hissed Mr Merridew, his hand again gripping my elbow, 'do you imagine, when you are snug in your bed, that you are still, whilst the world beneath you hurtles through the universe at 66,000 miles an hour? How will you sleep tonight? Will you feel breeze?'

I pulled my arm away from his bony fingers. 'But it does,' I said.

'It does?' he snarled. 'It does what?'

'It does feel like you're still.'

He stared at me, his eyes filled with hatred.

The bell rang and, 'So, gentlemen,' said Greg Kirrin walking towards, his hands rubbing together, 'are we done with this nonsense? Mr M, did you want—?'

'One moment, please, Gregory,' murmured Mr Merridew, raising his walking stick to block the shopkeeper' path, 'for it

seems that Peter here is making a stand. In the face of an un-
forgiving universe, Peter alone has the courage, strength and
fortitude to shape events to his own ends. Why, Peter, to do
so would make you a God amongst men, would it not? Do
you not see, Greg? Do you not see the determination with
which young Peter stands his ground in the face of chaos and
cries, "No!" ' and he stamped his stick upon the floor. ' "No,
this will not do!" He would stem the flood and banish disease.
Death and distress will wilt beneath his steely gaze; catastro-
phe will cower …And you, Gregory, *you* would deny him his
moment.'

'Well, Mr M, it's the fairies, you see,' grunted Mr Kirrin.
'It's the principle—'

'Ah, Peter,' said Mr Merridew with a heavy sigh and a shake
of his head, 'a shame, perhaps, but it seems that Mr Kirrin is
more determined still, determined that you are to be thwarted
and, therefore, where does your own determination leave you?
It appears that both you and we are to be denied your moment in the sun. Ah, well: for the want of a nail …' And then
he turned away:

'Now, Gregory,' he said, resting his hand upon Mr Kirrin's
back, 'I would speak with you on the subject of candles. I'm
in absolute darkness …'

And so Greg Kirrin and Mr Merridew went about their
business. Norman was slumped in the corner, his face like
washing-up water, his eyes defeated. It was over. And so I stood
there although I had no reason to. I felt like a stray dog, kicked
and starved, but I just stood there as if the only choice I had
to make was between sweets and a comic. I just stood there
although my eyes burned with tears and anger.

And, for a moment, I thought: what if he's right? It was
kind of nice, in a way, to think that it didn't matter what you
did: that you couldn't control things. It was funny that I'd

always thought it sounded such a terrible thing but it was like Anna-Marie's ten thousand men, I suppose. You know about how she said they'd be so happy. It was one or the other, wasn't it? There were either consequences or there was chaos and, suddenly, I thought maybe I could just go home. I mean if there was no point, then what was the point of fighting it? That's what Anna-Marie thought—I knew that now—and that's why she was giving up.

And I nearly did—go home, I mean—but, you see, the thing was that Mr Merridew was wrong. And Anna-Marie was wrong too. I knew they were both wrong. Absolutely wrong! But the thing is, even if they were right, well, just because Anna-Marie wouldn't fight for herself, didn't mean I couldn't fight for her, did it?

I felt the piggy-bank resting in my arms. Chunky and so full of change.

I felt my arms rising, slowly, slowly.

Well, I thought, if it's chaos they want …

The piggy-bank was high above my head.

… Then it's chaos I'll give them.

And I threw it down.

It crashed.

It smashed.

It shattered.

Tiny, shiny pink blades of pig and coins, bronze and silver went spinning and rolling and rattling across the shop floor. Greg Norman turned to stare at me and even Norman stirred.

And then I began to scream. And if you thought my grand-mother's screaming was loud, well, ha, you've never heard anything like the scream I did right then.

35

I was late of course. The leavers' assembly had already started and I could hear Miss Drew's piano booming out across the field as I ran along, tripping and stumbling. They were singing that song 'One More Step Along the Road I Go' which you might know. They sang it at my old school too, at the end of each year. It had always made me sad before but ...

I hoped I wasn't too late.

I pulled open a classroom door—I didn't even care whose classroom it was—and barged my way through, pushing tables out of the way and sending pencil cases sliding and chairs rattling to the floor. I ran down the corridor—the singing getting louder and louder—and pushed against the heavy doors before bursting into the back of the crowded assembly hall. All the children were sat in their usual rows. As it was a special assembly all the teachers were there too, sat on chairs next to their classes pretending to sing rather than drinking coffee in the staffroom or sharing cigarettes. Mrs Carpenter was right at the front, her voice louder and higher than everybody else's. But Miss Drew stopped playing, her fingers hung above the keys, and every child in the school swivelled to watch me as I clattered in. Mr Gale turned and glared at me and Mrs Carpenter shot me this stare.

'Well, well, well,' she said, her throat billowing like a snake's, 'it seems that Master Lambert has deigned to join us. How good of him. But perhaps he would like to furnish us with a justification for his late arrival.'

What could I say to that? Should I tell her? Should I tell her all about Norman Kirrin and Mr Merridew? All about the fairy?

She adjusted her glasses. 'Any sort of explanation ...'

What about the Lodge and my grandmother? What about Kat and Alice and the secret room?

'Don't stare at me like a landed fish, boy. Answer the question or see me later. I believe you know now how this school deals with such ... impertinence.'

All I could think of was, 'Anna-Marie,' but it was like she couldn't hear me. It was like no sound would come out.

Mrs Carpenter growled with disgust. 'Sit down!' she snapped. 'No, no, not there, you stupid boy: next to Miss Pevensie.'

As she didn't really have a class of her own, Miss Pevensie was sat a little apart from the other teachers on the chair closest to where I'd come in. She hushed me with a finger to her lips and waved me over to sit at her feet. I skidded across the smooth, shiny floor and took my place, reluctantly crossing my legs and folding my arms across my beating chest as I searched for Anna-Marie. Miss Pevensie looked down at me as if to say something but then I think that when she looked at me she realised it was already too late. I already knew all the secrets. She looked sad and gently touched my hair. I think she thought that sometimes it was better not to know. I thought she would be a very, very good teacher anyway and maybe, maybe she was right. I hadn't really had time to think about that yet.

'Well, moving on from that ... reprehensible interruption,' said Mrs Carpenter.

I was relieved. At least she wasn't cross.

She read the story of Lazarus. You know, about the man who gets a second chance. That was one of her favourites which was kind of pretty funny, once you thought about it. As she spoke she toyed with the crucifix that hung about her old reptile's throat. Her hair looked newly curled and gleamed like metal. And when she'd finished everybody closed their eyes and put their hands together whilst she hallowed God's name and asked him to forgive us our trespasses. But my eyes didn't close at all. They squinted through my armpit trying to catch Anna-Marie's.

I thought I'd seen her sat towards the far end of the back row but I couldn't be sure. It was like she was only half there, pale and see-through like a ghost, her eyes all red. It was like when you look at the sun but you know you shouldn't because it'll burn your eyeballs out and so you kind of look at it but look away at the same time. And when you wake up from a dream and the dream itself is in your head but as soon as you start thinking about it you can't quite find it: you look to the left but it's on the right; and then you look to the right and it's slipped behind you and in the end you're spinning round and around but it's too late because it's already gone and it's just you sitting up in bed in the darkness with your dad's breathing and your mum's crying and the moon through the curtains.

'Anna-Marie!'

But it was like shouting at the sky or down a long tunnel with the echoes bouncing back at me like rubber balls. Why couldn't she hear me? I imagined this picture of myself in the ground in a box—I suppose I mean like a coffin—and I was kicking and screaming and punching at the wooden lid trying to escape, trying to make myself heard over the silence which had been buried with me, stuffed in and flattened, packed good and tight with shovels. I hammered my fists and called and cried but Mrs Carpenter just kept on talking and the children kept on staring and the teachers just kept on winking to each other and smirking when they thought no one was looking.

I looked around the hall. The curtains were pulled back and the sunlight stuck to the windows like the sticky-backed plastic on the cover of my geography folder. It was hot and stuffy. Only the stupid children were still wearing their jumpers. Many of the teachers were waving sheets of paper in front of their faces to cool the air. The hymn books had all been stacked neatly for the end of term and all the children's work that usually plastered the walls had been removed leaving only big pale squares and pin-holes on the sugar paper that remained. All the P.E. equipment, like the big box that only the sporty children could really leap over and the thin mattresses that always twisted your ankle when you jumped funny, had been pushed to the side. The climbing ropes had been tied up and hung there like half a dozen nooses.

'Anna-Marie!'

This time some of the children nearest to me turned and stared. A couple of them exchanged glances and giggled into the palms of their hands.

'Peter!'

Mr Gale's eyes were bulging. His big stubby finger pointed at me and then at the empty space on the floor beside *his* chair.

'But ...'

At me. Then the empty space.

I slid across the floor towards Mr Gale, my backside polishing the floor as I went.

Mrs Carpenter had begun to ask the school leavers about what they wanted to be when they grew up. They used to do that at my old school too.

'Robert Sawyer,' she said, 'have you decided what you would like to be?'

'Yes, Miss. A Farmer, Miss.'

Mrs Carpenter chuckled. 'No surprises there, then, Robert. Like father like son. And what about you, Lucy? Lucy Carr? Leave her hair alone, girl. I'm trying to … ascertain your ambitions for the future?'

'Miss?'

'What do you want to be when you grow up, dear?'

'Oh, Miss. Sorry, Miss. Work in an office, Miss.'

Mrs Carpenter's eyes widened. 'Really? Quite the women's libber, aren't we, Lucy?'

Lucy smiled blankly.

'Peter Lambert! Will you stop fidgeting, boy!'

But I couldn't stop, could I? How could I stop? I felt like … Well, you know when people say they've got ants in their pants? Well, that's just how I felt then. Big ants. Small pants. You know what I mean.

'Anna-Marie,' I hissed, hoping that nobody would hear me but her. Everybody turned round. This time everyone had heard me. Everyone except Anna-Marie. Her eyes were open but—

'Goodness me!' cried Mrs Carpenter. 'Will somebody shut that boy up?'

Mr Gale put his big hand on my head and turned it to face him. 'Peter, for God's sake, what the … the … the hell has gotten in to you?'

'It's Anna-Marie,' I said. 'I've got to …'

Got to what? I didn't know what to say, did I? My brain was full of thoughts flying this way and that, crashing into each other like jumbo jets and so noisy I could barely work out what any of them were trying to say. Was he right? Doctor Todd I mean. All that stuff about what was real and what wasn't. I could see all the children right in front of me. They were real, weren't they? And the school, that was real. But what about everything else? Anna-Marie was real, wasn't she? And Tommie must be real. There he was in the middle of our row, glasses peering at me. Why would I make up a Tommie? And after all Anna-Marie had taken me to see my grandmother so I couldn't have attacked my grandmother if it hadn't've been for Anna-Marie. But then I hadn't attacked my grandmother, had I?

'And you, Marilyn?' said Mrs Carpenter.

My head was spinning like a tornado.

'A housewife, Miss.'

I didn't know what to think.

'And don't you let anyone tell you that isn't jolly hard work, Marilyn.'

'No, Miss.'

On and on she went, every job you could think of: a nurse, a drayman, a footballer, a mechanic until finally she was scouring the back row with lidded eyes. 'Well, is that it? Have I missed anyone?'

Mr Gale cleared his throat and Mrs Carpenter's head twitched towards him like a newspaper after a fly. 'Anna-Marie,' he said. 'Anna-Marie Liddell hasn't spoken yet.'

Well, I can tell you that that remark went down like the *Torrey Canyon* and Mrs Carpenter's lips did the can-can whilst she considered whether or not to—

'Very well,' she said, and pointed at Anna-Marie. 'You.'

The boy sat next to Anna-Marie nudged her. And then he nudged her again. She turned to look at him. She scowled. 'What?'

Again a flurry of giggles amongst the children.

'Miss Liddell, yes,' said Mrs Carpenter, sounding like the Queen of Britain, 'dearest Anna-Marie, if you would be so good as to grant us a moment of your *precious* attention, I am lead to believe by Mr Gale,' and the look she gave my teacher right then seemed to make him shrivel all up until he was sat on his chair looking like an old apple, 'that we should enquire into your dreams and aspirations. For my part, I can't imagine—'

'I'm going to be a teacher.'

Anna-Marie's announcement was greeted with surprised silence and then, among one or two of the teachers, by wide grins. Mrs Carpenter looked startled for a moment as if someone had unexpectedly driven a stake into her heart. And then she laughed, a hearty, throaty chuckle but chilling like cold rain sliding down the back of your shirt.

'What a thought,' stuttered the headmistress. 'I should think that, thankfully, highly unlikely, dear. Standards have fallen, of course, in the modern world but thank the Lord they haven't yet fallen to quite such ... subterranean depths that anyone in their right mind would allow the likes of you within a country mile of impressionable children.'

'I don't see why not,' said Anna-Marie. 'After all, they let you.'

A murmur passed among the assembled children. For most of them this was beginning to look like the best assembly they'd ever had. A bit more of this and the hymns and the Bible stories wouldn't seem so bad. Some of the teachers glanced at Mrs Carpenter eager for her reaction. They were enjoying it too.

'Be that as it may, my dear,' said Mrs Carpenter, through a tight lizardy smile, 'I at least have some mathematical ability. I think you'll find it hard to make a career in teaching when there are horses in circuses with a better grip of basic arithmetic than you.'

'So what?' said Anna-Marie. 'I'm going to be a teacher. I'd be a good teacher.'

'When it comes to maths, Anna-Marie,' said Mrs Carpenter, allowing each word to drip like hot wax, 'you are barely sentient. It doesn't matter, dear, how much you may kick and scream that the universe is unkind. You will never be a teacher.

As sure as I am standing here today. The sooner you adjust to reality the better for everyone.'

And then Mrs Carpenter smiled again and this smile made my skin turn all pimply like when I watch the Daleks or Cybermen or something on *Doctor Who* because I could tell that what she was saying was true. She wasn't just upsetting Anna-Marie for the fun of it, not only that: she was telling the truth. And when I looked at Anna-Marie, I could tell that she knew it too.

'Perhaps, my dear,' said Mrs Carpenter with a chuckle, glancing at the teachers, 'you should consider working in a shop. I am sure it could be a very rewarding career for someone so … dissolute. Or, perhaps, waitressing. Besides, they have tills, don't they? I'm led to believe a monkey could operate one.

'You are what you are, Anna-Marie,' said Mrs Carpenter. 'Do you imagine that life will be different at your next school? Do you imagine that you will be different? What you are now, Anna-Marie, is what you will always be: a rude, ignorant trouble-maker who thinks only of herself. It would be funny,' she said, 'were it not so … pathetic.'

Anna-Marie just stared at her, tears filling her eyes. I called out—'Anna-Marie'—but it was like she was at the wrong end of a telescope, so far away that I could run all night and never get to her. And then she stood up and, 'Excuse me,' she said very politely to the boy next to her in the row. He shifted his legs and Anna-Marie walked to the end of the line, stepping carefully over everybody's toes, and then towards the hall door towards the car park.

Mr Gale kind of raised his arm to try and stop her. 'Mrs Carpenter,' he said but Mrs Carpenter said, 'Let her go,' and, 'Good riddance to bad rubbish.'

I tried to stand up—'Anna-Marie!'—but Mr Gale's strong hand held me in place.

And then she was on the car park. Anna-Marie I mean. Everybody was watching through those big windows and this time Mr Gale got up. 'Mrs Carpenter, I—' but Mrs Carpenter told him to sit down and, 'Let her get on with it.' Just like that.

I'd leapt to my feet too but I was already too slow and Mr Gale had grabbed me by the arm.

'Mrs Carpenter,' he stammered, 'I really think this … this …'

I couldn't see Anna-Marie now. She'd headed off towards the playground, out of view. I was trying to get away from Mr Gale but he'd locked both arms around me so I could barely move.

'Anna-Marie!' I called out.

' "A man that is a heretic after the first and second admonition reject!" ' cried Mrs Carpenter, eyes blazing. 'Isn't that right, Mr Potter?'

The vicar had been watching events with a look of amazement and was startled to be suddenly asked to contribute. 'Well, Sybil, I'm not sure that I …'

Mr Gale was on his feet again, his big barrely chest heaving against my back, his arms still holding me tight. 'Now, Mrs Carpenter,' he said. 'Heretic? Is this … this …'

'This! This! This!' screeched the headmistress, phlegm and fury spitting from her lips. 'Get the words out, you ridiculous man! Yes, this *is* completely necessary. "For vengeance is mine, saith the Lord." Leviticus, I believe vicar.'

The vicar sat rigid on his chair, his face bulging like a big, fat plum.

This was no good. I had to get free. I squirmed and wriggled against Mr Gale's grip, twisting and turning, and as soon as I could I turned and kicked him in the shin. Do you remember when I kicked Anna-Marie that time? Well, it was just like that but about a thousand times harder. I was sorry to do it, though, because, in spite of everything, I kind of liked him. 'You little shit-bag!' he cried but he let go of me and clutched his leg as he fell onto his chair so hard it neatly toppled backwards beneath him.

There was lots of noise now. Mrs Carpenter was screaming like a banshee but nobody was really listening. A lot of the children were laughing or shouting or clapping apart from the infants, of course, who were all crying and being comforted by their teachers who were on their knees mopping up tears and trying to explain that everything was all right and that there was nothing to be worried about and that, yes, there was a lot of noise but they were just being silly, really.

Now I was free I stumbled between the rows of children not being nearly as careful of toes as Anna-Marie had been. I didn't have time for that and I didn't even have time to say I was sorry either. By the time I was half way across the hall most of the children were hurriedly pulling their feet back under their knees for fear of being trampled.

'Peter Lambert!' cried Mrs Carpenter above all the commotion. 'Where on earth do you think you're going?!'

'Go on, Peter. Go on.' It was Miss Pevensie out of her chair and waving me on. It was funny really because it wasn't like I even really knew her or anything. I mean I wasn't even in her class.

I ran out of the hall, through the lobby and out into the car park. I was pleased to leave all the shouting and screaming behind. And I didn't even need to look around to find Anna-Marie. I knew where she'd gone. I skidded around and nearly fell but managed to go so fast that I didn't. The gravel crunched beneath my feet. As I spun around the corner towards the playground I could see her. She was standing on the swing, clutching the chains in each hand. The chains of the broken swing hung beside her.

'Anna-Marie!' I cried, now running across the dried field and the broken grass. 'Anna-Marie!' as loudly as I could.

She looked up.

As I drew near I gasped: 'Anna-Marie, don't.'

She stared at me but not like she could really see me. It was like she'd seen a little boat on the horizon or maybe a distant swimmer waving at her as the sunlight twinkled on the waves.

I was right in front of her and held out my hands where they cradled the tiny fairy like a crib.

Oh, I didn't tell you I got it, did I? It was when fat old Mr Kirrin was scrabbling round on his hands and knees for all those coins on the floor. It was easy.

'It's all right,' I said, puffing for air. 'It's going to be all right.'

Anna-Marie frowned at my open palm and then squinted as if she couldn't quite see what I was offering.

'What is it?' she said.

'It's …' Well, I wanted to say that it was what Mr Merridew said: that it was something different from what it was. You know, like my mummy's ring. That it was a symbol. Or a … a token. But that would've sounded stupid, wouldn't it? So I just said: 'It's the fairy.'

And then her eyes lit up and went all wide. She whooped and leapt off the swing leaving it waving wildly in the air.

'It's for you,' I said as she drew close. 'I got it for you.'

'How did you … ?' she sniffed. 'How much did it cost?'

'Nothing,' I said. 'Nothing.' And then I said, 'I stole it.'

And then she smiled and closed her eyes. And then she grinned, and then she laughed her head off. Literally.

She reached out and took the fairy in her own hand. She looked at it. That was all: she just looked at it. And then she said, 'Thank you, Peter,' and I thought my heart was going to blow up. I mean like a bomb, not like a balloon.

Tommie came trotting up behind us. He was hooting with laughter too.

'It's complete chaos in there,' he said slapping me on the

back. 'They had to let everybody go early. Good for you, Pete. You're a hero.' He'd never called me that before: Pete or hero, but I kind of liked it. 'That,' he said, 'was the best assembly ever.'

'Listen,' I said to Anna-Marie, 'it's like a story.' I held her hand really tight. 'It doesn't need to be real. It can still make you happy or make you sad. You can make the story end any way you like and if you don't like the end of the story then you can close the book and make up your own.'

Anna-Marie made a face like a mad person. 'What are you on about, bean-brain?'

'We have to walk the lane,' I said.

'Well, that's just what I—'

'Shut up, Tommie! Why, Peter? Give me one good reason. Why do we have to walk the lane?'

'I … I don't know,' I said. And then, 'Just because.'

Anna-Marie gave me a heavy look but then she shrugged. And then she looked at the fairy and smiled. 'Well,' she said, 'that's good enough for me.'

And then I smiled too. And Tommie smiled although he didn't even really know why we were smiling. And then I began to cry. It'd been that kind of day. Anna-Marie gave me a funny kind of look and then glanced back to the swings and their long shadow; the chain, turning, creaking, the air still. She frowned again and then she looked back at me. And then she cuffed me round the ear. But not too hard.

'Oh, and, Peter, another thing,' she said.

'What?'

'Don't say "literally".'

Postscript

Everlasting Lane was fresh and new, as if newly washed, newly made, newly born. As if we, Anna-Marie, Tommie and I, were the first to see that sun and the first to taste that air. As if the world were untouched and unused like a box of paints, new out of the stocking on Christmas Day or a set of coloured pencils all the same length with perfect points or even that piece of wood waiting for Kat's magic to turn it into ... into something. And the day was still. As we walked the trees saluted us and Everlasting Lane unrolled itself like a carpet.

We walked on.

I was thinking about everything that had happened, my head spinning like a sixpence: all the stuff that Doctor Todd had said about me and Alice; and then when I'd gone to *Kirrins'*. And after that when I'd got to the school assembly and everybody was shouting at me. And Anna-Marie in the car park. And me running after her. It was like everything had happened at once. And then we'd started walking the lane: Anna-Marie, Tommie and I, just like we'd always—

'I wonder what's going to be at the end,' said Tommie.

I shrugged. I didn't know.

'I think it's probably going to just turn into this big road or maybe even a motorway. It might be like the motorway that my dad and I go on when he takes me to London. Sometimes we stop at the big service stations and have fish and chips or sausages or something.'

Well, I didn't really know but I could imagine my disappointment if he turned out to be right.

'It's the only thing that makes sense,' he continued. 'People don't just build *lanes* for no reason—I mean, any kind of road—all roads go somewhere. Nobody would build a road for no reason. What would be the point? Why would anyone do that?'

I didn't know that either but it sounded like the kind of thing that Mrs Carpenter would say. 'Maybe there isn't any point,' I protested. 'Maybe there doesn't have to be one. Maybe the lane just comes to an end because whoever built the lane in the first place just stopped because they couldn't decide where the lane should go.'

As we walked I began to wonder what other feet had passed this way before us; what wheels had gouged deep ruts in the wet mud; what hooves had clattered upon the dry, baked earth. It was easy to imagine the shadows of the past sprung suddenly to—

'But that would be stupid,' said Tommie. 'Who would start building a road without knowing where it was going?'

I thought about the roaring motors, bright lights and pumping fumes: Tommie's motorway. I didn't like the idea at all. 'Maybe it's just a normal road, then, with a few cars and bicycles,' I said.

Tommie grunted. 'Maybe, but I bet *that* ends up being a motorway.'

He was right of course. I know Kat had said that there was real magic but could that really be true of a road, no matter what its name was? Suddenly I wasn't so sure.

Once—it seemed such a long time ago—we'd wondered whether Everlasting Lane might be true. And then we seemed to have grown up so much that we thought its name could only be pretend. But then I'd thought, what if, after all, it was true? What if there wasn't an end? What if, maybe, it wasn't like a story with a happy ending all tied up in bows? Maybe Everlasting Lane was more like that programme *Coronation Street*, just endlessly unwinding and never reaching an end and never meaning anything; I mean anything that mattered. And, anyway, which would be worse: getting to the end or never getting to the end. I didn't even know.

But I was going to find out.

'Bill and Ben the flower-pot idiots,' said Anna-Marie. 'Flob-a-lob. Honestly, you two give short planks a bad name.' Tommie and I each caught the other's eye and blushed as if we'd been caught telling lies in class. 'It's typical,' she went on just like she was a teacher or something. 'You've been walking along, wittering on about what you're going to find at the end and you haven't even noticed what's going on around you now.'

'What?' twitched Tommie his head switching from side to side. 'What's going on?'

Anna-Marie shook her head in despair. The fairy was hung from Tommie's chain wrapped two or three times around her gentle throat. 'Come on,' said Anna-Marie, 'and, this time, at least *try* and pay attention.'

We walked on.

Acknowledgements

I would like to express my love and gratitude to the following in the hope and expectation that they will know why:

Dennis, Valerie and all at Melville House.

Eloise, Sam and all at Galley Beggar Press (UK). And Henry.

The ladies at EDGE: Ruth, Kathryn, Nikki, Bev and Rachel.

Keith, Paul and Tim.

The siblings: Iain, Harry, Paula and Brian.

Caren.

My boys: George, Charlie and Harry.

My patient and ever-loving wife, Kate.

And Carole and Wynne: Mum and Dad.

Four Questions
for Andrew Lovett

How did you come about writing Everlasting Lane?

The original inspiration was my relationship with my mother. It broke down when I was in my twenties and I needed to try and make sense of what had happened. I was also moved by the story of a little girl in the school where I was working with whom other parents wouldn't let their children play – she was the inspiration for the character of Anna-Marie. The title itself came from a residential road in the town where I lived. "Everlasting Lane" sounded so fantastical I couldn't resist pinching it.

Would you tell us a little about what it's like to write a child protagonist?

Childhood innocence is such an extraordinarily precious state, but, as Anna-Marie suggests, trying to capture it successfully on the page is like the difference between a picture of a tiger and the tiger itself.

I'm not sure I see Peter as being so very different from the average adult (by which, I suppose, I mean me). We all like to think we understand the world better than we do when in fact we're neither less confused nor less desperate for guidance than the average child.

Or is that just me?

What was the most challenging part of writing this book?

Digging deeply into childhood memories was a mixed blessing: sometimes beautiful, sometimes traumatic; always emotional.

The weaving of many disparate memories into a coherent whole drove me to distraction, but the fact that much of the book was written in the early kid-free hours or late at night probably didn't do much to help my mental state.

Writing the book was a doddle, however, compared to endlessly rewriting and editing it.

Who are the writers who inspire you?

My first literary hero and biggest inspiration was J. D. Salinger, the writer who made me want to be a writer. Others who influenced *Everlasting Lane* in some way were James Joyce and Christopher Isherwood. I like Orwell, Austen, Steinbeck and Updike. Paul Simon is a great short story writer who, unfortunately, has never written prose. A contemporary inspiration is Aimee Bender.

Reading Group Guide

1. In the beginning of the novel, Doctor Todd gives Peter a watch as a present, to help Peter organize himself. After receiving the watch, Peter destroys it. What might Peter's destroying the watch signify? Is this action a reflection of his feelings towards Doctor Todd? Is it something more complicated?

2. Peter's mother suggests she and Peter play a game in which Peter pretends she is not actually his mother, but his Aunt Kat. She insists he call her "Kat" for the rest of the novel. What might her reasoning be behind this? Do you think it's directly related to Alice? Why, or why not?

3. How do you feel that Peter calling his mother "Kat" instead of "Mummy," or "Mother," changes their relationship? Is it for the better or for the worse?

4. This is not the only time games are played in order to mask something more serious. Can you think of any other noteworthy examples in the novel when games are played? And why are games used in this manner?

5. What does Peter learn about the consequences of actions? The notion is first brought up by Anna-Marie in reference to a game. Are consequences a game to Peter? Give a few

examples of where such consequences play a significant role in the text.

6. In a general sense, what does Peter learn from the Scarecrow Man? Think about their first few encounters.

7. When Mr Merridew says there is "no difference" between a good man and a bad man, what is he alluding to? What does Peter learn from this conversation?

8. Memory plays an important role in this narrative. What were the most pivotal moments in this story, where memory changes your understanding of events, or the characters'? See, for example, pages 7, 212 and 323.

9. Why do you think Peter's memory is so hazy and uncertain? Is it because of something significant that happened to him, or is he simply forgetful?

10. On page 46, Anna-Marie tells Peter that his "grip on reality seems so … tenuous." Do you agree? Why, or why not?

11. The setting of Everlasting Lane is at once new and familiar to Peter. How is the setting a largely important aspect of this story? How does it feed Peter's unique imagination?

12. Peter's father is explored significantly in the novel's very beginning, as well as its end. How do you read this relationship? How is it an important relationship in the story?

13. Throughout the novel, there are moments when Peter is baffled by the adults around him. Sometimes their advice to him is contradictory. What lessons do you think Peter learns from these interactions? To trust grown-ups, or to trust only himself?